FIC RIC

RICHARDS, DAVID ADAMS

RIVER OF THE BROKENHEARTED

3 WEEKS

RIVER OF THE BROKENHEARTED

ALSO BY DAVID ADAMS RICHARDS

Mercy Among the Children

The Bay of Love and Sorrows

Lines on the Water:
A Fly Fisherman's Life on the Miramichi

RIVER OF THE BROKENHEARTED

DAVID ADAMS RICHARDS

Arcade Publishing • New York

Copyright © 2003 by David Adams Richards

FIRST U.S. EDITION 2004

First published in 2003 by Doubleday Canada

This is a work of fiction. Names, places, characters, and incidents are either the products of the author's imagination or are used fictitiously.

Library of Congress Cataloging-in-Publication Data

Richards, David Adams.
    River of the brokenhearted / by David Adams Richards. —1st U.S. ed.
        p. cm.
    ISBN 1-55970-712-7
    1. Motion picture theater managers—Fiction. 2. Irish—Canada—
Fiction. 3. Single mothers—Fiction. 4. Catholic women—Fiction.
    5. New Brunswick—Fiction. 6. Widows—Fiction. I. Title.

    PR9199.3.R465R63 2004
    813'.54—dc22   2003020368

Published in the United States by Arcade Publishing, Inc., New York
Distributed by Time Warner Book Group

Visit our Web site at www.arcadepub.com

10 9 8 7 6 5 4 3 2 1

EB

PRINTED IN THE UNITED STATES OF AMERICA

For my cousins Mary Baldasaro
and Cathy Richards Green
who know that though this is based
on incidents in the life of our grandmother
Janie, it is a work of fiction.

And for Bob Gibbs and Fred Cogswell.

"Because of their enmity you will be left alone.
They will cast you out and forsake you."

The Seven Storey Mountain, Thomas Merton

RIVER OF THE BROKENHEARTED

PROLOGUE

The graves of the Drukens and the McLearys are spread across the Miramichi River valley. If you go there you might find them—"run across them" is not the exact phrase one might want to use for graves—in certain villages and towns. I don't think we have hamlets here, but if we do, then in certain hamlets as well.

What is revealing about these graves is their scarcity. The scant way they are impressed upon the soil, dispersed here and there about the river. A river that stretches 250 miles from the heart of our province, a river of lumbering and fish and of forests running tangled to the water's edge. Our ancestors came and founded communities, and over time abandoned them for the greater lumbering towns of Newcastle and Chatham, so that only graves are left. One might go years without stumbling upon one, and when one finally does, an immediate reaction might be to say: "Why in Christ is old Lucy Druken buried way out here?"

I suppose some of the brightest of my relatives have lain forgotten for decades in the woods, forgotten even by their own descendants, in fields that have become orchards or mushroomed into forests again, the descendants having moved on, first to the towns and then west to the cities of Montreal or Toronto, or south to the great and frantic United States. The graves' occupants unremembered. Yet in what love and sorrow might they have been placed?

Two hundred years have passed to find what is left of us still here. Last October I came back from the train station in the debilitating gloom of a rain-soaked autumn day. He had demanded the key that morning, when I said I was leaving.

He spoke to me in his slightly limey way—being the only memory he ever retained of his father, and so the thing he held onto, come hell or high water, for a memory gone over sixty years. A limey with a Miramichi brogue.

"Yes—well, then—you can just give me the key, can you not—leave it here" His hand shook as he pointed to the table. "And we will think no more of it; I will not even call you a traitor—just remember I could not leave people in the lurch—as much as I wanted to—if they were lurching I'd stay!" he said turning away at that moment.

I found it hanging upon a string outside the winter door, waiting. I came into our small house, with the broken mirror in the foyer, to find him sitting in his straight-backed chair in the absolute middle of the small den, equidistant from the memorabilia of both British and Irish roots—the cross of Saint George and a broken Irish bagpipe, staring out at me in perplexity, his hair now thin against his fine head, his tie done up very properly, hankie in his breast pocket, dark high socks and well-polished shoes on his feet. Each shoe tied with a small bowed lace, which never really did anything but make my heart go out to him—especially when I realized it took upward of fifteen minutes to get each shoe on. He was drinking some mixture of aftershave and vermouth—a pleasant enough concoction, he said, to starve off his "dearth" of gin gimlet he might on occasion—at two in the morning, or five in the afternoon—go searching for. I told him I did not have anything on me—no Scotch or rum.

"Do you know," he said to me, "you are absolutely right, my lad. I have been thinking of giving it all up."

"What up?" I say, turning away so he will not see the gin I have tucked in my tweed jacket.

"This place—this house—sell it and go away! Is that a gin cap I spy—"

"Where?" I say, looking about the room. Trying to make no sudden moves, I pick up a cushion and hold it against my pocket.

"That cap?" He clears his throat.

"What cap?"

"Why, my son, the cap on the gin bottle—you have glided a cushion over it."

"Glided a cushion?"

"Is it glided—I'm not sure—?"

His fingers tremble just slightly. He is looking around for something—a cigarette, I suppose.

I take the gin out, hold it before me like a newborn infant.

"Yes—there it is—you are a saviour—I always knew you were—and foolish me in the process of changing my will—wondering who to leave all of this to"—he waved his hand abstractly. "You just went out to get me some gin—"

I go into the kitchen, get the glasses and pour out our libation.

"Gin's the drink," he says, smacking his lips and looking at the two glasses to see if they are perfectly symmetrical. He takes his, shakes just a bit getting it to his lip and, confident his immediate plight is over, downs it in a draught.

"You found the key all right?" he says.

"Absolutely."

I came back once to find 223 newborn baby chickens in the house. I believe it occurred when he upset a crate of chicks somewhere in his travels. He was imprinted on them and they followed him home. He came in the house, the front door left ajar, picked up the letter opener to open his increasingly oppressive pile of bills, and saw 223 little yellow chicks staring at him. He opened the door and told them to go. They did not. He then tried to hide them in the dresser drawers, and keep this from me when I came in.

"Do not say one damn thing about what you see in this house," he said.

I found them walking the halls, sitting on his lap, as he pretended not to notice. In fact, he remained until I bundled them up and took them away, ruefully dismissive of us all.

"I will not go," I say to him after our gin.

"And why not?" he asks. "Why won't you go wherever it is you are wanting to—go?"

"Because you're my father and someone needs to stay with you."

"Oh—well then—I see—very noble of you—Wendell my boy. Let's drink to nobility."

I guess I can drink to that as much as anyone.

My father Miles King told me that some are damned by blood, by treason, by chance or circumstance, some even by the stars themselves, or as Shakespeare, denying that, said, by ourselves. This in a way is a journey back in time to see how I was damned.

My name is Wendell King, and I have looked for these forgotten places, and found them in their quietude and hope, and have gone to the archives, reading old tracts, deeds, family history, searching out what I can, to try to dislodge the secrets that have plagued my father's life.

PART I

ONE

The McLeary family arrived in 1847. They left Ireland crammed into a ship's steerage with those like themselves, unseafaring and sick. The ship foundered in an autumn gale off Sheldrake Island, at the mouth of the Bartibog River, which flows into our great Miramichi. Having no help, they lived quietly in a cave near the bay.

"Well, it's a better cave than you'd ever find in Ireland," old Isaac McLeary would say.

From dawn till dark the children saw only trees, and the snow fell without much regard for them. Most of the children went into a stupor; then the "gales did come," as was written by Isaac, so he could no longer tell land from sky. He wondered what he might do to save his family, but there was very little he could do. He had no money for return passage, and no idea how to keep his children alive in a country where he had nothing to plant, and the very bay was frozen. He kept going out to look at it, and then sent his youngest to walk on it.

"By God—he's walking on water. Saint or not, I do not know—I only know that there he is, Little Hemseley, wandering about on a bay."

Five were lost. Their graves have been found by me, in an alder valley, forgotten under mouldy stone. I have read the transcript, at the back of the Bible that my father possessed: "I found them laying with their backs to trees only a few yards from each other. Three of my sons are gone. My oldest girl Colleen was dead holding her rosary. I find little Hemseley in a small shelter. He's gone to heaven yesterday. Isaac—January 25, 1848."

Unfortunately the old man did not know there was a church and a school and houses and stores a few miles away. And when he did find out he did not tell the others, because he was mortified by his lack of resolve in finding this out before half his family was dead.

With spring, what was left of the McLearys moved from the cave to the town of Newcastle, at the time a great lumbering and ship-building port in the north of our province. They lived in a small brick house notable for its lack of windows and its chimney leaning like the Tower of Pisa.

"It's not much better than the cave, but at least it's in a community where everyone helps everyone, and none are left to flounder in the cold," Isaac was reported to have told his children. Except that was wishful thinking by a man who never had the wherewithal to support himself. Soon very few helped them, and they became wards of the church, constantly at the point of beggary for almost twenty years.

Then, one cold autumn morning in 1868, old McLeary saw the very Irish family he had run from, all walking up the muddy street of Irishtown with trunks and suitcases, swords and guns. The Drukens had arrived. A strange name and a strange family. They were a wild lot, unfettered even by what was considered colonial civilization. The four Druken children were as tough as whalebone and went off to wars as youngsters go off to play baseball.

They settled as near to the McLearys as they ever were in Ireland. It made poor old Isaac's gamble of taking his family across the storm-boggled sea to escape the horde almost pointless. For once again, by sheer accident it seemed, they were all crowded together on the farthest back street of town.

There they were all cozy again, in two incredible small houses, in a back lane farther from the centre of the universe than they had ever been, so creating their own, a universe of blistered snow and dirt, rebellious sin, and a dozen childhood diseases that erupted each spring from the mud, an inferno where insults were drivelled toward each other and battles of hellish nature erupted on the street. Both families came with old men and children to escape the kind of poverty known to characters in Dickens—but poverty not as fanciful.

Both were Catholic, both hated the British with a dying hatred, and yet hated each other even more, the hatred of subjugated people propelled by subjugation. Both believed the other had betrayed them in a former time to British intrigue, in bogs and lands where death blows were dealt to children and women as right justice by those who nosed snuff and wore wigs.

They carried such hatred for each other that in Ireland they never wiped their blades of blood. Blood over someone snitching because both their families, and ten other families as well, lost boys to a British hangman in 1791, crowded in an Irish dungeon, chained together with one slop pail. Brought out, blinded and blindfolded, and dragged to the gallows, without pomp and ceremony. The other families had been killed off. Only these two remained.

The feud started on the day a Druken man was to marry a McLeary woman. Someone from their party threw a stone at a passing British horse, which threw a cavalry officer, reported to have been related to Lord Churchill himself. One of the wedding party snitched on the rest to save his life, and the British marched into the church to find them hiding. And from this report vague and unsubstantiated over many years, because the matter was incidental on the larger scale, no trial of any sort was held.

So who was the snitch, McLeary or Druken?

Both families, never forgetting their children on the gallows, carried this holy war against each other, a war of attrition, war of words and staffs and peevies, all the way from Ireland into each other's little houses and sheds in Newcastle, New Brunswick, a full century later. In 1875, a swaggering Protestant constable weary of their squabble told them their fight was over lives long dead and history past:

"History never passes, it forms," one of the Drukens said, putting his arm about one of the McLearys—whom he would protect to the death his right to kill. "So, my man, we're just getting started. And do not think we come from a nation without poets and gifts."

But the McLearys produced few men, and the Drukens' were more favoured by ruthlessness. The little solitary family who lived between them, by the name of Winch, sided with first one and then the other, seeing fine advantage in doing so.

By the turn of the century only Jimmy McLeary, the grandson of the first McLeary to step off the boat, was left to wage war. The remnant of a proud family gone, Jimmy was alone; his brother had disappeared, under mysterious circumstances. His oldest daughter, Agatha, had died. Only his daughter Hanna Jane was with him.

Alone Jimmy could not fight back, though he had his young daughter play tunes on the fiddle to gather courage, and would go out to meet the Drukens on the street. Paddy Druken was known to have cuffed him good as he called them forward to meet their doom; little Hanna Jane herself was taken to court once for setting booby traps near the well.

There was a squabble over the well because each family was sure the other had stolen gold from Ireland and hidden it there. A ludicrous assumption, but enough brainless among them to search. Paddy Druken, half mad with rotted teeth, guarded the well on pain of McLeary death—and the McLearys, in the hottest month of the year, squeaking for drink, had to sneak to the well to get their water. So little Hanna Jane beguiled them all by jawing a bear trap and placing it near where Paddy was known to sit. It did not catch his arse but a pad he was wont to sit upon.

"A booby trap that might cause a leg to break in half," the magistrate said. "How does a girl of six make such a booby trap?"

"With much patience, sir," Hanna Jane was reported to have answered.

"Whose well do you think it is, little Hanna Jane?" The magistrate asked.

"Whoever family is bold enough to lose a life there—it will be theirs by the grace of God." Hanna Jane scratched her nose. She wore her big straw hat and long dress, and carried a purse like a little lady.

She left school, this Hanna Jane McLeary, and went to work. At twelve years of age, she went to Fredericton, that city of stately elms and small minds, so she could find work at the houses of the genteel descendants of our good Loyalist stock. But she came home when her father took ill with gout and drink.

By 1915, Jimmy could not go without drink, and all fight was gone from him.

This was Hanna Jane's worst period, so bad that in 1918 she became briefly engaged to the young luckless Bobby Doyle, a cousin of the Drukens' from time gone by. Yet Jimmy's daughter had strength to care for him and found work playing her fiddle at local dances, travelling in winter by horse and cart, her fiddle in an old bait box she carried under her arm, and Bobby Doyle waiting in the snow for her money so he could drink.

"In those days," an old man once told me, "playing for our boys from the woods, or fishermen in from the bay with their sunburned necks, she was a wild thing with her hair down—and there was no one made fresh with her if she didn't want. But she could not continue with poor Bobby Doyle and be her own, so she left him that April, and gave back the friendship ring he had given her."

I am the happier. For this Hanna Jane McLeary, this daring rebel girl, this sweet lost light of Bobby Doyle's eye, became my grandmother, became in all her dancing tragic scope one of our great Maritime women, though she never wanted greatness—no, thrust upon her.

TWO

I was never to see my grandfather. There is a picture of him next to my grandmother, taken, I think, in 1922, where he looks a little like Fitzgerald, and she, a more beautiful Zelda. Someone once told me—wisely or not I do not know, or care, for the art of such wisdom as his changes—that my granddad never succeeded at anything very much.

"Yer grandaddyoo (he said granddaddyoo) was a howling failure— just like yer dad. It must be the English side of you."

I assumed this to be correct. Why not? A small theatre in a callow town is not the great world's idea of success. We had all failed, and he needn't tell me. We were failed poets, dancers, and musicians that had little enough moments of brilliance on a stage, in church basements, at weddings, or forgotten moments of sorrowful laughter long gone—say with a slight ballet movement in a stage adaptation of some composer in the lost summer of 1946.

George King, our patriarch, often failed too. Failed in youth by having both parents die, failed in the first war—the illness that he wished to end with a sudden crawl over the top prevented him from going to the front. His fiancée in England left him for someone else, assuring him, as fiancées often do, that she loved him still. So, broken-hearted, he came to Canada. His wife, my grandmother, was Irish Catholic with a broad Miramichi accent, and he Church of England. This caused a rift in the family for years, and pitted the town against us in a strange way. Like a curse not ended yet. Failed at family life for a son he did not know.

So many rifts, and so few years, my sister once commented as we drove to Burnt Church for a summer vacation that we never had.

My grandfather had come to Canada from foul London as a last respite against his sickness, and fought it here, on a playing ground unlevel at the best of times. He fought it with medicine from Dr. Giovanetti and what he called stingers—that is, gin and beer mixed; he fought it with walks and exercise, and camphor and morphine, and swimming in cold climates.

"I am Janie McLeary—from Chatham Street," my grandmother said to him when they first met—their meeting quixotic as it was assuring my birth, through the birth of my father.

"I am George King—and I'm just about done for." He smiled as he took her hand. "You don't have any home remedies, do you—some syrup or elixir you're hoarding for yourself? Give it up if you do."

He was a collector of small prints and silver coins and out-of-date things like tin meat cans from the Boer War and took his meeting with my grandmother to be destiny, for as he said: "Once on the ship—the *Lucy Corker* out of Liverpool—I had decided on Canada. Before that moment I had decided on nothing, not even whether I might climb the rail and jump, saying, 'so long now, my chippy mates.' Once in Canada, I took my travelling music show northwest. It could as easily have been southwest. At this moment, why, I might be in Boston with another lady altogether! And then to need someone to accompany me—in you walk, Janie McLeary—a nineteen-year-old girl carrying her fiddle. There you go—that's destiny. We play well together too. You don't call that fate—it is most remarkable."

They were married, much to the chagrin of her father, who said he had witnessed the English when he was a boy in Ireland (though he never was a boy in Ireland) and said he would hang himself if she went through with it. So he went off to do it, wearing a white shirt and tam-o'-shanter, and then because he couldn't bring himself to tie a rope to the Morrissey Bridge, asked his friends to hang him instead.

"Hang me, for I'm not fit company with myself."

After being drunk with him for a day, they said they would, so he backed off and went home.

The town took the marriage to be doomed, and since he was sickly, in bad taste, and her friends all decided she was insane. They would stand outside her door talking about her as she sat inside listening. One of the things against her was that she had been engaged to Bobby Boy Doyle, a man with passable fists who boxed in the golden gloves. It was just another family of enemies for my grandmother to have.

"She's just a damn cow, that Janie McLeary—"

"I am not," she would say. But they in their hats and skirts from Eaton's summer catalogue would continue speaking as if she was absent, paying no mind to her protest, and then all walk off together singular in their state of agony and in their affirmation of the mortal sin she was committing. All of them would ask her for money later on.

My grandparents lived in a rooming house run by the Dobblesteins, who owned a little mill on the back square. Janie was seen pushing her husband in a wheelchair the day after their wedding—he thirty-three, she twenty. George King failed at his first try and then his second in business, attempting to open shops in the listless, insipid summer of the flu, which, incidentally, he assumed would dispatch him with a quick cough and sudden heart failure. That it did not sent him back to reading Conrad, but saying that he found in life "not the joyous exuberance and overwhelming optimism Mr. Conrad himself finds." (I take this not as irony in the least, for my grandfather was little fit for irony at the time.)

And then on the back of a cold winter, Grandfather coming home from playing piano in Moncton for a penny or two, decided on the theatre. It was one thing the river did not have. He decided on a theatre when the train got stuck at a pass and he saw a white drift outside in the night, the snow wisping about, he said, like "frantic actors on the silver screen who have all suddenly forgotten their lines." All of a sudden the idea of a theatre, or a playhouse, was there, was born in morphine-induced love.

It came, spontaneously, in another man's mind as well: Joey Elias, who himself had escaped through England to Canada and who was strangely drawn to my grandmother's enemies the Drukens. So in one instant, two centuries of divisions were firmly entrenched, trenches fashioned for a century more.

Elias was after the same projector, but my grandfather managed to get it first, a mere ten minutes before Elias himself came with the money—from his friend (and silent partner) Mr. Harris of the Royal Bank, newly arrived in town. Both looked upon my grandparents' marriage with a good deal of self-righteous disdain, as did much of the populace. Elias's failure only solidified the disdain.

"Mr. Elias—he dead," my grandfather was fond of saying as he walked about the house, drinking his gin-and-beer concoction, browsing through Mr. Conrad's *Heart of Darkness*.

Our first theatre, the Regent, was down a gravel lane and stood with its back to the town. It had been built as a feed shed, and was bought by my grandfather for three hundred dollars. There were seven benches in front of the small square screen my grandfather had constructed, and at first most of the customers were men. My grandparents' first movie was a Tom Mix, and when he fired his gun, fellows from the woods who had come out to watch this display in a rather taciturn fury fell over backwards, shouting, "Me Christ, he's shootin' at me!" and scrambling over each other to find the exit. When they came back upon the theatre the next night, one brought his own revolver, to "pay Tommy back," and was talked out of it by my grandfather, who said he would only be "killing the air—and Tom would remain Tom."

This was not laughed at by my grandfather, for why would he laugh at those things that were natural, in support of what to most was unnatural? But he wrote a piece in the paper about how these sights were possible, on what small frames in a band of film they sat. As the months passed along, and winter came again, and more people were informed about trains seeming to come out of the air and pretty girls showing their corsets, more people came—and into this mix were the young women who had idols like Clara Bow and lovers like Valentino.

The silver screen brought our forefathers a view of New York, London, and Boston that many had never seen, and showed the Keystone Kops running about ragtag streets far away, and Buster Keaton and Fatty Arbuckle. The benches were replaced by seats and a carpet, and a refreshment stand was built. The price of admission was ten cents and the Regent became known as the dime.

The Dime flourished as few things did, and gave my grandparents the life they wanted. And it influenced people more than they would like to admit. The blacksmith because of his proportions became known as Pond Street Fatty, after Arbuckle, and a young girl who had a peek-a-boo hat believed she was the spitting image of Clara Bow, and to her beau, who cut hair in the square and shaved my grand-dad clean, she was.

But Mr. Elias bided his time, thinking that at death's door Grandfather would find it too taxing to run an enterprise such as a theatre and sell out. Yet night after night my grandparents played their instruments wildly and brilliantly against the backdrop of silent actors cavorting on the screen. To those early goers to our theatre, my grandfather seemed possessed. And after six luckless months Mr. Elias, who had opened his own little theatre, called the Biograph, went to visit the house of his opposition.

The afternoon was sweltering and light shadows flitted on the wall as the blinds blew forward in a gust of July wind, and my grandfather swiped at motes of silent dust every now and again. My grandfather was dressed in a wide-lapel suit and a housecoat, with his pockets bulging with strange collectibles, pins, buttons, Boer War medals, that he rubbed for good luck. Mr. Elias, holding his hat, his pin-striped suit also of a variety found in the 1923 summer catalogue, watched him with some dismay, and thought, as he admitted later, the old boy was bonkers. Mr. Elias humoured this insanity as best he could, and was to comment later that "all the Kings are insane—and George was the most insane of them all."

"It's horrible about your illness," he said after a time.

"My illness—what's so horrible about it? In illness you'll sometimes find—as in war—a horrible beauty is born." My grandfather gazed at Elias with a peculiar expression. Then he shoved a teapot forward for Elias to have tea.

"You'll probably find, Joey," he said after a moment, glancing through the drawn venetian blinds as he spoke, "it will not be any more horrible than yours will be—when it comes, which it will. Would you like a cupcake?"

Elias went home very distressed at the situation but willing to make some kind of an offer to amalgamate the two theatres under his control.

"Ah, that I were in England now that spring is here," my grandfather was overheard to have said that afternoon. Elias took this as a sign that the old man wanted to get the hell back to a place where he could be buried.

So while King was still alive, invalid though he was, Mr. Elias visited him on three more occasions. It was during that long, awful summer, when noise and light and heat bothered my grandfather excessively, that Elias was at the door. He was willing to buy the theatre for a fair price so King would be able to go back home to merry old England if he wanted. Elias brought over a nice reclining chair, for the "old boy" and some slippers for the "old boy" to scuff about the house in.

But Elias did not offer a fair price, for he had never before been an agent of fairness, and it was impossible for him to be one now. If he had, my grandfather surely would have sold—although returning to England was not an option.

Joey Elias waited for Mr. King to sell the theatre to him. He waited for three weeks. He delivered news on departing ships and waited word on the price of sale.

"The *Lucy Corker* is going back. Why don't you try to be on her, h'm?"

But it did not happen.

The last time he went to King's house to reason with him, King was gone. Where? Janie would not say. Well, when would he be back? Janie did not know. Well—shouldn't a dying man stay put? Well, said Janie, a dying man who does not know his options should.

Well, if he had gone without settling, he had gone off his stick, Elias said to his friends Phil Druken and Leon Winch later that evening. Both of these men loved his company because he supplied the town with rum—and on late nights, if you were in good with Elias you could get a drink. Phil Druken's young girl Rebecca sat on his knee and listened, with rapt attention, to the names of people, which is what she seemed to know more than any other child.

She looked at Mr. Elias in a peculiar way this night. For only a child still, she remembered him. It was Mr. Elias who had sold her mother medicine during the flu—sulphur mixed with milk, and rotted herring to ward off the germs—to her little brothers, the Druken triplets. The first triplets ever born in our town, they are known as the Druken triplets by the middle-aged grandchildren of those who once knew them. They were two years of age when the flu hit, and Putsy their oldest sister was seven, and Rebecca, who loved them most, was four. She put her faith in Mr. Elias and went outside to play.

Elias sold their mother, Patricia, these cures, posturing concern. They drank the tea, and walked about with rotted herring hanging by twine from their necks, and were found in an upstairs bedroom dead in a heap.

Elias, walking back and forth in front of Rebecca now, was saying that he did not want anything for himself—far be it from him to ever want something for himself—but there must be a limit to all of this. Janie had a son—"that little squirrel-faced fellow"—so how could she take care of a business as well as a son?

"Yes, yes," he said, disheartened, "it's impossible for her to oper-ate the theatre *and* be a mother." Then he looked up under his eyebrows and shook his head sadly. He saw Rebecca staring at him, fixedly, and smiled. "Come here, Rebecca, and give Uncle Joey a hug," he said.

THREE

No one remembers the town being disrespectful to Mr. King—people liked him, and went to the theatre regularly. If anything, the respect the town had for him transferred to Janie, and she was held in esteem as well.

Still, once Mr. King's impending death became apparent—that is, by Christmas other things came into play for those few who might gain by his demise. That he was dying was a shame. However, the other life, the life that tells people someone else's death is not a shame if it opens a door for themselves, was now opened. On Monday the tenth of January, Elias made inquiries into the state of the theatre, and met with the manager of the bank, certain that he would make the bank an offer on the Regent—for the Regent must fall into the bank's hands once King succumbed. Janie would give it up, wouldn't she, and go back to living a normal life? Besides, she was expecting again, so it was said.

Mr. Harris must have realized that the widow Janie King would not be a reliable sort to take over after the death of her husband, with one small child and another to be born. Elias added that her husband knew this himself. The bank must take it over, and he, Elias, might, if the price was right, buy it.

Yet Janie might have the ludicrous idea that she could run the place after King died. So, Elias added, now was the time to put a lock on the theatre door—seal it up before she got that chance.

"I see," Harris said, as men say who don't see at all. "You think so—board it up."

"It has been done before," Elias said. "Besides, the Biograph really is the legit place for the big Hollywood pictures. I can combine the two theatres to make one—it will save your bosses a headache—and you know the town can't support two places."

Elias liked to assume that Janie had done something deceitful to her husband at the moment he was dying. What that something was, Harris himself didn't know. But Harris nodded, stood up, and closed the door. Perhaps, Elias suggested, she was hiding him so he could not sell the place.

"Is that what is going on?" Harris demanded,

"I am not going to say anything," Elias said.

"Then there is the mortgage," Harris said. "I have never lost a mortgage in my life—but you see, I didn't give this mortgage to her—nor did I give it to him. Old McGrathon did."

Elias threw up his hands.

"Well, that's just it. I feel helpless fighting a woman—because I don't want to, but you see, if I don't, her theatre'll put us both out of business. I spoke many times about it with King—three times he was ready to sell and three times she says no. Now her husband is too weak to make any decision and decides to go back home or wherever. What we need is to do something for her so she can have some little money. I've known George King—he's an entertainer just like me—I understand him—I understand the practicality of the English. She doesn't!"

He said this though there were no mortgage arrears, and Harris agreed because he was terrified that there might be if she took over.

"I would have to get head office in Montreal to sign on that—to board her up," Harris said.

"I know it's a bother to you," Elias said.

"Oh, no—I can have it wired by Tuesday."

Elias glanced bitterly out the window, at snow falling against the paved street, and the flame from his lighter flickering on in the dusk. Then he sat back, legs spread, and puffed on his smoke, full of expectation and life. The intention was for both of them to show each other their solicitude for the woman.

But on Tuesday morning a storm covered the river. All businesses were locked, schools shut, and the telegraph office was blocked with snow. By now it was announced that King was dying.

Hearing from Usoff Assoff, the man who had come with his blind horse up the street to deliver coal, that they were thinking of shutting her theatre, Janie knew she had to act. She was twenty-five years of age and walking past the couch where her husband was dying. She took the shotgun and said to my father, "I'm going to the hall. Take care to stay here—I will try to get to the maid."

Janie, however, was not dispirited and walked through the snow toward the theatre with a shotgun under her arm.

She meant to guard the Regent against anyone from the Biograph or the bank, armed with a double-barrelled 12-gauge my grandfather had bought for bird hunting. And she had something else—she had the deed and the will that stated the business was now hers alone.

Harris, who did not get the go-ahead from the head office until Wednesday morning, found her there, pointing the shotgun at him. Shaken, he hurried back to the bank.

"She pointed the gun at me—a lunatic—it might have gone off, and then where would I be? Well, there you have it—I wouldn't be, would I?"

The mortgage payment was made that afternoon. It was brought to the bank by Walter McLeary, her projectionist and cousin. Harris informed Mr. Elias that his hands were tied for the moment.

"How hysterical she is," Elias said sympathetically. "But something has to be done! This is not the time to be weak—understand me, Harris—not the time. I have heard her shotgun is not a British but a Russian make. I'm not sure of her politics. Are you, Harris? She might be one of those Irish troublemakers we hear about from time to time."

At Elias's insistence Harris telephoned the sheriff.

This Russian-made shotgun was by the next day the topic of the town. What did she have a Russian gun for—what possessed her?

This talk was something that informed Mr. Harris, who was a moral man, in the sense that bankers are moral in their circumspection about whom they entrust money to. A hidden anger about his position at this lowly bank enveloped him. In his thwarted inner life, she was the key.

For the next two days, Hanna Jane—or Janie, as she was now becoming known—stayed at the theatre. She sat in the chair with the shotgun across her lap, under a lurid one-sheet showing Valentino. He was gone too, Valentino, his art dead at the age of thirty-one, with a gaze and a cigarette, and champagne on ice.

The phone rang. It was the police.

"How did you find me?" she asked.

She was joking. They weren't.

The police demanded that she give the shotgun over and stop the nonsense. They called her father, Jimmy, and he, plied with drink, came forward, his face pale, and pointed a finger at the theatre.

"Come on out—be sensible—come out, girl, and talk about this. Yer livin' life the way of perdition—perdition is all around you now—and it was what I was telling ya at yer marriage ya'd fiddle and fart until ya found perdition—"

She said only when she felt safe would she.

"I am yer father—can't you be safe with me?"

"Never!"

"Ah, yer an ungrateful girl—an ungrateful girl, Hanna Jane—"

He would look behind him to other men, shake his head, grin, turn back and ask her if she might be so kind as to loan him some money for a nice Canadian horse.

"Not on yer life."

"Ah, yer an ungrateful girl, Hanna Jane," he would say, scratching at his woollen pants while Harris and Elias kept telling him to keep at her and wear her down.

She hollered that she would fire at anyone who came to take the theatre from her, and die with gun in hand, as her husband, she was sure, had wanted to do years before in the mud of France.

"Honest ta fug, she's as mad as a defrocked nun," Jimmy said, looking back at them. By now the whole town had gathered to listen. There was Phil Druken, drinking and shaking his head. There was Putsy Druken and her sister, Rebecca, who had run to see them hang Janie. That she was not to be hanged disappointed them all, the children especially.

There was only one small detail. She had forgotten all about my father, her son. At midnight of the second day she locked the theatre doors (there were two, outside and inside) and went to her house.

When Janie came home from the theatre, she could see George King's arm hanging down from the couch, his white pyjama sleeve embroidered with gold trim. He was just forty years of age and had been on Canadian soil eight of those.

My grandmother never shed a tear, for he was, she said, at peace, and gone to heaven if there was one. The maid, however, had fled as soon as the man had died, and had left my father alone, to sit in a room for six hours with his dead father. Janie went quickly to her son, kissed him and made a cup of tea.

That night Janie sat in the room with her dead husband's belongings, clutching an old cane of his. Sleet fell on the roof above, which made all his collected trivials noticeable as she stared about the room. The house too was a monument against her and George. Bought by two upstarts who thought they were something, it was a house unfinished, the upstairs dark and undone, and two rooms downstairs left with studs bare. My father had faithfully awaited her return.

He often remembered her from his vantage point at the far end of the room. She was haughty and beautiful. She wore a black dress, done up with purple buttons, a dress she could never have hoped to afford three years before. She sat staring into the dark, unblinking, and every now and again she would look at him for a solid minute. He would smile timidly, and she would look away.

In the morning the minister from the Anglican church called her with some information about the service. It was a grey day, just right for such an event. Earlier, a casket had been delivered and the body had been taken away. Her one friend, Walter P. McLeary—her cousin, who was twenty-three at that time—did the legwork and got done what had to be done.

I was told that she worried about the last rites. So she sent the maid, who had returned that morning, to find a priest. The priest, called O'Hanrahan, came as a service to her. He asked for some clothes of the deceased so he could give them to the needy.

He said that he was uncertain about an Anglican going quickly to God. She answered with good dignity that no one knew God's arrangements with Mr. King but himself.

The drawing room was small, and very British. It had the British flair for clutter in leisure. It seemed that anyone in it should talk with an accent. It contained Mr. King's leather-bound books, which Janie never read. It contained his piano, which he had brought from England on tour, a picture of his schoolmates, all dead in the war. It contained his coin collection, started long before he crossed the Atlantic. She closed his drawing room and locked it, and put the key in her pocket.

When Janie left the house, the sky was bright and the windy air was filled with smoke. The day was warm for late January, and the snow was thick and pure white. There was no funeral procession. But Joey Elias went with about two hundred others to pay their last respects. A small stone carving to Mr. King's memory was erected later in the year, and overlooked a part of the Miramichi that stretched toward the sea.

FOUR

The first effect of Mr. King's death was for others to reinvent themselves as allies of his widow. For after his death he was thought so highly of, how could anyone have ever been his enemy or entertained a malicious thought against him or his? To me his life seems sad and woebegone, because I did not know him, and the idea of his death is a strange companion to his photograph before me, looking like F. Scott Fitzgerald, on the lot of MGM, where he went to be a scriptwriter after his life had failed.

Mr. Elias visited Janie twice, saying he had started a raffle for her. She thought he meant that they were going to raffle her off to another man.

"No, no, Janie—nothing like that, dear. I have started a raffle at the Biograph to show solidarity with you—some little things you might need now, dear."

Elias sat in her room, and put the boy, Miles King, onto his knee. Afterwards he spoke sincerely about how she was sad, how the house smelled of death. When someone spoke of Janie in an off-colour way, Elias shouted: "Her husband is gone—and she has the little boy to think of—and is pregnant again—so I want no one here to talk about her."

The little girls Putsy and Rebecca Druken noticed how their own father, who worked at Dobblestein's mill, withered under Joey Elias's gaze.

"We have to watch her like a hawk," Elias told people, "but it's for her own good, you understand. She may try to drown herself in a pool of water somewhere or other. Where's the nearest pool of water?"

"In the river."

"Go now and watch it."

"Watch the river?"

"Yes."

"It's January."

"Yes—so?"

"So the river is frozen solid—"

"Have you no sense? She will find a way to crawl in and finish herself, I am certain of it."

He spoke about how Janie's house was empty—the little child sat in the corner looking about. How awful that was to Mr. Elias. And there was wind blowing along the floor and cold winter light coming in—and how that struck him too, perhaps as a warning. Like in the Old Testament, when the plagues came—for wasn't money the root of all evil? Or was it just because King was a Protestant? Ah yes, that's the rub. And what did the priest say about Janie and her money? He said she would find no happiness. Though he did take her gift of a hundred dollars. Besides this, there was the emptiness of the back room, the unfinished quality of it, the locked drawers everywhere—and the closed-off drawing room; how terrible, he said. He wondered what could be in there that was valuable. And too, her great ignorance is everywhere—

that is what was so sad. Great beauty matched by great ignorance.

"Stupid" someone said, smirking.

"You fool," Elias retorted. "Not stupid—never stupid—brilliant, the way she plays her fiddle—but ignorant." And he added, "Poor old King."

For just five months before, he had been playing checkers with King, and King was talking about getting well. King had travelled on a train to search out treatment from Banting and Best, and hadn't he come home thinking he might get better? False hope, all false. Were they honour-bound to protect the widow from any connivance, even though she was Janie McLeary?

Here he gave Putsy Druken a hug, and patted younger Rebecca on the head.

How those two girls adored him—well, the whole town did. And he saw his life now only in this adoration.

A week or two after the service there was just a slight change in posture. Elias needed a favour. He went and asked Janie for the loan of a Mary Pickford film. He said he was in a pinch and would not ask her for anything again, but he knew she had an Arbuckle film she could run, and her theatre was not to reopen for another week, seeing that after a death in the family many family businesses stayed closed a respectable amount of time. She told Mr. Elias that no one went to Arbuckle since his problems with the starlet at his house. Being discreet she could say nothing more, only that she would lend him the Arbuckle.

"But I've run the Arbuckle—everyone has run the Arbuckle."

"Well." She smiled. "I wish you no trouble, but it is bad policy." She was trying to say that it was bad policy for him to ask this favour, but she held her tongue. "And as a matter of fact I am going to reopen sooner than I intended."

"Oh! When?"

"Tonight—so you see, it would be bad policy."

"Bad policy," he said, and looked at her curiously. It was the first time he felt her temperament—her will. And it was not like her old drunken father, whom he bullied and laughed at. He had not felt it before, not directed precisely at him. "But I raised a raffle for you," he said.

"I am grateful," she answered, "but Pickford is mine, and I will run it at my theatre—tonight."

"But it's just one film," he said. "And you could wait another day or so!"

"It is bad policy," she said.

"I see," Elias said. He went back into the cold street that smelled of ingrained dirt and soot and steel. He heard trains far away and had an idea.

"There'll be lads to handle her," he thought. And he further thought that she had done a very silly thing.

That night he came at his friends sideways with: Did they know that he had known King in England? And what had King's kind thought of him? Nothing. Now when it came down to it, who had arrived here first in this land of ours, this great Canada? Why, it was him, Elias. And hadn't he written to King to tell him to come over? Yes, he had—begged him, in fact, to come over to do a musical tour. And Elias was to be his manager. Here he showed a paper, with his signature and King's. Then he put it away.

It didn't matter if this was true; the paper indicated that it was. Legitimacy was everything to people like Phil Druken who did not read or write. Rebecca sat with him this night, in long, torn stockings with her hair matted and braided. She listened as Elias passed back and forth in front of her.

Janie opened her theatre again, went back to work alone, with the Pickford film to run. It created a small scandal, for many had convinced themselves she wouldn't have the audacity to open alone.

"I imagine," my father once said, "that my parents played their music in front of those pictures—those slightly absurd characters the silent films created with a great flourish—and once alone, she was somehow wounded. I remember her playing her violin. She practised every day in the upstairs chamber—yes, she called it a chamber—for her discipline was everything. And the secret was, she had arthritis in her fingers. The secret was, she was worried about Joey Elias's piano-meister—a Mr. Leaky, a squat, affable, beringed, bedazzled puff who came from Rogersville, thirty miles away, and liked to say he could outplay that "McLeary treasure" in seconds flat. My mother practised because of that, and after a time became as competent on the piano as she had to be—but it was her fiddle that saw her through. That this contest gathered the people on different nights to one place and then the other was good for both businesses. In truth, who knows, there may have been a vague collusion here, a collusion born of the whiff of enmity.

"'Can Miss McLeary'—they did not use King—'do this' Leaky would say, and he would run the gamut like a Liberace, his tails hanging from the back of his seat and helping Tom Mix or some other hero along the precipice where hung danger and desire.

"'Ah—can Leaky do this?' Mother would answer with bow in hand, and a delicate plucking of her string, her hair—she could not play without her hair hanging down—tossed reckless about on the storm of her own passion, as luckless John Gilbert strode into a room.

"Her going back to work so soon was unseemly," Father continued, "yet her great talent made them forget her bad manners, and soon they came back to her in droves. So did her better pictures—my father had seen to that. So Elias again was thwarted. The puff from Rogersville was fired. Elias decided that a local girl, Mary McCarthy, could play just as well—but she did not play as well as Janie. After this there was a phony war, so to speak, where nothing much happened for a little bit. Still, in order to facilitate Elias's ambition, a crime would sooner or later have to be committed."

"Would it?" I asked.

"Well—didn't it?" Father said.

———

For a while no one bothered her. It was during this time her second child was born. She named it Georgina for obvious reasons—she could not name a girl George.

Elias had a plan, and a plan wrapped within a plan.

"You know," he said to his friends, "King always thought he was too good for her old man. Now what if I operated like that—thinking I was too good for people? Bring the old fellow here. I want to talk to him. No—he doesn't have to come here—I will go to him."

Over the course of the next week, Elias enlisted the support of old Jim McLeary. He made an impromptu visit to the house on Pond Street. There was snow on the ground, and Joey entered and saw a little old man leaning over a plate of stew. One electric light shone from the side wall onto the floor, and the edges of the kitchen were in darkness. Now and then a mouse would run across that light and into the darkness again.

The idea Jim McLeary had always promoted, and was therefore promoted by Joey Elias now, was that he had loved his daughter and protected her reputation. But just the opposite was the case—there were many times he should have stood up for her when he didn't.

Now, for the sake of Janie's children, Joey Elias himself had come to him, eyes cast down and a gloomy expression on his face. He even entered the house timidly, in great deference. Then, taking some rum from his pocket, he spoke about Hanna Jane.

"Far be it from me to tell you what to do," he explained while immediately telling Jim what to do. It was the children they had to protect, or what was a heaven for?

"A woman should not work but should think of her children," Jimmy said.

"That's all I'm thinking of," Joey said, "all as I'm worried about. I don't even think that Georgina is baptized yet—and growing up without a father is terrible." He held his hat in his hand and smoothed its rim, bending it forward a little before putting it back on.

"I tried to bring her up right," Jim said in a feeble way as he looked at the glass being filled with bootlegged rum. "You know that, Mr. Elias."

"I know you did," Elias answered. "It wasn't your fault."

Jim drank, nodded, and was given some more. Did either Joey Elias or Jimmy McLeary know they were lying to each other at that moment? The fact was, lies had buoyed them both for a lifetime. Jimmy McLeary drank, and prepared to go fight the battle for the spiritual lives of the children.

He put on his tam-o'-shanter and strode toward the great house he had not been in before.

He knocked on the knocker and then opened the door. Janie came to the entrance and saw her father, already drunk. He implored her not to keep up this charade of a business when she had little ones at home. Everyone was talking about her, everyone was saying it was a disgrace.

"There'll be a death over this yet," he said.

That he was drunk did not surprise Janie, for during Prohibition— or anytime drink was scarce—a drinker would drink more, for fear of not finding it later.

His hands were red, his fingers blunt, his back arched forward, his nose pressed down like a beak. He tried to grab Georgina away from her, but Janie ran into the drawing room and locked it shut.

"I want to baptize the child!" He yelled from out in the hall.

"The child is baptized—I baptized it—I did."

It was almost poignant the way she said it, and he understood his shame.

He went back to Joey Elias in disgrace, and looking for more rum. Elias dismissed him, saying there was none available.

It was in March when Joey Elias began to talk about the Trojan horse. He had been reading about this horse in a magazine at the barbershop. He said that his luck was George King's lack of luck.

"Why?" Phil Druken asked.

He answered that he had been a bachelor all his life, but was it his luck to marry someday? He had grown up in an area of the world where having the upper hand had rarely if ever been used to exercise one's humility, and an excess of luck had almost always stipulated a lack of restraint. A look of triumph was contained in a cordial smile at a moment when the fading sun flushed his shaven jaw and crisp hair.

"You turn in one direction instead of another on a road," he continued, "that saves you, or someone detains you, and by that you are saved—or your opponent dies and, well, his widow is alive. Your mother makes a bad marriage—and then dies, and you end up with the bad luck." The sun hit his white face. "The world doesn't care much about an incident—if it works. It might be bad, it might be good—but it is all a gamble. For instance, the Trojan horse—who would have thought of that? The horse itself is neither bad nor good, and it doesn't matter. If it works, good was beside the point. Because the world is filled with achievements that have little to do with good."

Could he help it if Jimmy McLeary had ruined his own family? Or if Janie could no longer run a business? Someone had to take it over, and that was him. It did not matter how.

"And the Trojan horse?" Rebecca suddenly asked. It was the first time anyone could remember her asking a question of anyone.

"Oh, that's the secret—I'm the Trojan horse," he said. "It's what you plan inside, what others never see."

He began over the next few weeks to see Hanna Jane, to speak to her, to touch her hand.

Nor did he think—she being a silly girl—that Hanna Jane could nail his horse shut.

But only a few weeks later, by the middle of March, things had soured between them for good. After he'd been cautious, courting her little by little, all Elias's planning came down to one rash decision.

It had turned mild. The paved streets were soaking, while the dirt streets had turned to mud, and car lights glowed feebly through the fog. Then it froze at night and began to snow. Elias went out on the morning of March fifteenth to see her, while snow fell over those muddy streets and lonely car tracks treaded up the hill, and came back late at night. Others had an uneasy feeling watching him play cards that night.

This much is certain. He had attempted a kiss.

There must have been a moment, maybe a series of moments, when his heart had been truly usurped. But she had not reciprocated. More to the point, I think, she had no idea of his feelings until they were presented with a clumsy kiss on the theatre steps, with snowflakes falling into her face. She had laughed. That laughter, though unfortunate, was not meant to injure but only to show the absurdity of his proposition.

The consequence was a shift in his metabolism: he now became more convinced that everything he had done since the death of George King was done not to buy her mean little business but to protect her and her family. He turned in mid-stride and decided there and then—if he could—to prosecute her as stridently as possible.

Elias had, he thought now, begun his relationship with Janie for her own good; this was firmly entrenched in his mind. Now he needed to do something else. And soon. For just a moment everything had been right with them, but he had played his hand too soon, and she withdrew. This was a miscalculation.

Where was the kiss attempted? On the very step of her theatre during late afternoon. Who had seen his attempted kiss? Mr. Harris, the bank manager. Elias pondered what to do. Usually he would have the good fortune of meeting Harris on the street at some time. But this did not happen, and Elias worried that the avoidance was intentional on Harris's part. He had to regain his hand. He decided he must go to the bank and explain the kiss. And it all depended on how it was explained. He decided it was best to pretend that he did not know that Harris had seen him and Janie, and that he would ask discretion not for his sake but for Janie's.

He walked to the bank. Though his suit was cheap, and thin, and blasts of wind chilled his legs to the bone, he waited outside until mid-afternoon, when the bank was closing and the only light on was the lamp on Harris's desk. Then he went inside and knocked on Harris's door and, seemingly humbled, said, "I thought since I had a moment I would tell you that something happened last Tuesday evening of a strange nature. Janie kissed me." Here he held up his hands, palms outstretched, as if to block misconception, and shook his head. "Now don't hold that against her—I want you to know that she is suffering, and very lonely—and it should have nothing to do with your feelings in trying to help her. She knows I tried to help her husband—and it might have been gratitude on her part." As he spoke he manoeuvred toward the hard-backed chair. He felt its seat with his left hand before he slumped into it, feigning dejection.

"I see," Harris whispered.

"Do you? I was discreet enough not to stop her—and now feeling ashamed, she has reacted by rejecting a certain advance I never made, and has characterized the advance as one on her business."

Harris was silent as he nodded, his bald face flushing.

"It doesn't bode well for us, as far as the business is concerned, to try and help her," Elias said.

"I see," Harris said.

"At the moment she realized she had no ground to stand on, could not keep up the pretense of being able to handle a theatre, I found myself having to avoid her sexual advances—"

He cleared his throat and waited.

"Deluded, is she!" Harris said.

"Much of the time," Elias answered.

"Yes—well, I did see it," Harris said.

"You saw she was deluded, you mean?"

"Not exactly."

"Deluded—I mean—how did you see it?"

"From the street," Harris said, pointing. "I was crossing the street. So there you go." Then he added, "it's strange—"

"What is strange?"

"I get the feeling that she set it up—so I would see it," Harris said, peeling an egg and looking up at the face of his friend.

"I don't believe that!" Elias said.

"I think she must have wanted me to think—you were taking advantage of her," Harris answered. "My two cents—but it'll go no further."

"Thank you," Elias said.

I believe that if Elias had said he made the advance on Janie, and had done it for the reason he had, which was for the affection of a woman who owned a business, Harris would have been understanding.

Joey Elias said he would take over her theatre, as a benefit to the town.

Janie sent for Walter P. McLeary, her cousin who had taken care of the theatre since George King took sick. He fixed the seats, swept the floors, cleaned the foyer, did the advertisements. At five foot four, Walter was a humpback with a lame leg. Yet he was indispensable to the survival of her business. He had learned to run the projector, took care of her coal and wood, made sure the one-sheets were up, but like Janie he himself was an outcast of the first rank.

He informed her that the Biograph was ready to expand to a new building, and Elias was thinking of more theatres. Only her theatre stood in his way.

"Think of it as armies—your army is blocking his advance, because you have the first runs. He needs the first-run picture. They make twice the money his does. There is nothing you can do but fight him. You might not want to fight him, but we must fight. You are a McLeary—and so am I—so remember who we are. Our people came over on a boat, settling in this town on the edge of nowhere. You, after almost a hundred years, are the first McLeary to make something of herself. And now this. So you have to fight. You have no other option."

"Yes, I know," she answered, her voice remote. Her features had changed since her husband's death. She seemed closed off, more solitary than ever. In her mid-twenties and a young mother, she was beautiful, though somewhat tougher since her husband's death. Her money held no pleasure. She was very stern with herself, yet was kind to almost everyone else and to Walter—though once in anger she accused him of having two humps.

Walter had done nothing in the last few weeks but find things out about her enemies. That he was able to obtain such information was in itself unnerving for her.

He walked back and forth, banking to the left and blowing smoke from his oversized cigar. He told her that it was a consortium of friends that showed a complete and unswerving contempt for her. How was this contempt manufactured? Easily, indeed. A widow like Janie McLeary would know nothing about what movies fine and decent people wanted. And why? Because her father was old Jimmy McLeary the drunk. She knew nothing about business, and would be better taking care of her children, the way a woman should.

That aside, he said, he was concerned about something else. The movies came in by overnight train and often sat in the open at the train station. Walter told her she must be vigilant, for Joey Elias knew where the pictures sat, and knew well how to use anything to his advantage. So what if John Barrymore's, or Charlie Chaplin's, or Buster Keaton's new movie was hijacked by Joey Elias? Would the luggage department care who came to collect it?

And here was the rub. What if Joey sent her father to collect these pictures?

"Joey is your father's pal."

For if even her own poor father came to override her, Walter said, his right shoe scraped down, by the way he dragged his foot, who would not laugh at her expense?

"Then you must guard the station. And I will guard the hall," Janie decided. "And if they take my movies I will take theirs."

"You have already run theirs. You have the first runs. Georgie saw to that before—all of them—"

"I have the first runs? Who said so?"

"In a curious roundabout way, Charlie Chaplin said so. I mean, you signed—or your husband signed—a contract with the film distribu-tors who act on behalf of the companies, and one of these compa-nies is Chaplin's—so it's your move, Lady Jane."

The movies came in by overnight train, down from the great city of Montreal, on the *Nova Scotian* plowing snow in front of it all the dark winter, and long after those pictures arrived they would sit in the soot-darkened train station the whole of the next day, near the time slips for the freight workers. Elias would switch pictures, or had a station worker whom he sold bootlegged rum to hold Janie's movie back, telling her it hadn't arrived, until long after his movie had started. There she would stand, awaiting the arrival of the tins of film that sat four feet from her.

Now it was decided that Walter would go to the station each day there was a change and collect the tins and the one-sheet directly off the train. Meanwhile, Janie would find out from Montreal's distrib-utor in Saint John what Elias was running so she would inform the public before he himself did.

At first it was a contest of who rose earlier in the morning—Walter, who was loyal to Hanna Jane, or pale, trembling Jimmy McLeary, once again showing unwavering devotion to Joey Elias and the drunks in town, whom he needed more than his daughter.

Jimmy would turn up at the station with the filching, troubled expression of a man gone to ruin, playing his last seedless gambit against his own kind so he would be liked. Always little Walter McLeary was there before him.

"I didn't think my own nephew would act like this—against his own kind—his own flesh and blood—like that there."

Over the next month, not a movie was missed. The Dime became known as "Janie's theatre." All the people in town called her Janie instead of Hanna, whether to show familiarity or respect, she wasn't sure. But she liked the name. It made her feel independent, no longer the young Hanna that George King had spied in what felt like an eternity ago. She was waved to by patrons of her theatre when she rode along the street in the Ford car, still wearing black, with a shawl over her head, or when she walked, her hands hidden in a fur-lined muff.

Though she had money she was unhappy—just as the bishop had said she would be. "You will not find happiness in this life, Janie McLeary," he had said after her wedding in the Protestant church.

"Then I will not search for it," she had answered.

FIVE

Near the end of May things took another turn. When Janie came up the steps—two hours after the movie *Metropolis*—which was too inscrutable for the patrons, who wanted Rudolph Valentino or some other hero—Walter told her the mortgage was coming up for renewal and showed her the slip of paper from the Royal Bank.

"Tell me that isn't bad," Janie said.

"It isn't good," Walter said, scratching the top of his forehead with his thumb. "I think Harris will say he can close on you 'less you can come up with seven thousand dollars."

"That's impossible—" she uttered.

"What is—?"

"The seven thousand—"

"I know," Walter said.

"What should I do?"

Janie saw him in shadow, and looked at his shoes, shining in the light from the street. Kind, endearing, and loyal—all these attributes were somehow not enough.

"Have you ever noticed in the world there are different kinds of men?" Walter said in a soft voice.

"What way?" Janie said.

"Well, one is the kind that moves into a new town and within a week or two decides there is a cause to fit into, a cause greater than himself, which was waiting for him."

"I don't understand," Janie said.

"Mr. Harris. He is friends with Mr. Elias."

"I will go to meet with Mr. Harris," she said in almost complete naivety, which Walter could not help but notice.

"Maybe you could borrow." He handed the letter to her. She took it and tossed it aside.

"I will see to it," she said.

She went home and sat in the dark drawing room, surrounded by her late husband's sketches and books, his ink drawing of his son, his framed tickets to a concert he played that the Prince of Wales had attended.

She had already met with Harris once since the death of her husband. When she had gone to the bank, Harris was on his lunch hour, eating a hard-boiled egg. He cracked it with a spoon and asked to see her husband.

"He is dead," she said.

"Well, then—who runs the business?" he said, twirling the egg about in its egg cup.

"I do."

"What do you mean, you do?"

"I mean—you see me sitting here?"

"Yes," he said, putting the egg in his mouth and chewing it slowly.

"Well, I'm sitting here because I run the business."

"But the bank needs someone to take care of the mortgage. Who would that be?" He put his spoon down on the napkin on the table.

"That would be me."

"But it is he we were dealing with."

"But you were not dealing with him, because you were not here then. You are new here, aren't you. Now you are here and dealing not with him, who is dead, but with me, who is sitting here."

"But," he said in exasperation, "that's not the way it should be."

"I agree," Janie King said.

He nodded slightly and looked out at the bank clerk watching them, as he picked up his spoon again. "You agree," he said, showing some surprise in his voice.

"Yes," said Janie with a smile. "No idiot should ever be in your position. But since an idiot is and I am dealing with him, it is bloody unfortunate for us both." She rose.

This is how their first face-to-face meeting (besides the brief encounter with the shotgun) ended.

Well, she thought, perhaps she should not have called him an idiot.

Mr. Harris assumed she was clever and bold, but not brilliant or courageous. He knew her kind before he ever met her and, meeting her that once at his bank, had smiled in a way which informed her that he had formulated ideas about her based on gossip supplied by those he himself wished to impress. So she called him what he was, an idiot. Now she regretted it, but found no way to take it back. Taking it back would show weakness. That showed courage on her part. Moreover, taking it back would maintain culpability where she was not guilty. She was wise enough to stand her ground. Except she had hardly known what a mortgage was when she called him an idiot. Perhaps she should have found out.

But back in 1927, though she knew everyone who was against her, though she believed she had all possibilities foreseen, she was still not prepared for this.

The day she went back to discuss the mortgage payment, Harris moved against her in a way that seemed to show he was allied with her. He was concerned very much with what kind of impression he should make. So he came to the conclusion that there would be an association of overseers for Janie McLeary's benefit. And for her son and daughter, of course. Harris knew that if she balked at this new alliance she would be truly outcast. He knew this when she entered the bank. He felt it in the fibres of his suit coat against his chest.

Harris hid behind the precept that it was a bank's responsibility to assess a person's risk. He could not let on even to himself that this was not the case. In truth, if he failed in this, it would be an appalling indication of his lack of moral fibre. The way to pretend he had moral fibre was to succeed in this fabrication.

In a way, as far as Harris was concerned, Fritz Lang's masterpiece did her in, for Harris had in his possession the appalling result of this movie. He himself had not seen it, which was a little thing—but Harris was a little thinker. If he had been the sort of thinker he pretended himself to be, the smallness and pedestrian quality of his life would have appalled him. But this was not the case, for Mr. Harris believed all t's crossed meant all i's dotted. And Janie could do neither well. This was her secret. Her father, who could read, had not managed to get her to. However, she would learn, so by the time I was a boy, she wrote letters in the dozen—as if making up for a lack in her person that had caused so much pain.

Harris stood and warmly offered his hand. She took it and smiled in relief, until turning to a seat near the window, with a drawn green blind holding back the May sunshine, she saw the worst vision she could encounter at that moment.

Sitting in the other chair, on this warm spring day, wearing a pinstriped suit with a wide green tie, was Joey Elias, who had been asked by Harris to help him assess her "potential" as a businesswoman.

This event took place on May 25, 1927. Harris had Elias come with him to the bank. He had her last year's mortgage statements and a statement of the theatre's debt in front of them. When she entered she saw a trap. But Harris believed that if an illiterate woman, who was generally given to hysteria and shotguns, was so suspicious, how could she deal in a rational way with a public she depended on? And what would that say about the Royal Bank?

"Don't let us be angry. I've come to help," Elias said, touching her hand, and looking with concern at Harris.

Janie said nothing but stared straight at Harris. She did not take her eyes from him, did not motion with her hand, and though a deadly heat hung over the room, she did not sweat. Harris could not admit how treacherous his plan was, yet could not look at her, and each time he tried, her stare made him flinch.

Her silence lasted five, ten, fifteen minutes, while Harris went over the figures with Joey Elias's help, and pointed to certain ink marks that Joey spoke about with high seriousness. Janie could not look at them, for she did not know what they were. She had not made them.

Finally Harris had a solution. Let Joey Elias countersign her mortgage. If she could not pay it, Joey Elias would take over her payments and her business—but would keep the name of the theatre in her husband's honour and she would retain thirty-three percent of the holdings. Elias was willing to do this for her because he was a businessman and had given his word to the bank. And if she would sign it could be transacted that very day.

"I will burn in hell first," she whispered.

Harris held the paper as she said this. He looked quickly at Elias. None had ever said this about any transaction he had ever done or ever attempted to do. No one spoke like this in a bank. He didn't even know if they were allowed to. She was a lunatic—he saw that now. The knowledge that he was inventing a problem and fabricating a solution for the benefit of Joey Elias seemed remote after she said those words. She must sign before she left—or in a week he would confiscate her building and place it up for tender. He told her this in a voice he hoped would scare her. She made no sign it did.

Elias waved his hand to tell Harris there was no reason to be so stern, and he tried to reason with her. He spoke of how much he respected her for trying in such difficult times. Then he spoke of her father.

"You know your poor dad believes you need help with your business—is worried sick about you and your children."

Harris looked at her eagerly, and then at Elias.

"That is why I'm here—I've come because of my feelings for yer dad, who has been your only support."

"Don't turn your back on your own father, Janie girl," Harris said.

How horrible it must be to be Janie McLeary, thought Harris at that precise moment. She remained silent.

Finally Elias, infuriated by her silence, and seeing his chance slipping, picked up a pen, put it in Janie's hand, and tried to force her signature.

Then Harris said, "If you cannot read, you cannot hold a mortgage. If you sign this document it will prove that you can read." He looked sternly at her, while Elias doubled his effort. But Elias could not budge her arm. The strain on her face was visible, and his unmistakable. How strong she was, strong like the broken often are, at the very moment you think they will crumble.

She glared at Harris the whole time Elias was pressing her arm down. Then without a sound, she broke the pen in one hand, and left the bank.

The air was full of pollen, and children played on the sidewalk near the building. She believed that all was lost and carried her purse in both hands in front of her as she walked rapidly away.

"I will have to borrow the money," she decided, "from every Catholic in the town."

"Yes," the terrified French maid said, handing her mistress two dollars.

It was later that night, far past supper hour, and the sun was retreating. From the oval window halfway up the darkening stairway, Janie saw two men watching the house. Across the street in the cold, damp evening, two more men stood guard. They knew she had to make an attempt to seek money from the Catholic houses.

She changed out of her dress. After daylight had completely gone, she went to the upstairs French window that overlooked the back lane.

"Why aren't you going out the front door?" my father whispered.

"They are all after me," she said, without emotion or even worry.

"Who is all after you?"

"Everyone in the world," Janie said, "so I am acting on that theory. Yet"—here she turned to her son—"where will I go?"

"I don't know. I don't know where you're going," my father said.

She was now standing out on the ledge, wearing a pair of slacks and an old shirt, her hair up under her hat. She asked him to hold on to her leg as she stretched toward the tree. She could barely touch the nearest branch with her fingers. She would have to jump straight into the air—three storeys above the ground—and grab the tree. She had no other plan except to ask anyone she might for money. But she knew that Pond and Chatham Streets would be watched as well as her house.

"You will fall!" my father remembered crying, and my grandmother turning to him and saying:

"Shh. You have to let go of my leg now and let me jump—it's the risin' of the moon," she said with a kind of frozen spite.

As he tightly held on to her, tears running down his cheeks, she added, "And take Georgina to Walter if I fail."

Then, knowing he was unable to let go, she pried his fingers away, one at a time.

"Let go of me now. And don't clutch me again, or I will fall."

He drew back, and then leaned out the window again. He felt she was doing this dangerous thing out of spite for others and their dislike of her. In the night air the wind had picked up and rain began to fall out of the sky.

"Things are better when we are brave," she said, and dropped out of sight.

There was a silence, and then the noise of branches moving.

"I am on the tree," she said. "Take heed to keep the doors locked.

And take care of Georgina tonight—we have no one else, you and I! Damn, I think I broke a rib!" She disappeared into the shadows.

Janie made her way down the cliff path and out along the street near Castle Lodge. Two men were standing on the lodge steps: she could see their cigarettes and hear their soft, whimsical banter about nothing, and in one of those banterings, a word fell into the open—"Janie." She had wanted to go to Castle Lodge for help—she knew the woman there. But now she changed her mind. She stopped not a second too soon and stepped into the alleyway leading to the wharf. Here were other men, most of the spring lumber having been moved. They were sitting up against some pilings, drinking. Far across in the night air, on the Morrissey Bridge, she saw a flashlight. A fire was burning on the shore a hundred yards from where she was. There were men there also. One was her father, hoping to collect the fifteen dollars Joey had promised to whoever could stop her.

She began again, as she had over many days, to doubt her sanity. For when dozens in town say you are wrong, you will begin to think you are. Maybe they were all trying to help, she thought, and perhaps, just perhaps, she *was* insane, as Harris suggested. Perhaps their smiles and their curious looks were out of sympathy only. She cursed that thought—she was not so insane that she did not know a light on the bridge and a fire on the shore. She waited a minute and then two. The rain started hard again. Her right rib cage felt bruised and tender and pained when she breathed.

There was something else about this idea of insanity—all her life she had been forced to act in a way uncommon with others (her father's presence with the rabble was proof of this). Yet were *they* sane? Was sanity doing what they did? And if it was, was it moral or justified to be sane? In great part her reasoning was the reasoning of saints as well as sinners. How could sanity be anything but a ruse—and a feeble one at that? For if Joey Elias went to those men and told them they had to find Janie McLeary to really help her—they would nod, and agree. That is in a second they could be persuaded utterly by fear or self-interest into doing something else, and turning away from what at this very moment they took to be completely honourable.

And could Joey Elias have put a good word in for her with Harris, instead of that display of piety? Yes. And was she being too cynical about their motives when she thought this? Not on my life, she thought. She was not being cynical at all. And was it because she was a woman and therefore considered weak? Of course. And their profession of dismay over the English—those men who were sworn to "help her"—were they paid for helping deliver coal and building the house? Yes, she recognized them. So her husband's Englishness was an excuse—of course. And another strange thought—any one of them she could seduce completely in a second, and will him to want her—she could have any man over eighteen do her bidding. Of course. So she was insane? And if these men were sane and common men, were they like the majority of men? Yes. And if that was the case, would it be better to be insane? And if insane, how would she make it across the bridge—as Insane Janie McLeary? Well, what would Joan of Arc do?

Who could say she did not think this or think something so similar that the men became the very composites of the minions of some mad Torquemada, or some horrid judge in 1431, and her own father poor gulled Charles VII? She could walk by them—keep to the far side of them, huddled down. They might not see. Yet if seen? Ah, if seen, done for—the Drukens themselves there to add moral weight to Joey's search.

She looked at the black water and saw the reflection of the fire strut and crawl in the distant waves even as the rain pelted her face. She watched the flashlight from the bridge meander through gloom dark as a deck of spades. She looking back saw her great house, with only one light on, feeble as an invalid calling. She was overcome by a feeling of futility and sadness for the future of her son and daughter. Her breathing was shallow because of the pain.

"Goddamn them—"

That might have buoyed her resolve but it did not solve her dilemma or the pain she now felt striking under her breast.

In fact, there was no way across the great river, and anyway, what would she do once across? For in truth the lights across the river were as foreign to her as Lima or Lisbon. Her idea had been to go to every Catholic house on the river and ask for any money they could spare and that she would pay them back as soon as she could while offering masses and movies about priests. And they would have her word, for her name was Janie McLeary King. But would they help? Many knew her only as a name. Some for sure thought she was crazy, for Joey Elias had been whispering this for months, and the popular conception among many was that Joey was doing everything for Janie McLeary, who had kissed him on the steps of her theatre.

Still, she found herself getting ready to swim. She calculated the crossing—close to a mile here—like this—"I have swam almost that long, on shorter jaunts—so I will have to put these jaunts together—I have watched as others have swam the river on days long ago—and have realized that I could do it also—but that was long ago before I met my life—my husband—that last year with Bobby Doyle when I was eighteen—"

That all seemed not to matter now. She had a broken rib, though, and because of this could not swim overhand as she had learned as a child. Therefore it would take her much longer, and the current would move her away from those houses, not toward them.

"I will probably drown," she said firmly.

The water shocked her when she entered and asked her by its flow, Does this prove madness or sanity? She must act—she had to. Yet the act—for she stood a good chance of drowning—would be called insane. But the bitterness of her friends over her marriage, the hope her friends shared in her defeat, her husband's death, Joey Elias coming to her house, her father often enlisted in support of her enemies, the scorn of the bank, car lights on the bridge awaiting her crossing—all this showed her absolute clarity of reason and purpose.

And so before she could register the complaint her body now made, she was in the water, drifting almost naked toward the very bridge where those men waited her demise with a snigger. Not because they wanted to be ruthless but because they wanted to belong and to be liked more than the one who was outcast. She was the outcast, like her family before her and her family to come. Years—even centuries—of being an outcast played in her blood, and this moment I revisit for every one of her enemies then, and for the descendants of those enemies.

She knew something else. If she did drown, a weight would be cast upon those men's heads like a great boulder falling, and the rest of the town, secluded and insulated from the fray as good people always are, would turn on a dime and accuse her accusers, and damn them to hell. This was the lonely fate of the brave, and the prophet, and so had no more comfort to her than that.

She spat water that tasted of bark and her head was dizzy. Two minutes into the river she realized how cold it was. But far worse than it being cold—she had no light to follow except the light on the bridge. Therefore she was swimming toward the very men whose job it was to stop her. Worse, she could hear them speaking about her as she drifted toward them. Three men were leaning over the railing, looking into the black water and spitting tobacco juice.

A man swore. The others laughed and one snorted and leaned over the rail. His tobacco landed inches from her face. She held her side and gave a grimace, then quietly moved on under them and out into the channel on the far side, where three more men casually sauntered back and forth.

"This is nuts," one of them said. "She isn't anywhere near here."

Tired, and stopping to tread water, she looked far above her, staring in the direction of the men's voices and seeing their shadows.

In the tone of their faint laughter and bawdy talk was the tinge of envy over money and position they themselves would never attain—and so pretended not to want.

At this moment a pain shot through her right breast and she felt she would drown. She turned and swam more furiously into the black. Yet soon her arms became too heavy to move, her lungs ached for air, and water frigid as spring rain numbed her breasts and legs. She made the sign of the cross, half in hope and half in simplicity, like a child, and floated on her back, staring out at the rain. Then a youngster on the bridge shouted that he saw something in the water. All ran to look. But none could see her except the boy who yelled, "She moved out there—she moved."

"Don't be so crazy."

"I'm positive she's there—look—her arms—about two hundred yards—going toward Estabrook's landing—near Estabrook's boom— off to the left."

She maintained that it was the youngster's cry of Estabrook's boom that gave her direction and saved her life.

The water murky with bits of bark had closed about her face for a third time when she found a toehold in the mud, and then stood on a solid bit of earth chest high surrounded by a morbid boom of logs that had come out with the ice in the spring drive and had not suffered the fate of being laid up on the wharf. And a stranger circumstance was this: if there had been no quarrel over the wood between the sellers and the buyers, which had happened that spring, this wood, too, would have been sawed, and she, still two hundred yards from firm soil, would have drowned. But the wood was still here.

She moved her arms and feet slowly, knowing that to slip under them meant her death. She skirted the boom until she found the perimeter and was able to hold her head above it. And just as she panicked—for being so close to her prize she felt she was sliding beneath the waves— a hand grabbed her. The night watchman had waded into the water to grab her while her tormentors still faced the other way. He was unknown to her, except as a hand, and a form. He held her up and helped her from the water. There on the muddy and bark-ridden shore she stood before her saviour, barefoot and for the best part naked.

"Well—you've had your gawk; now go get me something to wear— I have a long night ahead of me."

"You don't remember me, Mrs. King?" He said.

"Why?" she said with defiant suspicion.

"It's Gully—Gully Taylor," he said. "You saved me during the flu."

"Ah yes—Gully," she said, and leaned against the old shed he had been standing in. "I need a blanket to wrap meself up in—and then something to wear."

He ran to the farm in the distance and soon came back with two towels to dry her and a dress borrowed from his sister. There in front of him she put it on, and turned to stride away.

"Mrs. King, there are some others on the road on this side," he said.

"Then I will not go up on the highway. I will go— Well, then, I will go to Estrabrook, to Estabrook himself," she said, her voice full of fire.

And she set out in the dark along the fishing path that youngsters made fishing eels, and found herself on Nelson Road at ten that night, barefoot and her hair soaking wet.

SIX

How do you greet a woman you've never spoken to before or thought of in any way except as the product of the worst of the town, who knocks on your door past ten at night to ask a favour when you are in the presence of a celebrated guest? If you are the maid that answers—the maid being a Jardine woman who held her position above others of her station—you would send her away.

"I will not go away," Janie said. "I will see Mr. Estabrook."

"And why will you see him? Do you have an appointment with him?" Mrs. Jardine answered.

But the study window was opened, and sound came from the back door, and a shuffle was heard in the study, then two voices—and one was Mr. Estabrook, saying, "Yes—of course."

So that night Mr. Estabrook left the study on his guest's instruction to bring the woman to him.

It was one of Lord Beaverbrook's favourite pastimes to recognize the friends or the children of his former townspeople and brighten their lives with an anecdote. He got a charge out of it, and it hurt no one. So when he was told that the woman might be a McLeary, he said, "Ah, McLeary. Not the McLeary who helped me deliver my papers years back?" And Janie King was sent for.

Estabrook, tall with a bent back and white hair, brought Janie to the study. She followed him with a good deal of self-possession, though she felt that at any moment the pain in her ribs might make her fall. This was the first time she had ever been into a Protestant's house (not counting her husband's). It was not only a religious difference. In fact, from the time of Mary, Queen of Scots, it had been not a religious difference but a cultural and economic one. Mr. Estabrook, whose children had been taught piano by Janie's late husband, might not recognize how well she understood this discrepancy, how she had played in its fire all of her life. Did Estabrook know of the events taking place to stop her? Quite possibly. But it did not consume his interest. His wood did, and the luxury of having at fifty-eight attained everything he had started out to do.

He opened the oak door, and as she entered she saw first the curtains blowing softly. Beyond that window, under a light, she saw a carriage, painted and restored, sitting there. So that's what that is, she thought, for it had been a mystery to her for years what sat in the dooryard of Estabrook's house. The house, compared with others on the river, was palatial.

Janie then saw the guest. She recognized him with a start—and Beaverbrook peered at her closely but did not quite recognize her, although he wanted to believe he did. He sat like a little imp in a chair, his feet just touching the floor, his pants held up by suspenders, his white shirt ruffled, the shirt buttons a little sideways.

Beaverbrook, the little town imp, one day would finance the Spitfire airplane to defend Britain against Hitler's Luftwaffe. But that was still a long way off, in a future he hadn't yet considered—though it was already in the thoughts of his friend Winston Churchill.

At this moment Beaverbrook was trying to think of who this girl was. Perhaps he had seen her as a little girl near the well. But he wasn't quite sure. He smiled, and his eyes narrowed. He had been telling anecdotes about Churchill and Lloyd George, saying that he felt Winston's career was over, an addition to the dustbin of history. It was a very common mistake made that year, and Lord Beaverbrook made his share of common mistakes.

"Although he might make a comeback, I cannot see it," he had ventured, boldly.

Now he shifted his weight slightly, crossed his ankles, and changed his accent to a Miramichi one, which he could affect as easily as a bawdy joke. "A McLeary. I bet you are Jimmy's girl."

She nodded.

"That would be it—Jimmy's girl. Has Jimmy gone to his reward?" Beaverbrook asked.

"Not yet—so the reward keeps dwindling," Janie said.

"Ah yes, a common problem." Beaverbrook smiled. He liked this girl very much. And wanted to know what she did. He suspected she did not do much. To him, Irish people were fine, but needed taking care of.

"Janie owns a picture show," Eastbrook offered

"You own a picture house?"

She noticed that he was visibly impressed, perhaps more because she was Irish and a McLeary than because she was a woman.

"Yes, I do, sir," she said.

"Well, I'll be damned. Good going. But don't call me sir."

"Do I call you lord?" my grandmother said clumsily.

"Call me Max."

"I think you have earned sir," she said quietly.

Beaverbrook liked this answer but made no more of it. Why was she wet—did she just get out of a bath? He smiled. She smiled back.

Then, addressing Estabrook (she felt it was in her dignity's benefit not to bother Lord Beaverbrook), she told her story. Estabrook must have known the story even if Lord Beaverbook did not, but he listened in silence and seemed to imply a steady ignorance about this:

The theatre would go in two days if she did not pay the mortgage. Worse, there were men from another picture house trying to stop her tonight. (She did not call them a mixture of Orange bastards and Catholic scum as she was known to call them in private.) Drawing a breath, she continued, she was hoping Estabrook would chaperone her to the Catholic houses, for they might be willing to loan her money, and they would not dare stop him.

Both men were silent for a time after she finished speaking. Both amazed that she had swum the river. It showed tremendous character—and a little insanity.

"Well, who holds your mortgage?" Beaverbrook asked.

"The Royal Bank."

"And have you been tardy in your payments?"

"Never."

"Then who told you you could not renew such a mortgage?"

"Mr. Harris, sir."

"And who is Mr. Harris, Janie?"

"Manages the bank here, Max," Estabrook said.

"And who would give a man like that a position here?" Beaverbrook asked.

Janie and Estabrook were silent.

"Well, this is bad behaviour," Beaverbrook said. "Your client's going in the night to beg money, swimming a river. We will straighten this out, won't we, Janie—you and I—we will straighten it all out."

"Yes, sir," Janie said.

"Churchill loves pictures. Do you, Janie?"

"Yes, sir."

"You see, you're just like my friend Churchill."

She knew that to answer flippantly would lose her the patronage she seemed to be acquiring. So she only nodded and stared straight ahead, feeling something biting her Irish heart.

"Come with me, Janie girl," Beaverbrook said. "As much as you might want to, you won't be swimming back. And you'll have your money—damn right you will."

It was after midnight, and the men who had manned the bridge— those brave fellows, my grandmother would sometimes call them— had dispersed but for a handful of hard-liners. It had turned to fog, and the boy who had exclaimed he had seen her arms moving in the water was now curled up on the side of the bridge road, making himself a bed. The fifteen dollars he had already spent fifteen times over was now drifting away in his sleep, toward Estabrook's boom.

Then he heard "Let it pass," and he jumped up, to see automobiles coming straight toward him—a huge black Packard with side lanterns and a car in front of it and a car behind. People—and the boy would remember this forever—whom he had believed and looked up to as men of tremendous worth now stood aside like children, and the cars passed by.

At first he thought it was Joey Elias. Then he heard the name Janie McLeary and thought, rubbing sleep from his eyes, Ah, they have her. Then he thought of the fifteen dollars. But no one made a move for her.

She sat in the back seat of a great car, with a fellow she seemed bigger than, and stared ahead—only now and again glancing from side to side quickly to see who it was on the bridge, as poor Mary, Queen of Scots, might have done on the way to the axeman in February of 1587. The plots were equally diabolical.

Janie looked straight at the boy now. He had never seen her before, but realized it was Janie King, sitting beside a man he recognized as Lord Beaverbrook.

A cheer went up on all sides as they followed the car.

"Good for her, she got across," the man who had spit his wad closest to her face said, as if he himself had nothing to do with trying to stop her. She might have heard it, for she looked back through the window at him, and then the car itself seemed to jump a gear and disappeared into the fog. The boy walked behind it, his hands in his pockets. The night was cool. He longed for bed.

Beaverbrook mentioned Janie King to Hoyt, the head of the Royal Bank of Canada, while Hoyt was in England. It was told in the company of Bennett and Churchill one evening that year. Churchill loved the story of the girl who swam the wild river—the outcast. He had become one himself by that time because he was considered a warmonger, out of fashion for his concern over this new man Hitler. Since it looked as if he could possibly lose his seat in the Commons, and his family home, he felt a kindred spirit in the "mischievous way all great men are linked."

So he said, "That cannot be good—you cannot have your clients swimming arctic rivers just to renew a mortgage. If nothing else it looks bad to the press, Mr. Hoyt."

"You are right, Mr. Churchill, I cannot," Hoyt answered with dignified severity.

Harris was demoted to a teller. After this he had not a friend in town—no one to tell him he was important or prominent. As a teller he found life difficult. He became a hanger-on and the butt of jokes in the dens of Joey Elias. He began to gamble on horses—something out of character.

My father once said that the first of his life was forgettable, "almost dastardly forgettable." He felt that his whole life was forgettable until he came back from overseas, after the second war, and had his children.

But it could not have been as forgettable as all that, for my father wanted to forget it, as many do who say that something is forgettable.

A year before his death he began to write down his story. In these chronicles he was searching for who he was, or what he was, and he had no one to help him navigate the terrain.

"There you go—I haven't left you much—but these chronicles make up for it. If I were you, I would settle for nothing less than what they give the next president for his memoirs."

Though startling and brilliant in spots, they also had pages of rhymes about pickles, notes on bargain hunting, fifty pages of attacks on his school principal in 1937.

They are written fairly unguardedly, and I have assumed his appraisal of the demoted bank manager—"Harris thought he was a bigwig, and played off others like a reflection"—is correct.

My father went on to write: "Harris realized his ambition had failed, realized in a habitual way—habitual to describe actions arising from a certain kind of shared mentality—action arising from a set of circumstances no different and no more dignified than common herding to please others. And how did he try to please others? By pretending to be something he was not. He failed, utterly—utterly he failed (how many ways can I put it?)."

This, my father called "reflection." Most of us have it. My father did not. He was too brave.

Janie King, who had been born with nothing, had beaten back a flood of enemies by stepping off the old wharf into the water. She had been called insane. Yet she still felt unsafe. In early summer that year, taking her son and small daughter to a relative in the middle of the night, her eyes glittering with anxiety, she said she had to go. She had an idea on how to change her fortune once and for all.

She boarded a train discreetly one late July evening and travelled in the terrible summer heat on a leather-backed seat southwest toward Toronto. She told no one, not even Walter. It was an unpleasant journey—the farthest away from our river she had ever been—and took almost two days, with a delay in Montreal, where she sat in a dull, sun-drenched building, alone, her purse clasped in her hand and the rudiments of her rural life showing through to the more worldly people about her. They would make fun of her, she was sure—her hat and her dress and her shoes all slightly out of step with those dressed like flappers on an outing. She even in her mid-twenties was more matronly, if not motherly. And what had she left behind? She knew it in her blood, like no one else. She had left a river, a great teeming river the likes of which would not be seen after St. Lawrence for two thousand miles or more. She had left a river in New Brunswick that would swallow you with its life, shout in its rapids, laugh in its eddies, create industry in its currents, a river of Irish and Scottish myth, wedded to the soil. She had left this to find and bring back a form of phantasmagoria that those who had grown up on it, lived life by it, and bled in its soil would trade their hard-earned money to see.

She would not be thwarted, even to the point of excommunication, which some in the church wanted to threaten her with. But she would not be frightened by this, either. For Janie in her single-mindedness could not be frightened. And she was doing this for no other reason than to spare her daughter and her son the poverty she herself had seen, the misery of the slop pail and the cold-water bath.

And our great sad river in New Brunswick, what had it created for the outside world? It had created the greatest ships under sail ever to be managed by a line, and that line was the Cunard shipping line. In like fact, it had created the man, emboldened and disliked, who would help Churchill win the Battle of Britain—Max Aitken, Lord Beaverbrook. Our great river in the north so obscure had guaranteed the Spitfire, had quarried the stones for the Parliament Buildings, had matured a prime minister of Canada and a prime minister of Great Britain. And now Janie wanted something from the great world to bring back home, to those hard-working and death-defying soft-hearted men and women she had known as a child.

She arrived to Toronto on a heavy, humid afternoon, with the taxis idling at the front of the grand station. She was not going to stay at any fancy hotel; art for its sake never impressed her. She stayed in the Simcoe Hotel, in a single room. She told me this when I was ten years old, for I was bold enough to ask. She registered under an assumed name, Janie Larson—a cousin of hers.

I went to Toronto years later, trying to get the feel of the same kind of day. However, when I arrived at the train station it was pouring rain, and I, unlike Janie, took a cab. After speaking with the manager, a fresh-faced fellow from the Ukraine, I checked the register in the basement, but it went back no further than August of 1942.

Why did she trust no one—what had failed in her? Well, how might others have acted, considering her life? "Betrayal causes a wound, the more to be vicious by," my father once told me. That was true enough.

I walked down Yonge Street reflecting on this, and in the heat singing Cockburn's "The Coldest Night of the Year." And reflecting upon those women who once had left cards to visit her, only to turn their backs when she needed them, and whose granddaughters became the indulged feminists of privilege who marvel at my grandmother in front of me, but if born in that time would not have shown her the spit off their tongues.

In the searing heat shimmering off the blue and inert lake, I followed her in my mind's eye as the next afternoon she took a tram toward her destiny, to a place with a few flashy posters and a "girl" of forty-nine at a typewriter, a prostitute in the shade of a building, and a wino lying in a yard. She gave them money. For she knew them all as people of her blood.

"What would you do with me?" the prostitute said.

"I would give you a meal," Janie said. "So get one now, dearie."

"If you are to buy wine," she said diligently to the wino, "buy Napoleon—at least you'll be in for a fight."

She entered the office, held her breath to stop the smell of sweat and cigar in the fiercely small room, with its couch with its dilapidated cushions and said, "I'm here to see Mr. Mahoney—of the talking pictures."

And when she saw him, late in the day—for he had business and was attired as such, and came in late—she asked him for a monopoly in writing for a guaranteed amount of time. She would stake her future on a roll of the dice. And that dice was a picture called *The Jazz Singer*.

If done on a whim, as Walter declared, it was a brilliant whim.

In August of that year she came back to her hometown with a four-year monopoly on the talking pictures. She heard that Elias had lost at cards and was fined for brawling, but she had no time to consider that.

PART II

ONE

By December of 1930 Joey Elias could not afford to heat his building and those who still went there to watch what was now a piece of entertainment history huddled in coats and hats, seeing their breath on the air, watching silent men and women who already seemed of another age and time walking streets forlorn and distant, climbing stairs already disappearing under their feet.

That winter was cold. The buildings were hard to heat, food cost an arm and a leg and many young men poor to start with were heading away on boxcars. Joey had heard that Roy Dingle, a former Dobblestein man, had almost frozen solid, and was down to snaring rabbits, living with an old drinking pal in a cave on the riverbank. It would be hard to live like that, he thought; but it also brought him pleasure, for Dingle was worse off than he was and, to be sure, the butt of many jokes.

Joey would go home, through the quiet snowy streets, and open the heavy front door of his house. It was a long, narrow house that stretched from old Chatham Street into a back field, where now and then a deer looking for feed would appear near some bald frozen maples. Upstairs it was cold and dark as well, and fit for him, who had no friends really. He would go into the kitchen and stare at the wall. Not a decoration was up for Christmas, and there was no joy in his heart. The last time he was happy was when he had fed his brother cake and jam on Christmas morning years before.

But the more he would talk to himself, the more his dealings with people would haunt him, and the more he would plead with some unknown God (a God he did not believe in) to help him. So he would drink alone, just as he lived.

When he was twelve in Poland, fearing he would be pressed into the Russian army to fight in some reckless war, trampled to death, or marched into oblivion to die in the ranks because of his nationality, he sold a person into conscription instead of himself, betrayed him and stole his boots and headed away. He was able to do this because the officer ready to conscript him owed him twenty-six rubles by gambling on the gaming pea—a game of chance where Joey hid the pea under one of three cups. But of course the pea was not in the cups at all but in Joey's hand. But then the officer was asked to fetch him for service, and Joey Eliseski sold his brother for the price of those rubles.

He made his way to England as a stowaway out of Norway. He went to Liverpool in a steerage filled with boards and rats, and made his way to London. There, off Soho, Neil Street or somewhere, he fell in with a group who made money gambling. He learned English and how to use a deck of cards. He was very young—the idea was to manage to live when the world was against your living. And so he learned how to palm aces. He did it well enough that he managed a card game in a travelling circus that went south of London in the summer. Here he learned another trait of human nature. Many people expected to be cheated. He liked his chances better after he discovered this. Really, he was not doing much more than what people who went to these travelling shows expected.

Before the start of the first war he tried to find his brother but could not. He heard that his brother had deserted back to Krakow and was beaten and taken to jail. Joey grew morose, and reckless. He got into fights, and somehow began to manage a boxer or two. He learned that most managers of most fighters kept most of the money if they were smart. He also learned that people longed for a white boxer—a Stanley Ketchel or Gentleman Jim Corbett, rather than Jack Johnson. This too could work to his advantage.

But when a boxer of his died in the ring, there was an investigation, and he fled to Canada.

Sometimes, closing his eyes he saw his brother. And when he first began to visit Janie he'd see Miles, who reminded him of his brother.

How could he do this to her? he thought. Hadn't he done enough? But the very fact that he had taken his brother's boots made him a veteran of acrimonious campaigns—so, in order to survive, he felt he must continue to do what it was he was doing. If he did what he set out to do, he was sure to win. How would he lose?

He realized that in order to lose he would have to go and hand his brother back his boots. Then be pressed into Russian service and die. What a silly thought.

Walter McLeary had "adopted" Phil Druken's family, for, as he knew, he had no other family to adopt. By now he had spent a lot of his money on them.

Since the family had fallen on hard times and moved to Tar Street, Walter visited them every spare moment. He could not think of Putsy without kindness and love, and a hope that went beyond hope that she might someday love him.

He always brought the Drukens something—a picnic ham, or a turkey, cigarettes or brandy for the old lad. He had taken Putsy and Rebecca to their first movie, a Clara Bow picture two years before. And both (Rebecca especially) had fallen in love with movies— with the idea of romantic heroes, or the idea of a young heroine given to melancholy because she knows how cold the world is. Sometimes these women would die in their men's arms, or sometimes the men would save them at the very last moment from a cold-hearted devil.

This December came the moment Putsy knew would come. Walter proposed. She had been waiting—expecting nothing less—for if he did not propose, she was hopeless as a catch, and, for obvious reasons, dreading the moment he would. She had expected a warning of some kind, or maybe a visit from Janie, whom she was secretly terrified of. Yet he entered the snowy yard one clear night, walked to her back door, and, standing on his canes, smoking his ridiculous cigar, asked her father for her hand, with his pale breath lingering under the old porch light. She was hiding behind the wood stove, but when her father called her out, she did not know how to say no. Without friends, or much of a future, a man who earned a good salary, no matter if he walked with canes, was a catch. And she told herself she should be grateful for it, and that it proved her more discerning than people would imagine, to marry a good provider and a decent fellow like Walter McLeary.

Besides, for her, Walter had asked Janie a favour. Flushed by his love, he asked Janie to help Putsy's young sister, who was known to have been in a certain amount of trouble.

The idea of Rebecca Druken having her own ideas was noticeable from the time she was seven or eight. At first things were done to please Joey Elias—just as children pray to please their parents, so did Rebecca act to please the adults she looked up to. She liked to win the approval of Elias, and studied how to do so. She studied the incremental desires of people. And she was equipped, with her open face and ready smile, to captivate others. She never clung to anything, that was her trick, yet from an early age she discovered that many people found her indispensable.

Now that she was fifteen she was sure of herself, and during the interview with Janie, she said that nothing in the world would be as fine as working for her.

"As long as you are good with kids you can work for me—if you are not going to school?"

Rebecca smiled. "What's a school that isn't life, ma'am?"

Rebecca Druken came to the house, to take care of Miles and Georgina King, in the spring of 1930. For a while she ignored Joey, but slowly (especially after Putsy ordered her not to) she began to slip back to the only life that truly excited her, that made her feel more important than anyone else in the world—the hidden life of the pea.

TWO

Joey Elias woke at three in the afternoon of December 20, 1930, and went to the skating rink. He sometimes went to watch the skaters. It took his mind off things.

Afternoon skating was just ending. Men and women holding hands glided before him. And who did he see in a long skirt skating in the centre of the ice by herself? The one person he knew who might work in his favour. It seemed inevitable that he meet Putsy Druken at this moment.

She skated toward him. She was tiny, had a peaked face but bold eyes, and an energetic smile, though her teeth were bad. Three were missing because her father had slammed her once when she tried to protect Rebecca. She had been at work in the shoe factory in Fredericton, but now she had come home. She had been with Elias for a while, but he always treated her meanly. And he teased her that Rebecca was prettier. This would send her into a fury.

Now she was engaged to Walter McLeary, and wore a pair of earrings, just visible under her dark hair. The engagement, for obvious reasons, wasn't widely announced.

Her father had worked for Dobblestein's. When the mill went out of business, Elias had put them out of the house he had rented them; he used to laugh that he had to fumigate it. Now that didn't seem the best way to have handled a bad situation. For he was thinking of Putsy and Rebecca again and of what use both of them could be to him.

They had nowhere to go when he threw them out, and Walter McLeary had helped them. That in itself bothered Joey.

But now Putsy looked up and saw Mr. Elias again. She still called him Mr. Elias, even though he had slept with her dozens of times. And she remembered all of the times she'd believed that Mr. Elias could help her family. Mr. Elias could get her father work if she was nice, if she did his ironing or his shopping. Always if she just did this or that, Mr. Elias would give them something in return. And she knew, though she could not admit to it yet, that she still loved him, and she was being cheated out of real love by being with Walter.

She smiled at Elias and undid her cap. The music played as skaters came off the ice and the lights dimmed.

"Oh," he said cavalierly, "Putsy. I hear you have something important to tell me." His smile revealed that he was amused by it. Then he frowned as if he knew it was an important matter for a young woman and so refused to be amused at her expense. Both looks she caught immediately.

She sat on a bench and began to undo her skates—newly bought for her by Walter, who could not skate himself.

"Well, as long as *you're* happy," Elias said, with an emphasis on the "you're."

Putsy nodded and pursed her lips as if she was about to say something.

He asked, "Is there anything about those talkies that are different—from mine?"

"Just the sound," she said. "It seems that in your place we've gone deaf."

She saw he gave a slight jolt at this, but then composed himself.

"But your place is just as nice," she whispered, standing now, her breath close to his face.

"And how do they heat their place? Do they heat it like I heat mine?"

"Oh, you must know now. They heat it with wood—just like you do."

"Ah yes. She's a fortunate girl, that Janie McLeary, to have all that dropped in her lap without fighting for it—like you and I have to. Her father tried so hard to do right by her and soon as she gets ahead she ignores him."

"What do you mean?"

"Oh, nothing—just a bit of talk. I think being married to an Englishman has gotten her where she is, that's all."

"Some are lucky to marry, some are not." She said this without thinking of Walter, but blushed after she had said it.

"He's good to you—that's something anyway," Elias said quickly, touching her face.

"Both he and Janie," she said. Of course Janie McLeary was Janie McLeary. Putsy could not look at the woman without feeling intimidated.

"You hang on to yer luck," Elias said, and he touched her shoulder with his hand to comfort her about this kind of luck.

Then he hurried away, having spied Walter.

Putsy Druken shrugged and waited as Walter hobbled forward. She walked toward him, trying to ignore his halting gait, and once looked back over her shoulder.

"I'm sorry I'm late," Walter said.

"Everything has a reason—as you yourself said." She smiled.

She walked ahead of him and he followed, puffing dramatically on his cigar, now and again looking behind into the crush of skaters, for he could sense something was wrong.

"Did anyone say anything to you?" he asked.

"Of course not."

He followed her out into the dark. Dark and Christmas, and lights twinkling on and off in small windows. Over at Beaker's store, a golden angel sat above the door, and a sleigh and horse waited for a group of revellers. Young men and women, all covered in bear rugs and sipping whisky, had stopped for chocolates and Player's cigarettes.

Two men saw Putsy and yelled, "Come on, we're going to the cove. Come on!"

She asked Walter to go with her.

"No, no," he said, blankly staring into the dark, the smell of diesel from the train yard beyond them. The bells of the horse were tinkling softly, and it snorted. It was a black Belgian with a fat belly and big hooves. Its harness was dressed with silver twine, and its tail was bobbed by red ribbon. All brought an excitement to Putsy—the smell of whisky, the idea of the bear rugs—all snuggled together. What would be wrong with it?

"I can't go," he said, looking back and forth, his cigar smouldering. "I have a movie in an hour."

"Ah yes. Every night you work."

"I told you I was talking to Janie about training someone."

"That doesn't help now."

Putsy kissed him on the cheek and started toward the sleigh.

"Damn it, Putsy, I can't go," he said under his breath, and as he tried to grab her his canes slipped out from under him and he fell, twisting his ankle.

She rushed back and tried to help him, but he waved her away. Other skaters ran to his aid as well, but Walter shouted to them that he was fine.

As he tried to find his canes in the soft snow, a man came up behind him and helped him to his feet.

"There you go, Walter," Joey Elias said, smiling and brushing him off. He handed Walter his canes.

Walter was too big a man not to thank him. The horse and sleigh had to go around them now, while Elias took the halter and motioned to the young driver to turn the horse back, with far more gravity than need be. There was some whispering from the women.

"Who is that?"

"That's who runs the movies."

"Oh, he has a humpback."

Though there was a commotion, and these things were whispered, he could not help but hear. Putsy pretended she didn't. The horse was whipped forward into the dark and went down the back lane, the sleigh slewing and all yelling and laughing. There was sudden silence, a whisper of smoke from the houses, and everyone began to laugh again.

Rebecca, who had come to find her older sister, stood in the dark near the side of the building and gave a flash of a smile to Mr. Elias, who just caught her out of the corner of his eye as he passed.

Elias waited until Putsy and Water were gone, then went over to her.

"Rebecca," he said, "are you ever pretty tonight" (just as he used to tell her sister when she was fifteen).

"As pretty as Putsy?"

"Oh, far prettier," he whispered, looking behind him.

"As smart as Putsy?"

"Oh, far smarter." He stared into her face. There was a sudden cruelness to it.

"Well, I'm not like Putsy," she said, biting her bottom lip.

"In what way?"

"I will do whatever you want me to," she said to him, "as long as you like me, too."

He stared at her and she looked up at him boldly, with a strange sullen curiosity.

"Then I'm going to give you a challenge," he said, "just a little challenge. I want you to tell me every word that is said in Janie's house tomorrow—doesn't matter how unimportant it seems. If you do that, I will give you another task."

THREE

Walter wondered what they had they said about him to cause that other laugh. Of course one could not be sure. But still, wasn't he used to it? Of course. And wasn't that part of the subtext—that is, his willingness to be made sport of? Walter was undeniably used to it, and would not even have flinched—if not for her.

Because he was used to something else; the subtext of a woman's pity. And for the first time he saw it in Putsy's gaze, and the undertone was fear and dislike of what her friends saw in him. Not fear of his affliction, but fear of the grief it would cause later in life. It was what Rebecca always saw when she looked at him—or looked through him, with a smile. But he had not seen it as yet in Putsy—not until this moment; when the realization that she would be left alone with him, as the revellers went on, became evident.

Though he pretended not to notice, or, if seeing that she noticed his gaze and then recognized that he knew what for a brief moment she let escape, he pretended not to care, and in pretending not to care he let out a laugh and shook his great head. Both of them saw Rebecca for a second. There was something strange about her, Walter felt. He did not know why, but she made him uneasy. Perhaps because she saw through his weakness.

He was left with Putsy, Putsy with him, and they moved into the dark together. He shook his head all the way down the street to the theatre, but he did not tease her, as he often did, nor did he ask her about her skating—she was deplorable, he knew, but this could not be said with humour or equanimity by a man with a bad leg.

He climbed the dark stairs to the projection booth and sat down to rest his right foot, the heel of which never touched the ground, the toes of which were as hard as cast iron. Then, after lighting his cigar, he checked the frames, spooled the reel, and waited for Janie's call up that it was time. The theatre was warm and cozy, and now seated 150 patrons, and on most nights it was full. Especially tonight with the movie *Frankenstein*.

"It will be time to start soon," he said. "Putsy, you may as well go home and see your mom."

"No, I will stay with you," she answered. "I want to." She sat down and stubbornly tried to make herself comfortable.

"Your mother wants you home," Walter said, "and I'll catch it if you don't."

Putsy, sitting on a stool at the back of the booth, nodded and, getting up, kissed him on the forehead. "Never mind," she said.

"Never mind what?" he asked with a blank stare.

"Never mind them!" she said, squeezing his hand, and she took her leave.

He flipped the projection lever and stared through the ghostly, vapid light at the great dark castle on the screen.

Then he sat down as the picture ran and read a mystery novel. "The woman was a floozy," he read. He put the book aside and thought. Yes, he convinced himself, she would get over this infatuation with whomever it was that she gave the backward glance to. Perhaps some young boy she was skating with. Besides, it was selfish to demand her complete attention. He could not ask what others asked for and feel deserving. Still, he was responsible for her now and acted circumspectly because of this. Though he was afraid to ask her what she thought of him! He could only imagine.

Some nights in the snow when they went out together it seemed as if she was travelling beside a gnome, a sin of which she was not conscious, having caused some grave sorrow in her life. For born witless in the world, skill demanded of us all that we managed as best we could against those who would be willing to destroy who we were. And the snow said this, and the ice and the hail, and he heard it every time he blanched at a young girl's horror as she met him on a dark corner. This was all intended to destroy something of his spirit—the great scope of his honour, the great pity of his heart, the great rendering of service to those of less fortune. Therefore over time subterfuge against others was demanded from him as well. How then could we not go into sin?

And wasn't he demanding too much from her? That is too much loyalty? This is what his part was—and he knew it. Still, he did not demand what others did—the attention span others demanded. And he believed it was a noble course he was offering, that is, marriage. Although even here, or I might say especially here, he understood what her limited options were in order to say yes to him. He put the book aside again. Ah yes, the pain and futility of her existence had caused her to grasp his hand. And her little sister whom she wished to take care of and keep safe from the clutches of Joey Elias. Rebecca! That is who she would die for, and so she was with him, Walter P., as a kind of death.

He hated in himself the vanity that had enabled him to cross that threshold and ask for her hand in marriage. He knew that her acceptance had extended fundamentally from her family's misfortune with their accommodations. A misfortune caused by Joey Elias, whom they had fallen from favour with. It was Joey who raised the rent on their small, rundown yellow house on Pond Street the very month after Dobblestein's mill, where Phil had worked for years, went bankrupt—and then, finding them no longer worth the trouble, threw them out.

So what had happened to Putsy except bad luck? When Elias took over their house on that fateful day he had thrown the teapot full of tea that they in worry and fear had made for him out the door behind them and kicked the door closed.

"I'll have to fumigate this place!" he had roared.

Elias was in a state where rage was enlivened with the possibility that people would stare at him, that they would think, "Ah, he's finally had enough. He's a great man but even a great man can have enough." And so he did what he did, picked upon one of the most miserable and servile families in town, and was rewarded just as he thought he would be. And something else was well known. Putsy as well as other young women had been his "girls." They would fight and call each other names because of him, and men he knew would listen to this, amused, and roar and laugh at their antics. Elias was old enough to be their father, though few told him that. Putsy was nineteen. She had been his girl whenever he wanted, and her only stipulation was that he not touch her sister.

On the day he threw them out, Putsy was at home.

"Oh, is there anyone going to help us?" said tall and thin as a rail Mrs. Druken, while Phil sat in a pile, oblivious to those around him, not only drunk but catatonic in his state of helplessness—as strong men of certain worth become as soon as that worth is challenged. Men who laugh at weakness all their lives, when suddenly pulled out of their environment, see weakness triumph over themselves.

And Putsy, with raven black hair and small, thin lips, kept trying to pick up their things. "Is there one man here, one man in all the crowd who will help?"

But the men at that moment were powerless—and Elias's men, like Leon Winch, believed they had won a moral victory. They cawed like crows over a piece of coloured string.

"Yeah, Philip, yer finally gettin' yers now," Leon said, taking a sniff and a spit. He stared around him, and seeing Putsy come at him he held her back as she spat and cursed.

"Yer not to go in there now—it's no longer yer place, you understand?" Winch said.

Rebecca Druken—wild red hair and green eyes—stood far down the street, her eyes fixed on Mr. Elias, at first perplexed and then amazed at what was transpiring. She herself did not enter the fray.

There was none to help, it seemed, in the whole world.

Yet who came along at that moment, from being at Easter duties, but the gnome, Walter P. McLeary of the orphanage off Pond Street, projectionist extraordinaire, a grand master of the defensive garble, a well-read provincial, with exquisite hands and a fertile mind. A cripple to boot.

Poor Putsy chasing her bland and not so clean corset that the wind had wired skyward. And now he had come to be her saviour. This was a defining moment in the destiny of our family—not only with Mr. Walter's arrival but in everything that had happened up until this point.

Added to the mix was his very strange soliloquy to God at Easter service, when hearing of the murder of five children in Strathadam by a deranged, out-of-work father, Walter had said, "Is there anyone going to be sent to help?"

And the answer came as clear as a tinkling bell. "Why, Walter P. McLeary of the orphanage off Pond Street, late of the beating nuns and hoodwinked by friends, I have sent you, sir—can't you see it?— I have sent you—you are called upon—and many are called and few are chosen."

He walked downtown muttering at the futility of belief, and ran into the melee at the bottom of the hill, and Putsy calling out for help.

And he (at first reluctantly) came to Putsy's aid. Mrs. Druken, she of the hard gaze who had teased him more in a day than most in a week, once calling him a weakling and a cripple, watched him begin to pick up their belongings, shouldering them and saying, "Come with me."

And she looked at him, her lips trembling not because of his help but because she had been reduced to help from him. Her family had always been at a strange war with the McLearys and had sided with Elias because he was strong. Now they were reduced to accepting help from Walter P. How could this be when they had long been in Joey Elias's good graces, when she had taken his part in any dispute with the McLearys, now be reduced to having a McLeary tell her, "Come with me"? Noticing also how strong he was, she trembled to think of all the times she had called him weak.

"Why in Christ's holy name should I follow you?" Patricia Druken said, blessing herself twice in rapid succession.

But young Putsy nodded and, clutching her loose garments, spoke: "Don't mind, Momma," she said. "If you can just put us somewhere tonight, I'll make sure we pay you."

"But why should we go with you?" Mrs. Druken said again.

"Because you asked for a man, and I am the one," he said, as heartily as he could say it.

Mrs. Druken gave a slight start, and then a feeble laugh, and off they followed him, old Phil Druken teetering on his legs, and Putsy holding a box in her outstretched hands, her face dirty and pouty, while young Rebecca followed at a safe distance, uncertain of her place.

"I will never speak to Joey Elias again," Putsy said. "It is not me who is insulted but my family now!" She took the Bible, there at that moment in the cold spring air and swore enmity against Elias, and spat.

After much searching and much inconvenience to himself, Walter found them a place on Tar Street, a smallish shed more than a house, yet warm and cozy enough, and he paid for it out of his own pocket. Putsy told him all about how Joey Elias had used her, seduced her, then beat her up.

"There is a better way to live," Walter said simply.

It was after this that Putsy became friendly toward him. She often went down to the theatre to wait for him, and they would go for a walk or sit out on a summer night. Rebecca often came along to watch the movies too, and they teased her about how susceptible she was to being the mimic.

So Walter as a mature man, spoke to Putsy about getting them a better situation. He took both Rebecca and Putsy to Miss Fish, the lawyer, to see if they would have some case against Elias, for his bad behaviour. But those most in need of the law so often have no case. He did, though, help procure Rebecca a job, taking care of Miles and Georgina King. Rebecca went gratefully enough, and he was happy. The idea that the Druken and McLeary clans were once at odds made her appointment more endearing to both families. And Putsy was profoundly grateful to him.

But was it subterfuge on his part—was he only doing it for the comfort of the young woman's companionship?

Well, no, because he had never known that the young woman would offer her companionship, or any part of herself for that matter. He had always thought Putsy was Joey Elias's girl, but she told him with her kisses that this was not so, and he believed her. She hated Joey Elias now—she hated Elias more than anyone. And since she was worried about Rebecca following her bad behaviour, she must change.

"But?" he said, "There is a but, of course."

"No, there will never be a but." She smiled and took his arm in hers as they walked.

But was that why she loved him? Was she willing to do this—to sacrifice for her family by marrying a cripple?

"I never think of it." She smiled again.

Then she was far more noble than he was, he thought.

Yet at the best of times he still hoped, and it was hope that now guided him. He had bought her new shoes just the other week, and new skates too. She could not pass a pair of shoes without wanting them. She had the mark of poverty, for wasn't it his experience that there were many things coveted by the poor—and one was shoes?

75

No. She loved him now, she told him. She loved Walter P. McLeary.

But now was the word—for NOW is what informed him, saying: "Before—when you asked a girl to dance, or visited her there was always that which prevented her—but "That" doesn't inform Putsy— Putsy Druken is different—can't you tell by her kisses. Ah yes, her kisses inform me, thought Walter McLeary. Her kisses were passionate, he thought.

"Can't you tell by my kisses?" she'd said one night.

Yes, she loved him.

Still, except for the kisses he had bought at the Sunny Corner Fair, he had nothing to compare her kisses to.

"Shall I compare thee to a summer day?" he said aloud now, and got up to make sure the reel changeover was still five minutes away. Then he sat down and fell into deep and pleasant thought. He thought of Christmas, how they would go to midnight mass, have punch later at the house, how her father and he would play checkers—he loved checkers and so did Phil. They would put the turkey on, perhaps wave the Irish flag, go carolling—and he would give her a diamond ring. Not even Janie knew about this.

Janie did not know something else. He had given Putsy a key to come and go from the theatre as she pleased, to save him from walking up and down the stairs to open the door for her. Because—well, it all came back to his paining foot and the unfamiliarity of love.

"You must never lose this," he had said, holding the key up to Putsy.

"Of course not," Putsy had said.

Still, who had she been looking back at? How could he not say he did not notice, and how could he not say her look was not even slightly eager to keep something hidden from him? He tried to think of the men he had seen talking to her over the last few weeks. Then he thought, Is she not allowed to talk? How horrible that would be for her if she was not allowed to talk to anyone. But still, as he made the changeover he couldn't help reflect on this again. On the screen, amid the screeches and howls of those in the packed house below smelling of chip bags and winter woollen clothes, was Frankenstein's creature, Boris Karloff, hideous for all to see. Never had the world seen such a monster, the one-sheet proclaimed. And the picture on the one-sheet was so horrific it was said a woman had fainted as she passed the theatre. When he heard the shouts of the common crowd chasing the poor mad beast who died for love, or lack of it, he remembered the scalding taunts of his youth, when he dressed in a tie and jacket his cousin Janie had got for him to go to his first dance. They had chased him too, until he met Janie on the street. She picked up a stick and, swinging it like a crazy woman, drove them all away. Then, putting her arm about him, she said, "You are my one favourite person, Walter P." It was hard to keep tears from his eyes when he remembered how noble Janie was as a girl.

He went downstairs and stoked the stove one last time. There were two stoves, a wood stove and a coal stove with a coal bin near it. They did not use the coal stove, so Walter had given the coal to the Drukens.

He went up to the canteen and took a Coca-Cola back to the projection booth as the patrons filed out. He preferred not to see them, or have them see him. At ten-thirty the last of the patrons left. He was alone, in his sanctuary. Far from the madding crowd, or any other crowd for that matter. He took his broom and swept under the seats and down the aisles. He closed off the cold air from the exit. Then he trimmed the Christmas tree in the foyer, put up lights over Janie's newly built ticket booth, ran an extra electrical cord along the front and put it under the carpet so Santa's face would light up every few seconds. He had angels and the manger as well. This manger, with its cows and ducks and sheep, and mother of Jesus.

"The mother of Jesus is everyone's mother—even Walter's," a nun in a prim peaked cap and with red-rimmed eyes used to say every Christmas. "Yes, even Walter's."

And the children would turn and look at him in amazement.

Walter went into his apartment behind the projection booth and lay on his single bed, with his clothes still on. Relighting his cigar, he whispered into the dark, as he always did, about something, love or goodness, kindness or fidelity. Like the scrofulous Sam Johnson with the orange peels, it was a sublime and private moment, a secret for the ages. (Although Sam probably used them to rub on his face and neck because of scrofula—for as Walter knew, Johnson—Sam Johnson himself—was hideous wasn't he, and had a wife older and far away.)

Once when he was whispering, Putsy said, "Walter, why don't you pray—say, for an operation to take your affliction away?"

"I could never do that," he said. "It would be breaking faith with God, who gave me life. You see, I refuse to call it an affliction."

"Why not? I would call it an affliction and I would blame God," Putsy said.

He looked at her and she smiled, but tossed her head slightly and averted her eyes. Ah, he thought, the poor girl has prayed for it herself because it is an affliction to her.

Perhaps he thought that life must come and go as if his affliction were a great heavenly checkers match between some damn arch-angels, or some bet such that to ask a favour, to be happy as others seemed, to have love and life and a woman's hand was to prove himself unworthy of the test he was engaged in. Strangely self-inflicted, yet still, with a humpback and a crooked leg, perhaps the only way to proceed. So he never answered an insult against him. Sometimes he would go away, as when Janie in haste said he had two humps, but he could never answer an insult. And why? Was he frightened of ridicule if he took action and failed? How could he be, for in many ways he had been ridiculed all of his life? And he knew he was strong enough to badly injure many who mocked him. No, his lack of action was far more subtle and far braver, for those who mocked him did not know it was bravery in its purest form, and that they were engaged in living God's pact with him—the allowable mocking of a better man. Walter was a sign of God's inevitable mercy—once it was understood that the mercy befell those Walter himself was most tormented by.

He stood and turned off the marquee lights. They went off with a pulsating flicker, and everything was silent and the Christmas wind blew.

There were those, of course, who had made something of a different pact, with the archangels of the other world. He tried not to think of how Joey Elias had come to him, offering him fifteen more cents a picture to change sides while the Englishman was in his bed dying. It was such an improper thing that Walter could not even tell Janie.

"You don't want to be mixed up with a foggin' Brit," Elias had said. "Now is the time to come with me." When a man was dying, when no one was there to look after the theatre—how could that be the time?

Walter said no. Elias sweetened his offer. Walter said no thank you once more. Then out of the blue one afternoon, in Walter's hearing, Joey said to his men as he passed by, "Yes, that's who Janie has managed to get working for her. He asked to come working for me, but I cannot take Janie's last—man."

It was meant for Walter to hear. And if Walter got angry enough to fight, Elias would beg off, saying his decency prevented him from fighting a cripple. But then later he got his three men—Leon Winch and two others from the shantytown on the bank—to beat him. This happened over four years earlier and Walter had never told a soul. He never went to the doctor and he tended his own wounds, his puffed face, swollen lips, and broken ribs as best he could.

"All three," Walter murmured now, thinking of how, when he swung his good arm, Leon was stopped in his tracks, and how he was able to throw the second man against the wall. But of course they came back at him.

He tossed his cigar stub into the sink and laid his head back on the pillow. Because of the number of times he had been kicked, his ribs still ached when he breathed at night.

The wind howled, and somewhere there was the whine of a dog, lost in the storm. Walter knew poor Putsy had once threatened to kill herself over Joey Elias. Walter knew these things.

Finally he fell asleep, the clock ticking in the corner. After an hour he woke, reached up and put his nightcap on, and fell asleep again.

FOUR

Putsy walked through the snow, up one street and along another, with her purse swinging at her side and her skates over her shoulder. At these moments her life seemed the best possible, far better than any other life possible. How could she want anyone else? Well, she couldn't and she didn't. And she would tell anyone who wanted to speak about it—although no one did—that her life would be set: she would be Mrs. Walter McLeary. One could do a lot worse, she thought. And opened her mouth to taste the snow falling out of a black, black sky.

Along Tar Street there were no lights, and three houses in on the left was her place, behind a pale plywood fence, and unseen from the road. There was a car parked in the snowy drive, a new Ford racing coupe. She stood silently and stared at it open-mouthed for a moment while catching her breath. Then she entered the house through the back door, near the large old stove.

Mr. Elias was sitting in the chair old Phil usually reserved for himself, and Mrs. Druken was running about trying to make tea in the pot Janie had given them since Elias had thrown theirs out the door. Putsy had always been spellbound by this man, and Mrs. Druken knew it and used it to the family's advantage—or so she hoped.

Elias stood and kissed her cheek, and asked her how things were, with the inflection that he was sad they had fallen out.

"I want a long talk, is all," he said, deliberately evoking a different look than he had at the skating rink.

"Oh, yeah—about what, now?" Putsy said.

"About you and Walter and how happy you both are," he said. "I simply need to know if you are happy. And as long as you are happy then I will be free!"

She felt the first twinge of jealousy, because in saying this did it now leave him free—for—she could hardly think it—Rebecca, who was fifteen now, her age when seduced. Well, however it was, she hated him now.

When Mrs. Druken came in with the tea, she immediately said, "Don't she look some good, Joey?"

"Yes, she does. It's too bad we all got in this mix-up. It's because I listened to my men—that goddamn Leon Winch who almost always sided with Jim McLeary."

Now everyone there knew that this was not true, but not one said it wasn't.

"And what's that that they told ya?" Putsy said, breathing through her nose, looking at her tea.

"They said ya were trying to cheat me—take advantage, but I was too quick to listen. You know whose fault this is—that Phil is out a job?"

"No. Whose fault is it?" Putsy said, trying to act nonchalant though her heart was pounding. And she knew, as she had from the time she was fifteen, she was once again vying for his attention with other girls in town. How she had loved that at one time. She wanted to say, "How are all yer other girlfriends, then?" but hesitated, fearful she might destroy something. And what was that something—a chance? What chance if she was to be Mrs. Walter McLeary?

"It is old Jim McLeary's fault. He caused the whole depression in Dobblestein's mill. I told him from the first to leave it alone, taking advantage of that woman, but he was terrible drunk, and he was bound to do what he was bound to do."

Everyone knew that this was not true either. The mill had collapsed just as others had, and neither Jim McLeary nor anyone else had anything to do with it.

Elias had a way of looking around when he tried to deflate someone's reputation. He did this with a look of astonished naivety, as if in sadness he had not forethought the fact that his argument would besmirch someone's name but had just come to the realization of that person's dishonesty at the exact same moment as those whom his words had just contrived successfully to convince.

"If we weren't so quick to vacate that day, that wouldn't have happened," Mrs. Druken said, kindly. This, too, was not true in the least—they were not quick to vacate. Elias had to haul old Mrs. Druken's left leg, and her shoe came off in his hand. But her saying this let Elias off the hook and allowed the infatuation Putsy had with him to continue.

"No, it was my fault," he said, holding his gloves in his hand. "It's what I realized last night. This was my fault and that's the end of it. But when I come up here and saw where you are living now, I couldn't accept this—couldn't accept it—I know we all had an argument that day and things got out of hand. You started for the door, and I thought you wanted to go—and I was sad."

"We were all sad that day, we all were," Mrs. Druken said.

"Yes, yes, that's right," Phil said.

"Shut up, Mom, Dad," Putsy said. Her eyes were wide. Her pouted face that always looked dark was beaming. He was lying, she knew. She knew and yet something about him made her not care, or not care well enough. "Where are you living now"—what did that mean when before they were paying for a rat-infested place he stole from them? The look on his face of shock at their living quarters made them ashamed, like the beaten-down so often are.

But there was something else Putsy could not admit. She was glad that Rebecca had not come home yet—for Rebecca, even at her young age, could steal Putsy's show.

"You know the Drukens and Eliases must stick together," he said, sitting down suddenly, and sighing. "No one here will help us if we don't."

These were all lies Putsy had heard a dozen times before. And every time she believed him, he was found with another woman or another plan that caused Putsy to dishonour herself in some way.

Joey Elias looked at Putsy. Putsy dropped four sugars in her tea because she was nervous. She suddenly felt that being engaged ruined everything for her—how could he come back right at the time she was being engaged? It wasn't fair, and her hand shook as she stirred the sugar. (She forgot what she had been thinking walking up the hill.) It was true, with her bracelet, her ring, and her long black woollen coat, she looked like a different woman—far more exotic, and she knew it. And sadly it was her innocence that made her feel it; though Elias had been her lover, he now looked at her with new eyes.

Then, drinking his tea, Joey stated his case. It came down to this. He wanted to make them rich—or at least richer than they ever were before. And with the Depression, anything would be an improvement, he said with a laugh.

He realized that Phil was the man he needed. Phil Druken could run his projector, by the by. But now he needed someone else, and he was here to ask Putsy a favour, a very small one, he said, yet important. Could she get Walter P. McLeary away from Janie, just for a month, to train Phil? Then, with Phil able to do the work, Walter could go back to being Janie's boy, he said.

Phil had already agreed to it, for he was only forty-eight years of age, and though his body had been racked by a number of injuries, running a projector for a theatre would be child's play.

"And I'll be getting thirty a week," he said.

"Thirty a week," Mrs. Druken echoed.

Now the fact that Elias had thrown them from their house didn't seem to matter so much, not if they were going to get thirty a week.

In the thirty-five years he had worked, starting on the boats loading lumber, Phil had broken his left collar bone, both arms, his right leg above the knee (very painful) his left leg below the knee (quite painful) his right foot, his left big toe—and had an ear removed on a saw at Dobblestein's mill. But now if he could—if he could—learn the projectors it would be blessed, as Mrs. Druken said.

"This is a new century fer sure," Mrs. Druken said.

"Wonderful, wonderful," Putsy said. All of a sudden the great world was alive with possibility again. In fact, her feeling was much like Walter's whenever he saw her. But her happiness unfortunately was not bound by Walter. Walter would not deny her this small request. He could not—how could he?

"Oh, I'm sure he will do it." She had to do this, to keep other girls away from Mr. Elias. She did not want to think this, she did not want to believe she was thinking this; nonetheless it was exactly what Putsy Druken was thinking.

Putsy knew that Elias was calculating something against Janie McLeary King. She didn't know what it was, but looking at him in profile, it was clear he had a scheme.

But if she said anything, or admitted it to herself, Joey Elias would disappear into that wonderful pink hue she now believed she saw. If she thought there was going to be anything deceitful happening against the McLearys, she had to pretend she did not. The McLearys not only had shone their lights on her, they had hired her little sister to take care of the boy, Miles, and the baby Georgina, had hired Putsy herself three nights a week for the snack bar, had made her feel wanted, and Walter had given her a key.

Her hands shook as she thought of it all. How much improved their lives would be if her father was a projectionist, though, and how much her mother, with her toothaches and her withered mouth, would be pleased by her. (It did not register that she was thinking like a single girl, and that if she and Walter were to be married in the spring, the same result would be forthcoming.)

Elias smiled at her, took her hand for a second, and said he had to go.

She walked him to the door, aware of every step she took and he took, and aware also that his body reaffirmed her feeling of well-being, just as it had before her father had been forced out of work.

"What if I can't get Walter?" she whispered. "I mean, he is busy." She did not want to say "He is loyal."

"Ah," Joey said. "I need Walter. It's imperative that he do this, for you. Janie can find lots of men to help her—she's a young widow. You have to do this."

And they both of them smiled at this at the same moment. But far at the back of her mind, in that anteroom of knowledge about true suffering and nobility that everyone, even Joey Elias at his best moments, knew and understood, Putsy Druken realized this: to take Walter from Janie, if even for a day, was to destroy Janie.

"I will ask him Christmas Eve," she said.

She went to her cubbyhole, behind the main room. She took off her dress and her slip and got under the quilt. Here she said her Hail Mary, and the Our Father, blessed herself and thought. Did she think she would be faithful to Walter? Why, of course— but he had to do this favour. It would be the only thing she ever asked—and no Druken had asked a McLeary for a thing before. So it was settled.

FIVE

"No."

"Why?" she asked.

"I cannot tell you. It's just no. You know it has to be no. For Janie's sake."

"But it's for my father and mother," she said, "so they will have something too. Why should everything go to others and they have nothing? That's all Joey is asking."

"I cannot tell you why, but I cannot go to work for Joey Elias. You are my fiancée. Rebecca is like my sister, and I got her a job—Janie treats her well. But if I did this and Janie suffered, I could never forgive myself."

"But that's nonsense! Nothing is going to happen. You can work for Elias—it's just on a loan, and after that, well, you will be mine and I will be yours. If you do this one thing, I will be yours."

"Is that what it all relies upon, Putsy?"

It was not, until he said it. They were silent. Time ticked by. What had happened in the intervening day was the prevalence everywhere of the rumour that Elias loved her again, and Putsy, no matter how she denied it, was frantic to please him. Rebecca had come to her and said, "He loves you again, so don't miss this chance. You are *so* lucky!"

So one more time true love was in the air, a true love that depended on connivance and treachery.

The conversation with Walter had been going on for two hours and it was Christmas Eve. They knew time was short. Midnight mass would start soon, and as Catholics of their time—which was a time of solidarity in a way of life, and a custom—they both wanted to go. Putsy was dressed in a dark blue coat with a fur collar. It was her Christmas present from Walter (she did not know yet about the diamond ring—he was far from rich, he had saved for a year), yet her very beauty in wearing this beautiful coat seemed to signal her independence from him. Or so other men had recognized.

"We better go along to mass," he said.

"It's just not fair—I—"

"Putsy." He smiled. "I can't—I can't walk out on Janie."

"You can't do anything, can you. There is nothing you can do, is there. You can't skate, you lumber about, you can't even walk right, so how can you walk out on Janie?" She gave a crude laugh.

He flinched. Then he shrugged. "You're right there." He laughed. "I am discombobulated when I walk."

"Don't try it on with fuggin' big words to impress me."

"Then please, milady, don't curse to impress me."

"We live in a place with no room, no furniture to speak of—it's terrible and everything—"

She said this looking away from him and he caught how beautiful she was—and how she did not love him. And as always he thought, like most men of modest attractiveness, "If I do this one thing, then she will love me."

"I told you I'd get you a new place at the beginning of the year— and I promise. Janie has contracted for other houses, small places on Weldon street. She could let you have one—or"—he took a breath— "you and me could live here. I have enough room in this apartment to last me forever."

"Yer just stupid if you think that's what I want. I want you to help my father. What's wrong with Joey Elias?" She stamped her foot, hard against the floor, so he took notice of her, with a changed expression on his face.

"I never said there was anything wrong with him. You did, Putsy."

"I never did, you did!" she screeched. She sounded like Putsy the little girl and her beauty became something vulgar, and savage.

"I will help your father," he said. "I will take him on as my apprentice. I've already spoken to Janie, telling her I need someone. Well, it'll be your dad."

This was a catch she hadn't expected, and she had to think quickly. Seeing this told him everything. It caught her like Hamlet's play, and he saw it. Everything became clear to him when she said, "For how much?"

"I don't know."

"How much, Walter?"

"I don't know. Twenty a week—"

"Ha! Elias is giving him forty," she said, though she knew it was thirty.

"Well, he better go with Elias, but I can't train him if he does." Then he whispered, "You must know why Elias is doing this—you must. He will do anything to destroy this business. To destroy us—"

"That's an awful thing to say about Mr. Elias," Putsy said. "You are a traitor is all what I know about it—to destroy us—you seem to be the one destroying us. You're the traitor!"

A traitor! He stared at her, and she looked back at him, her lips trembling like her mother's had that long-ago day. Then she walked out, and he couldn't find her in the crowd on the street. He went back to get his canes and made his way to church. The wind was blowing, and it was warm, with wet snow falling. At church he could not see her, and the very solemnity of the mass was lost on him. He looked at the stations of the cross and remembered the flickering candles and shadows of his youth—a youth of torment and bullying at the hands of others, of priests and goody two-shoes and choirboys. And why did he still go to church after they had dishonoured themselves like this? Because they weren't his faith. If they were, he would be nothing, and have nothing.

After mass he found himself outside, holding the rail. He inched along the steep stairs carefully, while boys and girls walked around him. Because his feet were such an impediment he had rings on four of his fingers, to make his hands more attractive.

"Putsy!" he called. "Putsy!"

People began to look at him. He hated being made a spectacle— he had never called out to anyone in years. He put on his floppy, peaked tam-o'-shanter and started for home. At the end of the walkway he was accidentally jostled onto a slick of ice the kids had used to slide on, and he fell—but was caught under the arms by two men.

"Merry Christmas, Walter," they said, slapping him on the back.

As he started down the street, the same horse and sleigh they had seen before went around him. He could smell rum, and perfume, and see a hand waving at him. He tried to keep up, thinking he heard Putsy. He started to run, and fell. This time he lay by himself in the snow, listening to the trees grate above him.

"Walter P. McLeary, late of the orphanage, crippled idiot," he thought. "Crippled idiot—crippled idiot! Thinking a woman would ever love you!"

He struggled to his feet, realizing his mouth was bloody as he lit his cigar.

He could not find her. The diamond he had bought for her was still in its box, under the tree in his room. He sat up all night waiting to hear her key in the door. Then, at midmorning, long after the bells for morning mass, just as he drifted off to sleep, Janie and her boy came in with their gift.

She saw the state he was in. It wasn't hard for Janie to decide that Walter could not be loved and should not take it seriously. She had tried to talk him out of any romance. It was for his own good—her own good as well. (Though she did not admit this.)

Yet for someone else to decide on the futility of his love did nothing to convince him to abandon it. In fact, he was more convinced of her love now then before. Putsy had probably tried to signal him, and had gotten mixed up, he told Janie. She was probably looking for him, as he was for her; perhaps she had wandered the whole night. Who knows why she didn't come back to the theatre. Maybe she had fallen—or falling ice from a roof had hit her and she was in a side alley somewhere. He had to find her before she died or was hospitalized with pneumonia. He knew she was fragile—no one more than he knew this.

He fumbled with his tie and rumpled-up shirt.

"She'll probably phone," Miles said. He looked quickly at his mother and then at Walter, nodding to both. He did not know that saying this deflated Walter's hope. Yes, she could have phoned, but she hadn't.

Walter looked at his phone and then glanced away as if scalded by it.

"That's probably it," Janie said. "She'll phone when she gets a chance. Maybe you should have Christmas Day with me," Janie said.

"It's just me and my children—Rebecca is gone as soon as we get home. The tree is up, the turkey just cooked. Miles needs a man in the house at Christmas—"

He knew secretly that this was a concession that pretended to ignore his physical limitation.

"I can't—I have to find Putsy," he said.

"Why don't you come with me?"

"I have to find Putsy—she's probably back home."

Miles looked at him, and Walter caught a sign of the boy's worry, and Miles, catching this, smiled again in order to be polite.

"If you won't come, I'll find the first derelict on the street to take home and feed, because as you know in the Bible—"

"I know quite well—the wealthy man invited his friends, who did not come, so he told his servant to find the poor and the crippled to share his meal. Well, this cripple is going to find Putsy before she dies in a ditch someplace."

"But where will I find a derelict at this time of day?" Janie said.

"You could try our old neighbourhood," he said. "There were many there when we were young."

SIX

It was now snowing gently all over town, and across the river the trees were blotted out, and down on the embankment huddled into the cliffs a few solemn fires were lighted, and up near the track, near Dobblestein's old mill, a few indigents stood close to a fire barrel. And then beyond this the little houses of Beaverbrook Settlement and Bellefond, nestled away amid the frozen trees, were silent, with a wisp of smoke trailing off their tin chimneys, their basins sitting out of doors, and here and there a French pudding cooling on the steps.

They left the "hall"—Janie always called the theatre the "hall"—and went in different directions.

She drove the streets in her new car, shifting gears with a clatter, as Miles sat beside her in his white shirt and vest. He wore a long London Fog coat over him. He was tall for his age, and thin, with very white skin (so much so a doctor believed he was suffering from hemophilia, like the son of the Russian tsar). His great attribute was kindness, his failing trait a kind of sad and acute gullibility and weak posture, so he walked bent over and often stared at the ground as if he was searching for a key.

Miles scanned the ridges and the small alleyways for a derelict. His mother would not be satisfied now until she brought someone home and then relayed the message to her father later. Miles's pensive face was racked with constant worry, and he sat close to the car door, in respect of his mother's accurate slaps.

He knew his mother was brave, and not to be trifled with. But she was alone. Her father, his grandfather, old Jimmy McLeary, would not come to the house. Once or twice in the last few years she had had to call a doctor down to his house. Again this afternoon she stopped at the little brick house and went inside.

"Would you like to come for a meal, Father," she asked, "to celebrate Christmas with my son and me?"

"Will there be a drink for me there?"

"No, there will not be."

"Then I have no intention to," he said.

"But there will be turkey and your grandchildren—"

"Turkey and my grandchildren—well, it's enticing but I cannot go. I am in no mood to either speak to a turkey or eat my grandchildren. I don't like Georgina's name—you should change it to Mary Beth."

"She is named after her father."

"Well, I still can't come."

"And why not?"

"The grubby fairies have stolen my suit."

"The suit I bought you—I saw in Larson's pawnshop," she said. "And I bought it again and have it for you now—and I will leave it here." She instructed Miles to go to the car and bring it inside.

"Yes, well, the fairies must have taken it to Larson's," he answered. "The bullies are sitting over there right now if you can see them—they all have a chip on their wings, if you ask me."

"I will leave your suit here, and if you wish to come, you can, at any time. You know that, Father."

"Then why did you kick me out of the house?"

"You were cursing and hitting me—and I didn't want to lose my patience and hit you back."

"I would never injure anyone."

"Not intentionally, no. Please come."

"I cannot do so and remain a man."

"A drunk loses that distinction almost immediately and with everyone knowing except the drunkard himself."

"You have sided with the Drukens against me—I think it was back sometime on the morning of October seventeenth, 1911."

"You know that is a lie, told by Joey Elias to make you hate me. I have never sided with the Drukens against you, and I forgive the fact that you have sided with Joey Elias against me."

Frowning and feeble, he looked away from her and cursed.

Now Walter and Putsy could not come. And Rebecca was told to go at noon. It was Christmas day.

"Do you think people are against me?" she asked her son.

"Not all," he answered, smiling, "I don't think all—I mean, I was counting them up and I am sure it is not all."

"Yes, all—all—do you understand, Miles? All!"

"All—why, Mother, I don't think all—"

Here she gave him a slap.

"Even who we pick up today?" he said, rubbing his cheek. She stopped the car and grabbed his lapel. "Even who we pick up today—*Yes.*"

He said nothing. Christmas had not been special for him. But he loved his little sister, Georgina. He had Rebecca take him to a store to buy a present for his granddad. Rebecca, angered by his money, told him she had nothing in her youth and could understand why he was bullied—for playing the big shot.

Now he asked his mother to go back and try her father one more time. To his surprise she took up this challenge. But the old house was empty.

"He is away," she said. "I'm sorry for that. We will have to find someone else."

Miles at this point in his life was eager to learn but had no one to teach him. He had not played baseball or hockey, or gone camping. Once he bought himself a hockey stick and took shots. Another time he bought a Swiss Army knife for the time when he and his mom would go camping.

He even suspected this neglect was not deliberate on his mother's part—but so many she had met had stung her, and to the end of her days she found it hard to trust them. So she tried to keep Miles for herself. She wanted him to dance on the stage, told him she would give him piano lessons any day now. But he waited and they did not come. She was afraid to give him piano lessons and lose him, like his father had been lost in England and gone to Canada. What if Miles learned piano and left Canada and went to England? The drawing room, where his father's piano sat, was in the closed-off part of the house, locked solid.

They were driving up a hill, on their way home to eat Christmas dinner in silence, without her father. It had turned unusually foggy, and the air seemed filled with icy pellets of rain. Suddenly in front of them a man ran out—others chasing him—and fell in front of the car. The men chasing him were some of the same that Janie had seen on the bridge. She threw on the brake and stepped out, pulling the tire iron from behind her seat.

"Ya'll not come at me as long as I face ya, ya bastards," she swore.

My grandmother looked at the men, and they turned on her. But they could not get at Roy Dingle, for that's what the man's name was.

He was a carpenter of sorts and a handyman as well. Janie stepped over him, swinging the iron at the men. Leon Winch advanced, and then stopped.

"Leave him to us, Janie, or ya'll be sorry," he said.

"I'm sorry every time I lay sight on you," she snapped, "to think that a man like my husband died and a man like you lives."

He laughed at this, but he was not happy. He roared that Dingle was hiding under her skirt.

"I suppose he is," she said. "All men do, sooner or later."

She backed them off and sheltered Dingle until they left. And they left because it was beginning to draw a crowd.

Janie McLeary got back in her car and started to drive away.

"You have to help him," Miles said, staring at the crumpled-up form of Dingle. Dingle in the snow.

"Whatsoever for?" She said. She put on the emergency brake and held him by the collar, almost spitting this remark: " You don't know him, do you. He is a Dingle—he was on the bridge—he was looking for his fifteen dollars just like the rest—and those chasing him today—the same kind of creatures. If I do any more to protect Dingle they will come back at us—you and I in some way. I'll tell you, boy— you do not know the history. I cannot have any of them in my house—it is a rule. Many Christmases we had nothing because of them. I cannot break that rule and not have disaster rule. If Dingle comes into my house tonight something bad will happen to me. It's bad enough to have a Druken as a maid; it's worse to have this man as a guest. You don't understand!"

"But he's hurt—he's hurt—so you have to break your rule. Besides, he'll be our guest," my father said, beaming.

Janie twice started to go, and twice my father pleaded.

"If I do, we will regret it all," she said under her breath. "Elias, who Dingle runs errands for, will seek revenge."

"We have to. How do you want Georgina to think of this Christmas?" he said. "Or be told of what we did if Mr. Dingle dies? If we went away and he died?"

And so she relented. My father would never forget the black back door of her Ford open and the wet shaking man being put inside. He helped his mother put little Roy Dingle into the back seat.

When Dingle came to, he reached over and grabbed Miles by the shoulder.

"Who are you?" he said.

"I am Miles," my father said.

"Ah—the Englishman's boy," Dingle said, with a glance at Janie King. "You are not a popular little boy. I don't think you are just hated, Miles—no, you are intentionally hated!"

Miles did not know what that meant. He stared at his mom, and then stared out the window of the Ford.

They got Roy Dingle to the house and put him in a spare bedroom. Janie brought in a towel and a basin, and helped him wash.

"I'm Janie McLeary," she said. "If you want to have supper with us, there's a pair of pants and a shirt in the closet. Come down in an hour if you are strong enough."

"Christmas supper with a McLeary—in one of the biggest houses in town. Times have changed," he said respectfully.

"Things don't change that much," she answered. "My father still owns nothing at all."

Rebecca, eager to leave, was now caught up with Dingle. Janie asked if she could stay an extra hour or two.

"Yes, ma'am, of course," Rebecca said. She went back downstairs to set the table, making sure Georgina was changed into her Christmas dress, but all the while seethed at her bad luck. Her one great desire this Christmas was to sneak away and be with Joey Elias. She was supposed to be gone, and light was now fading over the snow.

SEVEN

Putsy had been drunk since Christmas Eve. It was her great failing, though she did not consider it one when she was fortunate enough to have enough to drink. She did not know she was drunk, and then she did not care she was. She did not know how many hours had passed or if Walter was still looking for her. She was with Mr. Elias all Christmas Day, complaining about Walter.

"He is a cripple," Elias said matter-of-factly. "You can't live your life with a cripple—you know that. How can you, Putsy! I try to think of a way out for you, but what am I supposed to do if you are going about living with a cripple?"

"Oh, I don't know what to do," she said, wiping away tears with his handkerchief.

"I know you are loyal, and want him to be happy, but marriage is ridiculous. Hippy Skippy, we call him. And he's not honourable—don't think he is. He's a sneak—he sneaks about tattling on people, and he drinks too much."

On Christmas Eve she was supposedly in love with Walter and wanting to marry him. Now, by nine o'clock on Christmas night, she knew she was in a horrible position. How could she go back to Walter? There were moments when she wanted to. How could she stay in this little room, at the back of Elias's house, beyond everyone else? He was expecting guests, and he had made it clear she was to stay where she was. If she came out of the room he would hit her. But she thought she would rather be beaten by him than stay with Walter.

The only way she could stay was to drink more. That is the only way she could stand herself.

Where were her clothes? How stupid she was, after midnight mass, to have climbed into the sleigh with the horse with the black mane that had been hauling those university kids. They put the big bear rug over her, and she felt warm.

"We'll hide you," the oldest of them laughed, "and he'll never find you."

And suddenly she realized that hiding was a powerful anecdote to her feeling of frustration with Walter. Yes, she would hide from him, let him find her if he could. Then he would do anything for her, and she would be able to help Joey Elias.

"And if he doesn't, I won't go back—he isn't fair," she thought.

She could hear him calling her frantically. She could hear his canes in the snow. She huddled down further. The young chemistry student's name was Ed, and he said he would hide her.

They made light of her, asked her if she would please explain $E=mc^2$.

"Don't talk over her head," a girl said.

"I can't explain it but I'll be damned if I can't drink it—give me some $E=mc^2$."

She told Ed he was the cutest boy she knew. He kissed her full on the mouth, but she pushed him away. On they went, on toward the cove. Down the lane and out toward the river ice.

The horse slipped and fell, and kicked its legs, frantic, and all they did was laugh. The young driver was the only one angered. He told them the horse wasn't shod right and needed rest, and after rest, water and oats.

A dispute occurred and he left.

Ed took over and tried to rouse the animal. And though she felt sorry for the old animal, she laughed too. Ed kissed her again. She saw in his eyes the reflection of her hair and hat and the victorious idea that she was the young fiancée of the crippled man from the theatre, out for a lark with real men like himself. The snow fell as they watched her drink.

Then when they could coax the horse no longer, one of the boys got out and kicked it. While they watched this boy—the girl telling him to stop—Putsy put a bottle of rum under her new coat and climbed down from the sleigh. When Ed asked her where she was going, she told him to piss off.

"Hey, none of that language—there's a lady here," he said.

"Tell her to piss off too," she said.

Then she ran into the dark with the bottle before they spotted it gone.

She started off to find Walter. How could she have hurt him—how?

In the snow she looked for him. Then she banged on doors of former friends and found no one home but Joey Elias. She hadn't meant to bang so loudly upon it. She was ready to run away. But when he opened the door she cried.

"Joey, Joey—let me come in. I don't want him to see me. I tried, I tried."

And she had tried, and she had failed. She hugged him, and he brought her inside.

"I'm doing it all for Dad," she said, weeping, "I'm doing it all for Dad."

"Never mind," he said. "We'll figure something else out."

It was now nine o'clock on Christmas night.

She had looked so refined just a day ago. She sat on the edge of the cot, in his back room, with its cardboard boxes, where he kept gin and rum that he ran out to the Maine border. She watched the door, hoping it would open. She heard whispers from beyond the door; the loud talk of the previous few hours had stopped. She waited, and then a door closed somewhere.

"Joey," she called, "I need a smoke, Joey—for Christ sake—for Christ sake, Joey."

It echoed a dreary note through the dark house, lit here and there by electric candles, the rooms cluttered with furniture, the hallways smelling of Polish sausage and salt bacon.

Joey Elias barely heard her. He was sitting at a mahogany table, far at the back of his large dining room. And he was thinking, as he rubbed his hand through his thinning hair: Why had she come to the door on Christmas Eve? He wasn't planning anything on

Christmas Eve but to go to sleep. Then a knock on the door, which he very nearly didn't answer. He went down the stairs and turned on the porch light and saw her face through the smoky glass, while snow fell quietly on the street. It changed their lives forever.

There she was. In her beauty. In her wonderful new coat, and her wonderful saucy eyes—eyes that could turn most men weak.

And what had he been doing? He had been preparing to go to bed. He thought she'd have been at midnight mass, go back to her folks' house.

He wanted her again, in his maze of thinking and planning and orchestrating, but not on Christmas Eve—it had to be later on. He had no idea that she would come over so soon. And she wanted to drink with him. She held up the rum and laughed, and up the stairs they went.

But now, tonight—thinking over all of this once again, he wondered for the first time if he had done anything really. Hadn't all things been done not *by* him, but *to* him? He still remembered the feel of his little brother on his back when he laid his head on his shoulder and fell asleep. To know peace again, he would have to go back to that time, carry his brother again—he knew it. He remembered what Father Carmichael had said a few years before at midnight mass: "We live lives that are calculated to overrule our instincts toward good. We are always making deals with our better selves in order to escape our duty. It never works in the end. In the end we have to face what and who we are. All of us live another life. That is the real life—it just goes on underneath, like a great lost sea under the ice. And all of us are equal in that sea. We must go back to our first mistakes and start again. It is not easy to do, yet it is possible. What will people say if you give up the protection of this present life for the other life, the interior life? They will mock you—torment you. That is what you have to look forward to. But it is worth this—yes—it is worth every slander against you." He remembered that sermon. It was the last time he was in a church.

———

He tried to think. What had happened? Putsy Druken had knocked on the door on Christmas Eve. And it had started when he had seen her at the skating rink.

Later, after he had fed her a meat pie and put her to bed, came the fears from his youth, and again he had to walk them off. So, taking his brother's boots, he went out along the streets covered in newly fallen snow. Most of the houses were shut up, but there were still some revellers shouting and going on.

When Joey came home from that walk in the early hours of Christmas morning, he found Putsy. Her hair was wet, her eyes puffy. She was crying and said she wanted to go home.

"You can't go now—wait till tomorrow," he said. "If Walter sees you in this state what will he think? You will never convince him of your innocence."

He helped her back to the bedroom. It was there, while laying her on the bed, that he saw it. Time itself stood still. Kept in a small pouch in her silk stocking, on her white thigh near her triangle of dark, beautiful hair, was a key. He bent over and kissed her thigh and she tried to push him away. When he came away, he came away with the key in his mouth.

He knew it was the key to Janie's theatre—the skeleton key that opened both outside doors. He stood, coughed, tucked it into his vest pocket.

He told her he was lonely and asked her to drink with him. After two drinks of rye whisky, she fell back to sleep.

He became worried about her stockings—she would know if she woke and saw the key missing. So he undid her stockings and rolled them down and hid them. He did not care if she went home without her stockings. If she did, she would think herself responsible for losing her key.

He would put the key back into the stocking after he had used it.

He still wasn't completely sure what he was going to use it for, but he was glad he had it on him. He was filled with a sudden and desperate glee. Maybe he would go and look at the projectors, or perhaps sabotage one—just a little. Perhaps that would encourage Janie to distrust Walter, and Walter would come to work with him.

Putsy woke, and they spent the morning together. They had some drinks, and around one o'clock in the afternoon she went back to bed. She never mentioned her stockings.

He had forgotten about the key until two of his friends came to tell him that they had chased and beaten Dingle.

"I hit him for you, sir, just like you wanted," Leon Winch said.

"Good, good," he said, though he had already forgotten why he had been angry with Roy Dingle.

"Then Janie came along and took him in her car," the other said. "Then Leon ran."

"I did not—"

"Sure you did," the other man laughed. "Ran from Janie King—"

Leon, furious at this banged his fist on the table.

"Dingle is with Janie King?" Elias said, astonished.

He could not believe this, so he sent the men around to find out what was going on at the house.

"They are sitting about eating supper," Leon reported when they returned. "Dingle is wearing King's clothes—though he swims in them."

"And I overheard them speaking about you," the second man said. "Janie said you had a fatal flaw!"

"Me, a fatal flaw!"

"Yes—envy."

"Envy? Envy! Me! Who am I envious of?"

"Her."

Elias threw his cigarette holder across the room, and spat.

"I think they've always been in cahoots," Leon said, "or we woulda got her on the bridge!"

Now this seemed completely true to Elias. And if it was, then he had been played for a fool.

When the first man left (for he was not a man of Joey's inner circle) Joey sat down in despair that he was being treated so badly.

"Well, let's you and I get even with them," Leon Winch said. "That's what we have to do." He was terrified of Janie King and wanted to prove that he wasn't.

Now Elias put everything that was happening down to Janie's trickery.

"Do you want to get even?" Elias said, the intonation of his voice suggesting that only good men got even.

Elias slipped his hand into his pocket and fingered the key. It was cold and silent throughout the town. The lights were out and the buildings dark.

"What do you intend?" Winch said.

"I want you to go inside the Regent—and burn the theatre to the ground. Then we'll see how the Biograph does."

"If it's a break-in they'll know its arson," Leon said circumspectly.

"Then you'll need this," Elias said. He opened his hand on the key and smiled as if his answer had been preordained an eternity ago.

My great-grandfather had missed Janie by five minutes on that Christmas Day. He had gone out to a house on Pond Street to find a bit of cooking sherry he had hidden under a plank a month before. To his amazement it was still there, and he went back to his house, and while drinking his sherry—the dregs of the dregs—he had a visitor, Minister Whispers. He was frightened because Whispers was dressed completely in black and had a hawkish face, and small cupped white hands. This visitor was a lay minister from the Church of the Gospel of the Lower White Rapids. He visited Jimmy three days a month to try to convert him "to a sensible religion."

"And why in Christ would one want a sensible religion?" Jimmy said. "A sensible religion is like a frigid wife—polite, but a lousy piece of wisdom in bed."

The lay preacher's report was that they got into an argument about saints and hell and fairies.

"I will never go trooping off to a religion where fairies are mistreated—never, never," Jimmy said.

The preacher Whispers imparted his wisdom about saints. Catholic saints were not really saints, he said. Jimmy, angered by this, told the preacher, perhaps a little rashly, that he had a saint in a box in his bedroom.

"What saint is that?" the lay minister asked.

"St.—Hemseley" my great-grandfather was reported to have said, coughing at that moment so the preacher could not be sure of the name.

The preacher said he wanted to see the saint. Jimmy said it was a feast day for the saint—Christmas—and he didn't want to be disturbed. Then Jimmy, his voice filling with emotion, spoke in his still half-Irish brogue about his daughter, Janie—how he had always loved her. He began to cry, and said he hoped she forgave him for all the terrible things he said. That he had worked for Joey Elias against her, pretending she had done him wrong as a way to enable his habit of drink. But that she continually looked out for him, even after he had done this.

"Of course she's a saint," he said, his eyes bright with tears. "She brought me back my suit today even though I had pawned it—just to have Christmas supper with her and her boy and little Georgina."

The minister's face was intense and snail shaped, with the upper lip falling over the bottom, so the line from his nose extended almost to his chin. Now his lips curled upwards in a sly smile. My great-grandfather had the reputation that D. H. Lawrence's father must have had—that is, when Lawrence and his wife were forced to leave their house, who was at the gate scorning them but his own father.

"But she keeps movies," he reminded Jimmy. "The very reason you crossed her out of your life."

"Yes—that is true," old Jimmy said, looking up. "But even so, who am I or you, Brother Henry—I mean, who are we to judge?"

"But they are movies," the lay preacher reminded my great-grandfather, who had drunk every day of his life since his twelfth birthday.

"I know they are, Brother Henry—but—well—it's Christmas. Many a Christmases that child had nothing at all—nothing—nor her mother. And now with her big house . . . What friend does she have, and why does she not have them—because she is true to who she is. Isn't that something in the eyes of God?"

"She is not a saint—she cannot forgive anyone. And until she is reborn in the blood of the lamb, she is condemned to hell."

"Oh, no," Jimmy McLeary said, and he began to shake.

"Condemned to hellfire—black as night—blacker than night— and pitchforks burning like coals."

"Ah," Jimmy said, looking about the place and spying the knife he had cut the preacher's bread with. He shook his head and looked down at his feet and growled like a dog.

The preacher became uncertain, and Jimmy mumbled and glared at his shoes, rubbing his hands together.

"Out!" Jimmy yelled, pointing toward the door with his head still down and shaking it back and forth

"Why?"

"The bread and cheese you are eating are hers—are hers!"

"I don't see—"

"I have not thrown a punch in twenty years, but I can flatten you, you prickless wonder. You are talking about my daughter, a woman I should have had courage enough to respect—and I will make you respect." And he grabbed the carving knife and took a swing at the preacher's ear, yelling as fierce as any Irishman at the Boyne.

The ear heard the swish, and the preacher ducked and fled into the grey night, yelling: "I'll get the police!"

"And I'll get my fairies and St. Hemseley and we'll met ya at the door—and you'll be the first I kill. You hear me? You'll be the first I kill, you fuggin' prick!"

For he always said fuggin', like an Irishman.

But Jimmy was not going to stay there, not when the preacher would return with the police—whom Jimmy had had run-ins with before. So he put on the suit he had pawned, and got his old hat out of the living-room closet—a hat his father wore in the 1880s, a huge top hat called a skyscraper—for he had no other respectable hat, I am told, being a newspaper boy most of his life. He left and went into the dark little streets, passed buildings swept away from our river decades ago, his feet in small leather boots, each with a buckle, and his face shaven and haunted. He would make it up to her. He had to, for he was an old man. He would go to supper, he would laugh, he would hold the boy. And if he could he would take the pledge: he would promise never to drink, he would kneel before her, and ask her forgiveness, for he was old, and he was dying. And some of the things said about her in his presence made him less than a man should ever be made. He would never do that to her again, for her crime was marrying an Englishman who was as fine a man as Jimmy had ever known.

Why had he belittled her? Fear! Why had he mocked her? Fear again!

But no more fear—no more.

The blood of the lamb was right, and any man could find it—all they had to do was seek it. To say yes once, and mean it—that was all God required.

He came to one of Estabrook's lumberyards and sat for a moment on a pile of snow-covered boards. Before him, the little mill (Estabrook's third smallest) lay dormant, and wet snow fell on Jimmy's big hat. He caught his breath, and stood, and walked off into the dark. Two women he met, and he tipped his hat to them.

"A merry Christmas to you," he said.

"And a merry Christmas to you, Jimmy," they said.

He smiled at this, and because they crowded him a little on the snowy sidewalk he decided to turn up the first hill instead of walking to the second. Doing this, he passed Janie's theatre. It was strange. The door was open, and the theatre was black and cold.

More than likely Janie was there, he thought, and he would drive off with her to the house. Late for Christmas dinner but not too late, he hoped, to make amends. But did he have a present for the boy? He searched through his pockets and was surprised, and overcome, to find a present. He lit a match and looked. Ah—it was a present from the boy to him. Miles had snuck it into the pocket when Janie brought back the suit.

"To Grampie—Love, Miles."

How terrible his life. How miserably he had treated others. He blew out the match before it burned his finger, and saw in the pitch darkness of the building another match go out.

"What is that?" Jimmy thought. "Reflection of my own match or someone downstairs?"

He proceeded inside.

"Hello," Jimmy McLeary, my forbearer, my great-grandfather said, and then walking down the steps to the furnace room, added, "Oh, hello—Merry Christmas."

Leon Winch, a Norwegian who had played an Irishman, hugely gutted, squat, and broad-shouldered came back without doing what he was told to do. For something terrible had happened. And it was the key—the key was responsible. For without the key, what would have happened? Nothing.

The old man had come in, Leon told Elias in a strange hellish kind of whisper.

"Who? Walter?" Elias asked.

"No," Leon said, "it was just as you told me—Walter wasn't there. I had gasoline, and was lighting a match—when just as I did, another match was lighted on the steps. I could see this through the window. When that match went out, I blew out my own."

Jimmy started down the stairs. And there was no place for Leon Winch to hide.

"Oh, hello—Merry Christmas." His skyscraper touched the ceiling; he held Miles's present in his hand.

Then his face went ashen as he smelled the gasoline.

He turned his feeble old body and started up the stairs, holding his hat in place with one hand.

"I hit him over the head with a maple chunk—that I threw away in the snow—"

"He is dead?" Elias asked.

"I don't know."

"And the key—where is the key? I have to get the key back into her stocking."

Leon said, "I left the key in the door."

"You have to go back and see if he is dead—now that you have done this—it is kind of an accident—but you have to for all our sakes. I will give you a house—I promise the house I took from the Drukens. You have to go back and get the key."

"You go back," Leon hissed.

And Leon left him.

That was over an hour ago.

How sad this Christmas was.

For a long time, Elias did not know what to do. He sat in a stupor in the large room looking at his brother's boots, frightened to death. He couldn't bring himself to go and check for the key. He prayed—actually prayed—for the man to be dead. For only if he was dead could he not talk. But Elias hadn't done anything—it was Leon Winch. Leon did it, that was certain. He, Elias could say he had no idea of the key. But then this idea came. Putsy would tell on him. He had to do something.

He stood trembling, and went to her. She was sitting, half-naked, staring at him as he opened the door. For a fleeting moment he thought he might tell her what had happened. But he was weak.

"Will you marry me—now?" he asked. "As soon as you can. You will never regret it"

He talked to her for an hour, and when he left, she still hadn't decided. But he felt her being swayed. If she was married to him she would not testify against him. It was nearing ten at night. He promised he would injure no one else.

But when he came back along the corridor a hand reached out, and touched his shoulder. He turned very quickly and grabbed the person by the throat.

It was Rebecca. She had come to see him, and now he remembered having asked her two weeks before to visit him tonight.

"You have to do something for me," he whispered harshly into her face, so she turned her head away.

"What?"

"You have to go to the Regent and see if the old man is dead—and find a key—and throw it off the Morrissey Bridge."

"What old man?"

"Old Jimmy."

"What happened to him?" she asked.

"I can't tell you—well, he was struck. It was an accident—we just wanted to scare Janie a little—but he came along—"

"Scare her how?" Rebecca smiled teasingly.

"I don't know, a little fire or something. But then Old Jim came along. You have to see if he is dead—you have to take the key and throw it away—for my sake."

"Why me?"

Her smile unnerved him. It was the same smile she used to have as a little girl when she was frightened, and he was teasing her.

"Because—you need to. They won't suspect you of anything—you were just trying to help—you're just a child. That's if anyone spies you. Go—go." He held up two ten-dollar bills. She grabbed them as if snatching at a fly.

"Kiss me first," she said. "And promise me you will take me to Fredericton the next time you go!"

He nodded, kissed her, forgetting that he had just proposed to her sister.

Rebecca went down the stairs. He ran to the window, terrified she might go in the opposite direction toward the police station. But he saw her slink away toward the Regent Theatre. Beyond her, in the park, a youngster was moving away also. Elias knew him. It was the boy who had driven the old horse when Walter fell. But he was going in the opposite direction, so that was fine. Elias lighted a cigarette and waited.

Putsy sat alone all night. She vacillated from one position to another. But finally, having her third glass of gin, she thought they would get married. Like true lovers, they wouldn't care. Because true love does not care for anything—God or mountains or oceans in between, not real love. She couldn't wait to see him, to tell him this.

Dawn was breaking when he came back into the room.

PART III

ONE

My great-grandfather was found early on Boxing Day. The skyscraper was lying on his chest, his eyes were half opened, while his hands, bent and twisted by the years, were gnarled together. He was at the last of his life, and weighed only a hundred pounds. He could not have fought without benefit of his fairies or his saint, even if he wanted to.

A dull snow was falling and the area was roped off; two constables had been called to the scene. Their finding was simple: the old man, angered by the "truancy" of his daughter, had come in with an idea to set the place ablaze, but his drunkenness caused a vanguard against him and he slipped and hit his head upon the step.

"Death by misadventure," they reasoned within ten minutes, and the sad old body was finally removed.

The word spread throughout the town and spent itself in back-rooms and barbershops. It reached Putsy, hung over and sitting in her house, at quarter to nine that night.

Old Jimmy McLeary was killed trying to burn down the place— and it would have just been right, for Janie King was not a good woman.

Initially people believed the story that it was part of an internal squabble among the theatre management. But early on, even though the case was closed, there was a rumour circulating. Somehow the old man had surprised an intruder or intruders in the building. The possiblity that these intruders might have been looking to murder Janie McLeary was appalling. Yet some people still believed it was her own arrangement with the world that had caused it all.

Rebecca informed Miles about the rumour at supper hour a few nights later.

"It's the Dime," Rebecca said.

"What do you mean, Rebecca?"

"All sorts of crimes happen at the Dime," Rebecca said. "That's what the people are so mad at."

"Who are they mad at?" Miles asked.

"Why, your mother, of course—and you too, I think."

"Me?"

"Well, aren't you the Englishman's boy and didn't he start the theatre? And didn't he bring that kind of music, and all of that? And the movies, and all of that? And the loud pictures from Hollywood, and all of that?" Rebecca asked, cutting some gristle off her chop.

"Who says so?" Miles asked.

"Well, not me, Miles, dear—I am not the one to say you are a sissy. It's people downtown. I'm not the one to say it's Janie's fault—it's people downtown. I just sit and listen, a fly on a wall, I am. I don't think I'm better than youse is—it's people downtown. I don't think Janie betrayed her Irish heritage by marrying a Limey. As I say, it's people downtown. But as long as you give me things and be nice, I'll be nice to you!"

"What can I give you?"

"Well, don't you have an allowance? You can give me that. And don't you have a medal of the king? You can give me that. And don't you have Janie's picture in your room? You can give me that. You see, I haven't decided yet what you can give me, but it's all up to me and not up to you at all. So when I decide what I want you will have to get it—or I won't be able to help you with people downtown."

Meanwhile, Putsy asked her father what gossip he was hearing around town. Many still thought it was an accident and the old man had set out to do the theatre in.

"How did he get in?" Putsy asked.

"Everyone is saying he had to have a key," Phil told her.

She gave a start, and looked away. Dull cold clung to the window, but the sky was forebodingly clear. She knew the old man had no key, and her key was gone—and that was exactly why she had asked the questions.

"But some say it was Leon Winch and me," Phil said proudly, "but it weren't me."

"Well who was it, then?" Putsy asked, tears beginning in her eyes.

"No one is saying," Phil said, "and many think it an accident anyway."

That night the snow glittered under the moon. Stars filled the sky across the river, and the wind was soft. A night for a sleigh ride into the future.

It was seven o'clock, mass was over. She had gone and prayed—like a child she had prayed for a conscience as clear as the sky. She walked down the town hill to Joey Elias's house, large and dark, with a queer sense of foreboding in the windows. She tapped on the brass door knocker, and when he opened the door she clutched at him and told him about the key—the key she had wanted to return to Walter. Had he seen it?

"No," he said.

It was soon to be a new year. He looked pale and his head was balding.

"Where did my key go?" she asked.

"Like I say, I do not know."

There was silence, and they heard the wind. Some boys yelled across the street.

He put sugar in her tea, and as he handed it to her he said, "I have no idea what you are talking about, but if you had a key you had better keep it quiet. The last thing you want is to get involved in this. The police might think you are culpable of something." He tapped the spoon against the cup. "Or," he said, "I can get a lawyer for you tonight if you feel you need one."

The talk of a lawyer cast cold in her gut.

"I never did anything. But what should I do?"

"If I can believe you—that you had nothing to do with it—I'll protect you," Joey said. "Act straight. Go to the funeral and act innocent because you are. If you are innocent we will get married."

Leaving the house, going down the steps to the road, laying her hand on the brass railing, all of this that just a day ago had been pleasant now filled her with dread. Suddenly marriage seemed terribly anticlimactic.

The funeral home where old Jimmy was taken was ten houses from the police station. At the police station she stopped, looking at the footprints through the snow. Just then out came Rebecca Druken.

"Why were you in there?" she asked.

"Oh, they just asked me if Janie was in the house all night—that night. Well, you see, everything is now up to me."

"What do you mean?" Putsy whispered.

"Just what I said. Now people are asking me things, and I am more important than a lot of people ever thought, and I was at the funeral home where I paid my respects—and you should go too. People know now that everything is up to me, and people are being nicer to me than to you—simply because it's up to me."

There was a look in her sister's eye that Putsy had seen very early on, when they played in the wood chips at the mill. With wood chips over her freckled face and in her hair, it would come and go, this look. Putsy would call her into the house at night, and saying prayers with her would pretend that she had never seen this look.

One Christmas, when Rebecca was seven, she was upset with the priest.

"Why?" Putsy had asked, putting her sister's nightgown over her head.

"Because he said we would get a present at Christmas—and I was waiting for this special present—and it turned out to be nothing—it was just the Host—at communion!"

Rebecca smiled as the nightgown was being put over her head, but when the head appeared again, the look Putsy had seen at certain times had come back, strikingly intense—smart, illusive, predatory, and sad.

As they stood near the police station, Putsy Druken remembered this.

"Do you know anything?"

"Do I know anything? Hah! You might be scared of what I know."

Rebecca turned her head away in a sign of dismissal, the consequence of which was measured only by herself.

The effects of his house are by no means legendary, but I do have a copy of the inventory handed down by my grandmother herself. There was a globe that produced snow when turned upside down and when wound played "I Wish You a Merry Christmas." In the drawer was a tavern account from 1901 that had gone unpaid. There was a card sent him by Joe Tardy before Tardy went overseas —Joe Tardy being one of the fighting Tardy brothers. Nothing is known of them outside of my town. Five brothers—the youngest aged fifteen—who because their mother had died followed their brother to war, and died as well. Their house, in good Canadian fashion, was seized for unpaid taxes. The note to my great-grandfather was recognition of his kindness to their mother when she was sick.

In the box upstairs, where in more exuberant moments he said lay his saint, sat a lone paper bag that had held his newspapers and the twine that bound them.

It is strange to me that a man like my great-grandfather would have a friend—or, rather, friends who looked up to him.

But he had more than one. And they gathered in the house, and told stories about his bravery in fighting the Drukens by himself, and sent him to his reward as best they could. Putsy went to both the wake and the funeral, but spoke little to Walter, who refused to look in her direction.

Janie received a card from a man who had done her a favour some time before. "Remembering you in your time of grief," Lord Beaverbrook wrote.

I cannot find his grave in the old cemetery beyond the tracks, but I have been assured it is there, among my other ancestors who followed the sea to Canada.

Late in the week, Walter had a meeting with Putsy. She demanded one, and he relented, for rumours were rampant, insoluble like vapours. She came to the door of his apartment shivering in her blue coat with the ermine collar. She told him that she hadn't meant to harm him. He knew this was true, though it was no great comfort to him. There was an inch of grime on his window. She asked him how he could live with all those collectibles, old one-sheets, pictures of Tom Mix and Buster Keaton. They were once fascinating to her, but now they were just sad. The world had turned sad for her all of a sudden.

He asked her to return her key.

"I can't find it anywhere. I have nightmares to think of what might have happened if it had fallen into the wrong hands. If I find it, I will return it to you, I promise."

He stared at her for a long time. Then, standing on his canes said, "How can you marry him? Don't think because my leg is crippled I could not break him apart! But I can't prove anything—unless you come forward. I can go to church and pray you come forward, but I cannot make you—no one can. You had the only key—besides myself and Janie—and Janie does not know about yours. I could go to the police—I should go. Soon he'll take to beating you again, just as he did before."

She stared into the corner, saying nothing.

But for all his threats he could not bring himself to harm her. Old Jimmy's death lay on his conscience, but no one could find the key.

The meeting with Putsy took an hour. When she left he stood and took a small drink of rum, to help ease the pain in his foot. He went and changed the marquee, and the one-sheet behind its wired frame.

Angry that Frankenstein's creature reminded him of his own plight, his own dull mob that chased him with torches, he took the one-sheet and placed it in the wall behind his sink.

After this he became like the hunchback of Notre Dame, as played by Charles Laughton—burdened, alone, and swinging from his gargoyles in the dark.

TWO

Sometime after the death of Jimmy McLeary, my grandmother closed the Regent (which Walter kept as his house) and opened the Grand on the town square. For a long while it was the largest and most imposing structure in our town. It signalled in the age of the great production companies, the big studio lots—Clark Gable, Bette Davis, Jimmy Cagney. There were five hundred seats in our theatre, gold exit curtains tied back with gold sash, and the faces of comedy and tragedy at the four exit corners. Our carpets were red, and the seats upholstered, and the snack bar sold Cracker Jack and candy. A picture of our grandfather was in the foyer. Over time this would be replaced by a picture of Janie herself.

Miles entered the theatre with a gasp in 1931, and was filled with a kind of urgency to become, as he once told me, "a great man, and to do a great thing—just as those heroes of ours were doing on the screen."

Rebecca stayed with our family, for there was no one more dutiful in keeping herself and the children clean. Far at the back of the house she had a room. She was often seen walking the two children to church.

Roy Dingle stayed as well and, in a suit and tie, acted as something of a greeter at the theatre door.

So if there was no real bliss in Janie's life, there were moments of triumph.

The one in town who watched these events with skepticism was Joey Elias. He had people inform him about the change that had overcome poor simple Dingle. And he decided this change had come about because of exasperating Father Carmichael, who had spent his time with alcoholics and the mentally ill, here and in Saint John. He was a radical priest for his time, or for any time, and was suspected by the bishop and others. He had taken Dingle under his wing, and it was whispered that he had prevented Walter McLeary from jumping off the Morrissey Bridge when Putsy left him. Elias liked to tease her about this.

"Oh," he would say about Dingle, "he's like all the rest of them. I know better men than he start to act like him. He's changed aright. He had a little scare and thinks 'Ow, I'd better act better.'"

Elias's men would howl with laughter, even though many of them had been exactly like Dingle and from time to time sought some respite from the dark cold glazing their souls. But they had found Elias, and believed in him, for in money can morality be seen—watches and jewellery and better clothes signalled to many of them a respectable life.

One night when Rebecca visited her sister, he said to them, "I will tell you this—terms like 'good' and 'evil' are bygone words. They don't apply to us. That's what Father Carmichael don't know—nor does anyone. It stopped last century, those words. They were used in centuries when people did not know their own nature and relied on fixed words to explain unfixed man. There is no evil in the world any more. I carried my brother on my bony back all around Poland and not once did I think I was any less off than anyone else—eh? In fact I was better off than my brother, who was sickly and had a cold."

Putsy was the one who argued with him as Rebecca listened. "How can you say there is no good and evil—"

"Well, there you go, I've just said it—"

"Does that mean Jimmy McLeary trying to burn down his own daughter's theatre didn't matter?"

"It mattered only to those who could profit or lose by it," Elias said. "Profit and loss, that's what we're here for."

"But what about inside?" Putsy said, putting her hand over her breast and looking at him, and then at Rebecca, who looked curiously at both of them as if trying to fathom which one was going to win.

"What *about* our insides," he said, "filled with blood and bile and nothing much more?"

Here Rebecca laughed, for Elias made a funny face.

What he liked was this: how clever he would be to use Rebecca's arrangement with Janie King. It would be easy to do. Rebecca wouldn't remain faithful—most servants were not, especially if they wanted to impress people with knowledge of their employer's foibles. And Rebecca had already advised him on certain things that went on in the house, always saying as a prelude, "Oh, she'd kill me if she knew I told. But it's a little sip of gin from a spoon every night—and ordering special bloomers for the little girl. But the little girl loves *me*, not her. Now Miles is her momma's boy, but Georgina is all *me*."

After she had worked a few months, Joey knew every room and what was behind those doors. She was his mole. And Putsy was jealous of this. And so this contest, just like every other contest, worked in his favour. The more Putsy and Rebecca suspected each other and repudiated each other, the more it validated him as their protector who was disappointed with either one or the other.

No, Putsy was as wild as a cat, but she was no Rebecca. He needed Rebecca Druken now. Janie made the mistake of some employers— she felt that if she gave Rebecca a job, Rebecca would be grateful and therefore more loyal to her. And Rebecca did seem loyal. But Joey Elias could manipulate certain events in the house, little lacklustre things that might not be noticed. He told Putsy this as if she would delight in this as well.

In every advantage taken over the weak or unsuspecting there was a glimpse into banality. And it was that glimpse that caused Putsy not to laugh.

Instead she continually asked herself questions about that night. Had she been so drunk as not to remember where her key had gotten to? Had she been at Elias's house all the time? Who took off her stockings? Why was she so depressed now, when everything had turned in her favour? What did it matter if old Jimmy McLeary had died? It could have been any one of a dozen of his cronies from the past. He was always threatening the world at large with his saint, saying his saint would go out and beat them up.

She listened from the dark of their room. Their room was large, with a canopy over their bed, and pictures of stallions in a field. A large white bedspread, with soft pillows spread under her. She wore a full-length housecoat, and had her nails manicured and painted red. She was twenty-one years of age, and her husband was thirty-eight. Yet it was she who wanted to change, and not her husband. Besides, the marriage had been so hastily arranged and done so strangely, with a justice of the peace at the local courthouse, that she did not feel married at all. She had not wanted to be married like that. She thought she would have a white dress, but Joey said, "Who needs one? It's just for people to gawk at. Who cares? What are ya worried about—it's legal."

Legal, yes—but it had not made her feel any better. And two weeks after their wedding he had driven over to Fredericton to be in a big card game, while she sat at home. She asked to go, but he told her she wouldn't be interested.

"You'll have no fun over there," he said. "I wouldn't put you through that."

As always, the way he denied her wish was to make her feel ungrateful if she asked. Things continued like this, until one of her "best friends" wrote a note to tell her that Joey wasn't alone going to Fredericton.

"No," her friend wrote, "I have heard that Rebecca went with him—keeping it all in the family, I hear."

She knew by certain signs that this was true.

After the friend wrote this letter, she started to pack and leave but Joey came in, and asked her what was wrong. He looked incredulous. How could she think that—her own sister? Never mind what a man might do—for a man was a man—but her sister, now that she was married?

Putsy, confused and crying, sat on the edge of the bed, with her head down. Yet in a strange and very uncomfortable way—Rebecca always left a clue about where she was and what she had done. Putsy, not nearly as bright as her sister, had noticed this herself. And the clue she had left Putsy—a jigsaw puzzle that Rebecca loved to do—given as a present to Putsy three days after the trip. It was a jigsaw puzzle bought in Fredericton. The tag named a Fredericton shop. Yet Putsy could not be sure.

Joey Elias usually went to bed at six in the morning and woke about one or two in the afternoon. His day started with his strong coffee and a cigarette. He was usually uncommunicative when things were going badly—and things were.

One night Putsy woke to a racket, the sound of a shout and a chair splintering against a wall. Her husband had been drinking all week. He had invited men in to play stud poker and he had marked cards. Now she listened, as a man from Fredericton, who had won against Joey in the card game in Fredericton had come here. A lot of men were losing their money tonight. One was no more than nineteen, and he had every cent he had earned in the lumberyard in his pocket. He was engaged to be married, and was bragging about this. Elias knew he had been paid, and had asked him to the house to have a good time. The boy came, with a bright smile because he had remembered Putsy as an innocent child in the lumberyard. He wanted to see her again, yet when he did, his smile faded; she was no longer the child he had remembered, who had played with him in the sawdust, and there was something strange in his look—a look of searching for the person inside the person that had delighted him with her love of life.

He wanted to go home, but Elias asked her to entertain him for a while, and, like so many many Miramichiers, he was too polite to say no. Then, after the boy was drinking with her, Elias came back with the cards.

"Do you want to double your earnings, Danny?" he asked. "Well, I'll show you how to—it'll be easy for you. Look—I'll deal five cards, see . . ."

Now, she listened for a long time. She could hear the boy mumbling.

"What do that mean—I lose again? Well, no—look, I had three fours, so—oh, yeah, okay. No, I'm not saying you're cheating."

Then there was a great deal of laughter.

She turned her face to the wall.

What was good and evil? he had asked her and Rebecca that day. Well, he said, there was no good, no evil, and nothing in between. Just people, he said sadly, doing the best they could do. (He always sounded sad when he spoke like this, as if he was disappointed.) The world was against them from the start. Why worry if they attained some degree of comfort by doing something against the world?

Yet if that were so, why did he hurt her so much, why did he humiliate others? If there was no good, then the line she had heard, "every beast has pity except man," did not mean anything—no words used meant a damn thing. For what did it matter if man did or did not have pity, did or did not murder, did or did not care for his children? She asked this of Rebecca one day, but Rebecca was busy doing the jigsaw and did not seem to understand what Putsy was trying to say. She looked up at her quickly and smiled, as if she knew something and wanted to give a clue, and then looked at the jigsaw piece in her hand.

"It's all up to us, isn't it, Putsy," she said quietly, so that Putsy was not sure she had heard her correctly.

"What is?" Putsy asked.

"H'm?" Rebecca said.

Putsy could not help thinking that what Elias told her was wrong. For if it was true that there was no right and wrong, no good or evil, why did Elias become enraged at a slight? Why did she, why did Rebecca, why did anyone feel hurt and lost and alone when the world turned its back on their best intentions?

She had to go to confession and confess about the key, even though she did not know where it was. The priest would never be able to say anything, and she would be free of the guilt.

She put her head back into the sweet-smelling pillow and waited for the noise, the laughter to go away.

Or perhaps she had to go to the police. Go to the police! What would they do? She didn't know. Worse, she saw the poor old man. Sometimes she'd look over into the corner and he'd be there nodding his head at her:

"'Lo there, Putsy," he'd say. "It's just me, Jimmy McLeary. Do you know, Putsy my girl, I love how you used to say Jamie, instead of Jimmy. Say Jamie for me, Putsy. As you know I'm dead and don't hear it that often. Hey you ever think you might take a jaunt down to the *Police*?"

She decided to go and stay with her mother. But her mother did not want her there, for the little bit of money Putsy managed to give Mrs. Druken would stop if she left Elias. (Rebecca did not give money, though her mother and father could not do without her.)

"You're going to make yourself sick," Putsy's mother told her. "You're thin, and don't even look good. Go back to him now—you don't need to be here. He has done a lot for us—don't you hurt his feelings. One thing about Joey, he has tender feelings."

So, she went back to Elias's house. Janie had finally forced him out of business, but he was not through. He would open a dance hall. He needed some money in order to do this. So he took to gaming to try and get the money. He lost. Now he was cheating to get back what he had lost. Everything was that way with Elias and in every way he thought he was determining his own destiny.

Very early in the morning he came into the room, sat on the stuffed rocker in the corner and unbuttoned his vest. A loose card fell from his shirt, and he looked over at her. The ceiling lights were still on. Elias had played a trick on the boy who wanted to get married, and couldn't look at himself in the mirror. A dull dawn was coming. He took eight hundred dollars he had managed to win and put it on the dresser.

Elias didn't want to give up what he had, and he needed more. For if he gave up what he had, he would have nothing, he would be less than the people who looked up to him now. He was sure the man from Fredericton had seen him sneak the ace into his hand. Now, he would have to do something else.

So Elias left Putsy at dawn and walked along the street to the wharf. There in the empty and freezing wind, he turned toward the cliffs that lined the shore, craggy and pocked by caves. It was here he found Leon Winch.

Leon was not a stupid man, but he could hardly read and write, had no formal education, and was frightened of men who could talk well, like Elias. He was deathly afraid of Elias.

Leon barked an order, and a little dog came up from under a blanket and jumped in his lap. Leon had been put out of the house by his wife—this had happened after Christmas, after "the night." She did not know why he was so nasty and angry and terrified, but she wanted him gone. So he came here. Elias was afraid he would say something, and so had brought him some money—forty dollars. This is what Elias brought him every couple of weeks. But Leon had tuberculosis, and Elias was happy this was the case. Leon watched Elias carelessly and said, while roughly hauling at the dog's fur, "When will it be over?"

"What do you mean—"

"I mean, when will you pay me some of what you owe me?"

"What do you mean," Elias said, trying to sound stern. "I've already paid you"

"I mean, it's what Father Carmichael said to me. This is not the real life—this is the pretend life. The real life is inside us. That means something to me—as you know—and no one can stop the real life with the pretend life."

"You are not making sense," Elias said, bullying him to be quiet.

"Everything has become the pretend life!"

Elias again gave a sharp retort. "I just handed you forty dollars. If you think that it is the pretend life, hand it back!"

"So—forty dollars is nothing," Leon said.

"I said that night means nothing—it will never be found out, ever ever ever."

"You told me that before."

"Well, it's true, so I wouldn't worry about it."

And Winch, who was now dying of tuberculosis, thinking this was true and must be true said nothing more. And Elias went back home, still wearing his brother's boots for penance.

It was his brother who had started all of this. He couldn't stop and turn around now without walking all the way to Leningrad to find him. And he didn't want to do that yet. Someday maybe, but not yet. He had to make his name before then, to make it all worthwhile.

Why did he have to keep the meetings with Rebecca a secret from Putsy if there was nothing going on? Keeping something from someone was the one way to assure you were doing ill. Did he care for Putsy? Of course—he liked to tell other men that she had transformed his life. There were hard times everywhere and men were out of work. He should be satisfied with a beautiful wife and a large house.

But he met Rebecca and kissed Rebecca—and Rebecca knew it— at sixteen years of age.

So he decided this, our Mr. Elias. He decided, and he could prove it, that he did not tell Putsy of the meeting with Rebecca simply because he did not want Rebecca fired over it. If Putsy got angry she would tell Janie. He could not do that to the young girl. And he believed he did not want to hurt Putsy's feelings, or ruin her fragile trust. This was closer to the truth. But the real truth—the real subject of his thought—was that he would not be satisfied until he went to bed with Rebecca Druken, now or ten years from now did not matter a damn to him.

He wouldn't be at ease until he betrayed Putsy. This is what was going on and this is what both he and Rebecca knew. He could not stand that Rebecca was willing to do this against her own sister—she was talking as if she was in Putsy's place already—but he could not stop himself.

He was wary of Rebecca's certainty that anything she wanted she could have. For it was he, Joey Elias, who had taught her that. And now, it was simply that she wanted him.

Elias did not know that Rebecca waited by the cliffs until he went home. Then, spying Leon Winch, she told him she was the only one able to keep him safe. Not Joey Elias, or anyone else. Only her. But if it happened that the police blamed someone else, she could come forward with something secret that would prove his complicity in the old man's murder.

"What do you want?" He scowled.

"I want twenty of your forty, each time you get it."

She was handed the twenty. Grumbling, scared and confused, Leon Winch went back to his corner. Rebecca made her way, in the late-night filthy dark, to Janie's house, acrimonious beauty on her face.

THREE

As young as she was, Rebecca had her own interests in mind. After Janie hired her, not a thing went by in the house that Joey Elias did not know verbatim the next afternoon. Most of it was just laughable gossip. Some things, however, were more to Elias's liking. One was the story Rebecca liked to tell the kids that there was gold in the well, that the Drukens owned this gold but the McLearys thought they did. That gold had been hidden in this well had been a rumour for years, and Rebecca would tell the kids that she would one day get this gold and share it with them—if they did not tell things on her.

Elias was amused by this, by the idea of teasing Janie's kids—or her kind—just a little, for all the cheap things Janie had done to him.

"What's Miles like?" he would ask.

"Oh, he's a spoiled brat, just as you'd expect. Georgina is more to my liking."

"Really?"

"Well, as much as you might like a King," she said.

Elias nodded at this. "But Miles is different?" he asked.

"Oh, so proper. I don't like Miles!"

Then he told Rebecca to take a small bit of goldlike dust that he had and put it on her boots after she came back from the well and show it to Miles and to put some on Miles's boots as well. He told her to act like a fairy godmother and tell them the Mother Goose tale. It was done just to accredit the rumour and to have a bit of fun, and mesmerize the children with a good story.

Nothing else was intended. Except this: he had made a fool of old Jim in his day, and something about Miles rankled him. So if Miles got to the well—which he, Elias, now owned—maybe he could get some kids to put tar on Miles's nice pants. Maybe the Conroy boy who followed him about, or the Waltling boy whose dad owed him money, they and a few more so Miles would not get away. Even in this there would have to be more than one. That's the only way Joey dealt with things.

"Tar up his knickers," Elias said. This is how tormented he had been by Janie King, and the ruin of his theatre. The tar on the boy's pants came as a complete afterthought. But Rebecca turned to him and said, "Oh, that would be too too awful."

But both of them knew that in the moment, in the display of their features, this would not be too awful at all, but extravagant fun, for they were born in poverty, and wasn't he rich? And if he was, then what was wrong with it?

However, Rebecca said this would only be done, as long as she could have a favour too.

"And what favour?" Elias asked. "Whatever it is you can have."

"I want to come here and sit in Putsy's place at the table tonight, and I want you to serve me. And when she comes in for supper I want you to ignore her."

"Come on," Elias said, "what are you after? I'm just doing this as a joke. You don't need a favour like that."

"That's what I want," Rebecca said. "It's not so important."

"If it's not so important, why do you want it?" Elias said, knowing how upset Putsy would be.

"I want it because it is not important. It is not important that you took me to Fredericton either."

She started to walk away, so he grabbed her by the shoulder and hugged her. The complete idiosyncratic falseness of his hug was felt by both.

He then tried to be stern. He had taken her to Fredericton because she had demanded it as payment the night she had gone to the Regent. And also because he had not wanted to leave her alone with the knowledge of Jimmy McLeary's demise. But both of them pretended that he took her there because he was being fatherly and affectionate.

"You wouldn't say anything, would you?" he asked her now. It was a question asked as an afterthought, expecting an answer that was filled with appropriate assurances.

She stunned him with, "Only a clue here and there."

"What do you mean?" he stammered, his face frozen, suddenly helpless.

"Oh, everyone leaves little clues," she said sorrowfully, yet with a great mischief in her eyes, like a scorned lover. Then she whispered almost fiercely: "We can't help it, can we? Here and there—sometimes

I leave a little clue right in front of Janie, just to see if she'll catch it. She never does."

So at sixteen she had a tremendous power over him. He saw it at this moment in her blazing eyes and the somewhat peevish mouth, and her long red hair. Never before had he been in this position. And though he twisted and turned there seemed to be no way out of it except to trust her. Unless he himself could say that the death of old Jim was immoral, and take the consequences for it. Barring that, he was not in control. Nor had he ever been in control since the days he carried his brother on his back. And he was beginning, just beginning to realize this. Her breasts were freckled, as well, except near the nipples—he knew this first-hand, though he had promised and had sworn to Putsy that he hadn't touched her.

He did not know what to do, except play games and have her on his side in these games. And this was the principal reason my father, Miles King, became their scapegoat that summer.

"You wouldn't tell anything on me," he said, looking at her sharply.

She only smiled and shook her head. "Silly," she said and hugged him.

When Putsy came home, supper was ready, and Rebecca was sitting in her place, and Elias was serving her. He did not look in Putsy's direction.

At first Putsy did not mind, but suddenly the jigsaw puzzle that had come from Fredericton, her friend's letter, the lie, and the sitting in her place informed her of Rebecca's intent. Nebulous and yet completely obvious, if not obvious to Rebecca herself. And the talk at the dinner table about the King children, and Miles peeing the bed because of bad nerves, bothered her. She did not like the idea of tormenting him or Georgina.

"What's wrong with you?" Elias said.

"Rebecca is in my place," she exclaimed, smiling slightly in fear at the silliness of her remark.

Elias began to laugh. And so did Rebecca. It was the teasing that was worse than anything, for the laughter seemed to say that this was not important, while their very teasing seemed to make it so.

Putsy left the table, and went to her room. When Elias looked at Rebecca she simply shrugged and took a mouthful of her dinner, reached across the table for a piece of bread.

Putsy lay on her bed with her hands behind her head, staring at the canopy and crying silently. She was crying because shortly after she had received the letter, she had gone to Elias, and asked him if Rebecca had gone to Fredericton with him.

"She is my little sister—please leave her alone. I wanted to take care of her—and now—I mean, I got her a job with Janie—you see, and—"

What this did was make Elias completely indifferent to her. It seemed now that he didn't even care if she knew he was with Rebecca.

And all silly Putsy Druken could do now was cry. Cry and think of Walter and how she had treated him.

Rebecca's easy and offhand tormenting of Miles went on another little while. She reported that Janie became so angry with his laughable talk about the gold in the well that she sent him from the table. Miles would talk to Georgina about how they would find this gold. He'd warned her never to go to the well on her own.

"You haven't mentioned anything about this, Rebecca, have you?" Janie asked. "That old rumour almost drove my daddy crazy. I think he spent half of his life worried about the goddamn gold that didn't exist."

"I may have said there was a rumour, Mrs. King, but everyone knows there is a rumour. Maybe—I beg your pardon—it was Mr. McLeary himself who told Miles."

"Well, whoever told the children, I have not told them, and I don't want it talked about. You know how susceptible children are to rumours," Janie said.

That was true, they were. And Rebecca informed Elias of Janie's demand, but by this time Elias had a much more narrow focus. And he told Rebecca in dribs and drabs what this focus was. It was perfectly obvious to him that the Kings were greedy children, and it was perfectly obvious that he was teaching them a lesson, and it was perfectly obvious that he was right to do so. It was also obvious that others he told were amused by it. It was obvious that they should be, because there was nothing wrong in it. After all, these were not ordinary children, these were the King children. So why wouldn't it be obvious? It was obvious that Janie so spoiled them they had no friends. It was obvious that little Miles loved flowers just like his father—and no man would love flowers, as Elias and his cronies said. It was perfectly obvious to Rebecca and Joey Elias that they were doing this as a kind of future investment for the town—teaching that little snot Miles King not to be greedy. This was bound to be a benefit when Miles came to adulthood. Perhaps he wouldn't be as greedy as Janie and cause so much trouble. For Elias it all came down to Janie's greed.

Janie did not know how Miles got the goldlike dust on his bed but she knew it wasn't from the well. And all of this time, Elias was laughing his head off over it. Each time Rebecca reported on the progress, he would howl with laughter.

Thinking every day that this would be the day he would find the bags of gold in the bucket he lowered, Miles would sneak down to the well to peer in. And one day he came back to the house with his pants covered with tar. I heard even here my father had fought back—that in fact unless he was protecting Georgina he never ever ran; perhaps, as he was wont to say, he was far too stupid to run. He begged Rebecca not to tell, and begged her to hide his pants, which Janie had just bought. He told her that five boys had grabbed him and painted tar on them. But this to Rebecca seemed like a lame excuse.

"Why would you blame other children for what you did?" she said. "That's what always happens—the rich snots blame us for what they did."

And since this was true in other cases Rebecca knew about, and with other families, she now decided it did not matter that much if it was true in this particular case.

"I know you don't like me, Rebecca, but I'm not telling you a lie."

"What right do you have to say that I do not like you?" Rebecca said.

"I know you think I am spoiled and maybe I am. But if you don't tell, I will—give you a stamp from my collection—I promise."

He looked hopelessly at her.

"Of course he is spoiled" Elias said, when she related this tidbit of information. "He has always been spoiled. His father dying did not do a bit of good to make him less spoiled, for he is Janie's boy. And that's the problem—he is a boy being brought up by a woman. Don't you agree, Rebecca?"

"I agree," she said. "But what are we to do with him?"

"What are we to do with him—what are we to do? That's the problem. If he was my son—well, if he was my son he wouldn't be anything like Miles King. But since he is Miles King, a kind of whatchamacallit —spoiled brat that he is, something has to be done. And I tell you why, Rebecca."

"Why?"

"Because if we do not cure Miles now, we will have a hell of a time with him when he gets older and he starts to run things. Teach him to respect us now, and there might be hope. But he don't respect, does he?"

"No, he don't," Rebecca said. "He don't respect nothing."

"How is she—the little girl? Is she spoiled too?"

"She's a dear. Sometimes I rile her and she gets mad at Miles, and I like that. No—if I was to have a little girl, it would be her."

"Really?"

"She's a King but at least she is more daring then fancy-pants."

"Well, we can always deal with fancy-pants. Just leave his tarred-up pants where Janie will find them. He'll catch it after that."

And it seemed, once they started on this course, that this was done in fun and amusement and for the benefit of Miles King, who was terrified to show the tar on his pants to his mom, who worked hard day and night. Miles King would be taught something, like little lord Fautenroy—or whoever he was—as Elias maintained.

But then the pants were found by Janie, and she demanded an explanation.

"I hid them there, ma'am," Rebecca said, so quickly that she backed up toward the stove in surprise after she had said it.

"Why?" Janie demanded.

"Because I didn't want you to be angry with the boy," Rebecca said, "and I was going to take them out and clean them—"

"You can't clean them. It's impossible. Tell Miles to come here."

"Please don't be too hard on him."

"Just tell him to get in here."

By this time Rebecca was doing what excited her—tormenting the young boy who the more she tormented became even more a symbol of her own family's despair, of Druken backwater despair, and coming down to Elias on her day off to let him know.

To her it did not matter if Putsy found out she had slept with Elias. In fact, as much as she pretended the opposite, this was exactly what she wanted. Besides, Putsy wasn't as pretty or as bright as she was. Putsy had also lost three front teeth. Rebecca forgot that Putsy had lost her teeth protecting her as a child from her father's swats.

For as long as she could go on doing what Elias told her, making him happy, and startling him with how brazen she could be (and she continued to be more and more brazen), then the terrible sadness in her life, a sadness she had felt since a child, would be kept silent, muted and at bay.

But one day she came down to Elias's house, and saw Putsy on her knees, begging Elias to leave Rebecca alone. It was startling to see Putsy so weak. Elias walked around her, and Putsy, crying, tried to grab on to his leg.

"Leave me alone," Elias said.

Putsy looked up and saw Rebecca.

"Rebecca, you haven't—have you? Promise me that you haven't," Putsy said, bawling.

Rebecca looked over at Elias, gave the same slight start she had given when telling Janie of the pants, and backed up to the door.

FOUR

Putsy went back to her mother's house, back to her dear old folks, as she said, to get the pic, and to take it down to Chatham Street, to that place where just a month or so ago the best man she had ever met—so she thought—loved her and was ready to marry her. But no, he loved her sister. Now she would put the pic into her sister's back. She could see herself doing it, and then she would hand it over to Elias and say, "See what you did." And she would go to the gallows and everyone would say, in a romantic way—for Putsy was romantic—" "She killed for Love."

And it was very nearly done, except for one thing—one simple fact. Rebecca did not go to Elias's that day Putsy went back with the pic. Putsy waited that day, for hours. The next day she waited as well. But Rebecca stayed away. And the third.

Agitated that her desire would not last, she took her pic, and decided that Rebecca was not to blame—Elias himself was. She hid this pic under her coat and waited in the corner of the foyer for him to come back from his haunts. She held the pic by the handle. How worn and warm it was. Still, her hands were weak, as happened with drink. And so were her legs. Drink had done that as well. It had swollen up her legs and her hands. So she put the pic down and waited.

Her father had kept this pic well, and drew his living from it. He had bled from it, sweated over it, and slumped upon it exhausted. Now she would kill with it.

The life of the pic was interesting too, for it had come from Dobblestein's lumberyard, and had been used in a boom to separate that last corduroy road of wood. She did not know what Elias had done to diminish this yard, but it would be ironic, for Elias was visiting this yard when Putsy first saw him. He gave her two caramels, and she brought her sister to see him the next day, to get two caramels too.

Now she waited. She could smell the soup in the cold air coming from up and down the street, and the small Irish houses benefiting from at least a month of temporary jobs at Estabrook's mill. Then at six o'clock she heard him coming, grating his heels upon the snow. How she hated him—how terrible her life. She crouched down in the doorway and waited, her shoulders shaking. She heard the key, the door opened. She readied the pic.

"This is for Rebecca!" she would yell. Rebecca's name was on her lips. And then in the gloom of the March night, she saw a small dark hat, a scarf around a woman's face, her red shoulder-length hair, and a boy being led into the foyer.

Rebecca, audacious as always, had brought Miles King into Elias's house.

Putsy glanced at the child and smiled uncertainly. Rebecca looked at her sister, surprised, and then calmed herself.

"Oh—Puts," she said, "I has to go—I won't make it home to the pisser. So I've brought him in. Take him home for me, will you?"

Putsy took Miles by the hand and walked him home. She was silent for a long time. Then she asked about his grandfather, and if he was sad. And she asked about Mr. Dingle who walked about the yard and shook hands with people at the theatre, and Janie.

"And how is Walter?"

"Good."

"Is he mad at me—angry with little Putsy?"

"I don't know."

When she made it to the house, Janie asked if she would be so kind as to take a basket of clothes to the church for the lottery, for it would be too late for Rebecca to go. And off Putsy went with the clothes.

There she met Father Carmichael, who took the basket and asked, seeing her wince, if she had had problems with lifting, and holding.

She nodded, frightened that he would know what she had been thinking.

"It's your arms and legs, isn't it?"

She did not answer.

"And you've been drinking—having trouble sleeping, and worrying about something, h'm?"

"Yes," she said. "So what of it?"

"Nothing—only I might be able to alleviate it."

Father Carmichael told her to come with him. Up to the great old rectory they went with a few scattered lights in the windows. There he gave her some fireweed tea and told her to drink it.

She took the tea and drank it.

Suddenly she broke down and told him she could not go back to Joey. That with Joey she would sooner or later murder someone.

"Never you mind that," he said. "You will accomplish much in your life now."

He told her to pack her bags and he would find a place for her to stay with some people he knew.

After she regained some strength she got a job helping the nuns in the convent with washing and cleaning. Every evening she went first to the convent basement to wash and then to her room.

After a month Father Carmichael told her that things would change only if she wanted them to, that nothing could change until she decided, but that change did not come by her will alone but by the will of God. He said after her Saturday afternoon confession, where she told him of awful things, but not of the key, that life did not happen according to Joey Elias, or even according to Rebecca Druken, as much as they might want it or think it. Their lives accomplished only sadness.

"How does it happen, then?" Putsy said.

"It happens according to God. Now, we might not see or know or even believe, but that does not matter at all."

She said she believed him firmly, but he told her she did not yet, that she might in the future, but there would be times when she would be discouraged. Events would happen that would prove that the path she was on was right.

"Yes," she said, "of course—it doesn't matter."

And as long as she thought that most things did not matter, she was fine. Yes, the illness was to think that everything mattered because of you—because you felt, and believed what you felt, was more important than what others felt. A concern of hers no longer, she assured herself.

One day, floundering over what had happened to her, still depressed because she had seen Rebecca with the King children downtown, as unconcerned about her as if she were dead, Putsy found herself at church.

Carmichael listened to her and then told her it was possible to change if she did not lie. If she did as he said, she would begin to change. If she lived as he said she must, if she gave everyone what she herself most desired others to give, kindness and respect—when she did this, she would find not lying easy. "Do not speak, and you will not lie," the priest said.

As absurd as it sounded, she tried this about town during the day, and it worked, more or less. She found she could not meet old friends without lying because they expected her to lie, because they were liars themselves. So, standing mute in front of them, she would shun their questions or answer in monosyllables. Not only was this painful but people teased her, saying she lost her mind over Elias. So she would turn away when she saw any of them, and walk in another direction.

Rebecca came and berated her, telling her that she was a huge disappointment, and then, what was worse, bringing some of her things back from Joey's.

"What has gotten into you?" Rebecca said.

"Christ, I suppose," Putsy answered.

She worked, and lived in her room behind the convent, and ate sparingly, and touched no alcohol. When friends from her bad days would come by, thinking she had struck it lucky and would drink with them again, she would send them away. And she began to realize she would never have to take another drink. And this scared her more than anything else in the world.

The priest asked her to do charity work. He needed help taking food to those very men she had come from and drunk with and slept with. This charity was something Carmichael did, though many did not like what he was doing, for it kept men here who the community was hoping would move on to somewhere else.

"I don't want them to think I think I am better then they just because I've had some luck," Putsy said.

"Oh, well, firstly, its what *you* think that counts," Father Carmichael said. "Secondly, there is no luck. Things are designed in such a way as to bring us forward—I believe this, and all things are unified. There is a man, Einstein, who believes all things are unified, and I, as a priest do, too. Have you heard of Einstein?"

"No."

"Have you heard of $E=mc^2$?"

"I don't know."

Putsy thought about this. And here is what she thought: I am smart enough to bamboozle this priest, and pretty enough to seduce him here and now, yet he thinks he can instruct me. How can he instruct me? Do I believe that if I act as if I believe, then I believe? Is that what he wants? When she told the priest this, admitting everything, he answered, "You told me your husband is a gambler—he would gamble on a fly, and if it will crawl to the right or the left, and he will make strategies and waste energy trying to figure out how flies move. Well, gambling might be that complex, but I assure you life isn't. The fly will move exactly as it is supposed to. You just start to do and sooner or later you will become. It is better by far than gambling."

The fact was, Putsy had had little enough charity from her own. Her broken teeth and venereal disease proved that. So she took to doing charity work. And her first impulse was her most radical. She didn't want to listen to this impulse, for it went against the grain of everything she once believed. She answered Carmichael's call and took food to the very men that had accosted her when Elias threw her family out of their house. They were sitting in a tin shed halfway up the cliff overlooking Ritchie's Wharf. They were snitches, rats to the police, wife beaters, and drunks. They had fought and gambled and hurt others all their life. They were the friends of Joey Elias.

She called to them and said she was coming in. The shed was cold and smoky; the men had colds and were shivering. She did not know that Elias had talked about her to these men, and that Rebecca had as well.

So they laughed and teased her, and tried to grab her crotch, but they took the food. She found out that Leon Winch had died, and after all his vainglory and work for Elias, Elias did not even go to the funeral. Leon's child, Ray, was left as an orphan on the street.

Strangely, it was listening to Joey Elias that changed her destination, when most would not or could not be changed by it.

And so, she lived at the convent as a lay member of the community, went to church, and began to help Father Carmichael with his charity cases. She had to numb herself from her former life, endure the hatred of some of the nuns she had for years made fun of, decided to have her marriage annulled, and had to admit privately that she had allowed the key to escape her possession.

Father Carmichael, who was known as an oddball not only within the church, which disliked him, but within the community, which was baffled by him, insisted she eat his assorted herbs and weeds. Swamp milkweed he was fond of cooking for her, and other wild-flowers as well.

In secret (perhaps Carmichael knew) it was her venereal disease which prevented her from going back to Walter. However, Walter did pursue her, and one night he asked her to come and see him. It was a cold, hard night, and the streets were wet and empty. She asked Carmichael if she should.

"It will be painful for you, but it might help him. I believe you owe him that, but only if you feel strong enough."

"He will curse me and belittle me."

"If he does, remember you have been cursed by Elias for much less, and you stayed with him."

Walter had been running the picture *Of Human Bondage*. He felt Putsy was exactly like Bette Davis, using his kindness and his crippled body for her own ticket. He saw himself in Philip Carey and could not help being bitter. How could she have gone with Joey Elias again—how how how! He had a speech prepared to make her feel utterly worthless, and he had practised it over the last few days. Then she would beg his forgiveness and he would laugh.

When she got there, Walter was drunk. She tried to talk like Carmichael might have talked, but to no avail. She tried to leave, but he wouldn't let her go. She sat in the corner and watched him. He asked her to drink with him, and she said that she wouldn't.

He said, "If you don't drink with me, I will kill myself this instant."

And he took the old shotgun that had been at the theatre and pointed it at his heart.

Fearing he would, she desperately searched about for a glass and, hands shaking, poured herself a rum. All that Carmichael had told her had gone out the window. Then, hands still shaking, she nodded and said, "If I do this, you promise you will put the gun away."

She lifted the glass to her mouth. With a quickness that surprised her, he jumped up and knocked the glass from her lips, and begged her forgiveness. She reached out and gently stroked the top of his head, and he bawled like a child.

"Please, Putsy—I don't care what you do, just don't drink any more," he sobbed.

"I am not going to," she said softly, smiling, tears in her eyes.

Rebecca worried about one thing—the key. What would Putsy say to Father Carmichael about the key? She went to search Putsy out. She did not find her, and was on her way back toward town, cutting through the rectory garden, when she saw Father Carmichael himself. She asked him when Putsy could come home.

"That is up to Putsy," he said.

"Oh, Father, I thought it was up to you." She smiled.

"No, it is up to her," he answered, suddenly handing her a few of his parsnips to take home to her mother. "You could stay here too," he said. "It does not matter what has gone on before. You may think it does, but I am not concerned about that. You might have a better chance to help yourself if you did what Putsy wants to do."

"'What has gone on before?'" Rebecca asked. "What is it that you know?"

"There is very little that I know," Carmichael said. "I am only saying that you could stay here also, and realize that all things hidden will be revealed."

"Ah, well," she said, "I'll take my chances in the big old world."

"We all take our chances there—even if we are here," he said.

Rebecca did not answer this. She looked around the garden and then said, "People say you have herbs and cure people and know the future. What is my future? Tell me what it is and I'll pay you."

He stopped working in the garden. His hands were covered in dirt, his face red from the sun.

"Sadness," he whispered. "And I ask for no money in telling you so. Sadness for you and your son."

"Sadness—what sadness?" Rebecca said. "And I might ask, what son?"

Across the river the trees were in full bloom, and the great ship the *Poduddle* was coming into the channel. Then without looking at him, and with the expression on her face of a person looking into the distance for a speck, she said, "You have just made me decide never to have a son. And if there is sadness, it is because we Drukens have always been under the thumb of the rich—without any help. Why would Janie McLeary be so lucky as to have two cars when the Drukens have none? And why would my brothers die in the flu when other children didn't?"

"Your sadness is asking questions that cannot be answered. You will have a chance to change when you come back with your son. Sister Putsy will ask your son to visit her."

"Sister Putsy! My, my, my. And you think I am going away. I will never leave this river"

"Perhaps I am mistaken."

"You are. And it is a shame that Putsy is so frightened by you."

"It is not me Putsy is frightened of."

"Who is she frightened of, then?"

"You," he said softly.

This startled her, but she smiled and said, "Good that she is."

She turned down along the road, passed some summer-brown hedges, and looked back over her shoulder. He was gone, and it was as if this conversation had never taken place. She threw the small parsnips into a bush.

As for Putsy Druken, to the surprise of everyone, she became a nun of the Sacred Heart in 1935. She never drank again.

FIVE

Elias, however, continued on. In a certain way, a natural way, he felt things were turning out for him as well as he could possibly expect. He would have his dance hall where the Biograph once was. But still and all, it wasn't enough. The thing he worried over, as old Jimmy McLeary might have said, "like a bitch with a fuggin' bone," was Miles. He felt that Miles was the usurper of his own worth—Miles would be the owner of a business that within a certain light, and according to certain parameters of business sense should rightfully belong to him.

It was not only this. It was also the fact that Jimmy McLeary had owed him money from drink. He, Elias, decided this one day, and set about to get it. Janie, however, said Jimmy McLeary's account with the world was settled, and she need not settle it again. She wrote him a caustic note to this effect.

"Jimmy McLeary did at least some of your patchwork against me. Have the decency, sir, to write off what he owes you because of what you owe him and me."

This made his blood boil. Never before had things been so clear to him. She was keeping the business from him to protect her son.(Why he thought this unnatural I do not know.) After he had done everything for her. And in this state of mind he vented his anger about Janie on the street, but never aloud, only in whispers— to challenge her under the table, so to speak.

Even if he wanted to remain silent, it was bad morals not to challenge this. And he challenged Miles's right, at first to be the beneficiary of a business, but after this, his right to exist as a little boy.

My father was alone on the street from the time he was eight. He was left to his own devices because he had no father (as much as Walter tried), and his mother worked. Mrs. Redmond reported to me that she had seen him many nights walking along the street after ten lugging his pigeon coop home from a show he had given, with his cane and magic box. No one remembers him with a friend except Georgina, whom he would take care of most days by himself out in the yard, or take on little excursions with a lunch, to go fishing or flower picking.

"He goes out with the little girl," Elias would say, "what's her face— Georgina—and they go out into the field, and you know what he does? He *picks flowers*—black-eyed Susans and daisies and pussytoes, and he brings them home to his mommie. But his mommie ain't there, no, she's fuggin' at the theatre with her arsewipe Roy Dingle. And what do you think of Dingle?—Dingle isn't a man—she's never had a man—and now she has Miles."

And the men would nod, and agree, even though after a certain time they decided it was tiring. Still and all, they respected him too much. Rebecca was also attentive to him, and told him about the flower excursions that Miles took with Georgina on his back like a papoose.

And then there were the plays he was in, and his magic act that he performed in front of Georgina, who was his sole audience.

One afternoon in May of 1932, just after Janie went to the hall, Rebecca came to work. Miles was getting ready to go to his audition as Mr. Bimble in the school play, called *Bimble's Thimble*. He had been waiting to do this for a month, for the only friend he had was his teacher Miss McGrath, who had known Mr. King and Janie.

But seeing him getting ready to leave, with his top hat and tie, Rebecca, who was feeding Georgina, said, "You are not to go out today. You are to stay in your room and take care of your sister and you are to polish the silverware." She took the silverware out of the buffet and handed it to him. "Why should I be expected to polish what I never get to use? Now sit down and do it like a good boy."

Miles at first attempted to talk her into letting him go—then he proceeded to the door, but Rebecca picked him up by the collar. "Get upstairs," she said, "and take the silverware and the polish with you—and I do not want to see you until it is done!"

The boy went upstairs, and Rebecca sat down and lifted Georgina onto her lap. She began talking to the boy from the kitchen.

"Your father was a liar. He was coward, and didn't want to fight, so he came here. But the Drukens went and fought. How many? Ten or eleven from here alone. Your dad came over on a boat, just when the fighting got interesting—he run away. Did you know that the British hung us in Ireland? Miles, you understand?"

Miles didn't answer.

"Janie worries about you being bullied. I used to think, poor little Miles. I did at one time think that. But now I think, no damn wonder—with your pigeons, and top hat. Who ever heard of such a thing? Trying out for plays—no real boy tries out fer plays, Miles. I had boys in my family, my little triplet brothers—well, just let me tell you, if they were alive today they'd show you what was what—they'd show the likes of Miles King!"

Georgina listened, for some sound. But Miles didn't answer.

"So what I'm thinking is this. I'm sick and tired of cleaning up after pigeons—and I just might assassinate them. Fair is fair, Miles—fair is fair."

Miles didn't answer.

"Answer me!" she yelled, suddenly in a state of rage (which she had first noticed on Joey Elias's face when he kicked them from their house). "Answer me—is fair fair or not fair—is not fair being fair or what is fair!!"

Miles didn't answer, and Rebecca put the little girl down and climbed the stairs.

"Open this door, Miles—open it—open this door—"

But the door was easy to open with a nail and a push and a kick. And Rebecca opened it. There she saw Miles in the tree next to his window, trying to climb down, hanging upside down from a limb, with his top hat still on his head and his pigeon coop under his right arm.

Rebecca did not move, so riveted she was by his self-destruction.

Georgina, coming into the room, yelled when she saw him in such danger, and ran to the window to bring him back in. Just as she reached out for him Miles fell and lay motionless on the ground. The pigeon coop shattered and two of his pigeons were mortally wounded and one obviously very ill.

Rebecca then came alive. She ran down the stairs and outside. Rebecca lifted him carefully and carried him into the house. She put a cold facecloth on his forehead.

She tried to cover it up; she gave herself and Georgina a story. They were in the laundry room and did not hear.

"We did not hear, Georgie girl, did we? You say that and Rebecca will get you a caramel. We did not hear and we thought Miles had gone out. But he was scared because he messed his pants—that's what he did he messed his pants and wanted to climb down the tree for he was worried I would find out. But I didn't mind him going to the play did I, Georgina?" Her lips twitched as she spoke and her eyes glanced from side to side.

"It was just too bad that he messed his pants—isn't that right, Georgie girl—"

But Georgina was angry with her for the very first time, and would not speak. Sometimes frustrated with the lie Rebecca was trying to plant (like the planting of a weed) she would stamp her feet and cover her ears. Rebecca, truly agitated that she had lost Georgina's affection, kept trying to make it up to her. This time, however, Georgina would not sit on her knee.

The next day Rebecca, Miles, and Georgina buried the pigeons with great solemnity at the bottom of the yard. Rebecca was still frightened and kept trying to appease the children, but Janie found out what had happened from the neighbours. Mr. Rolfe came foreward with the information Janie King needed. There had been trouble all that spring; many times the boy was beaten and kept silent.

"If you don't get out I will phone the police," Janie said to Rebecca.

"The Drukens have done nothin' to you," Rebecca answered with complete calm.

"And that's the way it's going to stay," Janie said.

And as tough as Rebecca Druken was, she was no match for Janie McLeary King. But she said, "You make a mistake in making me an enemy, ma'am—fer I done nothin' to you—and Georgina needs me. Who do you think Georgina loves if it ain't me? You, ma'am, she hardly knows! Understand, ma'am—Georgina loves *me*. She is a Druken more than a King, and Miles is a foolish Winch more than a King. And that's what you're so jealous of—all the McLearys are jealous—and that's why you throw me out! This house was kept by me, ma'am, it was cleaned and cared over by *me*! I took care of it—see how spotless it is—well, one day, I swear to Christ with my last fuggin' breath, it will belong to me—Rebecca Druken."

Usoff Assoff had a coal horse and in the winter children would follow him.

On an August day in 1932, Assoff sat high upon the bridge and with a crank opened the middle span to let a lumber ship pass up the channel toward Estabrook's mill, cutting through the dark Miramichi. And in the summer whenever there was a ship to go through, Miles would be there. He would set the clock to get up at seven-thirty. At times he played his recording when he woke. It was a recording Walter had made for him at the Grand, over a period of three months.

In this recording he had gleaned phrases from various moments in a number of movies.

"Good morning, Miles. How are you today? How is your little sister? Are you going anywhere special or are you just off to school? Have a good day, Miles, and we will see you tonight."

At night alone in his room he would play the second part of his recording.

"Good evening, Miles. You are up late tonight. Is your sister asleep? Did you have a good day? Did you make some friends? I am your friend. I will see you tomorrow, Miles."

Miles King would awake and go to his sister's room, take her to the bath and put her in the tub, scrub her face and feet, dress her in her crinoline dress, with the white bonnet on her head, and manoeuvre the carriage into the street. Georgina made quite a splash sitting in her pink carriage, her hands in gloves upon the front bar, with the unicorn painted on the carriage roof.

"To the right," she would direct, "around that pile of poop. Miles," she would yell, "around that pile of horseshit on the road."

To the right he would go, and to the left he would turn. Miles knew which way to go to bypass the young Drukens, the young Winches, the young Kennys, who all seemed to be his deadly enemies, for reasons that were never quite explained to him.

He wanted to watch the span open, but often Georgina did not. Still, she was in his care, for she had no one else. He was never asked, he was never told, it was just expected. No one knew he had deadly enemies, for he told no one. He continually monitored where these enemies were, so he passed them in the shade of the trees and cutting across the park. Then he would rest, wash his sister's face with a pink cloth, or shade her from the sun with a lovely straw sunhat. Then she would motion to her arm, and he would pick a bug off her sleeve, or give her a drink, or do her a soft-shoe. To keep her entertained he would take out his comb and paper and play a tune: "I'm Over the Moon for You."

Or if the little girl demanded a story he would tell her one while he danced in circles and pretended a top hat rolling down his arm. There was a time when he would produce a pigeon, named Harry Feathers. But Harry Feathers had been the last casualty of the great fall of '32, and was buried at the edge of the yard by Rebecca herself. So Miles found a sparrow and put it in his pocket, with its feet in the air. Sometimes Georgina did not want to sit in the carriage and he would lift her onto his shoulder and carry her, while pushing the carriage with one arm, into the back lot of Hawkenbury's for flowers to put in a jar.

But all this was his way to get to the bridge, where he would watch the span with fascinated eyes. And he would say, "They have made quite a mistake here, Georgie girl—the whole span turns the wrong way. They would have saved six minutes turning it in instead of outward. I have timed it a dozen times. It is not as uniform as they thought, for the span to the west is shorter—you see? They haven't reckoned the footage correctly. I cannot tell you in the run of a summer how much that would save—in time and in money."

"Who gives a shit?" the little girl would say, sitting upright in her carriage. "I want to see Mommie."

He would undo her shoes to straighten her stockings, and then, realizing that the Drukens were on the prowl, he would head straight to the walkway that skirted the cliff, with his child bouncing up and down in the squeaking carriage.

Sometimes he would take her to the baseball game, though he was not allowed to play. He would tell her baseball rules, how the ball could be hit at only a certain angle of the bat. Then, seeing the Drukens watching him, he would put her in the carriage and set out straight across the field and turn into the alleyway in back of the closed-up and cinder-smelling Regent Theatre, where Walter lived. They would go there for candy and gum and stay a half an hour or so.

"Why do you walk so funny?" Georgie would demand.

"God made me that way." Walter would smile, thrusting a cigar into his mouth.

"Thank God God never made me that way," she would yell.

And off they would go into Pleasant Street. Then he would take her home for lunch. He would make her a sandwich of cold meat and a salad. Then she wanted a game of checkers, "for everything." Always she bet either the entire theatre or all their mother's houses, or the well where it was said the gold was hidden by bandits.

"The theatre's mine!" she would yell. "The well is too—you are left with none—you are left with none!"

He would put her into bed for her nap, promising to wake her at two. At two he would completely change her—new stockings, and another dress, an afternoon bonnet, a little purse, and brand-new purple gloves.

Today, this summer day in 1932, he was worried. They were going down to the cottage the next afternoon. That meant he would have to go to the circus today. If he did not go this day he would not go. And he promised little Georgina he would take her if she wouldn't tell Janie that he had bought a mouth organ. She had not forgotten his promise. It was on her lips when she went to lie down, and on her lips when she woke.

"I didn't tell about yer mouth organ—so take me to the circus."

The problem was, he had overheard the Drukens saying they were going to the circus. He knew well enough not to go when they were there, for they had beaten him silly before.

"If we see ya at the circus again, ya flower-pickin' bastard, we will rub yer face in the motors," John Druken said. Miles did not know where the motors were, but he didn't want his face rubbed into them.

"Where are the motors?" he asked.

"Go fuck yourself, ya pansy-assed bastard. Mommy's little flowered shit arse." They said. And John came back and kicked him good. "You'll find out where the fuggin' motors are," he said.

"And we'll shave yer head."

"And pour molasses over yaw."

"And have rats eat yer knob off like they did in that movie."

"What movie?" Miles said, looking up at them from the ground.

"You'll find out what movie, ya scab-lickin' quiff."

And so saying they left, complaining about the poor quality of the Saturday afternoon matinee.

Of course by ten years of age Miles knew that the problem with his life was that his mother had fought with everyone. She had fought all her life. Yet those she fought with were not above inciting kids to exact revenge on him. But he couldn't tell her this. It would wound her too deeply.

Still, he had wanted her to explain it to him, to tell him there might be a possibility that it would be better sometime in the future. But the only thing she said after Rebecca stole her fur coat was, "Everyone leaves me—but you won't, will you, Miles."

He had painted Rebecca from memory after she had gone away. He wanted to catch the particular effect she had on people. He did not know this is what he wanted to address in the painting since he was only ten; however, it was the primary reason he painted it. In his watercolour she was sitting on the bed, with her hands turned toward her hips, looking up at someone at the door. It was one of the first watercolours he had ever attempted. It is somehow striking how well he caught Rebecca's character with a dab of red to show her hair and opened lips, a dab of gold to show her hanging slip and slightly parted knees, a dab of blue to catch her eye.

He was patiently braiding Georgina's hair when he heard the first distant chord of thunder.

"We can't go today—it's going to rain."

"I don't care if it rains. We'll be under the roofs they have over the rides."

"But I just put on your new dress—your prettiest one—and your new gloves."

"So what? We will take the umbrella."

"But don't you think—?"

"I'm going—I'm going—and if you don't go I will go alone—and I will tell Momma you have the mouth organ—"

"I told you I would take you—so I will take you. But if you catch a cold it isn't my fault. And Mom can't know I've taken you—because she told me not to."

"Yes yes yes, I know I know I know."

And they started out across the darkening field in the pulpy smell of summer toward the distant grounds where the circus was, where the trapeze artist had climbed a wire and an elephant was laughed at because of the amount of dung he had left, where the Druken boys tormented the monkey, and Billy Pebbles got sick in the crowd. Miles clutching some loose change and a one-dollar bill and wearing his top hat in case a circus manager needed him to lend a hand. "A real momma boy shit arse," the Drukens would say. Georgina sitting up in the carriage yelling, "Hurry hurry hurry—Miles, hurry before the circus goes away."

And they bounced over the stony field toward the big tents.

SIX

My father never so much as opened his mouth to me about it, except when he was in the throes of despair. Never spoke about anything, really. I don't know where he lost her. I like to think of them as great birds might have watched them bumping their way across the red dirt field in the heavy air toward the circus with its animals and its games. She giving him orders—"Here, Miles, go here. Over this way. Stop. Turn right. Watch out for the dogshit, boy."—clutching the bar with her purple gloves.

What is known is that he went in under the big top. He bought a ticket to see the chimps who smoked cigars and dressed like a married couple.

That is what he had wanted to see more than anything else. She wanted to go on the unicorn, and he paid for that. He put her on one of the large seats, which meant she didn't have to stand. He watched to see she was safe, then ran to see half the chimp show, went and found her again, paid for another ride and her chocolate whoopee, and went back in for the rest of the show. He was sure he saw her when he came out—he was sure she was near the carriage. He went to buy her a hot dog, and when he came back she was gone.

He didn't know where she'd gone, and he was too shy to tell anyone. He kept looking. But everyone was going home, because of the thunderstorm, and the circus was littered with dead, meaningless trifles and empty rides, and squeals of people running with newspapers over their heads. He kept searching for her as rain pelted him. He had stayed too long to watch the chimps, and no one knew where he was when she got off her ride. Someone told him she was seen heading home. So he turned the empty carriage around and retraced his steps. He got to the house and no one was there. He went back to the circus. By now, it was deserted, and all the tents and trailers were closed.

That morning he had taken Georgina to the photographer. They had their picture taken, he standing beside her, she with her bonnet on, smiling. It was to be a surprise for Janie. It had cost him three dollars. The photographs would be ready the next week, when they came back from the cottage. Before she had her nap he had helped her pack her bag for the cottage, putting in her doll and her colouring book. Thinking of this made him frantically tear through the circus grounds trying to find her. But it got dark and then darker, and he went home again.

He walked up the steps. The door was open but no one was there.

He waited hours. Sometimes he was in a daze, broken only by the wind over the trees. Then after midnight he heard a sound and looked through the screen window. He saw a woman coming up the street. When she turned into the walkway, he closed the door and hid behind it. He was shaking so badly he was sure she could hear his teeth chattering.

"Miles—thank God you're okay, Miles, thank God—come—come," she whispered. "Come."

To Miles everything seemed so sad. All the elms had big wet leaves and if you ever saw pictures of them they were sad, and all the puddles were silent, forever and ever, and all the telephone wires were still, and the birds flew away all at once, and the woman, Putsy, took his hand and that was sad too, as sad as any woman taking a child by the hand in any movie that you saw, and no one would ever tell my father different as long as he lived.

He carried his mouth organ in his pocket, still had his tie and top hat on. He had done a good job, he had braided her hair, he had changed her stockings, he did a dance to make her laugh. He wanted Putsy to tell him where she was. But Putsy didn't want to tell him. No one told him for a long, long time. And when they did, he looked as if an eternal sorrow could not escape his soul, in grade five or grade eleven, or any grade in between. In fact, he never spoke a word for three years to anyone at all.

PART IV

ONE

My father did poorly in school. As a boy he would be gone to school when his mother woke, and would return to the house after she was down at the Grand. "With all her actor pals," he said. He would go upstairs, look over his homework, and then lie on his bed, staring into the dark, remembering certain frames of certain movies he had seen— for he had seen far more than most people his age, and could be considered in a certain respect, or in most respects certainly, as the son of an actress, for in her heart and soul Janie considered herself to be one, and, what is worse, had the temperament to prove it. As for Miles, he was left off centre stage, not unlike Edgar, he once admitted to me.

"Edgar—Edgar who?" I asked.

"Why—Poe, son, the poet Poe—born of a thespian family—a father and mother who died in 1811—when he was two. Well, just like he, some of my very dreams were dashed at the very same age— the age of two."

The drawing room was closed and the piano was off limits, but sometimes at night he would go down and listen, his ear pressed to the door, for someone had told him that his father was a ghost of a man at the end of his life and that the sound of the piano was the very last thing heard in the house on the day he died.

Miles had only been in the drawing room once, and not for a long time. And he, as he once admitted, had hopes that made him blush.

"Yes, Wendell," he said, "I had hopes to make me blush, but humankind has a way of dashing hope—and in fact that is what makes you blush in the end. In fact, all men should blush at the moment of death—just because of the great foolishness of their dreams."

After the death of his sister he never asked to play the piano.

"Though my fingers wiggled and itched," he said, "worse than my toes. And Mom would curse at music—what she loved she learned to hate after Georgina died, so it came down to hiding the fact that I wanted to play—or taking myself into the woods to play in secret. The biggest obstacle was, I could not get a piano into the woods—well, not every day—so I had to find something else. I found a Horner harmonica when I was ten."

My father, as he said, "did not press the piano." It was as if a self-imposed punishment had been decided. After the death of the little girl a great weight oppressed him. I learned through rumour and supposition downtown and in the barbershop where people gathered how Georgina had died. When I heard the cruel nursery rhyme: "Miles pushed/his sister fell/down Paddy Druken's wishing well," I pretended I didn't know it—to mention it to him would have been agony.

He spoke best in soliloquy, his voice though always polite was clipped halfway between a British laurel wreath and an Irish crown of thorns—not unusual for Maritimers used as they are to monologues and fist fights.

"After Georgina died, I was sure Mom would kill me, and I simply waited for the blow. Yet she did not strike. Of course she did not want to, of course she still loved me, and of course she did not listen to those nasty rumours that I had pitched and tossed my poor sister into the well. Of course she did not although once she came close to accusing me. Still, I was inconsolable at not being killed. Ten years of age is a little young to make a noose," he said to me, "though I know better children than me made a noose at ten—some in the wars must have, but I was between wars as you know. However, I will say this. I was in charge of the little girl, and I was rich, and my mother dressed me funny, and—well—do you know what this did, Wendell?"

"I'm not sure."

"I'm not sure either. Rebecca, while she worked for my mom, held me up to ridicule on the street, in front of her cronies from time to time, and gave me a sound knock on the head for their amusement, but what was that? I was still a player, as they say, in life. I had my pigeons and my tricks. But afterwards what did life matter? I don't think life mattered. I lived, I ate, I watched others do things that I might have once wanted to do. But some kind of gap was now in evidence between myself and my existence." Here I could see him trembling as he looked at me.

"That's terrible."

"At any rate, it did irreparable damage to the relationship between me and your grandmother. Or is it 'your grandmother and I'? The yard grew up about the house, and the trees grew to shade us, and the nights were soft and melancholy, and the rooms smelled of face powder and cosmetics and strong tea, and the wind blew along the hallways where I would sometimes stand for hours staring in abject desolation at emptiness. Georgina's room was locked, for my mother could not look at it in calmness. Nor, though she tried to hide it, could she look at me in calmness. So over time I became a kind of oddity—a Mr. Oddity, if you must know. I did not speak for several years, for my own thoughts about that day did not seem to matter. I could not remember what happened, yet people believed I only said this because of my own culpable, damnable heart. Rebecca was gone, and that was a good thing. She begged money or stole money and went away. Where had she gone? I wondered often enough. Some said she joined the circus to do a bawdy dance—I had no idea what that was, and could not conjecture. However in the summertime at night, when the wind blew, I sometimes felt she was coming back to see me, and I would dream of her in the midst of a bawdy dance, swaying to some doomed music at the other end of the house. It was known that she had had a falling-out with many people, and I always thought, ludicrous I know, that she would be back to seek revenge on us all, even against the man who taught her everything she knew—Joey Elias himself.

"No" he said, looking at me with a peculiar gaze, "none believed me. I was too witless. There is a conscious effort at times to see only the worst side of people, and I was the one they had singled out. I realized that by twelve years of age, but had no voting power to correct it. I thought that if I donated something to the town they might like me, so I began to save my money for a fire engine, knowing our town needed one. There would be no need to name the fire engine after me—we would name it after Georgina. But I could not save enough. That became the story of my life."

As a boy he lived a solitary life. If it was a mild night he would walk to the theatre and go upstairs and sit near Walter, looking through the projector's gaze at the movie, at Cary Grant or Irene Dunne. Then he would take out his sketch pad and doodle the actors, Fred Astaire in motion, or Clark Gable in full smile, until he heard Janie leave, and when the theatre, the great Grand she had built as her own monument to her own brilliance and talent, was locked solid as a vault, he would return home alone. He would walk back and forth on the street outside until he saw her lights go out.

His supper would be made for him by the maid and sitting out on the kitchen counter, cold. There was a new maid every few weeks. They could not keep one long enough to know her name.

"Mom, I was going to ask the new maid—my new 'pal' as you call them—to come outside with me, but I cannot for the life of me find her."

"She's gone, son."

"Gone. Where?"

"I did not like the look of her—"

"You did not like the look of her, I liked the look of her quite a bit."

"She had the 'French look.'"

"She did, she did. I admire that."

"Well, I am not fond of the French."

"Well, mother, who is? Yet is that any reason to let the poor girl go?"

He would go days without seeing his mother or caring if he did. For there must have been some idea, some grain of understanding, that a death he had forged had caused a shift in their destinies and in their loyalties to one another. That was the rub. The loyalty Janie demanded of him was not, evidently, strong enough in her to keep her from accusation, although direct accusation was never thought of. She could not stand any display of affection from him—no hug, and no kiss, and no gentle reminder they were mother and son. It was too painful for her, and became after a while too painful for him, until something inside him no longer cared.

Still, she was desperate not to lose him. So though he bought himself a Swiss Army knife, he never got to go camping, and a snorkel and fins were enough to cause frenzy in her gaze. The great damn river you see, terrified her, and although she had swum it herself, he must not—for losing him meant losing all that was left. She did not know, for he did not say, that there were certain moments when certain boys (never just one boy) held his head under water at Vye's beach to see if he would gurgle. He did not—learned to hold his breath for almost three minutes when he was fourteen.

Every fortnight, in a kind of desperate attempt to win her approval, he bought Janie a present with money she left on the table for him, and he left these presents on her bed table. Years later my sister, the sleuth, discovered these presents unopened in her cedar closet, all of them having notes attached.

"A little something for you, Mom, to prove what you already know, that if the town does not love you, I do."

Miles came and went alone from school, went to socials by himself and stood at the far end of the gymnasium in his bow tie and white jacket. He spied a girl at one of these functions as alone as he, and one evening at supper hour, when he was sixteen, he looked up at Janie and said: "Could you get Elizabeth Whispers a coat? It is cold out."

"Elizabeth Whispers. Who is Elizabeth Whispers?"

"She is Sammy Whispers's daughter."

"Who is Sammy Whispers?"

"He was the preacher who met his end at the hands of his congregation."

"Oh yes—that Whispers."

"Yes."

"Why can't she buy her own coat?"

"Because she cannot buy anything, let alone a coat. Her family has no money. And if you ask me I doubt if in a hundred years they will earn as much as you do in five."

"Tell her to come see me at the theatre tomorrow afternoon, and she will have her coat."

"Thank you."

The next evening Janie said, "I gave Elizabeth Whispers her coat—but I did not let on I bought it. I pretended there was a draw at the theatre and that she had won."

"Since she has never been to a movie it must have seemed slightly incongruous," my father said.

"Yes—whatever that means, I'm sure," Janie answered, cutting into her liver, which she insisted on eating every Wednesday, just as she insisted on fish for Friday.

Miles picked up his glass of milk, drank, and said nothing more for a week or two.

Then one night, unable to look her way, he said, "You lied to me, Mother."

She stared at him. "I am positive I have—but when?"

She discovered that Miles was talking about things she had completely forgotten. That she had told him many lies about many things to keep him near her bosom, to keep him safe, and to secure her legacy. She had told him that the river had great fish that would swallow him in "one godawful suck" so he would not go there and drown. She had told him when he was little that the forest held man-eating plants so he would not go into the woods, and lose his way, and she had told him that all the universities had closed down because everyone was poor, and he should not make any plans to go, that she had not gone to university and it did not bother her. In fact, she was twice as smart because she hadn't. She was at least as smart and twice as rich as any university professor.

So if he wanted to be a doctor as he said, what would happen when he was operating on a patient and she needed him at the theatre?

How many patients would he lose if he had to have two jobs? He would have to leave an appendix to change a reel.

"But perhaps I wouldn't want to work at the theatre."

Nothing struck her as more ludicrous. He should work for her—that is where he was needed. And the theatre would be the only place he was ever wanted. Besides, the whole world was against her, and he should not be as well. She told him that she had hoped Georgina would be here with her, but as he knew, Georgina was not.

"I'm not needed," he said.

"Was St. Patrick needed in Ireland?"

"Only until the snakes were gone. And it seems our snake—by which I mean Rebecca—has fled," he whispered.

He walked with a military air about him, and because his hope was to be a doctor, he carried a book of Boyle's *Anatomy*, back and forth from the Grand Theatre to the house. Most people thought he was the personification of a "creepy" egotist. Nor did he mind them thinking this, for it set him apart in a different way than the death of the child had. And in a certain way it complemented it—perversely, to be sure, but what else did he have to fall back upon if not the perversity of this kind of precedent?

Still, he believed in a kind of doomsday scenario for himself.

"Why do you have all the doors locked and every light on in the house—even in the basement?" Janie asked him one night in 1938.

"Because Rebecca is back in town with the circus, a hawker at the dart game, and seeking a way to do me in."

"That is nonsense," his mother said.

"Well, Mom, I realize that the carnie is the best place for any of us—there is a kind of emblematic understanding between those people, which in fact is rather sweet, and if not for her I could join. Yet my concern isn't nonsense. She wants your home and your business and is willing to kill me for it—I knew it since I was seven years old!"

"Absolute rubbish," my grandmother said.

The 1940s film noir seemed right for Miles—those films with Bogey and Mitchum, those with palm trees in the dark, those with stairways leading to forlorn patios, those with large cars and indifferent dreams, that ocean waves seemed to wash away. He in his cadet uniform smoking cigarettes alone in the dark theatre, looking like Fitzgerald himself, while the howls of moviegoers echoed around him and sometimes, for no apparent reason, at him. Or for the reason that he carried Boyle's book of anatomy while asking a girl for a date to the spring dance.

He was in essence forgotten by the town. The girls in their finery, the boys in their youthful swagger waltzed by him, in jaunty indifference onward toward a war, and Hitler in Europe.

He wasn't even worth bullying any more. Joey Elias told people: let him go, he is too harmless to harm.

"Janie's lad," he was called by everyone. Many had forgotten his name was Miles. Some would never know. He could have been Artie Shaw, could have been Benny Goodman, could have been anyone singing "I'm Miles Away from You."

He and my grandmother alone in a house that never reached grandeur and never quite captured despair.

After 1940 my father became the front for our family, the shuffling dancer with the smooth moon face, who could tap dance, sing, and do a sadly brilliant imitation of W. C. Fields. "Hello, my little chickadee," he would say, mostly to his newly trained pigeons. Once at a picnic in the honour of a middle-aged female member of our IODE he waved away her offer of ice water after the three-legged race with: "No, I don't drink water, ma'am."

"And why not, Miles?"

"Why not, ma'am—you ask why not? Well, it's because fish fuck in it." He bowed and walked away.

He was left alone, and slowly, quietly, he left the world, the church, the house he lived in, and began to drink.

After a certain day—I'm not sure what day this was—he never performed tricks with his pigeons again, though he had a budgie when my sister and I were little, and at times played with his bowler hat like Laurel and Hardy to make us laugh. Though he did not laugh when we did.

I did not know until I was sixteen and found a letter with his report card from 1939 that because of supposed psychological problems (sneaking a gin bottle into class), he never graduated, but left school in grade eleven.

"He's about as interested in school as a bag of dung," the principal wrote to Janie, one airy April day of that far-off year. "He must be taken to task. It is all well and fine to have money, Mrs. King"—by which of course he meant that it wasn't—"but responsibility is more to the point here, isn't it? He is simply not responsible—for he has money. Well, he might not always have it, might he not?

"So try him in banking (if someone will take him), as a teller, or perhaps as a clerk in a store. He may make a labourer, for he has the strength if he has the will. He cannot be much else. Do you know that he drinks?"

"I am quite aware that he drinks," Janie wrote back. "It is our family inheritance—which is more than an inheritance—over a hundred and fifty years from Boyne to our Irish famine—than you have ever had, you pickle-cheeked, squeamishly polite, kiss-arse bastard."

The principal, disgusted at her coarseness, did not answer back. I don't think he expected an answer and got one anyway. There is a life always and forever beneath the life led, and one signature folly of that hidden life is a perverse and private desire to cause pain. Janie, however, was willing to trade pain, so sorrowful had her life been. And she knew who he was, this man. He was, in his imitable tall and bony fashion, what so many men are, who have felt over the years a right to belittle people. He was this man, the frightened head of his own department and a complete arsehole.

The school was glad to be rid of my father, and I assume my father of them. Miles was perceptive enough to know that his torture came because of class. The Winches and Elias and the Drukens had tortured him because of class, and so too had those from the principal families in town, the Estabrooks and Blacks. For Miles King was considered rich by the poor and callow by the rich. He could do nothing about either perception. His father had been an eccentric orphan, his mother born at the intersection of Pond and Chatham Streets. No one had taught him a thing. His mother left him to his own devices. And he floundered in much.

One day the anatomy book was found in a back field, opened to a page underlined and annotated by studious juvenile remarks, left and forgotten as well.

There is a moment that this anatomy book gives us. We can interpret him leaving it in the back field like this. All his life he had believed Janie, and then, by the time he was seventeen, he realized half of what she had told him were lies to protect her investment in his life, because she no longer had her daughter. Nor did she mind him suffering over this. And suffer he did, so he began to keep up his father's flower gardens, and lavished the attention on them, and on the hummingbirds that flitted about them, that no one had ever managed to lavish on him.

Still, Gram spoiled him in other ways. She bought him a sports car that he never drove, and invited young people to his house that he never spoke to. One night when he was sixteen coming into the house late, he saw a most depressing sight. Young girls and boys jitterbugging in the drawing room—in his father's sanctuary—laughing and playing the piano that he had always been kept away from.

"I have invited some little people over," Janie said.

"Have fun, you little people," Father said. "I am off to bed."

Coming to his room later, with the melodious sound of Artie Shaw trailing behind her up the stairs, she looked in at his door.

"Look, I've been thinking. If you want to play the piano—you know you will never be as good as your dad, however—well, would you like to?"

"Absolutely not, Mother," he said.

She began to see then that just as she was willful, brilliant, and determined in a way that reminded one of a disaster survivor, so was he.

She tried then, to no avail. To no avail. When he was seventeen she decided to have him a birthday celebration, with papier-mâché decorations and young girls in sprightly attire invited. But he whispered in her ear: "Ten years too late, Mother. Not for the girls, of course, but for the party."

She faced him the next day as he stood ready to enter the back hallway that led outside. Her voice seemed to echo and engage you with its power and its tragedy.

"I was alone after George died. I don't blame you for being little, but there was nothing I could do with you. You could not help. It must have been a strange position to be in—you as a child—how you must have wanted to help, at certain times—like one of the princes brought to the tower. But if you play your cards well, you will someday inherit what I have to leave."

"I see. Well then, of course." Father smiled, lighting his cigarette with his engraved gold lighter. Then without finishing that thought he nodded and went out into the yard to attend to his father's flowers, and his own rock garden.

He loved all his life flowers, ground ivy, small white violets and purple loosestrife. They commanded our back yard in the summer, sadly waving like ancient talismans, brandishing bright colours and certain of a swift demise under the autumn sky. He kept them up at his mother's great grey house on the hill as well.

"If it wasn't for a dumb plant, I'd never get to see him—though I only see him from the hind end anyway," Grandmother once remarked to me when I was very little.

"What was Daddy like?" I asked, thinking she would shower me with information about his goodness.

"I'm not sure—I never got to know him that well" was her reply.

TWO

Just as abruptly, Miles quit high school, put his bright paints away, and became a cadet. In 1940, when Churchill came to power after years of being laughed at by the intelligentsia who now called upon him to save their arses, my father, telling his mother nothing of where he was going, lied about his age and went gaily off to war, hoping, like his own father, that a crawl over the top might do him in. He wrote to Janie from Halifax, jostled in among other soldiers in a crowded train station, waiting to take the *Queen Mary* across the pond.

"You might not know, but I have 1302 guppies in my room. You will have to feed them when I am gone—or feed them to each other if you can't manage it. I will be away for some little time—perhaps in Europe."

We do not know what happened to his guppies, but she did remove from his room his copies of D. H. Lawrence, his *Sons and Lovers* and *The Rainbow*. "Thank you, God, I now know what girls do— or what I am supposed (or allowed, or is it willing?) to do with them" was scribbled on both.

He spent most of his furloughs and nights out at theatres in London, and sent his mom postcards now and again from Piccadilly, about various theatres and theatricals he knew she would love. All of them were unsigned. A picture of him in a London pub, frayed and cracked, remains of those days. He is looking silently out at the camera. And the truth be told, no wise-ass friend or jaunty boyhood pal snapped this poignant photograph of my father when young, but the barmaid. For he, as always, was alone.

By 1944 my father had risen to a captain of artillery in the North Shore Regiment, and there is a story that outside of Caen, France, on a hot, dusty furnace of a day, he accidentally fired on his own troops, and took out a number of them, thinking them Germans. Whether or not true, it was never verified, and I did not ask him about it bluntly, though I suggested he write his war experience down. But he was only a boy of twenty then, and a captain of artillery is a fine thing for such a young, inquisitive gentleman.

In England he searched for his past, in Ireland as well.

He retraced his father's steps on King's Road and King Lane, into King's Head Inn, and King's Square, and found in a small upstairs room beyond Piccadilly an old yellowed piano that my grandfather had played his first piece on.

"The remarkable Georgie King of Blackhead's Lane," George King was once called. My father put the program in his pocket and brought it back to Canada, not to give to his mother (as one might think or infer), but to keep on his person.

He remained friendless, was the last one in and the first one out of the amphibian landing craft on June 6, 1944, walking with his gun over his head, far less worried about German assaults on his flesh than drowning, and in the process making a complete ass of himself, which everyone from the town of Newcastle simply assumed he would do.

"And what happened to that terrible Miles King?"

"Drowned within a second of leaving the transport."

"Ah yes, well—h'm—of course."

In 1946, he was released as a commissioned officer, with a long lanky body, and a white sad face. He came home with a plan to marry—his schoolteacher.

He went nights to sit with Miss McGrath in her parlour, drinking tea, talking about and apologizing for history lessons uncompleted in grade eight. She, who was thirty years his senior, tried not to leave a light on, yet would see him standing in her little living room as she sank back into a chair in the dark. Miss McGrath finally told him she was a friend only and could not make him happy. Nor, she said, did she have the inclination to do so. He went and got good and hammered.

"I've lost the love of my life," he told an old school acquaintance.

"Who? Diane? Susan? Who, who?"

"Miss McGrath," he said.

"But she's damn near sixty!"

"And worthy of every year God has decided to spend on her," my father mused.

The fellow told me that he decided my father was mad.

"In what way?" I asked.

"In a way that was charming and interesting," he replied, "and quite sharp—but nonetheless a little self-destructive, I think. No," he continued, picking up his beer, "completely self-destructive—frighteningly so!"

My father did perform at a St. Patrick's Day concert that March, which enabled him to do a bit of soft-shoe to a scratchy recording of Glenn Miller's "In the Mood," which he had to reset halfway through by shuffling over to the skipping record with a cane and, after resetting the needle, tapping back, twirling about. He was introduced as "our boy Miles" by Monsignor Hanrahan, and he seemed to like that, "our boy Miles" was the finest tribute he had ever received on the river. But St. Patrick's Day aside, he did not enter the church.

"Why don't you come to church?" Hanrahan asked him that afternoon.

"Because I wish to be a saint."

Miles was back home, pondering his life, his hope for a career in the later part of the 1940s. Certain he could not stay with his mother, certain he had to make it on his own, thinking again of medicine, he packed to leave one sweet soft night in July, with the crickets chirping under the window, and the smell of his father's flowers gentle in the garden below, leaves rustling soft like on the trees.

"Where are you going?" his mother said.

"I am going away."

"Don't be so full of nonsense—there is nothing out in the world for you. You have to stay here. Who will protect me?"

"You have Roy Dingle," he said. Roy, whom they had saved that long-ago Christmas day, was her male companion or, as she called him, "her pal." They were suited for each other, looking something like Percy Kilbride and Marjorie Main from Ma and Pa Kettle. Roy called her Mrs. King. Sometimes she would let him back the car out of her garage. He would shine it, wax it, and dust off the seat for her as he awaited her on Sundays to take her to church. They were partners at Auction 45, and went to bingo once a month. As for Miles's relationship with Roy Dingle, they were strained at the best of times. Many times Mr. Dingle would be known to turn away just at the moment Miles was to offer friendship.

"How can you leave? I need you to take over the business—you have to. Who will own the business when I die?" She burst into tears, looking at him through her fingers as she cried.

"Ah, another ruse," he thought, "in this sweet July evening, with the fireflies across in the darkening field where I have hidden my bottles since I was fifteen."

He left and neighbours actually heard her wailing at the gate.

He sat with his suitcase, his hair well coiffed, and his cigarette pinched between his manicured fingers, waiting to board the train, even an hour after it had left.

The next day he received a job offer, from her, in writing, to be Walter's apprentice—the apprentice Walter had been asking for for twenty years.

He was offered thirty a week and room and board. When he married, if he married, and depending whom he married (a qualification) he would receive one of her houses she had scattered about the town, where she put her money instead of putting it in the bank.

So Father entered the theatre as an employee on August 6, 1947, with five dollars in the pocket of his brand-new itchy suit.

THREE

Janie went every day, at four, accompanied by Roy, to her child's grave. She would stay there on her knees until the church bell rang out at five, in the wet or in the snow, it did not matter. Four o'clock was the moment the child had left my father's sight, the moment she had disappeared.

Most blamed it on Father. And Father, for some reason, suspected someone had pushed her, although he did not know who.

Rebecca had gone. He heard she had been married, and that she had been put in jail for performing an abortion. He had to look up what that was. Still, my father made little comment on anything people did. His ambivalence kept the terror away. Still, she had escaped somewhat—in some way from something. In poking around Miles found out that Joey Elias sent her money now and again, that she was a carny girl with a tattoo, and was living her life somewhere else.

"She has gone and I don't remember much about her—nothing really. In a way it is as if she did not exist—a phantom. So if she comes back will I know her?" Then he answered, "Of course—for she will make herself known to me."

"Why?" Someone asked.

"She will not be able to stop herself," he said. "You see, for the life of me, I do not think it is yet over."

In the winter of 1948, Miles, driving his old black car, with the glove compartment filled with whisky bottles, his suitcase sitting in the back, with a map upside down on the dashboard and the mirror tilted in such a way that he could read this map upside down, thinking he would make a dash for it, saw little Elizabeth Whispers hitchhiking home. He was escaping from his mother once and for all, escaping from her ironclad grasp on his life. But he could not help pulling over for Miss Whispers.

"I ain't getting in with you," she said.

"Why not?"

"I don't think you have a clue where yer going—not the way yer been coming back and forth with that map."

"Oh this—well, I'm going to Boston, to start my life completely over. You see, my mother runs my life—but if I go to Boston, she won't find me." He half whispered the last part of the sentence with his hand up to his mouth, to ward off spies.

"Well, I'm not up for Boston."

"Well, I'll take you only to what you're up for," Father said, folding the map and putting it away. "You remember me, of course," he said.

"Of course not," she said.

"I'm the rich boy."

"I didn't know there were any rich boys here."

"Well, of course there aren't, but they think I am, you see. And anyway, it was grade eight, and I didn't do my history and I was desperately angry with how we conducted the First World War—the Great War, remember? I was desperately angered about the poor Tardy boys—how they all were killed except—well, there you have it—I didn't speak—"

"Oh my Lord—the deaf and dumb boy," Elizabeth said, suddenly trying to look more presentable. "You're drinking now," she said.

He looked at her a long moment. "Quite," he said and shifted gears.

"I don't drink," she said.

"That's an affliction I've managed to overcome." He smiled.

Her face was deathly white, and her blond hair fell from her barrette, and her stockings were twisted. She lived beyond Renous, in a house with nine children and a widowed mother, and she was the eldest girl, and had come to town to try to find work at the new Eaton's outlet, hiring three "girls" that afternoon. She had walked all the way to town and didn't manage to get an interview. Now the winds had come up, in bits of blinding white and blue, against the blue of the sky and snow, and she had to go home to a house without supper.

She looked at his regiment pin on his lapel. "You were in the war," she said.

"Many of them," he said, smiling again, and taking a drink of vodka.

"How were you at the war?" she said after a moment, straightening the hem of her old plaid skirt.

"Not very good, I'm afraid," he said.

"Why? Did you run?" she asked.

"If only I could have," he said.

She smiled. "What, then?"

"I believe—I haven't been able to authenticate—or is it validate?—the account, and don't remember, but it seems—and seems is the word, Miss Whispers—that I fired on my own men."

"Good God. Did you kill any?"

"I think, perhaps, your brother Kenny—but—in the heat of battle—who can say—?" He took a drink while looking at her, with the face of a man as perplexed by his admission as she herself might have been; the bottle suctioned by his lip.

"Good God."

"Quite," he said.

My father and mother were married eight months later, after a meeting with Janie, I suppose to see whether she approved, although it would not have been billed as that. Janie did not approve, for Janie approved of so little. It may have been because the girl had grown up a Protestant.

Sometime in November of 1949, my mother's water broke when she was alone in our small bungalow, surrounded by mean little hedges and shallow trees gnarling up over the picket fence she had dreamed of having as a girl, and the beginnings of a flowering garden on a half acre of slope. My father was away, on an errand, across the river to pick up a movie from a broken-down bus, for in our family movies came before almost anything else. My mother always maintained that Janie knew she was about to go into labour and sent my father across the river anyway, to demonstrate her control over him and his loyalty to her.

"No one is needed at a birth except the mother," Janie once said to me, as if in explanation.

So with the trees bare and the sidewalks glazed with shale ice, Elizabeth made her way alone to the hospital. I was born that afternoon and placed in an incubator, where to this day I remember the glass and the lights in my eyes. Of course I am my father's son, so you may think this exaggerated.

When I was three, I began to smoke. (I know this sounds exaggerated too, but I could get them from my mother's purse without her knowing and smoke them under our porch steps.) My sister, Ginger, was born in 1952, and we grew up in a small grey bungalow my grandmother owned, at the intersection of Blanche Street and the street that was named after her by the town council, which wanted to do something to honour a woman most of them had scorned in their youth.

After my sister was born, my mother went to Gram to ask her for a raise for Miles. Never had Janie been so livid. How dared she ask for a raise of any sort. This was a matter only between her and Miles, and no one else had any right to say anything. Miles, on hearing this, did not take my mother's side, but his own mother's. And that essentially was how Elizabeth was frozen out of any decision in our family life.

Once, I took off my clothes in church, and I was forced to quit smoking when I was five. I was often put into the corner during supper because of some infraction, my father saying I could come out and join the family as soon as I stopped thinking of the chocolate pudding on the counter. An hour or so later he would tell me to come out anyway.

Very early on he gave me talks against alcohol. "It is a practice I do not want you to take up, for it is— Well, I see nothing wrong with it myself, but Miss Whispers, your mother, does, for some strange reason, religious or not I do not know. However, this talk is to humour her and instruct you and I will get nothing from it myself."

I remember how happy we were. The door would open at night and we would shout his name, and rush to him, my sister and I, and he with snow on the collar of his coat and smelling of a certain brand of what he called his tonic would put us up on his shoulders and carry us about the house. Now and again there would be a small dispute between him and Mother. My sister would cry and plead with them to hold hands, and after a time they would, and the fight was ended. Such gigantic concern and such easy relief was supposedly the life of children.

At six I began to realize that my father was somewhat different. I do not know to this day why I wanted him to be any other way—looking back now he was perhaps as good a man as most. But different. He spoke of flowers when other men spoke of sports. He talked about "the radiant leaflet I just found in the bog beyond town" to men who cringed when they heard such a thing. And why would they cringe? Weakness on their part, my father assured me. Did Walter cringe? No, never—for Walter understood the mind and soul of the dispossessed. So saying, he thought I would be relieved. So saying, I was not.

He took me fishing dressed in his suit and tie, and strode back and forth on the beach looking for strange pebbles or flowers, which he would dig up with excruciating care and place in the trunk of our car and bring home to his garden. Often he would carry his briefcase with him into the woods. And of course this caused a crisis, if not in his life then certainly in mine. It also caused hilarity among many people on the shore—hilarity my father never seemed to notice, though I would turn beet red. Once, some kids were pointing to him and laughing at his gentleman's attire as he carried a basket of flowers slung on his forearm.

"God, who in heck is that?"

"Hell, don't ask me," I said.

Still, when it became known that in that briefcase under his arm were not the papers for some business but a full bottle for anyone who wished to have a drink with a so-called businessman, they forgot he was a sissy. When they found out he could drink 90 percent of them under the table they suddenly decided he was a man!

And when it was discovered (or should I say "thought") that my father had a great deal of money, old army buddies came to our door in valiant attempts to relieve him of it, by investing toward a future moment that, they all said, would make us millions. And my father, the butt of army jokes, barbs of all sorts, had no idea why people were friendly with him now. Or if he did, and reflecting upon this, I am sure in some true way he always did, he never let on. That interior life that we all live day to day, the most important life, was hidden to others, who gloated at him like one would at a prize they had just discovered at the bottom of some Cracker Jack box in our theatre. They gloated at him as an inanimate thing that would suddenly make them better in their own eyes. They spoke about him in bars and at parties, saying, "There's the man that might help us." And surely if he did "help," it would be a benefit to everyone concerned. There was also hidden a slight anger here—for how could this man they mocked (and all of them had) suddenly hold the key to their future, without them having realized it when ingratiation was more readily allowable. But this anger could be masked in a kind of elemental rethinking of their position. Phone calls were made to him, invitations given, dates of meetings that were once unthinkable, now quite evidently assured. He and my mother were actually invited out.

"I think I have improved," he said to Mother one afternoon in the living room. "None of these chaps would speak to me in uniform. Civilian life has done wonders for me. Well, I am a finely disguised botanist, so perhaps it's my treatment of flowers that has reached them, and they have come down say from Grand Falls to see my fire-weed—you think?"

"I do not think that at all," my mother said, angry at the moral superiority that masked the avarice of these people. Moral superiority saying they were far too good for him when his money didn't matter, now making the case that he was morally sanctioned by them for his coin. My father of course knew this—as he looked at me one afternoon I was certainly cogniscent of the fact that nothing much escaped him. But he did not speak.

So it was our mother, who registered the intent of lackeys who had once smirked in his direction coming upon our house, in beat-up automobiles, briefcases filled with fabricated wealth, calling him their friend. Contracts for new knives that would be major breakthroughs in cutting through a steak stuffed in the pockets of their double-breasted suits, like well-attired gangsters; showing us the Hula Hoop, the spin top that spun for precious moments on my little sister's head while the man oohed and aahed at her ability to balance it there, her eyes focused upward upon it; and of course the best of the lot, the Slinky that wobbled down the stairs in unison with their open-mouthed gestures, as if they were cheering on a horse in the Kentucky Derby.

My father said, "My God, Elizabeth—it's a wire that moves. Now I will ask one defining question: does it move up stairs? I see how it comes down. No? Well, it would be splendid—I mean, even more splendid than it is right now—if it could climb up the stairs, saying at the top of the precipice, 'I'm off to bed, Dad and Mom—see you in the morning?—Ha."

Or he would say, "A knife! How does it work?" Astonished for the benefit of people who seemed to be much duller than their product. "Look, Elizabeth, darling—a knife. The man is selling—a knife."

They would stand out in our raining yard in the drizzle as Father punctuated about the June lilacs, saying almost nothing to them as they made their pitches, or saying:

"H'm—no—I am not so sure I could help with a marina—first because I am no boatswain—Mark Twain—ha ha—and have the unnatural ability to be deathly frightened of water—it took me some few years to get over my hubris but I now admit it gracefully."

Or sometimes we would hear from our small upstairs playroom, filled with a patchwork of sentiment, of torn colouring books scribbled upon and dolls with no legs, a volley of curses out in the yard, because my father refused to do what it was they wanted him to.

"You are a Christless stupid bastard who has never understood anything, and if it wasn't for yer damn mother you wouldn't be able to wipe your arse."

"The exceptional thing about that is," my father would respond as he clipped a pussy willow, "none of us would be able to wipe our arses—I mean without the help early on—or is it guidance, or forbearance even—of our mothers."

"Goddamn you!"

"And you, sir."

One of these men, Corporal Gary Fallon, came many days, sat outside in his old Pontiac and spoke to Father about dishwashers, how the modern married "girls" would go ape for them, how handsome I was and how a darling my sister.

Introducing me to this corporal, a dull mustached man of forty, with a loud voice and blunt unmoving eyes, a white shirt against the implacable grey pocking of his skin, the bloated August turbulence in the sky and with the innate complexion of a fish, Father said of me, "I was going to name him Harold, after Lloyd, or Peter, after Lorrie, but I thought he may well end up hanging from clocks or killing a pawnbroker—"

The corporal did not respond, except to look completely perplexed, as if the men continually scurrying through his brain taking orders didn't snap to this one, and I felt an acute embarrassment for him, and of course for my father, standing in front of him.

Still, whatever error people had of him, my father had either no ability, nor any interest, to make right.

I at that time did not know who Harold Lloyd was, or that the most famous scene in movie history was his hanging from a clock. I did not know either that Peter Lorrie acted in 1935 as Raskolnikov, who of course killed the pawnbroker (and her mentally disabled sister) in *Crime and Punishment*. But these things my sister and I would ferret out over the years, as if they were composed of vapours and thrown to us by a magician in gloves. I became better in the end to understand these signals from him.

One day, after he was cursed because he would not help open a restaurant for a man he hardly knew, I saw my father standing in front of me, holding a cigarette in his right hand, his eyes shining, his lapel carrying his regimental pin, and wearing a sad smile, looking somewhat like James Mason, in one of his finer British roles, acutely alone in the world and poignantly brilliant.

Still Fallon had talked my father into giving him three thousand dollars—for dishwashers. My mother, Elizabeth Whispers, found out about this, and rushed into the kitchen one morning while we were sitting at breakfast.

"You are not giving him any money—"

"I already have," Father asserted, buttering his toast and puffing out his chest, and looking at us as if we would stand up and cheer. "It seems like a wonderful deal—in fact, one of the stipulations is his help in gaining attention for my play."

"How in God's name is he going to gain any attention for your play?" my mother said.

"I have no idea—but in the middle of the conversation I said, 'What about my play?' and he said 'Of course, your play—certainly your play—' That made me believe that he would—it's a play about—well, I hate to harp about this, but it is a play about the poor policy of trying to do in widowed mothers."

He looked at me with a quirky smile, as if I, if no one else, would fathom what it was he was saying. And strangely, what I took from his smile, what I fathomed from this, is that my father actually wanted to die. And he was searching for a way to do it without God knowing. That's what made it difficult. He was trying to kill himself without God finding out—hoodwinking God into killing him, or killing himself behind a bush, and burying himself before God checked on him for the night.

I am certain of this—there was a desire in my father since that August day in 1932 to destroy himself. I know that he bided his time, went to work in silence and ran the projectors and walked to and from the theatre every day, even joined the Rotary sometime in 1955.

"I'm a member," he said to Elizabeth, "I am a member of the damn Rotary, although as you know I agree with Groucho, I'd never want to belong to a club that would have me for a member. I also believe that it was Mother that got me in, simply because they couldn't take her—being, as you know, a woman—so they took me, as kind of a backup."

He started calling other Rotarians Brother. "There's Brother Pete," he would say, and he would hurry me across the road to meet him. "Hello, Brother Pete. How are you?"

I was open to the wound of the Brother Petes and Brother Johns of our town ignoring him. Of course. And was this expected by him—of course. It had to be.

For inside, in the inner life, there was something, some Quasar pulse that I am sure said, at least once or twice a month:

"Well, my good chap Miles, why don't you take the shotgun there. See it, nice and shiny that it is. Well, boy, pick it up—yes, the same one your mother held at bay the jaunty riffraff of the town paid by Joey Elias to be morally outraged not only at her womanhood, but her mixed marriage to boot (well, it was the age)—and squeeze a fine spray into your skull—h'm? Your indeterminist struggle against indeterminist people will be over with a solicitous blast."

I surmise, and Ginger can verify this, that my mother had absolutely no patience with people who killed themselves, and forbade him to do it.

I do not know any more except this:

"Why would anyone blow their head off?" Elizabeth Whispers asked in rhetorical fashion one night, just at supper in February of 1955—which to me was as good a time as any for a speedy dispatch. My father had been pacing up and down and down and up, in a random self-induced terror about something that had happened to him as a child of nine, and about the idea that our lives, and especially the life of Ginger, would not be safe until he took some kind of action.

"Why blow one's head off? A change of pace, I suppose," Father said, looking over at her drearily. "A change of pace, my good woman—a change is as good as a cure, as they say."

"Biscuits?" she offered.

"Quite," he said, sitting down.

My mother was not like my father. She fought Gary Fallon until she got the money back. She phoned his family and told them she would go out to the house. But they said they did not know where he was.

"He's a bastard," my mother said.

"I've often suspected so!" Fallon's father exclaimed.

She went to the house—she was tough enough—and went about their windows looking in, as my father stood near the car with the door opened. It was one of the defining moments of my life—realizing how different Elizabeth Whispers was from my father, seeing how my father yielded to her the responsibility of taking on the world.

"You get out here, Gary, or I'll get the sheriff, I swear I will. I'm not allowing you to ruin my family."

"Do we have sheriffs?" my father whispered out of the side of his mouth rhetorically to my sister and me, sitting wide-eyed in the car.

Gary came out, this honour-bound corporal, hands in his pockets, and shrugged.

"I know you—you're a Whispers," he said. "You grew up without water and a shitter in a goddamn bog." He laughed raucously, and I am sure he thought we would all laugh along with him, for this is what he had laughed at all of his life—the tragedy of the poverty of others.

"And I know a thief and a corrupter of innocents," my mother yelled, her stringy hair falling down her back, her nose sniffing, her white boots covered in dooryard mud.

"And who is this innocent?"

"Why—him," my mother cried, pointing her clenched little fist at my father.

My mother did not give in, and our money was gotten back—well, except for five hundred dollars—and Gary Fallon was out of our life.

"Did he happen to say anything about my play? I suppose it's all up with that too?" Dad asked. My mother looked at him, and started crying in the car. She sat in the car for hours crying that night. She would not come into the house until eleven o'clock. And she cried for days after, saying she would leave, go away and never be back.

"Never!" she yelled.

My father would bow his head.

"Never!"

My father would nod.

"I said never!"

"Yes, I have heard you. You have said never. Well, remember it is you I love, my Miss Whispers!"

My father stood, sometimes in the den, sometimes in our hallway, smiling whenever my mother passed by, watching her collecting "things" to take away.

"Get me the box in the basement," she would say, "get me the box." And he would run to get it. "Get me the trunk in the cedar closet—go get me the trunk!" And he would run and get the trunk.

But she could not leave him. A week or so later he asked her not to tell his mother or press the matter any more, or what he was most afraid of: "Tell the press itself" and:

"If Janie finds out, I will never hear the end of it."

"You don't deserve to."

"You are right, of course," he said, in front of the hallway mirror, trying a Windsor in his tie. "Still and all, she is just starting to get used to me being down at the hall. You know, she actually introduced me as her son. Not that I mind if she does or does not, but then again, working where I am, it is nice to have my employer, who is also my mother, recognize who it is I am."

There was something my father snuck into the house and kept from my mother for well over a year, taking them out only when she was gone and looking at them in a kind of melancholy joy, like a child might look at a fishing rod or bicycle in a store window. Tuning forks for the piano he never played.

FOUR

Usually though, from mid-afternoon until supper he was at his garden, wearing a sombrero, and carrying a small spade, rooting in the earth about his flowers. In the winter he would sit in the far back room, looking out over the river, now and then sketching the trees on the far shore, and he would make his way at night to the theatre to run the projector.

But in the 1950s the world changed for us all. Television came in a kind of spite against us. My father started a campaign against television. For the first time in years he went to the church rectory and asked Bishop Hanrahan to shout down from the pulpit that TV was satanic, or at least imp-like.

"Anything that small has to come from the devil himself," Miles said.

Hanrahan of course would not do this, for he was watching television at the time; and something in him liked the idea of the destruction of Janie's business. My father knew he would not, but tried the gambit anyway. Then he went back to his work. The town no longer needed us, and for many months we ran to an empty house, John Wayne shooting out at empty seats, or Glenn Ford rounding up cattle to solitary lovers in the fifteenth row.

For the first time I saw my grandmother worried, for her lower take meant that many first runs were too expensive. Each night, driven by Dingle, she would come down to the house to see Father.

"We will have to ride this storm out," Janie said to us one night. "But there'll be no television for us, will there. You won't buy one, will you, Elizabeth?"

"Television is a gadget that won't work," my father said with conviction.

Dingle, feeling superior to Father, would glare about at us. Sometimes he would point his finger at Miles, when Janie was directing him to do something.

"I want you," Janie would say, and Dingle would point, "to go to Saint John tomorrow and see Mr. Winchester"—point, point—"and tell him for me, in person, I will not pay thirty-five percent for a goddamn Elizabeth Taylor. No matter what the take is in big cities, it is not the same as"—point, point—"here!"

Still, the first runs, our life's blood, were slowly drying up. The old Grand began to look dowdy, and though my grandmother put down new carpet in the foyer, spruced up the marquee, and advertised more aggressively, people no longer came in the numbers they had. In those years we had no TV, as if fighting against the modern world, in a similar fashion as the Whispers people themselves had no TV because of religious scruples.

Though Ginger and I longed for and lobbied hard for TV. We were found at night, on those soft twilight June nights when our mother looked for us around the neighbourhood, staring in the windows of houses where the artificial lights of the televised world had captured our hearts. I was more guilty than she, for I knew how my father plotted against TV, how he did a song and dance at times before the main feature to draw a crowd. My heart went out to him, to his wonderous sadness and his enormous plight, and I vowed I would not leave when I grew up, but would help him any way I could.

During these days my sister saved money in her piggy bank to buy one of our arch-enemies. And in 1956 (the worst year our theatre had), when she had saved eleven dollars, I took her to find the place the televisions were.

I found myself trying to haul her sled over dirty snow, with Ginger watching me with the most beautiful brown eyes of any child I have ever seen. I turned onto a side street, with the window shades down on most of the stores, and the sound of traffic disjointed and faint. It was late afternoon, late February. I entered a small, depressing shop, with my sister by the hand. I remember a big, silent clock on my right, and a stack of shoes, some coins under glass, and an old office fan. The radio was on, and a faint light shone under the dial. There were beaded drapes behind the counter.

"You don't get TVs in here," Ginger said.

I told her the man in here sold them.

Four gongs came from the radio, and I looked beyond the press on my right where the piles of boots and shoes were and saw a man staring at us from behind the beaded curtain.

"Who are you?" he said.

"I am Wendell," I said, taking off my thick glasses.

"You're Janie King's boy," he said. His voice was distant and cautious. His face was cleanshaven, with some red blotches on his cheeks. His hair was short and iron grey, his eyes steely, his pants rumpled, and his slippers frayed at the toes.

I shook my head.

"If you aren't Janie's, who are you?"

"I am Miles King's son."

"I didn't know he was married—or had children. How old is she?" He was staring at my sister.

"She's four. She is Ginger King."

"Ah," he said. "I'll tell you what I'll do—I'll get someone to take you home. So your mom won't miss you. Okay? You know Sister Putsy? Well then, if she can come, you will go home with her."

He picked up the telephone and made a call. Fifteen minutes passed as we sat near the door and watched him mend a shoe, which he seemed to tear at with no enthusiasm. Now and then he looked at us over his glasses, staring at my sister and then down again at the shoe.

There was a tinkling of the bell and Sister Putsy came in. We considered her our aunt, because of her closeness to Walter, the history of which at the time we did not know. But she was one of my father's few friends, and it was only to her he spoke those few times he went to mass. She sent us a card at Christmas, and except for the company card that Gram sent to us, it was the only card we received.

"Are they Kings?" the man asked, pointing at us with a worn black file in a kind of "I told you so" voice that made me shiver.

"They are," Putsy said.

"Well, take them out of here."

"Of course."

Ginger took her hand, and I followed them with the sled, and we made our way past Radio Street in the evening dark. Not knowing anything then of the world she and our father had lived in before we came, not knowing of the hilarity this man had created at my father's expense, the laughter and spite seeming to have dissipated among the tired old shoes. He did sell televisions; they were kept in the far room. His last gambit to destroy our empire. Hannibal still planning his revenge up to the moment poison was drunk.

When Joey Elias saw Ginger, she looked almost identical to her aunt. Chance was cruel to send this child, this changeling, into his life. It made him feel what he hated.

So he went to visit Putsy the next night. She lived in a small room behind the convent. Her walls were decorated with posters and pictures of people he did not know—the forgotten ones, some in wheelchairs, some obviously retarded, many having to be spoon-fed. Their names were written under their pictures, and the dates when they had died. These were the people she helped Father Carmichael with. Joey could not help but feel a kind of disgust at this—she had wasted her life.

"I'm doing fine," she said. "I cannot walk very well, but Walter has had much practice at that and helps me cope when he comes here to visit. We are like an old married couple except I'm in this room at the back of the convent and he's in the old theatre downtown." She laughed at this, showing her broken front teeth.

"But if you had stayed with me," Joey Elias said angrily, "if you had—I would have taken you to Boston, to New York, or the Mayo Clinic! I would have found out why you can't walk well—I would have taken you to the greatest specialists in the States. We'd go south, you'd get better there—to Baltimore or somewhere."

Putsy looked at him a moment. The reason she couldn't walk well was the after-effect of venereal disease, though there was no trace of it in her now, and it was her husband who had given it to her. Though both he and Rebecca had remained relatively unaffected, she had been in constant pain for twenty-five years.

"There was once a very rich man," she said, trying to sound like Carmichael, "and he lived in the places you just told me about. And his son was dying. And do you know what? He took his son

189

everywhere—for money was no object. And he went to Boston, and New York and Louisiana, and to the Mayo Clinic, but no one could save his son. And in the end, just a while ago, he brought his son here because of Father Carmichael. Because he had heard that the priest could heal people. Everyone thinks he can, and it has been documented on the radio that people say he is miraculous."

"I know that. So what?" Joey Elias said.

"But my priest could not heal the child either. And now of course people blame the priest for not doing what he never said he could, and the bishop is angry because it has repercussions here."

"What's the point?"

"Well, the man had already tried that which you wish me to, and came here in hope of trying what I already have. So you see it is not up to us to decide anything about our lives."

"That's nonsense!" Joey shouted. "When I saw you, you were a little gutter rat—you and your sister—and I helped you, both of you, I did, and you are not even grateful, either of you. I don't decide? I fought to make my way to Canada—I did what I had to do. Don't say for one second it was not my decision. If I had not bribed a guard and slipped onto a boat, I wouldn't have gotten to England, and I was little more than a child, so don't tell me that what we do doesn't matter. I was scared out of my wits the guard would arrest me on the spot, but I did it. So don't tell me that it doesn't matter. I was shaking like a leaf and I begged him—I begged him, peeing my pants—and he took me and hid me. Don't tell me that does not matter!" His hands were trembling and his eyes were watering. A cold, dark wind came up and rattled against the window.

"I didn't tell you that it didn't matter," Putsy said calmly. "I simply said you did not decide. You think it was you who decided the guard could be bribed? You just admitted you were terrified. You didn't know a thing, Joey. In fact, you expected the opposite."

"I did not."

"What if the opposite had happened? It would have been ordinary—maybe even expected—for the guard to grab you and hustle you off to the police. Taken the bit of money you offered him and then run you in. Your life would have ended far differently. It would have ended like it might have ended for your brother. No—you see, someone other than you decided, as always. And someone has decided for me. I found that out the night I lost the key. It was me who got drunk, yes—and I accept responsibility for anything that I've done wrong—but it has taken me years to realize that it wasn't my intent to loose the key."

"What key?" Elias shouted. "You keep going on about a damn key!"

"I know you had a brother who died in Europe. You came to me the night Georgina was lost, and you told us how terrible you felt, for you had a small brother who died in Europe—you couldn't get him out of Poland when you left. You told us that. Maybe that is *your* key. I'll pray that you will find your key and have peace of mind."

Elias stood, trembling, ready to strike her, and then abruptly left the room. All this time, unknown to Putsy, Walter had been sitting outside the other door of her room, listening. He slipped down the back stairway.

"Walter P. McLeary, late of the orphanage, I've sent you," he had thought when he first saw her in 1929. Yes, perhaps it had all happened just like that.

What in the world had happened to Putsy? Elias wondered. Where was that young woman who used to be so wild, who carried a knife, who seduced young boys and broke their hearts? She was with Father Carmichael at his little retreat taking care of people who couldn't live a day without help; they couldn't feed themselves or dress themselves; they would be better off if they had been given needles and put to sleep. And she read the New Testament and a little book called *The Way* and every day she followed exactly what these books said. A real martyr and stupid to boot. Her stupidity rankled him now, for he needed her. He needed her because he was growing old and becoming scared, and he had no one to love him any more.

"We lost her," he thought. "She's become a religious fanatic."

Well, how did this happen? It did not happen overnight. It took Joey Elias himself to do it. And in his heart of hearts he knew why. She could have forgiven him everything, except Rebecca. For the first time in almost thirty years he began to see what had happened. He remembered how strange Putsy had acted at the house, how he couldn't talk to her and then he remembered how she had fallen on her knees and begged him, how powerful he'd felt—for a second.

Anyway, all of that was over years ago, and he tried not to think of it. Yet whenever he spoke to Putsy, the same thoughts always occurred. His betrayal of her became fresh and new as a bright flower once again.

"But it was Rebecca's betrayal," he said now. "Rebecca betrayed her own sister—that's the kind of girl she is. She's a Druken—they're all the same, that lot."

He passed the place his Biograph once stood. In 1944 Janie bought the property and had it bulldozed into the ground, and made it into a park in memory of her daughter, Georgina King. He passed the little statuette of my aunt and made his way along Chatham Street in the gloom.

FIVE

We left at night, usually. It was my mother's idea, her hope assuring my sympathy, being still a child. It was her way to save Father, although I doubt that my father ever wanted to be saved from anything. But Elizabeth tried anyway. Everything was clean, everything was pressed, everything packed into four suitcases. Travelling light like escapees running for some damn train that kept moving just out of reach.

Sometimes our escapes were short-lived. On three or four occasions, Janie did not even know we had made a break until we were back at our place going about our business in the usual way. Sometimes we stayed away a month, living out of suitcases at various places.

We went in summer, when I could smell smoke off the wind, hear in the heat the short on-again off-again call of a crow in the dead silence. I remember air shimmering off a lone spruce tree in the middle of a field, while my sister was behind the vehicle being sick.

"It's because I'm skinny," Ginger said. "I would rarely get car-sick if I were not skinny—and it's just such car trips that leave me skinny—because I continually puke." She said this not only in defiance but as a celebration of her willingness to be pulled away once again from everything she knew, from house, from school, from Gram.

"You are doomed," I said to her.

"Yes. But no more than you, Wendy dear," she promised. (I invoked my mother's rule that she not call me Wendy.) Then she looked at me with her huge brown eyes and gave a smile, then immediately returned to her retching.

"I am a goner, unless—or is it until?—I have some kind of a strawberry milkshake," she said.

We laughed, leaving little echoes somewhere in the air beyond us, and got into the car again, and drove.

Many times Father could not continue without his libation. He would pull over on the side of the road, and while wind from other vehicles whipped down upon us, he would drink. Then, being at least a little drunk, he would ask which one of us—Elizabeth (who could not drive), myself, or Ginger—was willing to take the wheel.

Once, I woke in the back seat, the last rays of sun lingering like jellyfish trails on the wide, empty fields, to see my father slumped in the passenger seat, my mother sleeping next to me in the back, and Ginger herself, sitting on three books (one being Mother's Bible), navigating the turns of a solitary secondary road somewhere in the lost province of Nova Scotia.

Or piling into our Chevy, with Dad's budgie upside down in his shirt pocket—sure way of putting Budgie to sleep—and a road map, and snow against the flat green windows, off we went toward our destiny, perched on the swing of despair, sure to make it out of the birdcage and into our future, somewhere where my father's brilliance would be appreciated and my mother would not feel a complete and utter failure in the queasy company of her relatives, in a town that dispatched rumour against us at a nod.

We would wake to my parents arguing in the car when they thought we were asleep.

"A woman you proposed marriage to," my mother would be saying.

"A scurrilous rumour—I did not propose marriage to my mother."

"Well, someone very close to her in age."

"There was, I assure you, not only an age difference of upwards of four to five months but a—how do you say?—a certain joie de vivre—"

"Osteoporosis—"

"That too," Father would admit.

On these trips, precious as they were to Elizabeth Whispers to try and escape, to live a life as she said, "For her family."

We instead relived the harshness of her childhood. With a lightless, luckless, endless bunch of non-ecumenical Whisperses, sitting in the dry rooms while outside snow shuffled in a dance against them. From her moment of birth, brought to life in the bitter and blithe gales, the jaundiced afternoons in a house that went onward without end, seeing a small mud-racked dooryard and a mother alone with nine children.

So Elizabeth's life was retold in whispers, in "Whispers' whispers" when she thought we were asleep. Her mother alone and with nine children. Her marriage to our father, the promise once as alluring as a golden bowl filled with shiny silver shone out now in slivers of a life forgotten, mundane as bric-a-brac, and alloyed with anger and dumb courage.

We always came back to town, to try and try again, to the streets, the shaded trees, the nooks and crannies in the park, the small shops, the buildings stretched out like dominoes along the side of the river and around the sundial in the square.

She had rented a cottage for us in 1960, but Father would not go, for the memory of his sister who could not come. All that summer in the smoke-fouled heat, Mother would step out of our bungalow, shading her eyes from the sun, to wait for our father who walked up Radio Street and into the house at noon, and back out at two, and home at five, and back out at six, and home at eleven, wearing his suit and carrying a brief-case as a banker might (it contained his daily allotment of gin). My poor mother making futile ultimatums and Father answering, "Yes, of course we are going, and we will go—we are sure to go. You are right about the children—they cannot swim in the birdbath, I know that. You may think I do not—yet many times as a young man I was left alone with not much more than a birdbath myself . . ." And his thoughts would trail off, and he would reknot his tie, clutch his briefcase, give his wife a peck on the cheek, and be off down the street, with the wisest little clink of the gin bottle against the glass. (Or two glasses, in case he could find someone to drink with, which most often he could not.)

Janie and my mother were at constant war over the prospects of my father. My father tried to keep the peace between them, but it was not easy. A fight over a raise erupted every so often. Holidays as well. But all was forfeited to Janie's immaculate will. I would listen to them while I ate my breakfast in silence, or at night from the relative comfort of my bed, seeing the hall light shining against a small patch of carpet and hearing:

"It's my mother, you see—so I cannot go."

"Why?" Elizabeth would cry.

"I can't tell you why—I mean, if I could tell you why, I would be in Boston now, drinking with the Kennedys."

I always wanted to make it up to my mother. I would think that at a certain time, when I got a certain age I would take her on a trip to Disneyland. I prepared for it by trying to save money. I told her in my halting way one day, during an autumn rain shower, that she and I would go. She smiled at me, and then burst into tears.

When the fights got bad, Janie would distance herself from her grandchildren, and Roy Dingle would act as go-between. Or I would act as a go-between for ourselves, going up to her house on plain afternoons with the smell of varnish in the porch, to be hauled up on the carpet in my father's place.

"I think you are a miserable, ungrateful boy."

"Yes, Gram."

"Do you drive a bicycle?"

"Yes, ma'am."

"And do you know who bought it for you?"

I would be silent, hearing the clock sound far off somewhere, the shuffle of papers on Janie's desk.

"*Tarzan* or Randolph Scott for the Saturday matinee?"

"I'm not sure," I would answer. She would peer at me.

"Ginger wants *Psycho*—says the kids are up for it." She would pause. "*Tarzan* it will be."

She did not come to our house for two years, because of a misunderstanding over a box of jelly doughnuts, and we did not go to hers (except to be hauled up on the carpet), save for Ginger, who was "in her camp," as Elizabeth Whispers said.

"She is not in her camp," Father whispered.

"Completely in her camp," Elizabeth Whispers said.

"Good God—you think so?"

"Absolutely."

Gram, of course, had chosen Ginger as her own, a replacement for Georgina, in her middle age. It was not only easy to understand, it was also impossible to fight. Fighting against it was like so much salt to a wound my father himself had caused. And so Ginger was freer because of this than I was. Far freer. *Psycho*, indeed. Ginger was sought out and fussed over, and coddled.

So it was hard to believe that Ginger was not in Gram's camp when she went to Gram's wearing her white fur coat, or her navy blue London Fog with the wonderful high white boots and the peach-coloured butterfly in her black hair. She had her own room, her own bath, her own hair dryer to make her hair look like Connie Francis's.

"Convenience," Ginger said to me, with a worldly air, "is what I have—and you Wendy, my boy, do not."

It was Ginger who contacted Janie to tell her where we were the time Dad made his successful pitch to leave, in 1962. Ginger could not leave Gram in the dark about where we were, even though she had promised our mother she would.

"I will reroute your mail," Janie said, and hung up.

We had gotten as far as Hamilton then. We could look out our apartment window and see street lights below us, along the winding roadways, and smell the cadaver-like whiff from the mill against the placid lake. My father had taken a job away from his mother for the first time since the war. He began to eat better, and refused a drink—even to the point of pouring gin down the sink (though he closed his eyes and turned his head away as he did so).

"There is no need for this any more—I am absolutely cured of it all. In fact, I could be crushed by gin bottles without taking a sip," he said. "I could take a gin bath, right now, scrub my ears and my toes and my lips, and never indulge in so much as a sip."

He gave talks against gin to us. "Never drink gin," he would say to me, with an inquiry in his look, "and if you do, my boy, make sure it is nothing much more than a quart a day."

He had become a projectionist at a theatre in downtown Hamilton, a dreary place the colour of rainwater, where I was not allowed even on Saturdays, and Mother stayed inside in our eighth-floor apartment, sending me out to the corner store for bread. Though in essence we were in hiding, she and Dad were happy.

"It seems as if my past life is nothing more than a dream—unfortunate to have dreamed it, but nonetheless over," he said one night to all of us sitting about our little table, he at one end and Mother at the other, and since there was a wall on one side Ginger and I sitting side by side.

"Now I will produce," he said. "I will have my own studio and paint. I will be not of the fashion, though, for as you know, my Elizabeth Whispers, I never was." He cut into his beef. "I will paint grandly, and well. I am elated that I feel no compulsion to ever go back to our river—for I ask you, what has our river done for us?"

We had been away a month, and Janie was rerouting mail to our apartment. I remember, as one does, a seemingly insignificant event that made a profound change. An envelope came in April. It had been mailed to my father by Maurice the photographer, who, in cleaning out the leftover photos from his father's career before moving the studio to its new location, had found two photos my father had paid for long ago.

I had entered a school called the Gift of the Blessed Sacrament with kids professing worldliness and being intolerant of the country boy. I was lonely, and overprotective of Ginger. We would stand together in the playground as the sun glanced off the orange jungle gyms and swings that swung on rusted chains high overhead. We walked together to and from that school, with our clothes so well ironed they never wrinkled no matter how we tried.

And then one day I came home to see my father in the dark near the curtains, with his hat on his knee, and those photos from Maurice in his hand. He sat with the photos for three solid days, as Ginger and I left for and came home from school with about as much interest in life as he was showing. He did not eat, though plates piled up about him on TV trays, or speak. The budgie flew against his head, or against the curtains, a bird in the house. But nothing could prod him forward—not even a phone call from the dreary Hamilton theatre telling him he must go to work or be fired.

"Tell them," he said, "to fire me, please—or fire upon me, whatever they will."

Then he put the pictures on the small table and left the apartment for places unknown. For some den where he could drink. There he would drink our savings down to nothing—there he would drink away our rent.

"I can fight almost anything—except a ghost," my mother said.

I studied the pictures, faded with time, cracked and dazed by a kind of glow that made a halo around the child's head. There she was, my little aunt Georgina, shy after a fashion, just the way he had dressed her that day, in her dress and her hat and what must have been her purple gloves, staring up at the camera trying to look— what, into the future or her mother's gaze? There was a delight of life on her face; he, Miles, in his summer short pants and suit jacket with wide lapels, his top hat tilted just a spot back to reveal his dandy- ish toff of blond hair, a smile on his face and with a protective arm around her, keeping her forever safe in the quiet vagary of that bygone day.

The quick unknowing note that accompanied these photos said:

"These may be of interest to you, Mr. King—I do not know who they are of, actually—but your name was fastened by paperclip. They must have been taken when you were a child—by my father who you may have heard has passed away—they were found among paid for photos in the bottom of the 2nd drawer, and get this—just like one of your mother's movie plots—they come to us directly from 1932. Yours truly, John Maurice."

I was looking at my aunt, that child who had never grown to womanhood, and saw Ginger staring back.

My mother always blamed Janie for having those photos sent, calculating my father's response, to go back home in a rush. Like a man turning back toward an avalanche to save someone he had no hope of finding, or my mother as Lot's wife desperately trying not to be turned into stone.

We left the apartment in the dark and travelled east toward Toronto, onward to Montreal, and into the heart of Quebec, going ever east, past the lonely mountains toward our New Brunswick home, our great sad river of the brokenhearted, for no other reason than that my father was not free, and we had nowhere else to go but with him. And of course Budgie came back too.

When we came back, Janie ignored us for months, and our friends, as few as they were, had scattered.

I think my sister was as lonely as I was, as we spent most days on the sidewalk pavement, without our gram to come down with her jelly doughnuts (this is how she showed her love). There is a look crossing a child's face when they wish to share their parents' dilemma over something that was never done by them, to remain friends with whoever it is they need; you might see it in the sunlight refracted in their reflection against the bike's handles turning at the end of the street.

SIX

Yet the question remains—did my parents have any friends? None on average—one or two at the most, and they were my mother's friends, who liked her "in spite of Miles," and who felt sorry for her "because of Miles." My father remembered them from his youth—a youth he did not, because of shame, tell my mother about so she would not have to suffer with him the memories he had of pushing Georgina in her carriage, of the terror these good people (for they were in truth good people) had once offered him. He did his best (for sanity's sake, and the memory of his sister) to ignore them or, if that was not possible, and it often wasn't, to insult them (being, for the memory of his sister, duty bound to do so).

A few months after we got home, Elizabeth Whispers decided to have a dinner party—her first in twelve years of marriage—with the Waltlings and the Conroys.

"They all attacked me before—what should prevent them from doing so now?"

"Don't be silly, Miles. You were a child."

"What if it's an ambush? If it's an ambush, I will retreat to this hill. You, dear Elizabeth, will be left to your own devices."

She told him he was being silly. He said to her as a last resort, knowing that she had a tender heart and if she did not care how he was treated she could not be cavalier once she knew this, "Oh, yes, when I was small they clubbed a little flock of parishioners who had come to hear a tenor sing 'Ave Maria.' Your friends tore at them— it's on record. I was appalled. They look safe now, but I assure you, the clean clothes and the cherub children are an act."

He was not lying so much as he was simply terrified to meet these people in his house, on his ground where he would have to smile and mince willy-nilly with those from that bygone time. And of course he believed that cherub children were always an act.

So the night of the party he sat by himself in the room, in the dark, with his hat in his hand, near one door as the guests arrived at the other door. I remember the light shining on his kneecaps, and now and then the top of his hat appearing as if in mime, and disappearing again.

They would call out to him, in jovial mood while he sat morose and drinking, and my sister and I on the stair steps looking through the banister railings to the dining room one moment, to the knees and feet of our father the next. A drama was being played out here. Bob Conroy the effusive car salesman, the goody-goody cheery man, and his wife, high-haired Sandra, with her tiara and her looking quick as an assassin into the corner, to turn and giggle at her husband. (Told beforehand, I am sure, that my father was a witless fool, and believing it because she herself was one, nor was there a poetry course at university she would take in later years to make a statement about women, could ever help that.) My mother mortified; they—these good middle-management people of our town—the only people my mother was brave enough to ever aspire to, the Waltlings who owned a clothes shop for the "Fresh young man and girl."

"Why don't you come and join us, Miles—talk about old times?" Hal Waltling said.

"(Under his breath) Good God—(aloud) no, Hal, I'm fine by myself—thank you very much—You see I'm not much company without my medication."

"Oh, do you take medication, Miles?" Mona Waltling said.

My father poured a half glass of gin and drank it straight. Then, clearing his throat, he answered, "I have in the past, Mrs. Waltling, and I'm fairly willing to again, whenever I can procure—or is it obtain?—it."

"Please call me Mona."

"Call you what?"

"Mona—my name."

Long silence.

"Momma?"

"No—Mona."

"(Under his breath) It is I believe enough to make a man stiff—although I suppose I am."

"What's that?" Mrs. Waltling asked.

"Nothing—not a thing—thinking in some fashion or another to myself."

"And what medicine do you take, Miles?" Bob yelled.

"Ah—well—as much of it as I can—when I can convince whoever dispenses it to dispense it to me."

"And what is it, Miles—what is it?"

"It all depends on what the meaning of 'it' is, I suppose. So Demerol when it works, morphine if I'm truly lucky."

"I mean, what illness do you have?" Bob Conroy said.

"Schizophrenia, I believe. However, no one is certain at the institute."

There was a gasp and a polite giggle from Sandra Conroy, who in her life had always hoped others would be the butt of jokes she herself could never get.

"Miles, you don't go to any institute," Elizabeth Whispers said happily.

"Not any more," Miles said, and he cheered himself by pouring another glass.

"But it's our dinner party, Miles," my mother pleaded happily, coming to him, and beckoning with her fingers against her brand-new summer skirt, taken out of the box that day.

"Yes, it is—so go to it," Father whispered.

"You come," Elizabeth Whispers whispered.

"Oh, don't worry," the guests said happily. "He doesn't feel well."

"He's fine," Elizabeth said.

"Come here, Elizabeth, dear," Mona Waltling said. "It's just a little brouhaha—we have them too, don't we, Hal?"

"Of course we do," Hal said.

Bob looked most cheery. He smiled and clutched Sandra's hand for fear of another small giggle on her part. Elizabeth walked back to her seat, as if, I remember, something had snapped inside her. Her little jazzy record, whatever it was, valueless to jazz, I'm sure, but making a splash with the early-to-bedders, seemed distant and forlorn. The smell of my father's flowers came through the window, with a damp middle-hour air.

There was a long silence. The brouhaha comment seemed to have been forgotten completely until, five minutes later, my father answered thus, quietly at first and then raising his pitch until he was almost shouting: "What in God's name—in the pleasant sight of Christ's good blood—would you, Mona Waltling, know about anything approaching a brouhaha? Your stifling marriage, your rather too big ass, your compendium of knowledge about nothing at all, your listless gossip about me no doubt, even your troubles seem to be of the quality that would resist to the death any brouhaha. In fact, when you do have a brouhaha—you will, I assure you, never live through it. I myself have had, so far in my life, at last count three dozen brouhahas—the death of my sister and a major war."

Silence. Gin being poured into my father's suddenly gleeful cup. My father feeling he had gone too far, I think, stood and approached the table, weaving just a tad, but not much considering he had drunk almost a quart of gin straight in the last hour. He stood above them as my mother sliced the roast and put potatoes and gravy on the plate for him, set it at the head of the table.

Miles sat down, the budgie's feet sticking up out of his shirt pocket. He looked at his guests, lowered his head, looked up again, and tried to smile.

He looked across at Sandra Conroy as if she would be his only friend here (he as always about friendship was mistaken) and said, "Oh, be joyful." He lifted his glass and had a drink. Then, without glancing Elizabeth Whispers's way, he picked up his potatoes with his fingers and tried bravely to stuff them, all at odds, into his mouth. Another saturnine girlish giggle—which was more like a giffle—from Sandra.

"The gravy is now cool," he said, making two spots with his index finger and looking at his guests as he licked it.

"You are very tipsy tonight, Miles," Mona Waltling said.

"Not tipsy, Mrs. Waltling—not in the least tipsy. I am very *drunk*—and you are bone ugly. I will wake up sober, and you will wake up—bone ugly," Father said, quoting Churchill, of course.

Hal gave a smile. My father raised his glass to the joke that had gone askew.

The rest of the dinner was eaten—if eaten can be the word—in abject silence, bordering on incivility. The jazz record stuck on "a Caz Caz—Waz waz—bibbity bobbity boo." My mother said, "Uh-oh," went to the record player and released it for good. The budgie's feet began to pump up and down, and Father suddenly, like a magician—and of course he was—tossed it with a flourish into the air, where it landed on Sandra Conroy's tiara. She sat rigid, her arms flailing out in front of her, her expression a silent scream, Budgie hanging for dear life to a strand of dyed blond hair.

The guests were gone by nine. Ginger and I, waiting on the steps for our mother's instructions to rush forward and be introduced as the showpiece to these such clever people she so wanted to impress, were left on those steps, sometimes, I think, forever.

My father put an apology in the paper. Printed in uppercase letters it read: "I called Mona Waltling bone ugly. This, I realize now, is overstated. The word 'bone' should never have been used. Miles King."

No one ever said my father could not be cruel.

SEVEN

That summer my father's evening primrose won a contest, and he was very happy about it. 'Happy' is not a word I would use to describe my father's many moods, for to those who did not understand him they were irrelevant shifts in a landscape mute and undeterred.

"It shows me that I am doing something right," he told the reporter from the local paper. "I am oxidizing the soil and I am planting them as close to what I call their natural state as I can, without using the variety of artificial stimulants that have become so popular nowadays. I suppose you could say I am playing God—but not in an arrogant way. I let the flowers smell themselves, if you know what I mean."

His flowers were arranged in our back yard with a tremendous flourish, and my grandfather's flowers were still kept up each and every day. One of his roses had come through generations of rain and sleet and some spite, from his father's first perennial, to bloom again.

"A goodly amount of them I am pleased with, though I have not had luck making fruit pies with my pin cherries."

It was later in the year when I learned about the makeup of my mother's dinner party. I came upon it piece by piece, here and there—at grandmother's house and at Charlie's Barbershop in the talk of two elderly men. And even then in the vagary of children's concepts it didn't register in any real way for a while. Now, as I write this, it seems strangely monumental. Mr. Conroy and Mr. Waltling were two of the five who as children had been hired by Joey Elias to tar my father's pants. My mother did not know this.

When I found this out I approached him one night when he was watching television. (He had disobeyed his mother and had bought one with the money he had won in the primrose contest.)

"I'm sorry about your trouble—when you were little," I blurted too loud and fast, I thought, for I did not know what else to say or even what trouble he had had specifically.

"Ah well," he said.

"They must have been very difficult times," I said, trying to sound grown-up. "I mean, I heard about it in a barbershop—when you—were sent to the psychiatrist. I am sorry."

"Ah yes. Well—'tis no matter." He smiled briefly, went to take my hand, and couldn't quite bring himself to.

The next evening, he was sitting alone in the dark of the den, and the sun sank lower, and shadows crossed the hardwood living-room floor. My mother was out (where, I didn't know). My father's meal, of turkey pie and a glass of milk and lemon pie, was sitting on the table, resplendent in its stiff mundanity. The cage door was open, the swing hung motionless.

Old Budgie bird, companion of his many trips, carried in his pocket or his briefcase, and on occasion drinking companion and a tippler of gin, had died at some point that afternoon, lying at the very back of her cage when he went to take her for a walk.

"She has soared her way to heaven on an eagle's wing," he said, "and we will all do that someday, I'm sure, to meet those who have left us behind—unwitting champions of our sadness and despair."

Money flowed through and over Ginger. She could not go a day without buying something. It did not matter what it was, or how it fit into anything. A pin at a fair, a plate with a rooster on it. If she did not get the money from Mother, she got it from Gram. The great contest for her affection, which everyone but me seemed to want, was thus engaged. She was beautiful, and boyfriends aplenty courted her from the time she was twelve. She seemed to have more of it—that is, money—and do less with it than any person I knew. It walked with her, when that splendid young womanhood was formed, issued from her enchanting smile, and her long, dark hair, and her whimsical sadness, and her flourish for triumph, and her loneliness under the spring sun, and her small breasts, which she refused to cover in a brassiere, and her maniacal truths about injustice that the youth of the world have always carried, and it lay down with her in bed at night and arose again, to an ovation of tired birds.

Everything Gram gave her, Mom gave too, so she was twice invested, twice coddled, and she took it as her due, and strode off to school with it, or waltzed with it at youth dances in the Catholic church that Bishop Hanrahan chaperoned. It walked downtown with her on Saturday afternoons, and sat on cement fences smoking away the listless and bored Sunday afternoons, resplendent and insecure. Yet it was always alone. And so was she. And so was I.

In 1965, Gram and Mom finally agreed on something. After talking to Sister Putsy, they decided Ginger would be better off at the convent, under the tutelage of Sister St. Beatrice May, where she would get up at six-thirty in the dark of winter, shower with forty other children, make her bed, go to mass, have breakfast, and be in class at eight-thirty in the morning, where she would study the major courses, from Latin to theology.

At four-thirty classes would be done. She would have an hour of gym, then supper, evening prayers, study from seven till nine, when lights would be out. She would sleep in a dorm with those other convent girls, chaperoned at all times by two nuns. She would wear long, white gowns to bed and dress in a blue-and-white convent uniform, with the pin of her saint on her collar. Putsy would keep an eye on her.

I knew she was devastated, and scared. But no one had time for her. Walter McLeary was dying, his great spirit ebbing away. He had suffered a series of small strokes, and once fell down some stairs, and everyone was worried about him. My father's drinking increased again—instead of a quart a day, he would drink a quart and a pint. He still dressed impeccably, though, and went to work, and many nights did not come home, lying in slumber across the theatre seats. And on those long afternoons when I searched him out, I would see him alone at his favourite restaurant drinking gin.

"I can have my favourite saint on my collar," Ginger said, to Mom one cool, airy August day. "What saint would you choose?"

"Ask your brother," she said. "I am not informed on Catholic saints."

"St. Francis of Assisi," I said.

"Ah—everyone will have him. As a saint, he's the big cheese. So I must have a different saint, maybe the saint our great-grandfather had—St. Hemseley, is it, who died of rabies—or was bitten to death by rabbits?"

"Fought the Romans," I said.

"Oh—those guys," she said, tears in her eyes.

As August fled in shadow and wind from the bay, another year turning over, time itself fleeing somewhere, with short squalls against Father's flowers and rose bushes, the notice came from St. Mary's about enrolment and orientation. We told her we would be with her and make sure she was settled. But at the same time, Walter was taken to the hospital, and there was a smell of death over our house and business. And it left young Ginger alone in the house, packing by herself.

Walter pretended bravely that he did not know his death was pending. I went to visit him every other day. How strangely small he was now; even his head seemed tiny. Sometimes he was distracted by some mystery he was trying to solve. I asked him one afternoon what he was thinking about.

"I want to know why I was born like I was born—and no one can answer me," he said. "Not the nurses, not the doctors, not the saints, not even God. Father Carmichael said it was a great blessing, but he never had to walk a mile in these shoes, did he? See my foot?" He lifted his naked foot for me to look at and laughed. "Many a girl ran from that foot."

He flicked his cigar ash and spoke in a hoarse whisper as I wheeled him out onto the balcony. But after a few minutes he was tired and wanted to go back inside.

Putsy would come and sit with him, and I would go home, and then Father would relieve Putsy.

One day he was furious because the nurse took his cigar from him and threw it in the sink.

"I want to go home!" he yelled.

"When you get better," Miles managed to say.

"He won't get better," the nurse said, with perverse enthusiasm. "And no more cigars!"

"I'll get better," he said, clutching Dad's hand. "You and Janie can't do it all alone." Then he whispered, "Put a cigar in my housecoat pocket, okay?"

That night, he sat up, reached for the cigar Father had hidden in his housecoat, and suffered a massive stroke. He was dead ten minutes later.

Then next day Ginger went to the convent. That afternoon, when I went into her room to see how she was doing, she had already gone. On the bed was a picture of her and Mom, and a twenty-dollar bill she had forgotten to take, her small red purse open to the air, and four new scribblers left on the dresser. Everyone so busy no one reminded her of what she did not take. No one said goodbye.

Dark clouds conjured above our house, too stingy to rain.

As the business faltered my father became more uncertain about himself, and he found running the theatre sheer agony. Janie then turned on Elizabeth and did what to her was unforgivable. She called her a poor mother.

After this particularly angry exchange, my mother wanted Dad to go away again, and had a cousin of Bob Conroy's offer him a job in Windsor, Ontario, for more money than he was earning. It was a sound insurance job that he could just step into, be there in a fortnight in an age when insurance jobs seemed just the ticket. Elizabeth begged me to help her snare him.

"To sell insurance—good God," he said. "To be the thousandth-thousandth man in the last blush of innocent conniving and hail good-fellow-well-met cannibalism, against dour overworked and uneducated Canadians all reaching for the ever disappearing brass ring—disappearing so fast that the speed of light makes a kind of momentary curtsy on the screen?"

"I don't know what that means," Elizabeth said.

"You know something? Either do I. But I have bigger fish to fry, Miss Whispers, exquisite fish. Not like my age-old and long-gone guppies, I tell you that."

"What?"

"You will see presently."

My father decided to come to Janie's aid and to open a small drive-in to offset the Imperial's second runs. If the drive-in could book these pictures before the Imperial, it might stave off the inevitable, or so he said. He wouldn't be completely successful by this, but it was a flanking motion, which he being an officer in the artillery knew something about. And with that he took out a loan from the bank—the first King loan in forty years, a large amount of money as far as our mother was concerned, never having seen a cheque for that amount ever drawn—and bought a tumble-down drive-in on the outskirts of town, a woebegone place deserted as a village and tormented by crows, with a sad canteen and a dilapidated projection booth, with a multitude of Stingers surrounding it.

"I will strike a blow for Janie and end our estrangement. I look at this as a challenge in the same way Monty looked at El Alamein—though not as big a theatre. Ha! Get it, Wendy?" he said as we walked together one afternoon, one of the few of our walks, and he picked up stones to toss haphazardly at the bent and scraped speaker-poles.

Seeing he was happy, I gathered my nerve and asked him about our past, about Elias, whom I had been hearing about at school. Nothing so much to inform me, but enough to whet my curiosity.

"Oh—Mr. Elias. What about him?"

"I heard that he knows what really happened to my great-grandfather."

"You have heard that?"

"Yes, lots of people say so, but no one can prove it. They say he had something to do with it—and even Sister Putsy—lots of people."

"Lots of people say so. Lots of people say much about us, don't they?"

He sounded satirical at that moment, ironic and cruel, and I did not like this side of him—the side I had seen at mother's dinner. The night before, in some roaring torment, he had demanded I stay with him and work for him. I felt as trapped now as he must have once.

Sensing all of this, he said, "Never you mind, son. You go on and become a scientist or something—see, for instance, if ball bearings hit at a peculiar angle with a certain peculiar force will ricochet forever throughout our spinning universe. It would be interesting for me to know what you discover—and at the end of all of that discovery, that sense of wonder, that acute knowledge that finally things are not random in our life but stretched with purpose known only to God, you come back and tell me then what I do not know. On the other hand, I will now tell you what you have not fathomed, why it is I stay. It is my life's work to find out what happened to Jimmy and to Georgina, although I suppose nothing much can be done about it even if I do. There is something—was something—that happened, and for the life of me I don't know what it is. Maybe it was a bet, or done on a dare—or just a card game, the sprinkling of gold powder on my boots, the killing of Harry Feathers. Maybe it was something said in an alleyway my mother didn't hear. Maybe it was something done in anger over something said. But however it was, I am now past half my life and have not found it."

"Is that why you drink?" I whispered.

"No, son—I drink because I am an alcoholic." He picked up another stone, and tossed it into the grey-blue sky.

My father now booked for both theatres, and his booking practices were not completely successful, or should I say sane. Mother had much more sense, and she railed at him that he should not have given up *Butterfield 8* with Laurence Harvey and Elizabeth Taylor for *Revenge of the Zombies*.

He explained, trying all our patience, that it was not the entire picture he was ever after but the pure moment, brilliantly poetical or farcical, that he could embrace. That's why, he said, Lou Costello was as great an actor as Laurence Olivier—though Olivier, he maintained, had his moments.

During the summer, and in fact ever after, he continued in this way, with *The Creature* and *The Return of the Blob*. In an argument he gave up *Spartacus* for *Horror Hotel,* which he claimed was a better picture. Then, to offset the Imperial's *Carpetbaggers,* which the bishop had asked Gram not to run, he booked in *Plan 9 from Outer Space.* The last night of this movie, just seven people were in the audience—even though free popcorn was offered.

Still, he could talk about the brilliance of Hitchcock's *Foreign Correspondent.* Or the gritty truth of the *Blackboard Jungle,* the inanity of Bob Hope and Bing Crosby, the self-indulgent greatness of Brando, the wasted brilliance of Orson Welles. And he could talk of this at the drop of a hat, with no one, not even Budgie, to listen, as he sat behind a fairly sprightly bottle of wine. And unfortunately that was the problem—he spoke almost always to himself, and was almost always alone.

EIGHT

The most unpleasant allegation against Ginger during her first year at the convent, far worse and of a different kind than her unsuccessful petition to dress like a nun—"Why should they have all the glory?"—or have boys in for pizza, was the allegation about a note sent anonymously to the mother superior after the St. Mary's Convent Skating Party was cancelled. "No one is indisponsible—no one—poonted head—think about it and be wear, you sparrow-faced twit, be it at morning mass or vesper prayers, signed Anon."

The letter was forwarded to my mother, who took it to my father.

"Who wrote this?" she said.

He looked at it for a fraction of a second. "Squirrelly little hand. Misspelled, loopy connected words. Ginger—has to be."

"She sent this to the mother superior."

"Then deny it is her," he answered, handing it back.

My sister was difficult for both Mother and Gram. And each of them blamed the other for her poor behaviour, her self-idolatry, and her miserable fortune in finding even one friend.

She failed that year—it was the first time, so that June night she was contrite. She came into the front room and called, "Yoo-hoo, Mommsie Q. Where is my fraulein, my little smootchiepookin?"

But Mother wasn't home.

"How did you fail?" I asked. "You were locked up most nights, just to study."

"Anyone can rebel anywhere," she said. "Grammie said she read an article by a woman who was talking about women's rights and she said, no one came to her with any rights."

"And that's why you failed?"

She looked at me askance and smiled. "Where is Athens?"

"Greece," I said.

"And the Pyrenees?"

"Spain."

"And is there a Y poet and a K poet?"

"What do you mean?"

"I mean the Y and the K guys, who are they?" She was still looking into the mirror, adjusting her blouse, opening a button in risqué fashion and then closing it.

"You mean Keats and Yeats—"

"Which one wrote something about Easter?"

"Yeats."

"Keats tricked me into thinking it was him—" She sighed as she fussed with her hair. "So you put it all together—say you put Athens in France, a good enough place for it, and the Pyrenees in Scotland—

'Ya be in the PYRANNAS now, Laddie'—is how I thought about it. And then you say Keats wrote Easter and you fail that Latin they give you—it's like a foreign language with all those Latin words—and you've pretty well done yourself in." She winked at me. "There'll be no learning for me," she said with exasperating self-assurance.

She was known as a wing nut, and had made many enemies at the convent. Kipsy Doyle, Nancy Savage, and Karen Hardwick all hated her. In fact, it seemed everyone hated her. She had dyed her hair green and had placed the name tags of her saints on her convent uniform— St. John, St. Paul, St. George, St. Ringo. She had been punished by the mother superior and left alone in the hallways until lights out.

I wanted to tell her everything would be all right, but I didn't believe it. I had taken to drink, just like Father. With drink, I could leave town in the third-floor reading room of our old library. François Villon, Victor Hugo, James Joyce, and a bottle of wine.

Curse of the Irish and at times of British Kings.

That June night my mother was at the doctor's. She had gone for a needle. My father had watched her getting ready to leave, anxiously smiling while looking guilty, as if knowing her condition must have had something to do with his failure, though he tried brilliantly to mask it.

"What a lovely group of people the Conroys are, in fact, a lovely people—a well-groomed bunch too. Why, you take Bob—car salesman, is it? Well-adjusted, I wish I was. You know, he's never read a book, well, why should he? He berates everything we put on the screen, well, why shouldn't he? So well-adjusted. Lions Club, is it? As you know I've had my problems adjusting—forced to take a leave of absence from Rotary because of that tantrum one afternoon—in front of the premier—and lieutenant-governor—who knew they'd be there—well, who knew I'd be drinking—however—I do plan to make a change—a grand leap forward. You'll see a different Miles from the Miles of old—"

"Please, Miles, be quiet," my mother whispered, forcing a wispy smile as she walked slowly to the car, on my arm, and the soft wind blew at the bottom of her dress, showing in the evening sun her sunless legs. "I am in pain."

"Of course," Miles said.

My father came home that night after Mother visited the doctor to drive me to work (like a vampire, I came out at dusk). We crossed the bridge in silence, and felt the air on our skin.

"Wendell," he said quietly, taking a cigarette from his silver case and lighting it with one hand on the wheel, looking over at me as he took his first drag. "What have I done?" he asked me, tears in his eyes. "What in God's name have I done to my Elizabeth Whispers?"

I knew the question was rhetorical—no answer required.

September came, and the shadows swept over our floors and filled the hallways. Ginger was back at the convent when I found out, coming home from school, told by one of my "best friends," who thought I would not throw a punch when he said it. He told me Elizabeth Whispers had gone to a dance and was seen later in the back seat of a parked car.

She had waited until Dad had drunk himself to sleep, had put on a new dress and high heels, and left by the back door, around through his flower garden with his purple loosestrife standing soldier. She had gone with Bob Conroy, the car salesman she had known at school. She had had a crush on him in grade ten, when he played right-wing second line for the A-team Beavers.

"How could she go to a dance with anyone who shoots right?" Father quipped sometime later.

I felt sorry for her, thinking of that dance. I felt sorry for Mrs. Sandy Conroy with her tiara, smiling in jest at Dad, never knowing what his terrible suffering and instability would mean for her. I felt sorry for Dad. He would not eat the lemon pie my mother made for him the next night. And as far as I know, he never did again.

NINE

From the mid-1960s on, my grandmother would wake at night without breath, and sitting up in bed, she would haul on a cord, and Roy would come to her aid with an oxygen tank. He would place the mask over her face, and she would breathe, and push him away, until the colour returned to her cheeks.

One word could delight you, another send a shiver down your spine. So Roy was subjected to these changing volleys, and did his best for her.

"Roy," she would call, and he would be there.

"Yes, Janie?"

"I want to see Georgina," she would say, and he would help her from bed, an old chivalrous gentleman from a school long gone and mocked by the very films they once attended. He would go in and out of her closets to help her dress and, after backing the sky-grey Cadillac out of the garage, he would wait for her on the steps and drive her to the graveyard, she staring out the window at young men keeping the night search alive at three in the morning, her hand clutching the ceiling grip and her eyes searching for the bright red flowers she had left in the graveyard the day before.

"Roy," she would say, "you must not let on that I had any difficulty breathing tonight—especially to Miles or Putsy, for they'll want me in the hospital for another checkup, and I have too much to do. I have been checked up to my ears, do you understand?"

"Of course, Janie."

"Checked to my ears, you hear. So I want none of them to know, you understand. Now, where is that money?"

"What money is that, Janie?"

"The money I promised you. I had it in my purse—where is it? I had it here. Where *is* that damn money?"

"Janie, you already gave it to me," he would tell her.

"I did? When?" She would look at him with a kind of inquiring and tranquil timidity.

"Yesterday—at supper last night."

"Well. Don't tell anyone about that either."

And there she would be, on her knees by the graveside as the sun just lit the dawn, and he would help her to her feet from the grass and pebbles her arthritic knees had fallen on.

As Dingle drove her back to the house at dawn, she would close her eyes and try to straighten her right leg to rest her knee. She could remember most of the movies she had played, and she could remember her husband doing a little twirl when they had managed to obtain the projector, in 1919, and she could still lay into any radio commercial that wasn't well delivered.

Every evening about seven o'clock, the grey Cadillac would drive out from her gate, travel the same route, and appear before the Grand. Roy would get out, in his grey suit that she had bought for him, with his dark brown leather shoes and his wide-brimmed hat that made him in the fading light look like the elderly Hank Snow. He would step around to her side of the car and open the door for her, and stand and wait like an adjutant. Janie would slowly make her way out of the vehicle, refusing his hand, and walk unaided up the steps alone, now and then glancing from the corner of her eye at the gawkers who stood nearby.

By late December of 1969, she knew she had a cancer, and she was not about to tell people of it. Besides, what would they say to her? Over the last year, she had sold off all except two of her houses, my father's and one that she said would be allotted to Roy Dingle, her friend. She was also going to leave Roy Dingle six thousand dollars. He had a pension, and she felt he would be happy if she also gave him a Cadillac.

"I don't want it," he said, bawling.

"You will," Janie replied, writing out a cheque. Most of her money was in the house, under the mattress and in other places. She gave another three thousand dollars to Mr. Harris's widow. (She must have taken a little pleasure in this, and I refuse to begrudge her that.) Then she had Mr. Dingle go downtown and bring a boy to see her.

"Are you Danny?" she asked.

"Yes."

"You went up the ladder for me—in 1964—you were nine."

"Yes."

"Other boys wanted you to go swimming but you stayed and helped me, an old woman."

He nodded.

"This is for you." She handed him five hundred dollars folded in her fingers.

Then she telephoned Bishop Hanrahan, who had politicked against our theatre. "I have money for you," she said.

"Oh, yes," the bishop said with immediate world-weariness. "Did you want me to retrieve it, Miss McLeary?"

"I did not get it as a McLeary, I got it as a King. I will bring the money around," she said and quietly hung up.

She gathered the money in a large shopping bag and carried it down the stairs. She would ask Dingle for no drive today—nor ever again. She was born without a car, after all.

Holding the money in the shopping bag she started up the hill, past all those signposts of her life— Oh, here is where Daddy carried me on his back when we went to fight the Drukens two at a time, the bastards, but they wouldn't come at us one on one, and he could throw a punch, Mr. Man, could he ever—and Dad taught me the fiddle and said, "Danny Boy" and "The Risin' of the Moon" is where we come from—and here is the schoolyard where I stood turning to see a young man looking at me, and it was Mr. King, fresh off the boat, like a child lost, and he came over, and said, "Are you to play for me tonight?" "For a price," I said, "for I'm no one's fool." That was long before the theatre, in the long-ago days of my youth. Oh, the storms then—Christmas we went sliding and the boys always got fresh, You sit up here close to me, put your legs here, and of course we would pretend we didn't know or didn't want to—and this is

where Georgina—Georgina . . . Georgina is gone, Janie girl—
Georgina has gone away.

The bishop was having midday tea and a hot cross bun. He was arrang-
ing a trip in the new year to the Holy Land and to Rome for an audience with the pope, and Father Carmichael, the priest who had given
his life helping people like Putsy and Walter, was not. Still, there were
many who thought Carmichael could heal people—a great comedian
had come here, for his son, and others as well. The bishop was wise
enough to know that this was false hope. Just as some dull men believe
that all the wise men lived in the past, so did Bishop Hanrahan believe
that all true goodness, and miracles if there were any, were in the past.

Besides, Carmichael had caused problems in the diocese. He often
held mass in an open field, near where he had built his own home.
There, much to the distress of the diocese, he and Sister Putsy took
care of seven homeless retarded children, dressed them every Sunday
and brought them to church.

"They don't understand what church is about," Hanrahan told him.

"Christ, however, understands what they are about," Carmichael said.

Hanrahan hated this pious lie, and hated Carmichael. So he
forbade him to have mass in the open.

Janie liked Carmichael, for she, having had no education, and
having had to learn to read at twenty-three so she could sign a
contract, was especially humble around these people that he and
Sister Putsy cared for.

She now sat in the vestibule in her heavy fur coat, and the bishop,
who knew she was there, and waiting, let her wait.

"Oh, Janie—I am so busy today—I am on my way to the Holy
Land—"

"I have not come to see you," Janie said.

"Pardon me?"

"I wish to see Father Carmichael."

"Oh," he said.

She was in terrible pain but she could not allow herself the luxury of succumbing to it. As for the bishop, to appeal to the whim of a rich woman—which he pretended he was doing—was better than admitting he lived in moral fear of Father Carmichael. So Father Carmichael was summoned.

"I want you to hear my confession," Janie said to him.

Hanrahan looked upon her with the most judicious political look he could afford—afford because of Carmichael, who could see through this look, being there.

Janie went to have her confession heard by Carmichael, the priest that comforted her when Georgina died.

She confessed to three sins. She would not consider confessing any more.

One was keeping her son away from the piano. He had begged her to study it when he was a child. "Perhaps I should not have done that," she said.

The second was not giving him more freedom to do what he wished, especially as a young man. "Perhaps that was wrong," she said.

The third sin was the most grave. She had never forgiven him for Georgina. "Please don't think I didn't love him—or did not try to forgive him that day in 1932," she said.

"Your boy would have given his life for that child."

"I know, I know," Janie said, patting the priest's hand as if she was comforting him.

Then Carmichael helped Janie, who insisted she kneel for this confession, stand.

"Here," he said, "take this for the pain," and he gave her a small bottle of liquid.

She smiled. "Is this your newest concoction?"

"It's gin," he said. "Drink it tonight. It might help you a little."

Then, as if it was an afterthought, she told him there was something in the porch and could he go and get it. Carmichael did, and Hanrahan waited. The air was now stale, and winter light came through the side window with the lace curtain. There was snow left by Janie's boots on the mat, unmelted yet, in the coming grey of a storm and New Brunswick's night.

Carmichael came in with the bag of money, and the door was left open.

Janie said, "Old moneybags I was called every time I went to church and the debt was brought up. Who was going to pay for the renovations on the church? Not old moneybags, it was said."

"Who ever said that, Janie?" Hanrahan asked with a smile on his face.

"At any rate," Janie said, "this money is for you, Father." She turned to Father Carmichael and suddenly clutched his arm. "It is for your little group—the ones you and Putsy help."

"I can't take this," Carmichael said.

"I am too ill to take it back now," she said. "You make sure you say my funeral mass—make sure I'm buried beside Georgina, and God will figure out what do with the rest of me."

Then she went home, went into the drawing room and closed the door. She took the gin (which had morphine in it) and lay back on the very couch my grandfather had died on, at the very same time of year.

Roy came in with the oxygen tank an hour or so later.

"I will not need that now," she said.

Roy Dingle asked why he couldn't be buried by her. Janie told him he would live another forty years and have many girlfriends afterwards.

"I will not—I will never have another girlfriend," Roy said, bursting into tears. "You are the only one ever to be kind to me—ever in my whole wide life."

"I know," Janie said, patting his hand, "I know. Well then, good for me."

These were her last words. She slipped into unconsciousness, and died in the midst of the storm of December 29, 1969.

TEN

I did not go to university, much to my father's pleasure. I twice tried to get into business on my own that next winter. I started a small haberdashery, next to Joey Elias, whose little shop was closed, the blinds drawn. It was as if not only his generation had passed but his entire universe had faltered and fizzled. I felt sorry for him.

He told me stories about Europe. One day, sitting in a chair in my shop, he asked me what I thought of fate.

I was uncertain fate had anything to do with me. He shook his head at this and gravely said, "The older you get, the more you think you have escaped certain things in your past. But nothing ever goes away—nothing! In fact it has started all over again, I think—don't you?"

"What has started all over again?"

"I wish I had stayed in Poland and I wish I had helped my brother," he said bitterly. "Do you know, I have a son?"

I didn't.

"I've told no one. He is your age. His life is empty."

I smiled uncertainly. "Empty?"

"Yes—empty."

He went to Putsy at the convent and spoke to her while holding her hand. He spoke about the good deeds he had done, how he had hired Phil when no one else would; how he had married her to keep her virtue intact after Walter had "let her down."

Putsy Druken was his only hope now. He was staring into a grand darkness he had never stared into before. It was a darkness he had only heard about, had laughed at, and in health believed he was too brave to fear. Now he was in deep sorrow, and in the alcove outside the side convent door, with a wrought-iron gate closed to the side lane, a wisp of smoke from a barrel in Mr. Hollingshead's field, they sat side by side, a little old man with a felt hat and a little middle-aged nun without many teeth. Tears were often in his eyes as the sun lingered on the gravelled drive, but the windows on the second floor were blank and hidden. Sometimes the wind blew his hat away, and Putsy would run about trying to grab it.

He told her that people didn't know right from wrong, and that children had stolen some of his baseball cards that he had collected. She was silent as he ranted against this, his face red raw, his lips wet, and his hands shaking. He sat forward so he could look at her as he railed against all the terror of his life. She was silent.

"What can I do?" he said.

She said she would pray that Joey would find peace in the end of his days, as Walter had.

"Walter—you want me to be like Walter? For God's sake, is that what you pray for?" He felt the cold through his coat.

"At times," Putsy said.

"I'll never be like Walter," he said, twisting away from her, turning his back. He hobbled away without anything more being said.

Elias was obsessed with going to Europe. He told me he had made a fundamental mistake when he was twelve, and it would be nice for him to go back and correct it. He spoke so much about it that many thought he was mad—that is, if there was a time machine, he would go back in an instant.

"And what would you do?" people would ask him.

"I would put my little brother on my back and continue my journey. I would be pressed into the Russian army and then this life would not have happened. There would have been no crimes committed."

"What crimes are those?"

"I tell you—if I had picked up my brother and put him on my back for one more day, no crimes would have been committed!"

He went to see Putsy, to ask her for money. And holding her hand, in the foyer of the convent, he finally confessed to her what had happened.

His flight to England, his trying to manipulate Mr. Harris against Janie, his palming aces against the young man who was going to be married, his spreading fake gold dust on the children's boots—all of this came about because of some mistake he had made when he was little.

"You spread gold on Miles's toes?"

"Not toes Putsy, his boots. Yes—well, me and—Rebecca. That's what we did—she more than I—she was worse than me!" he yelled in spite. "She was far worse than I was!"

"That's very strange," Putsy admitted, looking around at the empty foyer and hearing a door close.

"Yes, yes. But you see, I have not treated people right—I must go home and see to it now," he said.

Putsy believed it was essential that she help, and so she went to his house, with money that Walter had left her, four thousand dollars.

"He would want you to have it," she said.

"Walter?"

"Of course. He would beg you to take it—and find peace with your brother."

However, the day did not come when Joey embarked for the old country. Something was stopping him, some bad feeling about the trip. Was the old country any longer the old country? Not at all. And were the Communists in charge? Of course they were. Besides, he was too old, and too sad. But worse—what might he find out about his brother? What torture might his brother have suffered? Who had fought on his brother's behalf if he, Joey Elias, had not? What might his brother have become if he had stayed to help him?

He simply sat and stared at the wall, seeing his life as if it was projected on a movie screen, seeing Leon Winch leave with the key and come back. Seeing Rebecca go again. So he sat, with the money Putsy had given him in his threadbare pocket, and he cried.

Putsy would drop in with some fresh fish and feed him, for if not, he might have starved. She would pray for a miracle and say that one would come.

"No—God does not love me."

"Of course he does." She would reassure him by reading parables and Scriptures. "Let not your heart be troubled, believe in God, believe also in me."

He yelled against this—and who could blame him? For what had God done for him? He grew up where there were palaces, he said, yet he couldn't keep his brother fed. God had a lot of explaining to do.

But that night she left the book *The Way,* and he opened it at random and read the exact same phrase—"Let not your heart be troubled"—as if it was not Putsy telling him this but someone else.

Yet he had gone so far on a road, how could he change now? It was not respectable to change. God perhaps did not want him to change—had she thought of that?

"Remember, you have been preparing for this moment all of your life," Putsy said.

"What moment? What moment have I be preparing for?"

"The same moment we have all been preparing for," she said.

"Damn it, what moment is that?"

"Death," she said.

For the first time in his life he was staring out at it and it was close enough to touch him, its great uncompromising gulf soon to sweep over him. And it struck him—this is what my grandfather was feeling while Joey had tried to take his theatre. For the first time he realized what a terrible thing it was to do to a dying man.

And then one day he admitted something else. "I have a son by Rebecca," he said, staring across the lawn at nothing.

Putsy did not know how to answer.

"How?" she said.

And so he told her. Rebecca had come back in 1948—she was running from a charge of fraud against her in Edmonton. It was then she became pregnant. She was frightened and wanted to get rid of it.

"Do you know what I mean?" he asked.

"I think so," Putsy said, hardly whispering and staring straight ahead. Wind blew against them and neither of them spoke for a moment. It was as if her womb, so silent for so long in such a bitter life, started to bleed again.

"She had gotten rid of a child before, she told me, frightened she was to have a boy. She aborted a girl child. Fate had been cruel—because she wanted only a girl."

"I know," Putsy said. "She would want a girl."

"Yes," Joey Elias continued, "she was frightened to have a boy—and I was afraid she would destroy it—so I kept her with me. And a boy was born here in 1949. You didn't know?"

Putsy shook her head slowly.

"But when she had it, no one loved a child more. She went away with him—I gave her eight thousand dollars, all that I had. I have not seen her since."

He stayed out in the cold far too long that day. But it was as if he was paying penance and had to tell her everything. And the very next afternoon, feeling that death was imminent—he felt the cold of death on his neck and shoulders, and remembered poor Leon Winch, whose funeral he did not attend—he broke down and admitted to Putsy the boots.

"The boots," he said. "I stole them."

Putsy said nothing.

"I gave my brother over to the Russians."

They were desperately silent for a long time. For the first time in his life he could picture his brother's smile.

Putsy told Elias he had suffered enough for this.

"How have I suffered?" he said.

"Your love for your brother," Putsy said, "caused you more suffering than your brother would ever want you to. I now forgive you on your brother's behalf."

"But you can't." He was sobbing.

"That's not true," Putsy said, looking up into the sun, "for I loved you as your brother did, and you abandoned me too, and that is all that is required."

Elias could not look at her. Putsy took his hand and squeezed it.

"You carried him three hundred miles, Joey. You were only a child yourself. What else could you have done? God did not give you any breaks in the matter."

"More," Elias blubbered, "I should have done more."

"You are forgiven," Putsy said. "I know it as I know my heart."

They spoke no more about it.

"You think I am going to die?" he asked.

"Very soon," Putsy said.

"What will happen then?"

"Pray that you will meet your brother, for he is waiting."

On Putsy's insistence he telephoned Miles and chatted about the good days. It was as close to an apology as my family ever got. Nor had Father ever solicited one.

"I wish your mother and I had gotten on," Elias said.

At any rate it was all Joey Elias could do.

The next morning Putsy went to his house, and found him dead, wearing the old threadbare shirt he had worn when he had carried the child so long ago, with the black trousers, faded to nothing, and the torn boots on his feet. His hands were folded, and Putsy took his hand and held it for an hour. Joey Elias had died holding a picture of his brother as a child in Poland all those years before.

I had been a haberdasher, and wore a tam-o'-shanter like my great-grandfather. But my little haberdashery failed.

Ginger Snaps wrote telling me I wasn't cut to the fashion of selling suits, and must go back to the business God created me for. She had been made to crawl along the floor of the convent as a punishment for some infraction done to Kipsy Doyle.

"Dear dear Wendy," she wrote, "of the luckless bunch of Kings, please think of your sister alone in this convent where the girls smell of body odour and everyone fights like weasels in a hole. Love, Ginger Snaps."

I went back to running the projectors, and I became a semicon-ductor of our old established business, with my grandmother's portrait in the foyer.

Sometimes I thought that the drive-in, staring out at the world from projection vents over the tangled bush and weeds to the giant screen showing kick-boxing and tiger lilies, would support us forever and a day.

Poor thinking is all. Poor choice of hat.

PART V

The New Age

ONE

My mother, Elizabeth Whispers, left when Ginger was in grade twelve. There was a fight, and my father sat near the mantel looking at the floor, a new hat from Zellers she had bought him about two feet away on the arm of the couch.

She reappeared a week later, and then two, and a month after that. We would see her at the door fumbling with her keys. Sometimes Father thought she had come back to stay and would run to greet her, only to discover someone was waiting for her in a car. Usually someone my father did not approve of but would not say.

She had come back for something, and what was assumed, by the friend that drove her, was that my father would understand, being a mature man. In my colder, or more lucid moments I would think she had done this purposefully to add a salt lick to the horrible wound she was causing.

She was never drunk like Father, but perhaps a little tipsy. People said she had gone to dances with various people who had at times various complaints about our business.

My sister, who could be unforgiving, wrote her a letter. "How dare you go dancing with your fancy feet. Your place is at home."

I do not know what Elizabeth and Father talked about in the last four or five years. I almost never heard them. She would come and go. My Elizabeth Whispers, with her long, blond, stringy hair and her scared, kind eyes. Twenty-five years she had put up with the great glowering business that had consumed her husband. And now, perhaps when he needed her most, she was gone. People rejoiced at her freedom from him, and this rejoicing left my father even more alone. His drinking increased threefold.

Some said she was having an affair with the car salesman who was at our dinner party, and that this was why my father would not eat his lemon pie. Others say (and I do not know what others—it might have come from the Whispers faction of the family—all skinny half-mad little poachers from Renous) that she had given father an ultimatum, another chance in the bevy of chances she had supplied. But though she loved him she could not stand it any more. She had to remove herself from the ghosts and go away.

My mother lived in a little apartment on Hanover Street, a place with small wall plaques and a tap that dripped time to some forlorn and inconsequential tune. My father, always a gentleman, never spoke ill of her, even though our business was faltering, and seemed to go into a spin after she left, and he became erratic and once threw French fries at a customer.

"You want fries—well, I will give you fries," Father was reported to have said. "I will shove them one at a time down your throat—sir."

We drove to the beach one evening after Ginger's graduation to look for shells he wanted to paint and place in his garden. We walked in silence for almost an hour. The beach stretched off into the corners where red tails of sunlight still rose and ebbed on the waves, and our shadows seemed somewhat blunted before us.

"I will tell you this, Wendy"—he broke the silence suddenly—"I have never had much stock in car salesmen." His lips trembled.

We were walking through some foaming wave. His pants were rolled up and he wore a white jacket, and little pinfish flapped around his bare feet. He reminded me at that moment a little of Stahr, from the *Last Tycoon*, out on the beach meeting the old Negro man, who was picking up little fish in his pails. Their conversation was philosophical as well. And about movies in the end. My mother's untimely decision to leave was the stone cast that in a sense had forced me to stay with him, and not go away and train to be, of all things, a police officer (something I never mentioned to anyone, but which came from wanting to solve the mystery that kept my father where he was).

"How long do you think we can hold out, Dad? They are stealing our first runs."

"I know they are, son, I know they are, but we can hold out like they did at the Alamo—for as long as our powder is dry—what?" He looked at me with a grimace that told me more than his words where he found himself now.

Stealing our first runs was not a euphemism. Our competition was brave enough after Janie's death to start doing it, knowing my father was something of an invalid. And now that Mother had left—driven away by father's irascibility, some said—he was more erratic. So it was time for the vultures to come. Little by little our first runs would end up on a bus going to another town, or would be delivered to Father three days late. He would drive like a madman in his rollicking old car, trying, with a gin toddy, to track our poor presentations down.

"Do you know?" my father said one evening in late June, the summer after our mother left, sitting in the pleasant small back veranda that overlooked his flower garden, the lady's slippers and the blue oxes. He swished a slender stick at a fly and looked at me, in a kind of tired and forward perplexity, as if he wished me to answer definitively the question, "do you know?" and then realizing I could not, continued.

"Dingle is unfaithful to my mother's memory."

"In what way?"

He paused a moment, shoving the slender stick into the dirt, to make half a dozen little nubs, and then said, "In the most common way, Wendy, the most common way, indeed. The man has a girlfriend, and is quite unabashed about it. Some person he knew when he was young. She has come back to town. I believe there is an arrangement of sorts. I don't wish to speculate any more than that, but he has grown his sideburns. She says she is a doctor—I believe, if I believe in anything, that she would be much more like an apothecary, whoever she is—a performer more than a surgeon. Did you know that I wanted to be a surgeon? She has Doctor in front of her name, which is more than I have ever attained, and the respect of Dingle, which is something more as well."

"She's probably taking him for his money," I said, thinking she must be in bad straits indeed to have to take Dingle for his money.

"Oh, of course—but we must not tell him this. She is a woman who has come back with her son to the town of her birth and lassoed poor Dingle, I suspect. There is even the idea—well, more than that, even—I heard it at the barbershop, so you can put as much faith in it as you will—that the boy is Joey Elias's son, and she came back to see what money he had for her. Finding him dead did wonders for her relationship with our man Dingle."

I thought nothing more of this for a week or so. Then one afternoon I saw Dingle with a younger woman. He was trying to look like a younger man, with his hair grown over his ears. No longer did he need us to bring him over Sunday dinner, or bring him to our place for Easter duty.

I realized I had seen this woman about town for almost a year. I had seen her son also.

The woman's gaze was remarkable, her stance, the way she hooked one leg slightly out, memorable—and reminded me of nights at the drive-in, or perhaps just of loneliness. Her hair was orange and brushed back on each side—in a severe way, not to say butch, and she looked tough, with cold, fearless eyes—undaunted by my staring, at any rate. She wore a T-shirt that said "I'm a tough nut" on the front, and on the back, "To crack."

Her name was Abigail Mahoney, and she had lived here as a child. She came to me as a kind of mirror into the river's past, for she knew about things like Dobblestein's mill. I wondered briefly if she could tell me something about my father's past. She had a degree from a place in Chicago as a psychologist and matrimonial counsellor, with just enough hint that it was bogus. Anything associated with harmonizing matrimony seemed bogus in these days, what with my mother and father.

There was also about her the impression that her purpose in life had just begun, which to me is an unremarkable trait in middle-aged women.

Now she was with Dingle as his caregiver, and worked as well as a counsellor to some women in the subdivision above us. She had her sign up at Dingle's house. She told fortunes on the side. She had also made inquiries into Elias's estate—a man she knew—and was distressed to learn that Elias had died with nothing.

Dingle had begun to live the high life, spending money for taxis and Chinese food in buckets.

"He has a way with the ladies I can't manage," Father said, "and now the poor fellow is wearing bell-bottoms and smoking grass, with a pipe. I am no prohibitionist, but I do feel you need time to develop a rapport with these things. You just can't start at seventy-four with a hash pipe, can you?"

It is a truth that the people I often thought could not flourish in the town did so much better than Father and I. And soon enough this woman and her son did also.

She insisted on being called Doctor. She was interviewed in the paper and said she had had a very harsh life, and people my age were suddenly drawn to her, and she was being celebrated as a survivor, and a liberal, by simply saying, "Kids today are just having fun—no one has any reason to worry about them." But she never looked in my direction, and as in most cases I seemed to have missed my opportunity to impress either her or her boy.

One night, an hour or two after I went to bed, I woke with someone in my room. The window at the foot of my bed was open, and the curtains billowed softly, and as if in a feverish dream I saw my father watching me. He was trembling and pale.

I sat upright. "What's wrong?" I whispered.

For a long time he just stared at me. Finally he spoke in a hoarse whisper.

"I went over to see for myself how Dingle was doing, and saw his woman, this Dr. Mahoney, as you call her."

"Yes?"

"Well, I'm afraid something peculiar has happened." He looked first one way and then the other. "She has metamorphosed into a Rebecca Druken."

"What is a Rebecca Druken?" I said, knowing who Druken was.

"She who is living with Dingle. It is she. She and her son. Oh, she is much different—at first I didn't know her at all. She has not lost her looks, but she has changed them radically."

"You can't be serious," I said.

"Quite serious, oh yes, quite, quite serious. Besides, I have checked in recent weeks. Noel, you see, is Joey Elias's son."

"It could be any number of people."

"And of course she wouldn't admit it to me. 'Rebecca' I said, pondering how incapable drink sometimes makes me, thinking I had gone somewhat senile. She didn't answer, 'Rebecca,' I said." He paused. "But of course she glanced at me in a kind of recognition that kicks you in the teeth—I was introduced by Dingle himself: He said, 'This, Dr. Mahoney, is my stepson.' And she said, 'Oh, how are you?' like that, all warm and fuzzy-wuzzy. She gave me a kind of searching look, as if trying to recognize who I was through the age, trying to fathom what my life had been like, so she could capture my soul in a bottle. Dingle is very pleased to have a doctor sitting about his house. She had made up a list of things that she felt Joey Elias might have left her, and was upset to realize he was not the grand man he had been."

"Does anyone else think she's Rebecca?"

"I went to see Sister Putsy. But Putsy is now almost totally blind. She doesn't know. Perhaps, but part of her still believes her sister died as a nurse on a military ship in the war even though another part believes she had a son by Joey."

"Well, if she doesn't know," I said offhandedly.

"Rebecca has snuck back and it will happen!" he said harshly.

"What—?" I said.

"Her plans to destroy me, bit by bit—don't you see? She brought her son home to accomplish this. It has been written, it has been prophesied, by Carmichael. But he is no longer here. He is somewhere up in heaven, I suppose. After being gone three-quarters of her life, she is back in the fold. She has made more friends and acquaintances in four weeks than I have managed to in forty years. She has tacked up a diploma on the wall. I refuse to honour her by calling it bogus. I am already in terror of her son. I wonder why. I am thinking maybe you should kill him. No, that's not the best idea. Prison food and all that. I am sure she is here to help your mother."

"Mother?"

"She is Miss Whispers's new friend—counselling her. She was the person who advised your mother to go. She helped her get the apartment up on Hanover."

All his life the one woman he worried about (rightly or wrongly) was now friendly with his ex-wife. If I had ever thought of leaving him, I could not now.

"Are you *sure* she is Rebecca Druken?"

He didn't hesitate. "I am."

I was silent. He was silent.

"Well," I said, "perhaps she *is* Dr. Mahoney."

"Well let me relieve you of the burden of lucidity," he said. "Consider that if she did not want to be known as who she is, there is one of two explanations possible. First, she has a grand largesse and wants to give it to the town—some fire truck or new building or peanuts for everyone—and remain anonymous—or she has hidden her true identity as long as possible to infiltrate, surmise and decide what she will do clandestinely. To me. For it has to be me she has come back for. Like an assassin—Mata Hari perhaps—or better yet Tokyo Rose."

"But maybe she *is* Dr. Mahoney?" I said, exasperated.

"And maybe Tokyo Rose was not Tokyo Rose—but Osaka Rose?"

He gave me a telltale smirk.

She had not looked at all like the Rebecca he described to me, or as he painted from memory. She was just a small, wrinkled, tough-looking woman, and she chain-smoked, wore jeans, and a T-shirt. No earrings, no makeup. Of course she was past these things, not for any reason, but she deserved to be. Coming by Dingle's at dusk I saw her sign out on the porch, "Dr. Mahoney—certified psychologist," creaking a little in the rain, and waving trees.

I asked about her downtown over the next few days. Few remembered Rebecca Druken. Those who did had not the slightest belief that she was in town.

I began to watch her coming and going along our street. She wore an old rain jacket and jeans, seemed more imperturbable to changes in weather than most people. She always kept to the far side of the street, close to the buildings, hunched over when she walked.

Her name, Dr. Abigail Mahoney , Health and Happiness Consultant, appeared in the telephone book. Over the next year she and her son became part of our town. But Dr. Mahoney hardly spoke to us. It was as if she did not think we were important enough to talk to. Perhaps she knew we were conservative—like a sixth sense you have about people in a waiting room.

Putsy sent Dad a letter about her sister, believing also that she had died on some military ship as a WREN in the war.

"Ships and men, and a good fight—is how she described it to me in the last letter I ever received," Putsy wrote.

I discovered the letter sometime later in his haversack of letters in the corner of his room.

One day I ran into Noel.

"How do you like being on the river?" I asked.

"I like it okay," he told me.

"Noel thinks it's a backward place and everyone's an asshole," Cassie said. Cassandra Avalanche was Dingle's cousin's granddaughter, and we had hired her one summer because of this, but it had not worked out, and she resented us all. She had been caught trying to steal a freezer full of wieners.

I looked at Noel, and the summer wind blew against his brown shoulder-length hair. Noel made the mistake many youth make, that to be rural and innocent of kinds of vice was to be ignorant. And Cassie liked this mistake, because it carried in its lie a supposed urban virtue that she could easily attain without virtue itself standing in the way. And then she could hold this virtueless virtue up to me and find me, and Father, who she once thought was sophisticated, lacking.

Noel was handsome, almost tragically so. He was empty too, in the way certain youth of my generation tended to be. That is, he was innocent because concern had so far escaped him. Or, rather, moral concern was foreign to him.

Noel's fame was that he had friends in Dorchester Penitentiary. One was Ray Winch, who he told me was getting day parole soon. (As if I should rejoice, like him and Cassie.)

My father, never receiving the gift of day parole, sat listless and depressed in our house of shadows and empty bottles and empty dreams, and fantasized his empire crumbling with the Druken return. Though I did not think there was evidence of their return, I was plagued by how easy things seemed for others, and how bright he in his monumental failures was.

"Do you know who Mahoney was?" he asked me.

I did not.

"Mahoney was the fellow who sold Mother the monopoly on the talkies. There is something in a name, after all—or a name borrowed. Diabolical, isn't it?"

Often Ginger and I found it difficult to rouse Dad to go to work. He kept staring into dark corners, mumbling to himself.

But then questioning him one evening about his paranoia, about Abigail, who after two years had done nothing but tell fortunes, give out home remedies, he simply smiled and said, "Ah, you have not reckoned on one particular fact, Wendy, my child. Poor Miss Whispers has not, poor Ginger flying toward her doom has not."

"And what is that?" I said.

"Simply that I cannot pretend that I do not know what it is I know—even if it would make my life better."

So with darkness creeping on, I would go to run the drive-in projectors, my father insisting that we run old black-and-whites—musicals and singing cowboys—to draw the crowd. Even then he could not understand why our lot was only a quarter full at best. He wanted to live the last years of his life in a kind of nostalgia, where the drive-in continued memories of dances and singalongs and top hats in a parade along the white picket fences of middle America. Ginger and I would fight with him over this, of course. But he was unperturbed by our protests. Of course.

One August evening Father paced back and forth in a particularly agitated mood, drinking from a bottle of gin. I have to be fair and admit that we were both old-fashioned, and the world was rushing away from us in wondrous exhilaration at being free. We were not free, and everyone else, including my mother, now seemed to be.

Days would go by and my father and I would be alone, caught up in the horror of what we saw or, worse, expected to see. Ginger was exceedingly short with us, because of our conservative natures and our arguments with how she dressed and where she went.

"We will not stop them," Father said, "and they will not stop themselves, for they do not know what they are doing. But her main objective is starting."

He squinted at me, to make sure I was who I was.

Then at the den door, in the crowded heat, he said, "My God—she's come back for Ginger."

"Who?"

"Who? I speak of only one person. She has come back for our Ginger, and it is imperative we stop her! It will be like Georgina all over again!"

Janie had left almost everything—the great house, two cars, the major share of the Grand, and a partnership in the drive-in to her.

This is what bothered us without either of us saying it.

The next day, when I went to Janie's house to see Ginger about booking some new pictures, I had a surprise. She and Gus Busters, who had graduated with me—in fact, the only one whose marks were consistently higher—and fresh from three years of failing one university course after another and taking part in radical campus protests over library books and distribution of free hash, were sitting on lawn chairs on the sunny side of the yard.

TWO

Gus Busters's fiancée was Kipsy Doyle. The Doyles were a large clan on our river, so breaking up a relationship like that made enemies of half of our clientele. But Ginger was irrepressible. By midsummer she was deeply in love.

"He is so independent and lovable," she said to me. "And he doesn't drink."

He did drink. Most people knew that. And he did something she did not know about—drugs. He got them from Noel Mahoney. But in the dry afternoon air I was averse to telling her this. And of course I knew nothing said by me would stop her. Busters drove a Vespa scooter, with his chihuahua, Scoop, in a basket.

At the circus, when she was fifteen, Ginger had wanted to get her face tattooed. The tattoo artist refused. But there was something about this request that made us realize she was entirely and fundamentally vulnerable to making a huge mistake, the kind of mistake the McLearys had always made. The kind my father made in one unalterable moment in 1932—to see a retinue of well-heeled monkeys at the circus on a rainy day.

A mistake the caliber of which would inflict a Picket's charge of the spirit, calculated to destroy herself and us. When she walked by me, in a cloud of mystery, I realized her childlike skip could become the scaffold kicking out from under our family's feet.

My father realized this too, but he was unable to do anything about it.

To her he was a failure, a man who had chased his wife away, and a drunk. But most suspect of all, suddenly, and in parenthesis, he was a man. And as James mentioned, "the agitation on behalf of women," had swelled and she was part of this, had flowered in it—used it to her own advantage.

There was a sense that the King dynasty was a matriarchy, that had to be preserved in spite of Father. His failure at life brought life to her.

Kipsy had loved this fellow Gus since she was a child. She believed that her marriage was guaranteed. Yet he made a delivery of frozen hamburger patties to the drive-in and Ginger came out to get them. He lingered by the freezer door, in the fury of a cloudless May night, and in giddy exasperation tried to swat bugs with his hat, and she said, "Oh, Gus—I remember you playing badminton. When you hit the bird it made me shiver." He had made it to the semifinals of the provincial championship in grade eleven, on those long ago gymnasium floors and contests of the will now forgotten, with cheering teachers and seeded opponents on the sidelines watching.

There was some question to whether or not Gus was brilliant. My father came to me one night to ask me if he was.

"Perhaps," I said, "but socially he is not very astute."

"Are any of us astute socially?" Father asked.

"Well, no. I am twenty-three years of age and have yet to meet a girl that likes me, or have a friend. It would seem to me I have quite a bit of the old Gus Busters in me. Busters continually makes the same mistake. He trusts all the wrong people."

"Yes—" Father said, "really the damn thing is, you see, that that person—oh, his whatchamacallit—his mother—phoned to warn me, that he drinks. Well, I thought—if he drinks and cannot afford it, he will be a burden—but if he drinks and can afford it—a blessing sent. So I thanked the mom and hung up. "Brilliant" is, however, not the word I would use to describe Mr. Busters—a village idiot like ourselves perhaps—h'm, Wendy, my boy?"

His mother was ancient when he was born, and Gus grew up like a grandchild on a forlorn lane. I felt sorry for him. I knew loneliness, and the absence of a father had caused him to trust others who so easily and cavalierly had little care for him. Kipsy was his high-school sweetheart, the one who did care in spite of others, but her influence was coming unglued after he met Ginger.

And Ginger was determined to be married, as a way to be out from under and on her own. Though Father thought Ginger getting married would save her in another way, he said after supper one evening with the small grandfather clock ticking away monstrously, our time devouring earth, he had to warn her. He could not live a charade. "You see," he said, "if I don't speak up, am I culpable the way a father should not be? Shouldn't I say at least something?"

"You mean, tell her he takes drugs?" I said.

"Yes—tell her of powders and sauces and stuff that he sniffs. She is a Puritan, our little rascal, isn't she—at least where it concerns libation. I made her that way and am sorry for it. However, the problem is what do I do, for I am far more comfortable with Gus Busters's predilections, such as they are, than with her sermonizing. However she is my daughter."

"So you have an obligation," I said, warming to the moment.

"Obligation. How wonderful that word, but what does it mean? It means becoming a snitch. No, that's not being a gentleman. I must also say that these things they take—heroin or whatever it is they drink—is fine by me. I've tried it myself many a night."

"You have not," I said. "In fact, I think, and I know in saying this I sound conservative—but I think you are very different from those we are now discussing—there is a different temperature to your doom compared with theirs—a difference not in degree but in kind—part of my love for you is that your doom is very different then the doom of those we have been speaking of—their doom is a greed-filled one—not Buster's but many he knows."

"Thank you. However, let's just say I might have drunk heroin if given the opportunity, so being in the moral quandary I find myself, I must let it go for now. I am a wonderful drunk—perhaps one of the finest who has ever lived. Gus and I are the same. The silly fellow thinks hash medicinal and non-addictive. I believe gin is addictive if non-medicinal. So," he said, shuddering as he looked down at his lamb chop, "we are somewhat kindred spirits, just the kind of son-in-law I need. He will be ineffectual but a presence enough to keep the wolves from the door."

"Gus will need a job," I said, lighting a cigarette from his silver case.

"I suppose she will have to hire him—just as my mother felt she had to hire me. So send him to me and I will see him."

Then I asked the question on both our minds. "Do you think he will bring her to ruin?"

"Vigilance," Father maintained, setting his lamb chop aside with a weary grimace.

Gus came to the house the next afternoon and sat in our den, his bony knees thrust out into the middle of the floor. He had a red afro and a freckled face, and the skinniest legs I had ever seen in shorts. I kept him company while Father readied himself in the bedroom, gargling.

Then I heard my father begin his walk down the hall, banging off one wall and lurching into another.

"Where is he?" he said, waving his hands for me not to try to steady him.

"Right here, Father," I said, smiling sheepishly.

Miles looked about.

"Where—where?"

"Here I am, Mr. King," Gus said, giving a kind of tip off his hair, with his finger.

"So you're the one?" Father said.

Gus nodded.

Miles looked down at him, completely baffled, turned and whispered to me, "Wasn't it the other Busters who lived in Fenwick Court by the old pool hall?"

"Pardon?"

"I said wasn't it the other Busters who lived in Fenwick court by the old pool hall?"

"No—it's Gus."

"I have to prepare another speech," he whispered.

"Pardon?"

His face went beet red. "I don't know him. I thought it was the other Busters."

"Pardon?"

"Are you an idiot? I said I don't know him—"

He turned to Busters and nodded civilly, and left the room. Then he called me into the hallway.

"What are you going on about?" I whispered.

In the hallway Father believed he could speak as loudly as he wanted.

"I thought it was the other Busters, or VanBusters, or whoever the hell they are who lived up in Fenwick court."

"Well, it's not."

"Is this the guy who does drugs?"

"I don't know. Shut up!" I said.

The interview was effectively over.

So we prepared for the wedding as best we could. They were to live forever all at once. She was to have a long, white dress with a train and have two bridesmaids, the other two girls of the triumvirate whom she had won over, Nancy Savage and Karen Hardwick, to isolate Kipsy even more.

Gus became (since I was to manage the drive-in) our projectionist. It took him only two days to learn everything he needed to know, his little chihuahua, Scoop, sitting on his head as he made his way around the theatre checking the wiring on the speakers. My sister went about with the diamond, tapping it against glass and filling French fry cups with delight, handing over the cups of fries with her diamond showing.

THREE

My father was in anguish after the wedding. Mother would not come back, and this further alienated him from the world. He plodded about the yard as November came in a drizzle and a blanket of frost, in hat and scarf, without a coat, feeding winter birds, and not reading the paper when his neighbour yelled across the street that Elizabeth was picked up and taken to the police station.

When I went to Mom's apartment, I couldn't bring myself to broach the subject. Her place was cluttered with knickknacks and wall plaques of winter scenes. She had not caught the whiff of intrigue, and did not associate Dr. Mahoney with Rebecca Druken. Neither, still, did I.

She spoke about how kind Dr. Mahoney was, how she had given Mom a special pair of oven mitts. It was as if she had never gotten anything before from anyone, and when I was leaving I realized that Mother probably hadn't.

As I was going down the stairs she rushed out after me and said, "How is Miles? Tell him I'm fine, not to worry, and tell him to eat his vegetables, please."

There were tears in my eyes.

Then in March money went missing. Ginger had sent it to Mr. Dingle to get his dentures fixed. Gus Busters had delivered the envelope and left it, he said, on the hall table. They looked for the envelope in every room and could not find it. They looked in the car and up and down the streets to and from Ginger's house. It was nowhere. When Gus went to the house a few days later, no one spoke to him, while Dingle with his loose dentures tried to bite into an apple.

Dr. Mahoney maintained that it was very strange that the money would have disappeared. She said she did not think Gus very honourable if he would take his wife's money—money given to an old man to fix his teeth.

But in truth Ginger also suspected Gus. She could not help doing so.

Soon after, Dr. Mahoney took Cassie Avalanche into the den and closed the door.

"You are like my child," she said, sitting very close beside Cassie and now and again stroking her hair, "but I've been in a man's world long enough to read people well. I want to help Ginger. She is the only one among them worth anything. I've seen too much abuse in that family—as you know yourself."

"What do you mean?" Cassie said, smiling uneasily.

"Well, you come from a hard family life and so do I—but we prevailed."

"That's right—we prevailed," Cassie said. "I remember the first time I saw them—in a new car up at Gary Fallon's house."

"Well, there you go," Dr. Mahoney said, thinking the child stupid. "So I'd like to see how Gus thinks and how he handles a crisis. That will go a long way in my understanding if he is worthy of Ginger. Noel did everything for him, yet he is continually letting us down. He makes fun of your uncle Mr. Dingle too."

"Oh, I know," Cassie said.

"Gus is a big talker, you and I both know that, so I want to see how he acts when push comes to shove. Take the money and buy something nice for yourself." Here she handed Cassie the envelope. "But don't tell anyone you did. I have to know this about Gus, you see, so don't think it is wrong—think of it as being helpful. That's all you and I will be, dear—helpful. Remember, there is very little that is right that can't be wrong—and anything wrong can be right, given the right conditions."

Her breath was close to Cassie's ear, a seduction of power only. The only kind of seduction Cassie would succumb to. The doctor pressed the envelope into Cassie's pudgy hands.

"Oh, that would be too awful," Cassie said.

Dr. Mahoney, whom she respected so much, nodded. "I used to think like that, but I've seen too many women tortured in bad relationships. Now I realize I have to fight fire with fire. This is my main object—get Ginger away from that man."

"Gus—"

"Yes, dear. And that other awful man as well—Miles, is that his name? He must have been an awful child. There was a little girl, wasn't there, that he pushed down a well? Now he is doing his work on poor Elizabeth and Ginger."

Cassie knowing when it was fitting to be sentimental, became so.

"Who will ever help them?" Cassie said.

"We have to," Dr. Mahoney said firmly. "Miles put Noel's father, Joey Elias, out of business and never batted an eye. So what if we do a little back to him? Do you remember Joey?"

"Not very well," Cassandra said.

"He was as close to a genius as you could get around here, so I want beyond anything else to fulfill his legacy. Do you understand?" Dr. Mahoney said. "I would have married him, but I am an independent woman."

Cassie smiled again, knowing this wouldn't be too awful at all, but appropriate for people like Gus and as privileged as Ginger.

Except when Ginger was present, Dr. Mahoney never spoke of Miles in a favourable light. And each thing she mentioned, each small boy she saw as spoiled, each man she knew was inept, every fellow who couldn't handle something became to her the embodiment of Miles King, the bully who'd pushed his little sister down the well. It allowed others to see Miles in the same way, not because they had ever thought this themselves, but because someone who had so much power over them did. It was the same power Joey Elias had wielded over Leon Winch and Patricia Druken.

Mahoney patted Cassie's hand and cautioned her, while folding the envelope into it. She said this had nothing to do with hurting Ginger and everything to do with young girls getting married to men who would abuse them.

"That's what I thought," Cassie said sadly.

She could be sad or happy at any given time, and Dr. Mahoney knew this, because Dr. Mahoney could too. She had learned it as a child, sitting on someone's knee.

To Cassie this was the kind of intrigue she had always sought. It was a positioning of events in certain people's lives in order to act out a certain scenario, for their ultimate benefit. What did it matter if it was also for your own benefit? She always practiced this, but had learned this better from Mahoney herself; this tough little no-nonsense woman who had prevailed who had gone back to university in her forties and became a doctor, a Ph.D. behind her name. What a happy age, Cassie thought (or actually felt a sensation with), that these things being done are to be now considered considerate and moral. What a happy age that I am gifted enough to be a part of them. But as sophisticated as this seemed for Cassie, it was only child's play, the beginning of an intrigue.

Cassie was inspired by Mahoney; and beyond anything else there was the idea that some sin in the past was to be rectified here.

"Was there a sin?" Cassie asked.

"Oh, yes—a deep sin," Dr, Mahoney said. "There was a little tyke called Georgina—I believe she loved the nanny more than she loved the Kings, and I think they destroyed her and the nanny. She clung to the nanny but they fired the poor woman. I do not want to see this happen to Ginger."

"Why didn't I ever hear of that when I worked for them?"

Dr. Mahoney lifted her eyebrows, just as Joey Elias was known to do, to show naive astonishment at the subterfuge of those they were discussing.

Mahoney, who had done wonders with my mother, now tried to improve Ginger's life. The greater the risk, the more inspired she became. She believed that something wrong was in fact right when it helped others. Therefore, the money could be taken, since in this case it would help Ginger.

She told Cassie this had been her primary belief since she was sixteen. Back then there was something disastrous she had to prevent and she had taken it upon herself to do it. At first no one else seemed to understand this belief of hers, but now it was considered only the "besting of an adversary."

The money was taken, Gus was blamed, and for a long time things seemed to deteriorate between Ginger and him, and him and everyone else in town, who now took him to be a shadow of his father-in-law, Miles King. He found himself unable to eat or sleep and he began to lose weight. And it was not at all violent—only vigilant. This was an accepted thesis.

My father, hearing of this in bits and pieces, saw it as the first volley in a war to capture the heart of Gus's beautiful wife. He wanted to catch Mahoney. "We will lasso her, and hide her in my house for sixteen years."

It was at this point, on a day when he drank two quarts of gin and got in a fight with his shoes, that I knew he needed psychiatric help.

In May, just as the drive-in was re-opening, Dr. Mahoney decided it was time to speak to Ginger, and picked up the phone.

Ginger hesitated when she discovered who it was. It was a telling hesitation, for she had promised Gus she would not speak to this woman again, but from the moment the doctor had taken an interest in her she had felt special, and she wanted this feeling to continue, because no one had ever agreed with her so much, so much so that her thoughts seemed to be read.

"It is uncanny, and she is uncanny," she would tell me on those rare occasions when she told me anything.

I heard this from other people as well. Mahoney had an uncanny ability to read them. Gus himself admitted this. That is why her accusation that he took the money was in one way so difficult to discredit.

Dr. Mahoney always told the truth initially and let the other things she said ride upon it comfortably. She said she had been thinking lately that Ginger had found herself in some untenable position. She also understood that Ginger's grandmother had many similar difficulties. Since both these things were true (Gus and Ginger were on the outs, and he had broken a vase), everything Dr. Mahoney said must therefore be true.

Ginger knew one thing: nothing had been done to her. And she had actually been getting along with Gus until the doctor's accusation over money. Still, as long as he didn't suspect her of talking to Mahoney, times were pleasant enough between them. More pleasant, however, was for Ginger to hear Dr. Mahoney agree with her. There was something else—her willingness to be duped by Dr. Mahoney because others less intelligent than she had been duped as well, and she wanted to be included.

"Why can't I be gulled as well to love her?" Which is to say at some point on the moral compass, somewhere along the thin line, the truth was known, and dismissed as unpleasant, because what was pleasant was untrue. This, in fact, had been what Ginger had done most of her life. Ginger knew the truth instinctively but simply dismissed it if it did not suit her. All of her life, Ginger had dismissed a message she did not want to hear. Throughout the last month, Gus had sworn that he hadn't taken the money, and Ginger realized that he had not been high or drunk for two months. He was frightened of Dr. Mahoney, he told her. "She is trying to do something awful." The moment he said this Ginger knew it was true, but she laughed and mocked him—because she needed to have power over his seriousness. It was not enough that Gus told the truth—it was how he said it. The way he said it was a flag to the bull—common sense to her precocious whimsy and will.

"I know you're not my best friend," Mahoney now said to Ginger over the phone. "Cassie is your best," she said quickly. "But promise me one thing."

"Of course," Ginger said.

"Don't remain in a bad relationship. As a psychologist, I can guide you a little. Whatever you do, remember Miles and your mother, and how much better off your mom is now."

"Yes," Ginger said. Although the fact of the matter was she did not visit her mother—almost no one did any more—so she did not know how her mother was at all.

Women were in tough places and in bad relationships. That was well known. And to Mahoney, just like Joey Elias before her, it did not matter precisely if Ginger was in a bad relationship. It only mattered that Ginger could be made to think she was. And if she did think this, Mahoney the psychologist would be there to support her. This was up to Ginger and up to no one else. And Dr. Mahoney was there to safeguard her choice. But Ginger, in talking to Mahoney, knew in the end what Mahoney thought her choice must be. And she also knew that she did not want to disappoint her by making the wrong choice. Still and all, this could not happen if a relationship was not fragile. Nor could it happen if Dr. Mahoney's real motives were honourable. This is not to suggest, however, that they were completely unknown. In fact, the truth here played a little like the votes in Comrade Stalin's axiom:

"It does not matter who votes—what matters is who counts the votes."

Whatever it was Ginger came to count on these phone calls now.

One afternoon in the tavern a tall hard-living farm boy stood up, grabbed Gus by his skinny shoulders, and kicked his behind. "That's fer stealin' yer wife's money, ya priceless prick," he said, to the roaring approval of the crowd.

Gus hobbled to the door. He knew well enough that Mahoney was up to something. But he could not tell his wife about the bruise on his backside, and she wondered if he was keeping something from her. Some people suggested to her that he was taking needles.

Each thing Mahoney discovered about Ginger caused her to suggest another. Her love of Janie. Her dislike of Miles's ineptness.

So Dr. Mahoney one day asked her why she felt so betrayed. Ginger said she did not know she had been.

"But certainly you were," Dr.Mahoney said, "certainly they've kept it from you."

It took a week for Ginger to realize that she had never forgiven her family for sending her to the convent. They had not said goodbye to her the day she went, and she had forgotten her twenty dollars on the bed. She had made no friends there, and in that curious place of piety and cant, she had tried to take her life. No one knew this, she admitted, but Dr. Mahoney.

Dr. Mahoney told Ginger she hated the convent as well, and spoke about it, ripening once again all of Ginger's wounds: the smell of suppers, the dark corridors, the mass each morning, and the nauseating feeling of snow and claustrophobia.

The next morning a letter arrived at the door, in a pink envelope with a happy face. It contained a twenty-dollar bill, with a note that said only, "Love, A. Mahoney."

Ginger sat on the couch, hugging the letter, tears flowing down her cheeks.

Ginger was now aware, as everyone else was, of Gus Busters's serious problems with drugs. She had found blotter acid in his pocket, mescaline in his drawer. At first she did not want to admit it because of her father's history, a history she believed she had overcome. And at first she believed it was only an occasional use.

But Dr. Mahoney made her see the truth. Did she help Gus? Ginger admitted that she had. Gus had owed money, which Ginger had paid twice.

"Why, then, should you be duped a third time by this fellow?" Dr. Mahoney said. "What, in fact, has this fellow ever done for you?"

Ginger said she did not know. And then she said, "What do men ever do for us?" She had wanted to add, "Except love me more than anyone else ever."

Now Dr. Mahoney suggested to Ginger she was an enabler of weak men. "Only a few facts are missing in the jigsaw puzzle, Ginger, but we are getting somewhere."

"Yes, thank you," Ginger said happily. Still, she had to admit that Gus had behaved himself recently and had not asked for an extra cent.

Then a week passed and no phone calls were made. Ginger, feeling left out, telephoned the doctor to see if she was ill.

The poor doctor said she was busy with many other people, many who had been abused far worse than Ginger. She also said she didn't think Ginger liked the calls.

"But that's not true," Ginger said. "I enjoy our phone calls."

"I didn't think any progress was being made."

"Why not?"

"Well—perhaps you don't take what I say seriously enough."

"Of course I do."

"Well, perhaps you should do something about it."

Ginger was in an unenviable position. She realized she had no reason to blame her husband. But if Gus was blameless, Dr. Mahoney would have no reason to phone, and it was Dr. Mahoney's interest in her she wanted to prolong.

The day after the phone call Ginger demanded soup. Gus, red afro, apron tied behind him in a bow, made it, sleeves rolled up in the oppressive afternoon, trying his best to stay sober and shaking just a little as he carried it on an old wooden tray up the three flights of ever-narrowing stairs. Yet when he reached her room she was sleeping.

"Ginger, your soup. Ginger, wake up. Soup's on!!"

"How dare you wake me up for soup?"

"But you wanted soup—"

"That was hours ago—take it away."

He went, and meekly waited for another order, knowing that what she suspected of him allowed her to be cruel. Yet secretly he knew she didn't suspect him—Dr. Mahoney did, and Ginger was under pressure to suspect him as well. There was no fighting this;

Ginger was obligated to think little of him in order to please someone else.

He discovered how easy it was for her to make him do things out of fear. She could not help bossing him. The more orders she gave, the more pleased she thought she was. And the more pleased she thought she was, the more pleased Dr. Mahoney would be with her, she knew.

One day, sometime after the soup, he, gathering gumption, told her that if she "continued being unreasonable" he would leave. She countered by saying perhaps he should—that her life was misery and everyone in town knew it, and that Dr. Mahoney knew it.

"What does she know?" he asked brokenheartedly.

"She knows—she knows," Ginger said. "So just you beware."

Gus left the house, wandered the streets. Lived in a shed downtown, and drank by himself. Everyone knew he was having a miserable time and he wanted to prove how wretched he could be, to himself as well as Ginger.

"Let her see how low I can sink, then she'll be sorry."

But he would always creep back to the house dejected, and go to bed alone.

Catching a whiff of this when I spoke to Ginger now and again, I got an inkling of why Mahoney should be feared, every bit as much as, if not more than, our former nemesis, Joey Elias. So things became worse, and Gus more desperate.

"You take all my friends," Gus complained to her one day, "and you use them for yourself, and that's not fair. I have no friends now, and you have a whole pile."

"Then just go and live somewhere else!" Ginger Snaps said.

So her husband came home the next morning drunk, covered in dirt, and missing a boot. The night before, he had gone to Dingle's and demanded he see Dr. Mahoney. Dingle had to restrain him, choking him until he passed out.

"The last straw," Ginger said now. "Dr. Mahoney was right. You don't want me to have a life or a friend!"

Gus drew back to strike her, but stopped himself and left the room. "If you hit me I will tell the police!" she screamed after him.

Gus was terrified of the police, because Kipsy Doyle was an officer now. He begged Ginger not to say that again. She relented finally because she knew the police would ask questions if they searched him and found drugs.

Gus left the house, and for days no one knew where he had gone. When he came back he and Ginger lived like strangers. Worse, he had no money for anything. He kept asking for advances from our father, who would say, "I have already paid you up until the turn of the century, my good boy. Do you need money for the new millennium as well?"

The only thing Gus wanted now was the new drug around town, cocaine. Sensing this, as a shark senses blood, Dr. Mahoney went to Noel's friend Ray Winch with a proposition. Now that Gus was back to wanting some "things," let him have some "things" free. Ray Winch feared her deeply. He had seen her twist phrases and tell lies without batting an eye. He felt the only way to end her control over him was to kill her or to become a saint. Both were feasible but unpleasant. He could not say no to her, so he asked what her reasons were.

She said her reasoning was extremely moral and timely. She wanted Ginger to share in a freedom the young woman's mother, Elizabeth, never had. She said that she wanted to prove that her world and her view were every bit as moral as those of a woman she knew who was a nun and whom, she often maintained, she had been in a great contest with since she was a child.

"You would not understand," she told Ray. "It is a woman thing. But this nun and I have divided the world between us. She thinks her world is the right world, and I know mine is. She is superstition. I am logic and control."

Ray Winch was born on the river but had grown up in the south end of Saint John, with an aunt. He had met Mahoney there some years before. He remembered her quite differently then, with her long red hair. He was even sure she went by another name at that time. But he knew her logic and control were like a bear's vise. The secret was, she had many things on him, and he was frightened of whom she might let know.

Out of jail again, Ray Winch ran a small bottle exchange. Selling amphetamines and hash, and more recently cocaine and PCP, was far more profitable. (He was not unlike his father, who in a previous generation sold rum for Joey Elias, rum that at times tore out the throats of First Nations men and women.)

Like many people from all walks of life, he believed selling drugs was not a crime, and these things should be legal, though at the same time he did not want them legalized, for he would miss the six hundred percent profit he now enjoyed. So in this disjointed world, he was a master of contradictions—hating that the police kept him down, and yet needing them to, to sell his drugs at such a profit.

Dr. Mahoney, sitting on a pile of empty bottles, her arms folded, knew all of this, of course, and much, much more.

The idea (far from true) was that Ray understood Noel like a son. Ray secretly found Noel a bother. Dr. Mahoney understood this as well, and placated this by giving Ray Winch what he needed (but not everything he needed). Ray, who was in fact a bad man, kept Noel out of harm's way of other bad men. But he did this because he feared Noel's mother. None of this was ever mentioned.

Dr. Mahoney told Ray this town was hers. She could have anything she wanted in it. Years of observing people had taught her exactly who was vulnerable and who wasn't, who needed things and who didn't. Like Joey Elias before her, she was titillated by the fact that many people expected to be cheated. Many were vulnerable. But most of all, the Kings were vulnerable.

"How is that?"

"Trust me," she said. "They are a family falling apart. I, as a trained psychologist, know this, my good fellow."

Now Ray had his doubts about her. She had been under observation by police in other towns, with her sign out and a Ph.D. behind her name. But to be humoured delighted her, and he was willing to do this.

She said that as a registered psychologist she would accomplish something fine and leave something spectacular for people to remember her by. And as much as she respected Joey Elias, his name would be eclipsed by her own. She brushed her hair back and gazed at him. Even Ray Winch could not stare for long into her eyes.

"How will you do this?" he asked.

"What have I discovered since I got home? I have discovered that Miles King had a child, Ginger."

"So what?" Ray asked. "Everyone knows that."

"Well, I will tell you," Mahoney said. "This was an unexpected bit of luck—with my son, Noel, coming into his own. A man who understands women and treats them with decency!" She looked around to see if anyone else was near. She began to speak in the curious self-justified way of a professional paid to pass judgment on others. "Miles is a drunkard. I knew from the time he was a child he would be. He was weak and would take to sucking on the bottle."

"How did you know that?" Winch asked.

"I was here some time ago, and knew him as a boy."

She smiled. Furthermore, she said, people had tried to do right by him from the time he was a boy. But they could not prevent him ruining himself and the business, even though they had tried. The theatre was a mess now, and whose fault was that? "Joey, kind heart that he was, tried—to no avail," she said sadly. "And Janie put the poor man out of business."

It was also a fact that Elizabeth had suffered terribly because of Miles's behaviour.

"That's true," Winch said, who actually liked Elizabeth Whispers, and was therefore easier to convince now.

"It is certain that Ginger suffered because of Miles's drunkenness. Any psychologist will tell you as much. She in fact is an enabler, and wants men to be drunk and weak. And it is also certain that because of this suffering, Ginger is attracted to men who will use her for what they can get. Because she lacks self-esteem, and does not believe that she deserves her money. This is certainly true in Gus Busters's case. He is a phony. I knew that right away."

"Yeah, I can see that," Winch said, proud to discover the same powers of observation that she was exhibiting.

It was also true that no one cared that this was true, except Mahoney herself, and maybe Ray Winch and Noel.

"Of course I care," Winch said.

So it followed that Mahoney could not let this man, this terrible Gus Busters, destroy this wonderful young woman, whom she was just getting to know. So give him what he wants, and let him destroy himself. It was for Ginger's own good. And in the end for Gus himself, who might get clean and sober and start his life over in another town. All of this would work to their general favour. In a way she would be doing a medical service, just as she had done in other towns across Canada and the States.

"How will it work in our general favour?" Winch said, using a file on a metal crate, his huge arms moist with sweat and his eyes half covered with hair, and chewing gum in boredom.

"Oh, I have something very big planned for us." She shrugged a moment and lit a smoke. She knew Ray Winch was a strange man. He was amoral, but there was a certain code by which he lived and worked which others could admire. This woman who was just "feeling her way into town" knew she had to handle him with kid gloves. But she knew this also, our doctor of psychology; she knew she could make Ray Winch believe what she wanted him to, because of his greed. In all her life, she had never lost at that game. Besides, he was already indebted to her. She had hired him to work at Dingle's, and he had come with some plaster and drywall and had charged three thousand dollars. Ginger had paid for this. So he had cheated the young woman and now must continue.

"When will Gus pay us?" Ray Winch said. "I'm just getting by, by the skin of my teeth, as it is."

"Are you so poor you can't bide your time?" the old woman asked, almost ferociously, so Winch immediately cowered. "You leave that go for just a little, and we'll see what happens."

"For how long?" Ray said.

"For as long as we have to," she said matter-of-factly, her gaze cold and her hair brushed back severely from her forehead. She thought a moment and threw down her smoke. "I have studied these cases all my life. I have helped families from one end of the country to the other. I came here and saw Elizabeth Whispers—what a horrible life that woman must have had."

"Yeah, too bad," Ray said sadly.

"Well," Mahoney answered, "if Gus starts to mess up, he has a young wife who is not going to stay with him. Oh, he loves her, but she is already getting tired of him. Why shouldn't she? She is the most precious woman I've ever seen. Besides, this is a new age. The last thing a wealthy, independent woman has to put up with is someone like Gus Busters, taking her for everything—isn't that right?"

"Of course not in this day and age," Winch said without the least emotion, but suggesting, in his tone, that Dr. Mahoney had no more real concern for Ginger than he had. He paused, and said, "I have some fairly good coke, and I have some that I cut a bit. So what do I feed him?"

"I don't want to talk about it," she said sadly.

"Then there is this," he said. And he brought out something that only a few on the river had tried: angel dust.

"That could make him sick," she said.

"Yeah, very," he said. "If he doesn't ask what it is . . ."

"Well—that's up to him isn't it?"

It was said so matter-of-factly, so ruthlessly, that he shuddered. He looked at her and, putting the small bag away, said, "What is this *really* about?"

Mahoney looked behind her, and then went and closed the warehouse door. She came back and sat on the same crate of bottles. "I am only helping Ginger King. I got my new idea one day while walking downtown. I was wondering what in heck am I doing back in this small, out-of-the-way place. Where did I, Dr. Mahoney who knows most things, go wrong? Why did I bring Noel here? What would happen to Noel in this place? I knew he was in trouble and I know he is a handful, but so much of that is other people's fault. Then I happened to look up, and I saw it."

"Yeah, and what did you see?" Ray Winch asked.

"I saw the statuette of Georgina, Janie King's little girl. I remembered the story about her, and I had a feeling that it was destiny that I be back in town and that something great would happen for me!"

"Oh, yeah," Ray Winch said, still plying the file to the metal crate.

"And," she continued, "that Janie herself had led me toward this decision. I stared at the statuette. Janie wanted me to see this, to make my mind up. It was as if I seen the world clearly for the first time, and was given an insight others did not have. It comes down to that. I decided that Noel and Ginger have to be united. Janie would want me to take over—she's letting me know—so if I have to do something ruthless to take over, I will have to do it—Janie herself wants me to keep the business going. It's as if she spoke to me from the grave, saying: It is up to you, Dr. Mahoney, to see this through. Her son is a weakling and Ginger needs help from a woman. I want Noel to settle down and get away from those people—and I want him someday married to Ginger."

"Yeah, and what's in it for me, Doctor?" Ray said, caught by a woman he knew was far too devious and brilliant to be actually insane.

"Doncha worry your little head. You'll end up with as much as Noel and me."

Still he tried as best he could to warn her now, just once:

"You should leave everyone alone—go away for good."

But she knew that wasn't possible. It had taken her almost a lifetime to get back here at the right time. She had waited for Janie's death. Just as she said to a priest long ago that she would never go away, she felt she could not now, and that her fate was sealed.

She left him and walked back down the hill on the street named after my grandmother. She was hunched forward, her feet moving in their new sneakers, chewing gum and huddled into herself, a sad strange little creature no one knew, in the midst of our town.

———

Gus Busters had left his wife and lived his days in the back sheds in town, with young boys who mocked him. He had no friends any more.

"Please let me come back, Noel," he would ask, standing about ten yards away from his friend.

"No. You displeased Momma," Noel said.

"But I won't no more."

"It's up to Momma."

Then it happened. Depressed since his argument with Ginger, and feeling like a bad son since his mother's death six months before, much to his surprise he was given two grams of cocaine that Saturday night, in one of those small sheds filled with the scent of beer and urine, as the sun faded over broken shards of glass and threw glimmers of orange light on the wooden floor.

"What's this for?" Gus said.

"For you," Ray said.

"When will I have to pay you?" Gus asked.

"You want me to take it back?"

"Of course not."

"Well, when I want you to pay me, I'll let you know." Ray patted his skinny shoulder, and rubbed his mop of red hair.

Some of the coke was cut with powdered sugar, but some was pure. And some had been cut with PCP. Noel and Cassie had cut this by themselves, for they were more daring than any of the others and liked to take it. Nothing could give you more energy than PCP if you could handle it. And if you could not, it was even money whether or not you would live.

Gus, shivering with good luck, took it home, the first time he'd been home in two days, holding it under his faded shirt. He ran past Ginger and into the upstairs bathroom, where he spread it out on the cracked hand mirror. Then, in leisure, listening to the tap dripping, he did four lines.

He was fine. He sauntered downstairs and began to laugh and talk with Ginger, making up her plate of dinner. Then, suddenly angered by the peas, he tore the stove from the wall.

Later he found himself out on the highway, in his underwear. Seven police officers wrestled a rolling pin from his hand. Kicking, screaming, frothing at the mouth, he fell to the dirt, had a seizure, bled from the nose.

Dr. Mahoney stayed by Ginger's side in the hospital waiting room.

"He's ruined himself," Ginger whispered, rubbing her hands, tears in her eyes, "he's deliberately ruined himself."

When Miles came to the hospital in trepidation (fearing to go into buildings where they might admit him), carrying a box of chocolates, Ginger, in kind of an epiphany, yelled and screamed at him in front of Dr. Hardy and Dr. Wise, and cried on Dr. Mahoney's shoulder.

My father trembling his mouth unable to get words out, simply called everyone—even two of the youngsters from the shed, Doctor.

When Gus came out of his coma four days later, he was 126 pounds, morbid and ashamed. It was raining, and the first thing he heard was an intercom. He felt for the first time that it was useless to live. He wrote my father proposing that he take his life, and asked Miles how he might accomplish it.

"Without giving up any secrets, you seem to be doing a good job now," my father wrote back. "But I believe, my dear boy, without laying blame, that all of this seems to have happened because you are popular and visited Dingle. If you shoot yourself, leave a note which says, 'I was cleaning my rifle and as you by now may have guessed I did not know the damn thing was loaded.' That might throw the scent a little. But I will also tell you this—you would be sorely missed by me, my fine chap, if you did."

The week after Gus was released, Dr. Mahoney went to see Ray Winch. She said he should press for the money now.

"Now? He's so sick he does nothing but puke."

"Now," she said. "He owes you thirteen hundred dollars."

"More that that."

"There you go."

"What if he tells?"

"He won't," she said. "He's too frightened of displeasing Ginger."

The cards she was playing were played in the finest sequence she knew. She was doing this for Ginger and Gus's benefit and not her own. This is what she told Cassie, who had been under Dr. Mahoney's mentorship. Just as Joey Elias had confided in a girl called Rebecca Druken, so now Abigail Mahoney confided. Cassie said she could help if need be.

"In what way?" Dr. Mahoney said.

"I know exactly what to do to sabotage their business," Cassie said with a forced smile. "Not that I would want to. I mean, the drive-in screen will tumble in a second."

"Why would we want to do that?"

"Perhaps you might want Ginger, one day, to start another business."

Mahoney sat back and looked at her young protégée with increased admiration and just a slight tinge of alarm. Cassie sat forward and grabbed one of the chocolates from the box Dad had bought for Gus. They had found their way to Dingle.

Ginger went to Dingle's the next day and found Dr. Mahoney at the table doing a jigsaw puzzle and having a gin and tonic.

"I wish I could be that happy just once," Ginger said.

"Here," Mahoney said, and poured some gin into a spoon.

"I don't drink," Ginger said. "Because of Daddy—and Gus—as you might know."

"I know," Mahoney said, touching her shoulder and smiling. "And I know your grandmother did not drink because of her terrible father, going to the theatre to burn it down. However, she did take a tablespoon at night."

"She did? How do you know?"

"She admitted it herself in the paper—I wanted to read about her when I came here. She was a pioneer."

"Yes—I remember now," Ginger said. As if Janie had mentioned this.

"Of course. And that helped her a lot, in making her great decisions," Dr. Mahoney said.

Ginger nodded, not at the prospect of having gin but at the prospect of making great decisions, closed her eyes and opened her mouth like a child.

FOUR

My father's past was always around a corner, and at times I could hear him pacing all night long.

"I find it hard to sleep," he told me. "I find it doubly hard to have to live through the conspiracy against myself." He took a drink, and spoke about letting the cup pass from his lips ("I cannot allow any cup to pass") and about who was going to kiss his cheek, etc. "Not, I hope, the doctor—or, for that matter, any doctor!"

Over the winter of 1979, it emerged that my mother was dating Noel Mahoney. There were a number of different stories about this, all of them fatal to Father. She arrived alone at certain bars, or dance clubs, but late at night, after many drinks, she would leave with Noel, always out the side door, thinking she would not be seen. She gave him money, bought him clothes so he could take her out.

On February 14, having bought Mother a gigantic Valentine's card and signing his name to it shakily (I helped him pick it out, and helped him hold the pen to the page), only to find out she was not at her apartment, Father threw one of our potted plants across the table, and smashed it to bits, cutting his thumb. Fearing he had murdered "one of God's fellow creatures, so to speak," he staggered away and lay down. I heard his laborious breathing, and saw only the bottoms of his shoes sticking up at the end of his bed.

Later he came out to the kitchen and said this: "I keep trying to figure it all out, Wendy. I'm unhappy about Dingle and what I started in 1930, in the damn snow."

"What do you mean?"

"My mother said I'd regret having Dingle as our derelict, and I already do. Well, forty-five years have passed, but still, I already do. He is a great foil to us. I never particularly cared for Hank Snow— oh, except for the yodel. Having a young woman to sit on one's lap is worth a yodel, I suppose."

He still couldn't bring himself to blame Elizabeth. Neither could Ginger, who now saw nothing wrong with my mother's attitude. (She had heard nothing about Noel and Mother.)

But I had to be firm. I told Miles bluntly that he had to get help with his drinking. He nodded. But a week went by and he did nothing. I pressed the matter again.

He looked at me a long moment, and answered me with the strength of conviction. "I am not able to. Do you understand, Wendy, my good man? I am no longer able to stay sober—to see things that are there—to remember going to the store with Rebecca to pick out my granddad's Christmas present—or to remember Georgina and how she would get so upset when the wheels of her carriage got stuck in the mud—she would yell at me, you see:

"You—you are an idiot, Miles. Everyone says you are and you are my brother!"

He laughed slightly, and then taking and pouring almost a complete tumbler of gin, and sprinkling it with just a small dash of tonic water, he whispered, "I am so—sorry."

But he was not whispering to me.

Spring came and my father was hospitalized for the first time. But he stayed only a day or two, and came out, and had a nice gin, and forgot what the doctor had told him.

"I am as fit as a fiddle," he said, "and am willing to take on the world."

I had made myself a room in the basement of Dad's house. Here it was cooler in the summer, and I could come and go up the back patio stairs and not wake my father. But one morning I woke to a cacophony of senses. I walked into the living room, drapes still drawn against the terrible conspiring light of day, and saw Elizabeth Whispers, tipsy and slightly staggering, but trying to be a lady still. My father, always a gentleman, was sitting in a chair with an aperitif in his hand, listening to her with rapt attention, like an old stage play we might have seen where some hidden dagger was soon to be revealed. The rapt attention could only be given in a comedy, so early in the day. It was 7 a.m., by the dining room clock. Of course the aperitif was being drunk because the gin was gone.

"Six-thirty," he once advised, "is far too early for an aperitif. But 7 a.m.—is high time we had one."

My mother had come to berate him for a host of things he was doing, which as far as I was concerned were none of her business even if he was doing them. (He had in fact one date in this time— and she was angry about it.) But her main concern was his trying to take Dr. Mahoney's friendship away from her. Dr. Mahoney had helped her move into a little apartment, was the kindest person she had ever met, understood the trouble she had suffered, and had done, she said, "everything for me." Then she added, "I will be lost without her, and you are trying to take her away from me!"

My father, always mortally aware of the way life and rumour inter-mingled, said nothing for a brief moment. And then, as if finding respite in the process of raising the aperitif to his lips, said just before he drank, "I am sure you know I have no love for that woman— Mrs. Mahoney, as you know her—except the love of the virtuous test of enduring her—not unlike Walter's test in being considered Frankenstein's creature for almost sixty years. I was hoping you would see through her generosity in helping you establish yourself as an independent woman—at my expense—and with, of all people, her son, but I was proven wrong once again."

My mother gasped. Clearly, she'd had no idea that people knew about Noel.

Miles lowered his crème de menthe with a gravity he reserved for his staff, and tilted his head slightly to the side to listen to her once more. She complained that Dr. Mahoney and her son had no more time for her, did not answer her frantic calls, and kept the door locked on her at Dingle's.

"Last night Dr. Mahoney said you two were on the best of terms—and that she understood Ginger, and loves Ginger more than I do." Here she slapped her hands together.

"This woman no more understands Ginger than she does herself, which is both her own and Ginger's tragedy and will envelope our son Wendy, standing behind you, soon enough." He drained his glass and poured another and sat back in the leather chair, staring gloomily at his slippers. "Do you understand they have set out to use you to get to Ginger? Don't you see this, my Elizabeth Whispers? Unless I kill her—or her son—which I refuse to do, at least for the moment . . ." He paused. "Now they no longer need you—yet you could have been here still, where we loved you."

Elizabeth turned to me, startled, and waved her hand, as if she did not know until that moment, in this terrible half-darkened little room, what her dalliances had caused. Oh, she knew of Miles's pain. But now she was beginning to see how severely opportunistic his enemies had been, at her expense. It was a momentary reflection, for both she and I staring at each other. But also in this moment was the shame of her own conduct that sprang out of giddy hope of independence, and was dashed in local gossip and smut.

Only now was she beginning to see it all as others did. Or, what was worse, I suppose, as Father did.

My father pretended he would never suspect Miss Whispers of any more then a "dance somewhat too close with someone I don't approve of," as he told his fellow Rotarians at a meeting one day.

"You are conspiring against the angelic—yes, angelic—reputation of my wife, Elizabeth Corinth Whispers, of Low Bottom Road, Upper Renous."

I tried to get Elizabeth coffee—but she said in a kind of inimical embrace of her own desperation that Father and the Grand and Janie, and Ginger, too, had betrayed her. And that her one friend, Dr. Mahoney, whom she liked talking to about books and music, no longer wanted to see her. I asked her to stay, but she said no. I asked to go with her, but she forbade me. Then she left, her body slightly tilted as she walked along the street, at eight o'clock.

Keeping the Grand open was the only thing Father wished to do. Nothing else mattered, after the death of Janie. It was to honour her, in some sad way to worship her, and he did not care how he went about it. Except to say, in a very principled way, his drinking did increase, and his unkind remarks were more exquisite, and of greater volume than before.

The movies I booked had to be of a certain "quality." It was, I told Ginger, our only hope. *Sagebrush Trail* was replaced by *Lust for Her Bust*. *Truck-Stop Women* replaced *A Song to Remember*. Not that Chopin would have minded, Father said. *The Story of O* replaced *Red Dust*.

"Don't you think, Wendy," Father would say, lighting a cigarette and pondering this, "that's why I've always run old black-and-whites? I want the crowd to breathe in a kind of unique staging, setting, and—what else?—character."

"Of course," I would answer. "But *Shane* will bring in thirty cars. *Sorority Girls Meet the Boys from Hell* will bring in a hundred and thirty." I had to book them, over his protests. I had no choice.

Miles never watched these movies. He was by now too sick at heart. Usually he was gone wherever and returned after the movies were over. In the long afternoons when it was a vacant lot, the drive-in looked vanquished, as if we had fought a tank battle here and lost. Weeds grew up inside the projection booth, the speakers were broken, the lanes unpaved, and dust clouded our view on a good night. The screen was my family's only refuge. The screen was where we lived. It came at a price, but it gave us our sadness and our laughter.

"I did not know monopolies would have such immense power," he told me, "but it seems to me that if you own three hundred theatres you have more pull than the chap who has one. Why would that be?"

Still, he would fight the Imperial for the Grand's first runs. But how did he expect to make his case, if when thwarted on *Star Wars* with Harrison Ford, he turned to the representative of MGM, and said, listing slightly to the right as he did when he drank, "Well, fine. The only thing I will say to you, since you have cost me a picture I had already advertised and you had already promised, something your father, who I'd worked with for years would never do, since you give your word to me over the phone, only to retract it in front of a Famous Players' representative now, and send it off to the damn Imperial, is that at this moment, sir, I fart in your general direction."

"He is dying," I told Ginger over the telephone. "We must do something."

As a last resort Ginger phoned Mother and asked if she might try some kind of reconciliation. So Mom and Dad went to counselling. I don't know how successful counselling can be in the Catholic Church. But the priest was, as my father called him later, "the new breed of priest." He played guitar at mass, invoked the names of psychologists and popular singers. Ideas came and went, but the predominent one was that my mother had suffered at the hands of the Kings, and that my father was unwilling or unable to accept this.

"Don't you think that was true?" the priest said. "The Kings the Kings, it was always the Kings."

My father blushed crimson that this gay twenty-six-year-old priest would say this to him a man twice his age, with such moral ferocity.

My father said politely that he disagreed, if he was allowed to disagree with a representative of the church or with the woman sitting beside him now. And if it came down to the insurance job, he could not in all conscience have taken it when his mother was ill. Nor did he have a right to abandon his uncle Walter at that time. Now that they were dead, insurance was out of the question, for he had a business to run. "If we cannot see this," Father said, "then something about our own humanity has gone, hasn't it?"

"Who said it was the insurance job?" Elizabeth asked.

"Well, considering that was perhaps the last true conversation you and I had, I simply assumed we were picking up from there."

Elizabeth started crying, saying that not one of her dreams had ever come true.

"Then I am sorry about that," Father answered, "but I thought I was dreaming when you got into my automobile that first day."

Then the priest said to my father, "Oh, yes—you're a man of the eighties all right—the eighteen-eighties."

My father sat still, with his hat in his hand, feeling the rake of humiliation across his face. Worse, he had stayed sober to come here. What nonsense—what utter nonsense not to be fortified with a simple libation, like a quart and a half of gin. I think it was, or I believe it had to be, facing that priest that caused the absolute dissolution of their marriage.

"But you are a man of the eighties, I suppose," Father said, "and you will almost certainly pay for it with your spirit."

When they left the rectory, Elizabeth stood with him on the walkway and tried to take his hand. Their fingers touched a moment but that was all, and Father said he would not go back to her apartment for supper.

"But I have lamb chops for you, and we planned," Mother said, getting flustered. "I planned it—and I got a new record for you. You like Orville—Packerton."

My father touched her raw cheek. "Peterson. Oscar. Yes. But I can't possibly—though I do love you—or is it I did—I am not so sure any more. But there was a moment, without casting any stone, that you turned your back on me, and I was left entirely alone."

He turned and walked toward our house in the gloom. She called his name once, twice, to come back for supper, before turning away.

It was the last time they were to see each other. The wind blew in from the north, the streets turned to sheets of ice, and the trees grated and called out in their pain. Deer were shot and driven on the back of trucks around the square, and winter came.

She was leaving the Legion in December, after the party, or during the party. Mother was a bit of a hanger-on, during the shuffleboard tournaments and, at the end, was often seen with Gary Fallon, who owned the new video store, and sold cassettes.

At four o'clock, someone saw her in her old red coat, just as the door closed after her. The place smelled of smoke and was lit by neon beer signs. Her coat belt snagged in the door. She pulled to free it in the gale, and slipped on the top step, falling head first to the cement; strangely, dead, a second later. She was tiny, really, not much more than five-three and revellers passed her inert body by for two hours or more.

I found out that she had one girlfriend, named Dolores Hughes. They went to bingo together.

My sister never forgave my father for this, and in the other world, the interior world, it allowed a crack wide enough in her soul for Dr. Mahoney to enter with her nightly sip of gin that would drown the rocks of despair, like rivers of old.

The next year was a watershed year in Ginger's life.

Her divorce was messy, and revealed a kind of trauma on-going between women and men. He had stolen from her, and from the business, she said, and she could not let that go.

She also accused him of battery. Nonsense, Gus said. He had to fend off her tantrums, her penchant for throwing things directly at his head. She accused him of taking the banister down so she could not get upstairs. He agreed. He did not want her up there, especially when she was insulting him, which, he added, was every night. She accused him of stealing to pay for his drugs, and in particular of stealing our grandfather's coin collection.

Then he accused her of theft of a different kind—of ruining his relationship with his former fiancée. Why? Just to prove she could do it, and because she disliked Kipsy Doyle.

"And could she do it?" Ginger's lawyer, Ms. Devon—well known in our area—asked.

"Of course she could—look at her," Gus said.

The debate continued. Where had their money gone? Why had so much been spent after only a few years of marriage? When was the last time there were sexual relations? How had the Cadillac been damaged? Neither of them wanted to answer these questions.

Ginger, sitting in her plain dress that showed her soft throat and bare shoulders, said he caused in her several nervous breakdowns, and wouldn't cut the lawn. Gus blamed her fragility of temperament, her tantrums, her flaunting her once-prominent position, on her grandmother, who had instilled in her a sense of superiority that she did not think she deserved.

Ginger countered this by saying Gus was terrified of high places, and wouldn't rock climb with her.

Then the first day of the proceedings were over.

"Thank God," my father said. Then my father went with the rock climbing.

"Yes, no matter how acutely psychotic we may be as a family—no mountainous terrain is going to give us nightmares—are they, Wendy?"

The next afternoon, leaning in the heat of midsummer, it came out, as indecisive as anything else in our family. It came like hash through a vent, like a dozen little boys whispering their attentions to her when she was thirteen and had breasts before any other girl.

There it was, the seemingly most modern of accusations, in the most modern of settings for our new generation, the hint of incest that Gus assailed her with, the hint of Father's relationship with Ginger one night when she was four or five.

"She admitted to me that her father used to pick her up and carry her from her room to some secret place," Gus said. "That's why she is so messed up. That's why she hit me with a rolling pin. That's why she loves to walk around naked as a pineapple." Why pineapple, I do not know.

Late in the day I confronted my father with this.

"Of course I carried her out of her room," my father told me, his legs and his arms trembling, "and put her on a comforter in the closet—and closed the door."

"Why, in Christ's name?"

"I was hiding her. Don't you see? I had to hide her."

"Hide her from what?"

"I don't know—I honestly do not know. But I had to—I had to hide her like I should have hidden Georgina. Don't you see?"

"Not at all," I said.

Then he told me that though he could not remember the specifics, he did think that when he was little Rebecca used to give him sleeping pills so she could rifle through his mother's closets. He said that he used to wake up and see other people in the house, and it terrified him. That was why he put Ginger in the closet.

"Christ," I said. "Father, are you ever fucked up."

"But not so much as to harm a little child," he whispered, "or anyone, for that matter—even if," he added, taking a drink of cool Scotch, "they have injured me."

Even I was now a suspect. The great house with its gables and its pot of Irish tea, thick and dark, was a place of haunted memories that had transfigured us all.

It was a relief to me when the divorce came in silent August. However, my father was thought to have screwed his daughter.

"I know many do," he said one day when he was alone at the restaurant with one sandwich slice and four double gins, and ladies from the IODE were looking across the room at him, "but I assure you, my good kind imperialists, I am not one!"

But Ginger did not refute the suggestion of incest, in court or anywhere else.

"That poor young girl needs so much help, after something like this is done," Dr. Mahoney told Ray Winch, echoing the sentiment of much of our town. "But she has me now, and I will never leave her side."

Her statement, of course, crept back to our house.

"I must get my theatres back," my father said, holding an umbrella one cloudless day. ("To ward off the tomatoes they will pitch at my head.") "But I do not know how. Right now she has too much power over me. I hate to say that, but it's true."

"Give Ginger time. She will settle down. If she could only find just one friend who would truly care for her."

"No, son—she is ripe for the grand mistake, the great finale," he said softly. "She is ripe for a quart of gin and a driving lesson into the sea."

She had no idea her life could be so disastrous—and I suppose she had no idea that disaster could follow her all the days of her life, that "surely goodness and mercy will follow me all the days of my life" could easily be "surely terror and heartbreak will too."

She was heartbroken, over her marriage, yes, but mainly over her lack of knowledge—her part in Yeats's poem, that of flattering beauty's ignorant ear, her part being, I know now, the ignorant beauty—and still being in love with trying to do something right. That was her tragedy.

"Did you know," she said to me one day, "that girls went to school and burned their bras and have marched for their rights?"

"Of course I knew this," I said.

"What do you think of it?"

"Most of them are privileged."

"Well, Wendy—there you go."

But "there you go" left her at a loss, and in some despair of ever being taken seriously. All those young women whose promise once seemed less than hers had leapfrogged into a new world, leaving her behind. In a small town theatre started fifty years before by her grandmother.

FIVE

I suppose if any girl would fall for Noel, it would be Ginger. Here was someone who was more dangerous than anyone, greater than anyone, someone who did not believe as others believed, who could make his own way as few others did. Father said, "That is what he has managed to convince those easily convinced that he is."

But there was something else—something that Dr. Mahoney in helping Ginger could never have foreseen, which played into her hand, like the age old game of the pea. Ginger knew that I feared Noel was the one person who might seduce her, and in that way capture some of Father's business. Now Ginger—like a fly testing the strength of a spider's web—must see for herself what I was worried about, to rebuke me as her stuffy big brother.

Looking back, I see that it was part of Noel's greater tragedy to be beautiful and empty, and to be controlled by his mother who applauded beauty and emptiness as a virtue. He was like a shell Dad placed with artistic flourish in the garden. It was part of Ginger's tragedy to be beautiful and to have the required money to pour into this empty shell. Noel believed he deserved this, and no one told him differently. Women gave him money; it was part of the universal plan.

In all its frantic searching, the age allowed this vacancy. It allowed for despair in finery, in doeskin coats and suede gloves. It allowed just once more what Camus understood about ancient Greece. It allowed for Noel's tragic beauty; the harshest and most barren of all.

The month of my sister's divorce, Dr. Mahoney brought Noel into her bedroom and closed the door and, sitting on the bed, said, "As you know, I am not going to live much longer. But I want one thing."

"Tell me and you'll have it."

He saw how her hair, brushed up red over her ears, made her look manly, how her white T-shirt showed freckled and sunburned arms. He remembered hundreds of nights with her alone in empty places, always seeking a moment that was destined to come. He remembered she had taken a course in university, he did not know what, but if people were suspicious of her credentials, he defended her with viciousness. He would tell the Lord himself she was an accredited psychologist if she wanted him to. And she did.

"I want you to get married. And then I can die in peace."

"What about Cassie?"

"No, someone special. This has to be a secret for now."

"Who?" he persisted.

"Someone I think might be worthy of my son. That is all."

He was good with older women, those dissatisfied that the world had left them out, and this is what he was thinking she must want. And he was not averse to this.

That week, Ginger met Dr. Mahoney at the Palace Bar. Ginger had come to see Dr. Mahoney as the touchstone to a world she wanted. The world that Dr. Mahoney understood, women like Ginger deserved. And Ginger wanted more than anything to succeed where her mother, Elizabeth Whispers, had failed. More than anything Ginger wanted this.

Mahoney ordered a gin.

"I'll have my spoonful," Ginger said.

Mahoney looked suddenly angry.

"What's wrong? What did I say?"

"You are not a little girl now. You can have more than a sip a day! In fact, I think you should. Throw off the damn yoke."

"That's right," Ginger said, and she too ordered a gin. She felt nervous about this, for she did not trust herself when drinking. But besides, there was the idea of gentle hypocrisy here. What had Gus or her father done that was much more than to go to a damn bar and throw away some yoke?

"You," Mahoney said, "are a freedom fighter."

"No," Ginger said, blushing.

"Of course you are. You finally handled your disastrous marriage. But I don't have much time left."

"No—don't say that."

"It's true—and I have never lied to you. But you are a real fighter. You own a business—you and your grandmother did more for women on this river than anyone—and I spent my life studying women in society."

She smiled and took Ginger's hand. She looked at this hand, with the wedding band gone and the small graduation ring still proudly displayed, and remembered what Cassandra said about sabotage.

"Did you ever think of having another business someday, something else altogether?"

"I haven't thought of it," Ginger said. "You know Dad—he still thinks it important to keep the business going."

"Well then, at any rate, I am lucky to have you to talk to, Janie's own grandchild," Dr. Mahoney said. "Look out for Noel—just look out for him. There are too many women who want to lead him astray. If he only had someone to ground him—like you!"

"You're my friend," Ginger said spontaneously. "You are the kindest person I've ever met. Of course I'll keep an eye on Noel." She said this like a child, knowing she was not mature enough to do what she just promised.

But Mahoney's faith in her brought tears to Ginger's eyes. The doctor ordered another gin and wiped tears from her own eyes as well.

"What is it?"

"My son—he has such a crush on you. But he's so shy. And he didn't want me to say a thing, because you were married and are such an important person—"

"Do you mean it? Noel?" Ginger, who was more than slightly drunk, said, her eyes glowing. She found it unbelievable. But she also knew this was the reason she visited Dingle's in the first place.

Did Dr. Mahoney believe anything she was saying? At this moment she believed every word. For in her life, from the earliest time until now, she could never remember telling a lie.

———

The next afternoon Mahoney waited for Noel to come back from Bathurst, and when he finally got home, she said, "Someone whose people own a business that we must take over!"

"Who's that?"

"The marriage. She loves you, I can tell."

He looked outside over the dark lawn, the brown fence, the trail of smoke from a barbecue and heard the shout of a child.

"Who?" he whispered.

"Ginger King."

He leaned back against the door frame. Ginger had just been divorced. It was perfect timing. His mother simply stared at him, with her green cold eyes, her figure still remarkable for a woman her age, waiting for his decision.

He remembered his mother speaking once in fury about the Kings years before, and though he had forgotten it until now, by chance all of this was to come about, and it was as fresh in his mind as if she had just said it.

But Dr. Mahoney made him promise not to say anything and contact no one in the next week or so. Ginger, she said, was a flower already bruised.

So, following his mother's edict, Noel made no attempt to contact Ginger—now that the "cat was out of the bag" and now that she was free. The idea of being free, Dr. Mahoney told him would allow her the choice not to be free. This was the play they were making—subtly indifferent to freedom that it was. How could it be indifferent to freedom—simply put, there could be no freedom without forgiveness. It was something our psychologist did not contemplate in her life of helping others.

After a week Ginger impatiently sought out Dr. Mahoney again.

The woman sat in Dingle's living room. Her sign was still up in the yard, faded now and lacking the punch it once carried. For there were complaints, not spoken loudly, that her only interest was in herself and that she took money from unhappy, hopeless people.

Ginger was one of these unhappy, hopeless people. "Were you serious?" Ginger asked.

"About what, my dear?" Mahoney was wearing a bright yellow shirt. Ginger could see the tattoo on her arm beneath the fabric.

"About Noel."

"What about Noel?"

"That he likes me."

The woman sighed, as if she were truly pained that Ginger would doubt this.

"I told you, he's just been through a terrible relationship. She was a liar and told him she loved him but didn't, even though I tried to keep them together, and I don't know if he wants to take a chance. Men are far more fragile than we are, really. Something like that they never quite get over. Besides, in my profession I've always cautioned young women against jumping back into a relationship. But then you strike me as being—more mature."

"Well," Ginger said, exuding all of her considerable charm, "you just tell Noel that I've been through a terrible relationship too, and I am mature—though I'm not a very good catch, I guess."

Dr. Mahoney picked up a grape and gave a smile, as she looked around at nothing. Everything was coming about because she wanted it to, and she was doing everything for Janie's grandchildren, just as the men on the bridge were doing everything for Janie's children. In her travels she had discovered one fact—many people wanted to be gulled. It was what Joey Elias had discovered at the circuses when he was sixteen. And it was what he had told Ms Mahoney when she was someone else all those years ago.

Later she told Noel not to go to Ginger for a week or so.

Noel liked teasing people. He enjoyed harming people too, but he never admitted that, for he was under his mother's thumb. He had taken money from older women who could not afford to give him any (Elizabeth Whispers being one). He smiled when they handed it over, for he disliked women, just as, he sensed, his mother disliked women.

He liked harming Mr. Dingle as well, stealing his pension cheque and hiding his medication, but he did not admit it. His mother, who saw these traits in him, refused to acknowledge them, not because she did not want to admit it but because he reminded her of herself when young. But it was also the one thing she worried about, for Dingle's pills and cheques were missing, and only Cassandra and Noel would have had access to them. That could be the undoing of her plan.

Contrary to his mother's instructions he kept his girlfriend informed. Cassie remembering how vaguely charming Dr. Mahoney was, felt duped. She told Noel that she would not stand for this. He could not marry that rich quiff, she said.

Noel assured her everything he did would be done for her. That they would get a lot of money and be together, perhaps go to Mexico.

"Well then, you must marry me first."

"How could I do that?" Noel asked.

"Who would have to know?"

Cassie was under investigation for stealing funds that were meant to buy team jackets for the high-school volleyball team. She would do some time over this, she said curiously without emotion, so she wanted his loyalty.

He said once she got out he would make sure he had done what he must, and they would be free of everyone, and have lots of money. He understood, our Mr. Noel, that she would not be there if his money was not.

"Mexico is fine," she said, and she smiled.

At week's end, just after work, Ginger was walking along the street above ours and saw Noel approaching, head down, deep in thought.

"What are you afraid of?" she said timidly. "I won't bite."

He stared down at her.

"Now," she said, taking a deep breath, "here we are—" And she reached up and hugged him.

He grabbed her and took her to a corner of an old warehouse where my father once drank as a boy. It smelled of silt and soot and old creosote logs. He wanted to tell her what was going on, just to torment her. He wanted to tell her about Elizabeth, just for fun, just to see how she would react.

"I'm broke," he said.

She put her fingers to his lips and kissed him. "I know," she said. "But if we care for each other, so what?"

My father began to react to all of this by staying almost drunk, almost always. I would hear the phone ring for hours, it seemed, while he sat beside it in the kitchen staring at the wall, or quoting from some obscure journal neither I nor anyone else remembered. Then he would leave, only to be brought home by a neighbour or two who were still concerned enough about him, or about our neighbourhood, to act in a conscientious manner.

His new escapades catapulted us into the paper again that fall, after all this time. He ran for mayor. "I believe that all enemies of the Kings should be drowned in their own urine," he would declare.

So Father's health became my primary concern. On a bright special day, he woke early—for he had slept badly, and was bleeding from the mouth. The night before, drinking with him in the den, with only one turtle-shell lamp illuminating our faces, he said to me, when I ventured that he should quit drinking, "It is impossible to drink with you—you are not a drinker, I find, and you have a limited conversational ability—and the reason is simply this, Wendy—after three or four days of drinking you sneak away for some food."

The next morning he woke early, dismissed the bit of blood on his pillow as some kind of lubricant for his tonsils, and turned on the ancient recording he had made as a child, listening to the old warped scratching of it. "Good morning, Miles. How are you today? Nice to see you. Have you made any new friends?" It played over and over and over, for upwards of forty minutes. Then finally, and thank God, he replaced it with Chet Baker, and as the melancholic West Coast jazz came slowly drifting to me, I heard him say, "Ah, no, I have not—not one friend in fifty years. Not even my son. It may be my fault, for a man to fire on his own troops should have the decency to expect to live alone. But there was that moment, once, when poor Elizabeth Whispers held a party. I did not realize that it was not they but I who was the main guest. I was the invitee, she the inviter, into a new life I would not step—and so then you see, it follows—her coat got caught in the door."

They were powerful lines for me, for they peeled more of the harsh onion away.

He was shaking and blue, and seemed to have a slight problem catching his breath. He opened up some cooking sherry and had a small draught.

"I must go back to England and find my father's relatives," he said to me. "There lies my hope. I will become a landowner somewhere in the midlands, and tend sheep by the flocks. I am not made for Canada, or at least not exclusively so—for the first part, a political correctness is rampant here—and for the second part, I am not sure how much longer I have above ground, so I must pick my final resting place with acumen. Perhaps, then, my cherished home in Ireland, wherever it may be!"

I did tell him that Ginger was in some strange way captivated by the doctor. She seemed to be in her company day and night now. I was reminded, in a flicker, of *Gaslight,* with Charles Boyer and the incomparable Ingrid Bergman. Ginger looked like Ingrid Bergman, at least to me.

"*Gaslight,*" Father said spontaneously, as if he had read my thoughts, "You have told me something, sir, that I have no power to stop—" He said this with gravity and aplomb. "Besides, I ask the startling question, Is she really a doctor—does she know anything really about doctoring—is she even a Mahoney—or is she someone else? No, son, I will not be so measured by the temperature of the moment—I have a longer memory concerning the history of events."

———

I went for a beer as soon as the tavern opened. When I got home later in the afternoon, I got a call from the police. Could I come and see them? What had happened? We will be here when you come, I was told.

I had a strange foreboding that my father was either dead or, worse, had run someone down.

He was sitting in a cell, in his bathing suit, holding his briefcase on his lap. He had gone for a walk wearing a bathing suit and carrying his briefcase. He appeared before the bank manager, demanding a loan.

"Of how much?"

"Eighty-seven thousand dollars, sir. Just enough to ride this tempest out."

"What tempest?"

"Ah—what tempest. The tempest I see all around me—the tempest from Famous Players, who have my first runs. The tempest of the cable company who runs *Playboy After Hours*, the most sanitized of sex, don't you think? The tempest"—here he whispered—"from a woman who has ensnared my daughter's innocent heart. Besides, I need a new screen at my drive-in, and it would be handy to have a screen in order to run movies—don't you think so, sir?"

Sweating, smelling of gin, not having eaten in a week, he looked—well, not dishevelled because he was wearing only a bathing suit—but more than a little under the rails.

When the bank manager, a well-kept, blow-dried fellow of twenty-four asked him to leave, he said he would stand his ground come what may. Then police bringing him to his cell, they discovered twenty minutes later that he was sitting with his briefcase before him, being used as a table, and a quart of gin sitting upon it, the gin cap beside the quart, and the quart half drained.

"We didn't check his briefcase," Kipsy Doyle told me. "We thought it held important papers. Well, he *is* a well-known businessman."

I did not tell them they had shirked their duty, for I knew them all by name, and rather liked Kipsy Doyle.

I brought my father home, where he was most excitable and truly discouraged about being called a businessman. Nothing, he said, was further from the truth. He was a magician and a song-and-dance man, a hoofer, if it must be said, who could still do a tap for damn St. Patrick.

"Remember Cagney," he said. "*Yankee Doodle Dandy*," and he did a shuffle into our favourite drinking lamp.

In the hallway of our house, the picture of my grandmother Janie seemed ambivalent to it all, with the light crossing her face at an angle that hid most of her expression. Yet in her expression was a foreboding, as if she was saying, Wait—and see—and you will know. All will be revealed with time—and time is on the side of the dead, my boy.

SIX

It was Labour Day of 1982. For nine years, every Labour Day—the last big weekend of the drive-in—my father had played *Gone with the Wind*.

"Rebels as poetry," Father said. "As far as I'm concerned, I always went for the rebels. When Clark Gable announces at the first of the film that those damn Yankees would win, I feel disheartened. Why? Not because I believe in slavery (except perhaps my own), but like my Irish ancestors, that great part of my blood has always agreed with the rebel yell. However the Irish from Boston and New York, some of my own relatives, fought for the North."

A Miss Larson—the granddaughter of the man who had the pawnshop where my great-grandfather pawned his suit—sold tickets, wearing earmuffs, and seeing her breath. A slight north wind had come and chilled the grounds.

The drive-in was about half full. There was only one short, for the movie was long—and no trailers about upcoming movies, only a thanks to our patrons for another wonderful season and our ongoing hope that they would visit our concession stand for the creamy hot chocolate and the one-sheet showing Kathleen Turner in *Body Heat.*

It was cool and rainy, and I ran the projectors, shivering and freezing because the heater was broken. Just when the damn Yankees were advancing on Atlanta, and just when the young girl shouted, "Miss Scarlett, I don't know nothin' 'bout birthin' babies," the screen collapsed.

There was kind of a hush as it wobbled, so I tried to adjust the lens to keep the picture in focus, and then it fell completely, utterly and forever. My father's great and somewhat triumphant right flank of the business reduced to a black inscrutable sky. The cables had loosened and stretched over time, and the old screen fell. A screen with no insurance.

I had the unpleasant task of going home and reporting this to my father. The drive-in was like our last panzer move, and now we fell back on our heels. My father looked not only heartsick but frantic.

Over the next week or so, I conveyed to him my regret that our empire, such as it was, had dissolved.

"Sabotage." He looked at me.

"I'm not sure—neither are the police."

"I did not imply a question but an assertion. It was sabotage."

"Who?" I said.

"*Gaslight?*"

"Oh, come—not our Dr. Mahoney," I said (like a grade-school teacher).

He did not answer my extraneous outburst, knowing in a way that was all I had left.

So, like Lee, I went to see General Grant. Ginger was in her office at the house, opening her mail with an old silver-handled letter opener.

I told her that she could get my father to sign, then I would sign too, and the Grand would sell. The drive-in would sell as well, as lots, or a subdivision.

"Don't be sad, Wendy," she said. "The business is gone, but it had a good run, sixty years or so—that's enough. On its ashes we will make our fortune—like Dallas."

"You mean Phoenix."

"Well, I knew it was a city somewhere down there."

I nodded and went, walked slowly past the houses that my grandmother had built, toward the house where I lived. If the screen had not collapsed, we might have held out indefinitely. Now the business would be sold, my father in retirement, and who knows, I might want to someday go to university—the privilege of others I knew. There I could meet fine people with solid motives who would never in their lives think of betraying or cheating anyone. At least the brochures never mentioned it.

Miles tried to write a letter to Ginger about her life and the life of the theatre. He knew that Ginger wanted to sell, but he feared that Ginger would no longer be her own advocate in this. He also feared that she would be an advocate against him.

But he had no letter after ten days; he only had a pile of papers on the floor about his desk, some drawings, scribbles and scratches, and a poem to Mom:

> "Miss Whispers, my love
> a sparrow in the trees
> a sweetness in her eyes
> before the blast of winter storms
> made her sad and wise."

And a line to Ginger: "My dear, dear girl—love, Dad."

It was crumpled up in the corner, and nothing else was said.

A month or two went by, and an offer was made to buy us out by the very mill that helped my grandmother all those years before.

Yet to sell we needed my father's signature that day, and I could not find him.

His room was empty. The bed not slept in, the closets with his shirts and ties were empty.

It was cold, and I could barely afford to heat the Grand. I opened it to a few patrons twice a week, I ran second- or third-run movies, from the backlots of Hollywood, where actors and actresses of the third rate tried to look like those who had made fortunes with a certain chin or coif of hair. They reminded me in their stilting way and poor scripts and halting motion of all the florid glory days of my father's life, the late 1930s and early 1940s.

Though Ginger and I were ready to sell everything, we could do nothing until I found Father.

I did not tell my sister that I began to get postcards.

Dear Wendy,
I'm here in Petra, where the wise men stopped for frankincense and myrrh. What is myrrh? Anyway will bring you home some—don't worry, I have learned the tricks of the camel—every few days you just have to replenish their humps, somewhat like a good drinker.

Dad.

A week later, another:

Dear Wendy,
Have crossed over to Cairo—the place I always wanted to see—going to the pyramids tomorrow—the valley of the KINGS, ha, ha. Will bring back some sand for you.

Dad!

P.S. Have not had a drink today and feel that I might get away with not having one tomorrow.

P.P.S. Remember that terrible movie "Murder on the Nile"?
Now that could make me drink.

Of course the postage gave him away.

I drove on a bleak afternoon to a small resort outside Charlotte-town. He was living in a cabin, the kind that Elizabeth Whispers had rented for us the year we never went. He had locked the doors, and sat with a thousand dollars' worth of booze, and was busy writing his memoirs. He was stuck on page three, and so was busily revising page one and two. The early years—

I helped him dress—he picked out his finest suit, and a new pair of shoes. I asked him if he had ever worn jeans. (That he didn't had always embarrassed me.)

"Good God," he said, tying his tie with a practised hand, and slipping on his rings and Rolex watch. "Why?"

"Not even on holidays?"

"I never took holidays," he said, straightening his cuffs and glancing at me in a kind of silent rebuff, a look of sardonic hope that I hadn't joined the tribe against him. He arched his eyebrows slightly to accomplish this.

"Well, you should have," I answered.

"You're right of course. I'll certainly drink to that," he said. "At any rate, I will probably have holidays from now on, won't I?"

I helped him to the car. For the first time in his life he had trouble walking.

On his return, Father was under enormous pressure to sell, not only from me but from his creditors. His face was often contorted by inde-cision. He refused to take Ginger's calls.

Then one afternoon at the office, as he was looking through the files that covered decades of moving pictures, he suddenly blurted in naïve astonishment: "We have not run one Canadian film. Do they even make them?"

"Oh, I'm sure they do," I said.

"I'm not sure—is it a bad thing to have adopted the heroes of another country?"

"We are good at adopting," I concluded, telling him that many of the actors we showed on our silver screen were Canadian—who themselves had been adopted by the States, or for that matter by Britain.

"This won't do," he said, lighting the last cigarette in his silver case. He then told me that he might have been fooled by this movie business. "I feel I have missed my calling. A great philanthropist wouldn't have sat at home taking orders. Do you think Gandhi was bossed about by his mother?"

"I can't see it," I agreed.

He motioned sadly at nothing. "It is time now to close the book and snuff the candle, what!"

"Yes," I said quietly. "It is."

So, after sixty years in the business, my father suddenly and conclusively (if I can use that word) decided to sign and get it over with.

He stood, straightened his tie in the mirror, fastened his cuffs on his white shirt, and buttoned his immaculate heavy winter overcoat. He picked up his leather briefcase, gave me a wink, walked by the cans of old, used reels, and turned out the marquee lights.

PART VI

ONE

For a while I went during the day downtown to the library archives, searching in the papers, back to that distant time when my father was a child, to try to help him solve some mystery I still didn't believe existed.

I saw a picture of the Regent on the day of Jimmy McLeary's death. Two officers stood there, not looking at the camera. The doorway was open, but looking with a magnifying glass I could not see the key in the door.

I filed on through them, one picture or piece of paper after another, until, "Little Girl's Tragic Mishap" came before me in letters a mile high. It was the local paper.

"Janie King's girl—you might have seen her and her brother, Miles, around our town—curly hair, sharp grin, and a feisty manner were her trademarks."

"Janie works outside the home. Left in the care of older brother, Miles (there was a picture of Miles in his top hat)—Miles was told not to leave the house or yard."

"Miles last summer sang 'Paddy's Boy' at our Dominion Day celebration—a bit of the dandy."

"A bit of the dandy." "Janie works outside the home."

What a conscious bit of terror heaped upon her and her son at that time of grief.

The next week I went over the investigation into Jimmy McLeary's death.

"Fatal Mishap Saves Regent. Angered by unmarried daughter's profession, scandalous pictures, and nightly ways . . . Gas and other combustibles found in basement of Dime . . ."

"You see, I don't remember," my father said when I began to hurl questions at him. "Please, please," he said to me, "I have my poker and my service pistol but I don't know if I can protect myself. Can't you see I am growing tired?"

He did not want to talk. So we drank in silence. That night, his head drooped forward and his wedding ring slipped off his finger and fell to the carpet with the tiniest of hushes.

I roamed the past in those archives while my father spoke about the great plays we would one day either write—no, I think they were already written—or produce, for the large theatre. We would go off to New York. And one day he came in with a map of the city, for our great journey south.

"Stay at the best places—go to the Brown Derby."

"That's not in New York," I told him.

"Well, I'm sure there's a watering hole or two we might find in Manhattan."

"I am sure there will be," I answered.

We could talk this way when we were drinking. That was the characteristic way for us to be men.

"We will make a scene—better than the movies—"

"Yes, but we are very bad actors," I said.

"Then we stick to doing Shakespeare and no one will know."

I found, in looking in the past, little slivers of grass and fields he had passed when he was a boy. I found streams he had taken Georgina to fish in, now dammed up solid—buildings he had roamed alone, long-gone ghosts. The river had changed so much since those days, subdivisions with grey roofs blocked the sun or held snow in the winter; pavement and concrete stretched down in redundancy from Beaverbrook Court to the square, and apartment complexes uttered nothing from their blank windows, their listless suburban sashes, and their mute satellite dishes, eclipsing any triumph my poor grandmother ever had, making all her lonely effort somehow vanish away. The great dark Grand that I wandered in alone—the seats removed, the faces of Comedy and Tragedy torn out to make us faceless once again, the old gold cords and curtains toppled.

I questioned Dad about that Christmas. Where was Jimmy McLeary when they went to the house the second time? Could it be that he was already on his way to meet someone, or to go to the theatre?

"More likely, son, he was out trying to find a draught."

"And why do you say so?"

"Because of Minister Whispers, who came calling after we had left the second time."

"But he died with his suit on."

"Then he put it on after the minister left."

"This only gets us to the outside of the Regent."

"I suspect we can get no farther this evening, so let us have a drink."

Then one night I broached the real subject, that August day of 1932. How did that day start for him? What had he done? Did he remember dressing Georgina?

Then I discovered something very painful, though he tried to tell me how compellingly comic it was. Rebecca had taught Georgina to tease him with certain words. When I asked him what these words were, he put his hands over his ears and told me quite plainly, "Wendy, will you please be a dear and go fuck yourself."

At this time my father was trying his own homeopathic concoctions to reduce the painful swelling in his legs and his difficulty with urination. He used pulsatilla and aconite, made, he told me, from blue monkshood. Very sure these two homeopathic treatments would cure all his ills. If not he would go to the more radical belladonna, poisonous but highly effective. He also told me that silica—flint—would help if he was restive and depressed, or had genital warts or a splinter—neither of which he had at the moment.

But it was seeking a cure for, or at least some relief from depression, and the spite of others, which forced him to try these things. The spite of others, he bluntly told me, had lasted far too long—he had become an icon among town pariahs, which only added to the powers of his enemies.

For a while he drank only dispirited beer (and now and again a brandy). Then we heard what I had been dreading to hear. Ginger was getting married again.

Father wrote Ginger a letter.

Please realize that there will come a time when you will look upon this letter, this seemingly irrelevant page, as the last link to our former life, when we were if not happy, then at least not so dispirited as to go off with bad company. I am not a philosopher or a very good writer—though I have a few poems I'd like you to see—but I can predict with a steady gaze that your marriage to Noel (if not an entire fabrication) is convenient to him and not to you (and most convenient to his mother, our psychologist). And as soon as it is no longer a convenience to them he will let you go—so it will destroy you—sooner or later. Now that I have said this, I am certain you will go through with it—to spite me and the truth of what I have just written. However, I will offer you a carrot with the stick. If you put your marriage to Noel off—for, say, thirteen or fourteen years—I will quit drinking. Yes, you have heard me—I will quit—at the end of those fourteen years as your wedding date approaches. All I have to offer you is my bad liver—but I am doing it with grace and courage.

Love,
Daddy

It went unanswered. This was the enormous mistake, the Pickets charge that Ginger's undaunted spirit had to make. It was what I noticed at fifteen when she wanted her face tattooed at a circus.

———

The town, the quiet unassuming town, however, looked upon this as incredible fun, behind her back. And they had great fun, enormous fun, with the trauma of my sister's life, just as they had had with my mother before her.

My father found this out late one grey afternoon when he managed to walk downtown to get shaved. (He found it horribly tricky to shave himself, since his hands trembled so.) The barber began to hot towel him. He was lying back with a hot towel on his face, and he heard from one of the more galling people on the river, a useless good for nothing, that he had heard that Miles King, who was such an oddball, had long had relations with Ginger.

"Ginger would fuck a mule now," the man said.

"I do not believe that is true, sir," Father said. "Ginger King with a fine education and enormous self-discipline, would never—as you put it—fuck a mule."

Still with the towel pressed to his face, and slightly, ever so slightly, altering his accent, he continued. "And as for the father— well, the father. You see, I know the father—we've had our difficulty, but I'm friends with the father. A better man you could not meet. No, he would no more commit an act against his daughter than he would rape a goat itself, or your wife, for that matter—even your wife—who is, as you know, somewhat goat-like in appearance, my fellow. And the scurrilous whispers against Miss Whispers were entirely unfounded."

Then he added to the barber, "Feeling a little queasy that I might slip with the straight razor, I, with great comportment, have walked down here. Do I need to listen to the licentious talk of fleeting and galling tavern bullies, men who on their own could never find the urinal by themselves?"

The barber told the man to shut up, and the man suddenly realizing who my father was by his impeccable suit, hurried from the shop.

"She will not marry that fellow Noel," my father whispered. "I will take a gun—I will take my service pistol—and do him in. As you can see, I'm a desperate man. Look into my eyes—a desperate man."

The barber began to shave.

That summer, my father went golfing. He was going to become the relaxed and tanned enthusiast of the coffee-table golf-book set, or so he said. He even bought a set of secondhand clubs, and some Titleist balls. He told me it was high time he became social. For man was a social animal, and the termination of his work might enable him to have, if not friends—for who would ever be his friend?—perhaps acquaintances. He said this as he sat in a chair in an empty room. I told him he might even find a lady friend again.

"No one could replace Elizabeth Whispers," he said.

But I tried to wax enthusiastic so he would do it, and even mentioned Dolores Hughes. "A wonderful new world," I said.

Yes, he said, he would get in shape playing and be the specimen he knew he could be.

I smiled. "The young artillery captain again."

He smacked his lips over a Chardonnay at noonhour. Then he said, putting the glass abruptly down,

"Well, perhaps not—but the once-again president and only surviving male member of the Harkins High Glee Club of 1937."

"Where you fell in love with Miss McGrath," I said.

"Never mock June–September love." And then he added, "Especially when a boy has no one else, and his pigeons' necks were wrung like chickens'."

He was, however, worried about social intercourse—that brand of talking and bunting with a society that was underneath, for him, crass in its supposition and knifelike in its responses. But I left him to it, and he went in July—and I deceitfully followed him about, in the woods near the old drive-in, where I, knowing the area, could find him on any fairway. Each day that I went, he stood off by himself, in solitude, came politely to the tee on his own, whacked to the right and left in a skitter of balls, his hair pinched in a clubhouse golf cap that didn't fit, his mouth in grim determination to not make an utter fool of himself, his golf clubs' vinyl bag with the ticket attached to signal his beginner's fees were paid. Sometimes there were squalls that blocked the sun.

"How are you doing, then?" I asked him on July 9.

"Absolutely peachy-keen. Warren and Don and I make a great threesome."

"That's great," I said.

"Well, it is great," he said defensively, "and they are great. But they do not drink—and so I am as a man obligated to go to the nineteenth hole alone. That's why you saw me alone when you came by today."

"Well, a beer is a beer," I said.

"A beer is a beer is a beer," he added.

"We should have one now," I said.

I stayed at the old drive-in lot, now full of backhoes and graders making it into something else, wandered about it, remembering nights of lost and lonely movies, and the twang of Duane Eddy coming from the speakers, while those girls and boys in heat swam in my fading memories to the tune.

Over time his enthusiasm for golf faded, the golf clubs abandoned in the back corner of our empty garage.

One afternoon my father went out for a walk. He stopped at the side of the street, and looked in both directions. Then he came back.

"I have nowhere to go," he said, "so now, what do I do? Do I go to a bar and sit? With whom? I am much more comfortable imbibing alone. I have always imbibed alone. Those children who drank years ago—started at the old age of seventeen—I already had eight years of professional drinking on them."

Then he turned on me and said, savagely, "What a waste—what an incalculable intellectual waste—for you and Ginger never to have gone to university. You have become nothing more than smalltown peons—unread and, as far as Ginger goes, sometimes unwashed. How wretched that must be. What an insipid time of life. So Ginger senses she must make a grand statement now or be forgotten. I know this. It is what happened to poor Elizabeth too."

I told him a little angrily that it was as much his influence as my grandmother's. And I unkindly added that he himself wasn't the song-and-dance man he had started out to be.

He nodded abstractly, and sat at the table with his rolling machine. "Reduced to rolling my own smokes. Christ bless me, what's next."

Bills were outstanding and he had to pay them. He had not eaten at home since our mother's death, but dined daily at a restaurant downtown, even though he ate almost nothing. Those bills put on one of his four credit cards were sapping him. He bought food for the poor, and gave tickets to dances to couples he hardly knew. Looking over the bills, I saw he had purchased three winter coats. They were not for him but for people who lived on the street.

I took him for a drive that night. But as soon as I got to the highway he wanted to go home. I mentioned the bills.

"Yes," he said, "I think I will have to pay these bills sooner or later. Why don't I have the courage to change?"

I was silent. He had more courage than most men I have ever met. He just did not know it.

I walked around and opened the door for him. He got out slowly, held his coat together, and looked up at the stars—at all those magnificent ragamuffins over our heads.

"What is wrong with me?" he said. "Why have I gotten old?"

He went to sleep on the couch.

I went into his office, where the bills were piled up in neat bunches, to look over them, and see which ones should be paid. Most of them were for heat and lighting, and his secret daily supply of booze. There was a cheque written for a bird sanctuary on Miscou Island. His note, in his shaky hand: "For the seagulls and the terns."

He had also taken a writing course to hone his skills for his masterpiece. Reading the comment of his professor, I could tell he found Father amusing and talentless, and I hated the bastard.

"I do not wish to be as great a writer as Henry Wadsworth

Longfellow," my father had written. "Well, who could be—you see, I am not vain. But I would like to be able to tell my life story in a way which might attract a feeble bit of attention so that my life will not have been lived totally in vain—for the memory not of me but of my little sister, who unfortunately fell down a well when she was four. I was taking care of her that day, and we started toward the circus, with such a bright bit of hope. Little did I know the little thing would not be home again. The dang problem is, you see, I have a difficult time remembering anything about it, or my life for years after. And I do suspect some people of laughing at me because of this."

My father had struggled for six months in this course offered by one of the fresh-faced post-modernists, in a way trying to remember and atone for his life; then at the last realizing literature no longer wanted to atone for life but only to smile irreverently and mock it, he gave up, and did not receive a passing grade.

He was being destroyed, slowly, and he desperately needed not to be.

He woke up the next morning at six, saying he was on his way out to kill Noel. I found myself wrestling with him in the street, he with a service revolver in his pocket. I got him to the house, I put it back, and I realized it was unloaded.

In the late summer, Putsy was on her deathbed and asked if she might see Noel and Ginger. After she spoke to them, she reached toward the table to give them her prayer beads that had been blessed in 1935 by Father Carmichael. Noel made a cross with his fingers as if warding off a vampire, and began to giggle. For the first time Ginger saw a banality in her future husband's gaze. For his part, he was angry that Ginger did not giggle as well.

Putsy said nothing. She handed the beads to them both, and made the sign of the cross, and kissed Noel on the forehead. When she looked at that broad forehead, the magnificent shoulders and wide grin, she shuddered slightly, and said, "God be with you, son. I believe you are who I think. Father Carmichael spoke about you years ago. But have no misgivings, he loved you too. He loved your mother as she should be loved—and loved your father, Joey, more than you could ever know."

Noel stepped back and then stood out in the corridor, with a tired-looking nun, while Ginger lingered by the bed.

"Come on," he kept saying, interrupting Putsy as she tried to speak. "Ginger, come on now."

Noel thought it ridiculous hocus-pocus, for one reason—if he did not think it so, he would have to respect or believe. Since his mother spent her entire life proving this was a lie, a way to enslave, he could not respect or believe. He was angered that Ginger did not mock it too.

"Dumb, superstitious old bat," he said. "She'll die alone, having done nothing in her life."

"That's not true! She helped hundreds and hundreds of people!"

"She hasn't helped who my mother helped. My mother helped young women get abortions. She never done that!" he said victoriously.

Dr. Mahoney went to visit Putsy that night. But the old nun, tired and broken from years of duty and prayer, had slipped into a coma. Her hands were thin and ghostly white, her mouth turned down in a little grimace. Above her head was a picture of the Madonna and Child. It was raining outside and four candles flickered in the quiet room. Beside her bed, four ancient nuns, and a group, equally aged, from the Catholic Women's League, were saying decades of the beads.

"She wanted to know if you were her sister," a nun whispered to the doctor.

"All women are sisters, aren't we?" Dr. Mahoney smiled in her best and most understanding way.

Putsy died the next morning, fifty-one years to the day after Georgina. The sun was soft on the milky water.

In the grand old church, my sister looked like a little waif at the pulpit, reading from St. Paul's Letter to the Corinthians, tears running down her face.

We came home from the funeral, Father and I, and sat for a listless four hours staring at nothing, except the subtle gusts of wind over the trees in the summer distance, the sound of faraway traffic going to our pulp and paper mill, and the occasional laughter of a child, who by dusk had not yet known pain.

TWO

In our own bungalow Father and I lived as disgraced members of the larger community. Ginger had made her choice. She had tried, she said, to no avail, to be kind to us. Do not think I blame her—both of us were alcoholic, and had no say in the greater world. And no one listened to what either I or my father said anyway.

So the very form of our house, the very notion of my father's flowers, from pin cherries to daisy fleabane, left us lepers in the noonday sun. So the two of us drank together. Really, we had no one else. And I was slipping into melancholic drunkenness as much as he.

"It must be a sad day when the only one you have to drink with is your father."

"Don't be silly," I said. "You are a professional drinker, just like me."

"Thank you."

"You're welcome."

Then, remembering his past, his voice rose as, banging a fist weakly on his knee, he said, "How can you say that a man who sells used cars in the useless humble-bumble of his life and attracts your wife so she is out selling Amway to make her fortune and hanging about shuffleboard tables is a man? Still you are not allowed to say he is not. Especially if you are a King. We are not allowed to, my boy, that is the thing."

"So for our kind it is best to be silent?" I asked, grabbling with him for the bottle.

"Yes," he said, grabbling with me to take the bottle back while I tried to pour myself a drink.

"Why?" I said, when I finally wrestled the damn gin from him and poured myself a header.

"The world seems against us," he said, looking at me, his fingers twitching.

On occasion he would have to go down to see Ginger and ask for money. Often Dr. Mahoney would open the door for him, and leaving the door opened, turn away:

"Ginger, it's your father!" she would say with a wistful sadness in her voice, for she knew he hated her.

And Father would stand in the foyer of what used to be his own house, and wait, in his ochre-coloured suit and tie. From behind one might see a few slight wrinkles in the jacket. The morning sun would be up over the trees, a godawful time of day, and Ginger, sleepily coming out in her pyjamas, would say, "What is it?"

"Oh, it's not much of anything, really. It's just that at this very moment I am just a little light in the pocket—too light by half."

"You want money?" Ginger would say.

"Shh," Father would say, cringing. "It's not like that exactly."

He would look around, smile at nothing, his lips trembling, and feel the emptiness that one does on particular mornings when there is a slight breeze on your face after a night of imbibing. "I do not want to be a bum—but as you see, this is a certain stretch in my life when it seems that—I have been up against it—so a few dollars maybe— just to stave off elimination—I mean"—here he would chuckle—"you must realize I am in the elimination round."

He would take the money and sneak back home, at times cutting through a neighbour's yard, with the bottle under his jacket. This particular neighbour did not like my father and would often shout at him or throw a stone to move him along. And my father would start to run, as if a dog was chasing him.

"Here we are," he would say to me at ten in the morning, coming over the back fence. "Now we must take it easy with this reprieve, and make it last as long as we can. Let's not open it until supper hour."

I would agree, and go back to my room.

"How dare you slam that door!" he would yell.

"I have not slammed it," I would answer.

"See that you don't!!"

Five minutes later he would be back in the kitchen, calling out to me. "Wendy, I think, however, I will open it now—and have just a touch—a tad, a reminder of old days—of those bright days of youth when I was in a London pub."

The reminder of old days would be gone in an hour. And we would wonder at eleven-thirty in the morning where the rest of the day was going to come from, or how to get it to go away.

One day that August my father brought home a full forty of gin. He sat it on the kitchen counter. He went to the cupboard to look for some tonic water, and bringing out a terribly flat half-empty bottle, he set it beside the gin. Then he went to the far end of the kitchen and folded his arms in determined vagrancy. He looked acutely uncomfortable.

"My God," he said. " My tie—has a stain from an egg. Look at that. I was at Ginger's house with a stain."

And he tore it off, and set it on a chair.

"Remind me, Wendy, never to eat another egg. That was Miss Whispers's idea—eggs and cauliflower and all of that. I'm an independent man now, I make my own decisions." He slapped his fist into the palm of his hand and nodded to himself.

He went into his bedroom, put on a fresh shirt, and put on a new tie. The heat had made him woozy, he said, and he was wondering if I could drive him to the beach that afternoon, for his yearly supply of seashells.

"Of course," I said.

"You know, of course, if I drink that, I am doomed."

"Why?"

"There is a certain sacred rule that will be broken. You see, I went to the house this morning—my mother's house, now in Ginger's name—and I was ready to confront Rebecca, a.k.a. Dr. Mahoney, ask her how she had managed to skewer so many of my sayings in the bloody paper when she recently told her life story, which in a way was my mother's life story. 'I swam the river' is a godawful exaggeration. I was going to get to the bottom of all this—are people intentionally hauling the wool over their own eyes, or is she a master criminal? That was my intent in seeing her."

"And did you?"

He looked at me a brief moment with a quizzical expression. "However, she talked me out of any confrontation with—this." He pointed a shaky finger toward the bottle of gin. "She had it waiting for me, as if she knew I would be there to see her. She smiled and handed it to me, and patted me on the shoulder like a nanny who had told me to go to my room—or polish some damn silverware, which I still insist was more than her job—her duty to Mom, in a certain way—and—well, you see—I'm in a luckless position now. 'You must must call me Abigail if you take this,' she said, eyeing me, holding the bottle up to my nose. So"—here he cleared his throat—"for the fucking bottle of booze I did. Besides, I am not overly overjoyed by the colour scheme she is using on the front foyer."

We both stared at the bottle.

"So you have given in and called her Abigail? You can give no argument now, can you?" I laughed.

"You see," he said, pointing to the gin again. "This is what Joey Elias used to do with old Jimmy McLeary, although Jimmy was a real Maritimer and drank rum. I prefer a more toxic libation. However, that woman is doing it to me—it's the same old world, just another go-around. Abigail I must call her—if I drink it."

"That's terrible," I said with compassion.

"What she is really doing is taking advantage of me."

"In a way she is," I said.

"Well then, I won't give her the satisfaction by drinking it."

"Of course not. Pour it down the sink."

"I should," he said, shaking his head bitterly. "That's what I will do."

"If you do pour it down the sink, you still have the moral right to suspect her. But one drink—you lose that right. I think that's what she's saying."

There was a long pause. Old hedges, old flowers, old child's cry, another hopeless summer day, without the requisite tallies and cans of film for our drive-in, our innocence in the kind of debauchery we were forced to run at the end, my father looking at these movies with the fantastic and fatalistic gape of a child. "Well yes, you are right there. However, I am more sensible than that, Wendy. I know this is a one-time thing and I will drink it—and it will be the last drink I have. And once I am sober I will be able to call her whatever in hell I want!"

I would not take a drink of it, and watched him agonize over every glass he consumed. I was very jealous that he consumed it all.

"I have just discovered something."

"What is that?"

"Her gin," he said, pouring out the last glass, "whatever her name is, is as good as any other."

In those intervening evenings, the slow drooping evenings of summer, when we had nothing to do except watch the pitch and toss of a baseball game on TV, a bottle would now and then find itself on our doorstep, put there by an elderly woman driving a Cadillac.

One night I told him that this settled it. He could not go about calling her Rebecca Druken any more. I would not listen to him if he did.

He looked at the bottle of gin, and like his grandfather before him, he gave up.

"I will not mention it again," he said.

One day when I woke I saw him pacing in the kitchen, with a kind of determined startled agony on his face.

He looked at me, detached, and sober, and said that he had to go out. I helped him get ready. He shined his shoes with the deliberation of a man being hanged in the morning, and brushed his jacket with the slow care of a shopkeeper you want to get away from.

"What's going on?" I asked him.

"All in due time," he said, looking in his top drawer for his regimental pin, and making a quip as he put it on, that the pin was just about the only thing left that was "top drawer" about him.

"Don't be ridiculous," I said, picking a piece of lint from his collar. "*You* are top drawer, sir."

"Thank you, sir."

"You are welcome. But what is going on?"

He turned toward the bedroom door, a bedroom smothered in wretched closed-off summer heat, passed a picture of his mother, and one of Elizabeth Whispers, and said as he walked away, "Mr. Dingle is coming here."

"Your stepfather."

"Yes—well, sort of—they were not married, and he did dress like Hank Snow—however, I just got a call."

"He is no longer able to be at his house, I take it."

"Quite."

"And his friends are gone."

"It does seem that way."

I drove him across to Dingle's in a car that sank on its tires and wobbled about the bumpy turns on the side lanes of town.

He lit a cigarette from his silver case, and now and again shoved the thinning hair from his eyes. He looked remarkably calm, except now and again his fingers trembled slightly.

Mr. Dingle was now a tiny man of almost eighty years old, with a blue suit and tie, and heavy, almost bombastic-looking shoes. His hair was gone, except at the very back, like hair that sometimes remains on the head long after the body is in a coffin. He had been left by people, by Dr. Mahoney, who could no longer care for him, and then after her, Noel, who had listened to his stories about theatres that he owned and had waited for his pension money, until he had exhausted that.

It was obvious Dingle did not know where he was any longer. There was a mark over his forehead where someone had hit him with a frying pan. The house was a shambles, holes in the living-room wall covered by velvet paintings of Elvis and show horses.

We took him home and put him in the guest room. He was the only person to ever use it. Over the next few days medical statements arrived, as did his medicare number (he needed a new one because someone had used the original in a scam for amphetamines), and a referral to a Dr. Hardy, three bottles of pills, morning, noon, and night ones, and a few letters stating his condition and the advancement of Alzheimer's—perhaps he would go in the next few months, perhaps not—as well as a picture of him in Saskatoon with a woman in 1956, with a pencilled line on the back: "Your daughter."

"Somewhere along the way he must have forgotten her," my father said. "How fortunate for him."

One of Dingle's arms had been pulled from his socket in a dispute over a bottle of ketchup.

"It seems he lived in a room in the basement of his house for a number of years," my father yelled. "That, I suppose, is like living somewhere south of hell."

My father laboriously went over all the notes, the instructions for diet and pills, and he would shout out to me from the other room, as if we had a brand-new reason for living:

"He is not to have any chocolate. Hide the chocolate."

"I don't have any chocolate—when have you last seen two practising alcoholics eating a chocolate?"

"Ah yes," my father said, pausing a moment. "And it says here he is not allowed to smoke in his room—grab his smokes."

"I'm sure he doesn't have any on him. That's just a reference point for you, Father—"

"Oh—he is not to have any alcohol." There was silence. Then Father muttered again. "He is not to have any alcohol. Those bastards."

"We'll give him a drink," I said, "if he wants one."

"Of course we will—for Janie's memory. That is, if we have some to spare," Father answered. "He needs a bib to eat—a bib to eat, Wendell! Do we have a bib?"

"We can use a dishtowel. I've seen it done with regular babies."

"Oh, yes. Okay, fine. He still has his three meals a day, and he likes singsongs—"

Here my father stopped, and his throat caught as if he was ready to weep. I looked into the room, and saw him with the letter in his left hand, while his right was patting Mr. Dingle on the shoulder.

"It's okay, Miles—it's okay," Dingle mumbled.

After we put Mr. Dingle in his room, I watched my father nervously fidget and move papers about. "You don't mind keeping him?" I asked.

"Of course not."

"Are you up for it?"

"Absolutely!"

"You mind that he never liked you and always took Janie's side in disputes over the management of the theatre?"

"Of course not, you—you PROSECUTOR—PERSECUTOR," my father said. "NOR do I want you to say anything about this in front of Dingle. Bygones are bygones!"

Then he took his fingernail clippers out and began to trim his nails, not looking in my direction, but breaking out in a whistle.

It was strange to get up the next morning and see this little man at the head of our table, almost bald, yet his skull looking ancient instead of young and new, with his huge bombastic shoes on our front mat, and being spoon fed a mashed boiled egg. I went to the fridge and had a beer, the place smelling of sweat, and the lingering scent of the mill over our bushes outside. My father watched me drink the beer, and then told me he was worried about his own drinking.

"I must stop drinking," he said, "at least for a time—it's unsavoury to have your nurse dead drunk in the middle of the day." He wiped Dingle's tired and pinched little mouth. "Besides, if I have to see about a new medicare number and getting pills, I can't be slurring my words as I approach the authorities. What would they think? They would think I wanted medication for myself. They have no sense of humour—most of the bastards are my former fellow Rotarians."

He did stop. He put the cork in the bottle. Sometimes he would clip a flower or two and put it in Dingle's room. He cleaned spittle and changed diapers, and said not a word to me, who couldn't do it. He dressed in immaculate fashion and curried favour to get what he needed for his "stepfather." He took him for drives and wheeled him out among the petunias to take the sun. He read to him the stories of Sir Walter Scott in his amazing voice, pausing now and then to tuck a blanket about the man, and turning pages with a practised finger, until the old lad fell asleep.

He informed Dr. Mahoney, who had always made much of the fact of her relationship with Dingle and how much she loved him, and asked her if she wanted to come up and sit with him awhile.

She did come, and held his hand, and spoke to him, tears running down her face, her hair just as severe, her forehead seeming to thrust out.

Father told her he wanted and needed help, and smoking a cigarette, looking over at a pile of old magazines on the bookshelf, he asked for it.

"What kind of help?"

"Well, if it is possible, Dr. Mahoney—excuse me, I mean Abigail—perhaps some help changing his diapers and feeding him one meal a day. I can handle most other things. You could sit with him a few hours. Perhaps at night, if he needs to be moved or put on a pot—"

"Change diapers." Abigail smiled. "What do you mean?"

"I mean, without being indelicate, Mr. Dingle needs his diapers changed. But since you were once his best friend, in a way, and taught him to 'groove' in a new way, and grow his sideburns, so to speak—Abigail, his sideburns didn't do that much for him—Abigail in a way!"

She did not come back.

Ginger helped with money and time, and came over every day for a while, wearing her light blouse, diamond earrings, and summer skirt that seemed in our house of dark furniture and old wars to embody the naïve and terrible wonder of the outside world that blew in with summer gusts from the door. But then she forgot, or had other things to concern her, so we were left alone.

We hired a day nurse who had a gruff sense of detachment and humour and carried Dingle back and forth from the bath to the bed.

The old house with the flowers and seashells, and nature trails concocted by the former artillery officer, had a visitor from our past.

Some nights Dingle would wake and scream, "The bastards are coming! Kill them all!"

And my father would rush in to him, yelling, "A fine idea! Kill them all. They who would not let you move beyond that basement room."

Once I woke up to a scuffle in the kitchen in early morning. Dingle was trying to down all his pills before breakfast. He was hunched over with his bib on, fighting for his pills and trying to bite my father's nose. A week later, I saw my father hobbling about the living room, rubbing his leg.

"Got me with his damn wheelchair—came at me like a tank," he said, looking up at me, his face showing as much inquiry as mine.

I realized that at night, when the streets were dark and lovers lay abed, as Thomas might say, my father was having a horrible time. I stayed up with him, and took turns, but there was a night when I went into the kitchen and saw blood on Miles's face, where he had been scratched almost to the bone.

"He was almost sure I was a Winch," Father explained.

The next day, Dingle remembering nothing about this, obediently sat at the table awaiting his boiled egg.

But something else occurred. It was said that because of this day nurse (whom Ginger had helped pay for) we had "alienated" Dr. Mahoney. In fact, the day nurse, a Mrs. Lovett, hated her and had threatened to slap Mahoney if she was rude to Mr. King again.

"You are—whoever you are—a damn fraud," she said.

We had not known that this Mrs. Lovett was a downriver Lovett and her sister's girl was Kipsy Doyle.

"There's something not right about Mahoney," she told us one day. "I don't know what it is, but I am certain it is something."

Father, smoking a cigarette, asked, "Do you think she is a trained psychologist, as she wants us to believe?"

"She's trained at something, and she's exceptionally bright—and very dangerous," Mrs. Lovett said, but would not go any further than that. Mrs. Lovett came even when Dad's money to pay her had gone.

In the months he lived with us, some eighteen thousand dollars was spent. But poor Dingle did not know this, sitting in the corner in his Hank Snow hat.

And one day, after picking up the fallen leaves in the garden and bringing them over to the compost, I came about the corner near the snug green hose and saw Mr. Dingle, frightened of falling as he stepped among the spent coltsfoot, hugging my father for dear life, and Miles, somewhat unsteady on his feet himself, and whose cheek still bore the lashed scar, saying:

"Don't worry, my man—I got you—I got you, and I won't ever let you go."

"You're not that Mahoney boy who knocked me with the pan?"

"No, my good fellow. I am the little English King you knew when you were young."

Dingle died in November. It was a bright, clear day, and children were off to school, children the age he was when he joined the Canadian forces and went overseas and fought like a son of a bitch in the trenches that they leased from France.

In his last rambling days he was still searching for something, fortune or peace or his daughter, I do not know.

He was buried alongside my grandmother with almost the exact same funeral entourage. He seemed to be the very last link to that former age, and my father was surely adrift.

PART VII

ONE

My father, having exhausted what funds the sale of the theatre had afforded him, and realizing that Ginger controlled the rest, and dispensed with them as she pleased, took a job as a crossing guard about fourteen feet from his house—which meant at times he could be a crossing guard while sitting in his house and staring out the window, through the shrubs and beyond the front-yard birdbath, assortment of homegrown flowers, down to the tired driveway shale.

He would open the door and signal the cars to stop. "There's a crosswalk," he would call, waving a red kerchief, and then slam the door shut again. I told him this was not the best way to endear himself to the school board.

"They are a bunch of hacks," he told me. "School board—politics for the sake of it."

Out he would go, dressed in bright blazer with black buttons, with rotund sign, and in practised comedy he would lead kids across the street who did not want to go.

Our house, that fall, was becoming more dilapidated than ever. A squalid yellow bungalow, haphazardly standing amid a multitude of flower lakes and gardens intertwined, a foundation that was crumbling, and numbers of small detached hothouses stretching their way to the back fence, hothouses built or reclining together over the years. One can see Mr. King's fantastic hope of making it into a kind of fairy land. One might see my groping upon it as well. A place of conical seashells and whispering lilacs blowing all our sadness away; shrubs named for Elizabeth Whispers, flowers named for Georgina, and a potted plant in a wire hanger for Ginger.

317

For Ginger to have stolen away Gus Busters those long days ago was not an astonishing feat. She could have done it with one subtle movement of her hip, or arching forward to whisper in his ear, driving with her light-as-breath smile every thought of Kipsy Doyle into the dustbin of history. I thought of this the last time I saw Gus Busters, getting on a bus at midnight, on his way to Moncton to try and start his life over, to get away from the reputation he now had in our town as a hopeless former husband and a snitch to the police.

My father was worried. Dingle's funeral took much of what was left. Often he would be seen staring at Dingle's old wheelchair and remembering some terrible day. "Why did he wear such large shoes, when he had nowhere to go?" he said one day.

At other times he would be dressed to go out of an evening, sure to make a splash, he said, in a nice pinstriped tie and grey-flecked jacket, only to find that he was once again short of funds.

"Can you loan me a ten-spot, Wendy, my dear boy?"

"No, I cannot."

"Is there anything we can drink here?"

"There was a pint of cooking sherry."

"There is no more."

"Some debilitating aftershave?"

"Gone as well—all gone."

"When do you get paid, Father?"

"Pardon me?"

"When do you get paid?"

"I have quit my job. I have quit. How many matinees have I run in my life?"

"Thousands."

"Thousands are right. Well, you see, I will not be cursed at by a six-year-old"

"A six-year-old."

"Absolutely—she was six."

"She?"

"Absolutely, she was a she."

"What did she say?"

"I simply said, 'How are you this morning, my darling little miss?' and she said to me, 'Go fuck yourself, ya prick,' as she lugged her burdensome book bag across the street."

"Times have changed," I said.

"They have at that, Wendy, they have at that. Besides that, the book bags are getting more and more burdensome, and those dark school hours never ending, and the mentors less and less helpful. Perhaps if she knew who I was, that I was Miles King who once owned the theatre, who fed her mom free jelly beans—"

"Then she would recant," I said. "Then she would recant."

"By gum," he said.

During the late fall he would spend days looking through the old cracked pictures he had got from Maurice the photographer, staring at them and pondering what he or his mom might have been doing at the moment the picture was snapped.

He would then, to save himself from despair, speak about the Grand, the plush seats, the carpet running along the aisles to the bottom floor, the great gold curtain that folded against itself at night. He would remember with exquisite aplomb Vincent Price. And he would remember people coming to those movies in a way no one did today. It was more than just an attraction then, it was a counterbalance to their entire lives.

And of them all Bogart was his favourite male actor, Audrey Hepburn his favourite female.

"But," I said, "you are far more like Olivier."

He paused, trying to get a drag from his rolled cigarette, and whispered, "Out, out—all out. Life but a walking shadow," and left the room. It was as if the entire Grand and sixty-five years of movies were swallowed up behind him as he moved.

Now former businessmen, his fellow Rotarians looked askance when he went for his walks, shaking and trembling; trying to avoid him, for he would stop them and say, "As you know, I have been a principal shareholder of a major business, and I will be again, so if you could spot me a dollar or so, I will take it under advisement that you have been good to me. Not only will I take it under advisement, I will do more—much more, I will take out an advertisement that you have been good to me. Your name will be published beside mine, and over time our names will be synonymous with goodness, kindness, and truth."

He sold his regimental pin, and drank the reprieve that it afforded.

This was Janie King's boy at sixty, trembling and reduced to begging, just as his grandfather had been. I would bring him home, but he would be gone again, secure in his fatalism and his assurance that there was some mystery to solve.

Once he was tripped crossing a street. He hobbled home along the sidewalk, his coat and pants ruffled, and his hand cut.

"So," he told me, "it has come to this. I am the almost perfect reincarnation of one Jimmy McLeary, for not only the imbecilic finery of the town smirk in my general direction when I go about asking for a dollar, but the fierce and malicious and poorly coiffed riffraff as well."

There was something else that he had, besides his paintings (which he could not sell or even give away) and his three-page essay on his Blue Bead lilies that he had revised sixty-four times and had paid to have typed on transparent typing paper. A man came one night in March, and went away with it in its case.

The man was leaving as I walked up to the house.

I found my father with the little pile of money before him.

"How did you get the money?"

At first he would not tell me, but I became so angry that he finally confessed. He had sold his service pistol.

"Well, he has mice in his shed and he has to get rid of them somehow, Wendy—so what am I supposed to do?"

"You are not supposed to sell your service revolver," I said. "To the very man who tripped you—to Ray Winch—Noel Druken's bodyguard."

That was something Miles had not known. He had forgotten all about Winch.

"That was Winch? That was *the* Winch—the last of the Winches?"

"That was he. Winch whose task it is to take care of Noel."

"You don't say."

We both stared at the crumpled-up money.

"Don't you see," I said, "Noel wanted that pistol away from you, for you told the barber you would use it on him."

"On the barber?"

"No, not on the barber—on Noel—and he has bided his time and sent along Mr. Winch to get the gun from you—he has taken your pistol—" I yelled. "And Noel will marry Ginger for sure."

"Well, we cannot pick and choose our relatives, now, can we?" Miles said, defensively, drubbing his fingers on his knee, and then brushing away some imaginary lint. "If only we could—some industrialist millionaire or some such—beverage maker, perhaps."

"Dad, this is the worst of the worst mistake," I said, almost in tears.

"Oh, I am certain I have made worse mistakes," he countered. "*Plan 9 from Outer Space* over *Star Wars*, with Harrison Ford, when I come to think of it."

He looked at me, and nodded in sharp compliance with my judgment, and in self-scorn. Then he stood, straightened his jacket like a gentleman, tersely turned, and went into his bedroom with the money clasped tightly in his hand. It was awful to be so reduced, and to remember what a brandishing of promise we once had, a few short years before.

We began to drink that very money away the next morning, both of us—although I stayed in my basement room while I drank mine.

As spring came and the wedding approached, Dad was increasingly bothered by the old pictures he had acquired from Maurice's studio. Hundreds of them, without names or dates, lay across his bed. He looked at them through a magnifying glass that he had received as a promotional gimmick from an ancient Sherlock Holmes movie star-ing Basil Rathbone. At least thirty shoe boxes crammed with pictures.

"It will be the first Druken–McLeary wedding since 1791," he told me. "That was a mistake, and this one will be as well. Our paths have crossed before, my good man—yes—and not so many years ago. Well, two hundred. I doubt this time if we will be hanged, yet I am sure some of us should be—and you see this is the fodder for intellectual play—our families hanged when innocent, and a short two hundred years later applauded when guilty. That's progress for you!"

Then early one Saturday morning he came out of his bedroom, and laid an old black-and-white on the kitchen table.

"It's the tent—where I went to see the monkey show."

"That very day?"

"I don't know."

"That means you might be inside the tent right at that moment," I said, smiling, thinking it all wonderful for a second.

"Just over on the right—you can see two of the children's legs."

I looked at the small stockinged leg of a child being whirled about, up and down in a circle of joy a half-century before.

He went back to his bedroom and closed the door. Thirty minutes later he came out again.

"But if it was raining, it might have been the last shot he took that day—everyone running for their cars." He paused, looking at the picture again. "I'm not looking for Georgina," he said, "if you think I am."

"Who, then?"

"Rebecca."

"What do you mean?"

"One second of frame for fifty years—from anywhere I could find it—"

"Why?"

"She took my sister that day."

I stared at him.

"No, I'm perfectly sane—I think. She loved Georgina, not me, and coveted everything my mother had. Georgina wasn't looking for gold or anything people imagined or put in the paper. Nor did I abandon her, as people have long told me I had. She was taken from me, to get back at Janie. She slipped and fell, and that was that."

"How can you know?"

"I can't."

"Then don't talk about it."

"Right," he said, laying the photo aside.

He cut himself a half a grapefruit and, putting a tiny bit of sugar on it, began to eat.

"Only one small incident tells me that I am right," he said, laying a seed aside with his spoon and looking up at me. "I did not remember anything about this until one night Dr. Mahoney came into the Grand with Ginger by the arm. Then I started to remember it, slowly, little by little. Perhaps I drank to forget it."

I did not answer him.

"Only one small incident in my entire life—are you listening, Wendy?"

"I am listening."

"Well then—do you want me to continue?"

"Sure."

"Good. It's been slowly coming back to me since that evening. I was jolted into a clarity about something—I'm not sure it is everything, but something. Rebecca had me by the hand one day, and took me to Joey Elias's. I believe that if it wasn't for Putsy at the door she wouldn't have let me go home—she would have taken her chances trying to get money from Janie. But the way Dr. Mahoney held Ginger and the way Rebecca held me was exactly the same. I don't mean somewhat the same, I mean exactly—the way she turned in her leg and crooked her elbow—which means that they are the same person." Here he paused to spit another seed on his spoon.

"Well, if that's true, how the hell is she going to slip up," I said, "after fifty years?"

He kept eating his grapefruit, and then he shook his head slightly and said, "Because she wants to—in a way she has to. That's one of the main reasons she has come back—to prove in the end she is Rebecca, right when we least expect it."

"To tell you?"

"Yes, she has to tell me in some way what she did, to show how much more clever she is than my mom."

"Like Moriarty," I said, staring at the magnifying glass.

"No, no. Just like Rebecca, poor distant cousin of Janie."

"Cousin Bette," I said.

"Who?"

"Balzac."

"Ah well—Balzac," he said. "But you see, there is still in her that spark of decency, the very human longing to be caught."

"Raskolnikov."

"Who knows if we can find the literary equivalent?"

He seemed dissociated from what he was saying, as if he was looking down upon himself from the ceiling and he was pushing the child's carriage across the fields. The early-morning wine coupled with grapefruit, perhaps.

Still, I had to tell Ginger, in private, and she decided for once to keep it in private. We met across the river, at a restaurant close to the golf course where my father once thwacked his rounds.

"Perhaps we can get Dad psychiatric help," I advised.

"We asked this before when Mommie was alive and he didn't go," Ginger said. "I don't know what happened to him as a child, but many men grow up with domineering mothers. You cannot blame this on Dr. Mahoney, who has no idea what in heck he is talking about—except to say it is a way to dominate me even more."

"I believe so," I said.

I saw the light reflected in her eyes, and realized how fragmented our lives had been.

Ginger was willing to pay so Dad could get help. But the help he needed at a private clinic would cost thousands. I told her the first thing I must do was persuade Dad to take the help.

"There's another summer coming," Ginger said. "Will he even be alive for our wedding? How many more summers will he have?"

I went back home and opened the door of our yellow house. Miles was still talking to me as if he did not realize I had left two hours before. He was sitting in his room, thinking I in mine, and he was saying, "Yes, I have every intention of figuring this out for the memory of my family. It is simply an extension of the sleeping pills Rebecca gave me when she wanted to rifle through my mother's closets. I have no hesitation in saying that she might be a master criminal. Are you listening, Wendy? It's shocking to hear, I know, but, you see, that's the trick—she has never realized she has committed a crime. Her son's marriage to Ginger is a perfect example. There is a seed of conceit in there, Wendy, or deceit, if you prefer. Everyone believes her, thinks of her as Dr. Mahoney, yet I myself will not be won over so easily. You think this paranoid. By this marriage to my little girl she will have everything she wanted from the time she was eleven and went to Janie's theatre for a Saturday matinee—everything she wanted she will have attained by this. What will she do, Wendy? I will tell you. She will throw it in my face, to prove to me it was calculated all along—even though it is as random as the handkerchief falling from Desdemona's paw. Are you listening, Wendy, my son—my son, my love?"

He went to sleep in the chair that night. The next day he was unusually chipper, going about his yard and raking last year's twigs out of the flower beds in the lower part of his garden, with his brimmed hat and his bare feet (for he found it troublesome to put on socks or tie shoes). He came into the house for some lunch.

"I am proud of you, Wendy," he said, sitting heavily in the kitchen chair. "Well, to a certain extent—let's just say I am at least as proud of you as Mommsie is of Prince Charles, that idiot—if I may say so— so I am as proud of you as a prince. But you have not figured out what

I have. Our Mrs. Lovett has figured it out. That's why Dr. Mahoney feared her. You see, Noel's mistake was taking money from old Dingle. That's what is being investigated, the beginning of the falling dominoes—so they must do something very quick and very big to go. They must get some reward for their terrible effort, and leave. That is all they are working toward at this moment—to get Ginger's money and go. They have to hurry now, or they'll end up in court. But a hurry will cause a mistake sooner or later. Then they will begin to squabble against one another, a little here a little there—vultures at a carcass picking out each other's eyes."

"What carcass?"

He poured himself a drink. "What is left of our business."

I caught a glimpse into Father's terrible world I had always known was there yet had not seen (if it was true), walking around, inhabiting the same space as we did, yet invisible as specks of hatred in the eye (if it was true). Brilliant as Lowry, as understanding as Orwell—yet a curious difference; the great shame of knowing and never being listened to.

He downed his drink with a wonderful thrust of his hand, and looked at me with a merry, merry (insane) eye. "It's all a seamless thread. How do we get Mr. King (that is me) to sell the business—the Grand? We destroy his right flank—the drive-in. We cut the cables to the screen and make it fall. Cassandra helped Dr. Mahoney see this. Gus Busters, who owes money for many draughts of cocaine—is it draughts?—I am unsure—realized this and is set to tell Ginger. Mr. Winch comes to my house and buys a pistol. Gus Busters was the mouse. The mouse runs away."

"My God," I said.

"My God," Miles answered, "has nothing to do with it. He only wills or allows. And in this case he allows."

He stood and took the bottle of gin from my hand. Then he sat down and poured another.

He complained that his pants had not come back from the cleaners because of some silly bill he did not know he was supposed to pay.

His breathing was laboured. The wedding was in two weeks, the party planned, the caterers hired; sorrow, sorrow, sorrow.

TWO

It was completely beside the point that I had totally forgotten Joey Elias, and had forgotten what I had heard in my childhood about the hidden life. There was something from this hidden life now pushing Dr. Mahoney forward, faster and more recklessly than she had ever wanted to go.

Telephone calls came from Sleepy Hollow prison for Women.

Cassandra was as a protegé at the apex of understanding. And what had she understood? She had understood Dr. Mahoney's thesis— nonviolent intervention as a way of interjecting oneself into someone else's life for one's own benefit. And what life had she wished to interject herself into? It was none other than the life of Dr. Mahoney.

The phone calls came at random, and at first were simply annoying. But then one afternoon the conversation took a more deliberate turn.

"It's just that I feel so lost," Cassandra said, "now that everyone is getting on with their lives. What's in it for me?"

"Well, dear, haven't I given you some helpful hints?" Dr. Mahoney said.

"Of course you have," Cassandra said. "I'm just thinking."

"What are we thinking, dear?"

"I'm just thinking about how terrible we treated poor Mr. Dingle."

"But did we treat him so terribly? I don't remember."

"Oh, I wouldn't say anything about it. But what might Kipsy Doyle say? There's all this talk of old people being beaten up. What if someone thinks that's what we did to old Mr. Dingle? I have a good rapport with the warden here, and she is interested in me also. She wants to see me get out from under this mess and make something of myself—instead of all that violence."

"Is this an outside line? This isn't being bugged, is it?"

"I don't think it is," Cassandra said.

"Well, all as I can say is, it is up to you how you want to take what I have shown you."

"But it's not up to me, Dr. Mahoney. It's up to them—it's them we have to fool."

"What do you mean, dear—fool?"

"Oh, you know—we always try to fool people."

"Who would I try to fool as a certified psychologist?"

"No one, but if they do get fooled we must help them."

"Yes, yes—but who is fooled?"

There was a long pause. Then, "Ginger."

"Oh, I've never heard anything so foolish—"

Cassandra hung up.

The doctor could not get in touch with her again for four days. She could not sit still, and barely slept.

But after four days—in which poor Dr. Mahoney had not slept, the phone rang.

"Will you accept the charges?" the operator asked.

"Of course. How are you, dear?"

There was silence.

"Cassandra, dear, how are you?"

"I have the envelope."

"What envelope?"

"The envelope that held the money Ginger sent with Gus—you gave to me—Ginger would know."

"What would Ginger know?"

"That I stole the money. And you told me to blame Gus. It would be awful for her to know that—if she was about to get married."

"I never heard anything so misunderstood. I never told you to steal. Besides, you might have got an envelope from anywhere!"

"Yes, except that it has the note."

"What note are you talking about, dear?"

"The note to Mr. Dingle telling him to get his teeth fixed. That's what made me so sad about Mr. Dingle and worried that we had fooled poor little Ginger."

There was another long pause. They could hear each other's breathing.

"But I thought you knew why we had to do that," Dr. Mahoney said.

"Oh, I know why you *say* we had to do that—but I don't know really *why* we had to do that. I don't think any accredited psychologist would say that."

"For her protection, dear—for her protection from Gus."

"But you know Gus couldn't hurt a fly, Dr. Mahoney."

Mahoney tried to sound stern. "I don't know why you are going on like this and I don't know why you are changing your mind when we settled on something and—"

"I'm afraid she might find out, too, about something else."

"What else—what else could she find out?"

There was another long pause

"You and I are in the same boat," the doctor continued. "No one has done us any favours. That's why we tried to help Ginger."

"Elizabeth and Noel. What would Ginger do if she found out about Elizabeth and Noel?" she said, and hung up before Dr. Mahoney could answer.

Three days went by before the next phone call. On a Wednesday night, Cassie asked for some money.

"But I have no money," Mahoney said.

"I worked very hard for you to catch Ginger—like starlight in a bottle, you once said. Perhaps you should help me!"

"I see," Dr. Mahoney said. "Well, you are being very pushy indeed."

"Not at all," Cassandra said. "I am only besting someone in an argument. It's what you taught—nonviolent intervention. I'll be out of jail soon, and I want things settled. I think I should have some money too—if everyone else has."

There was a long pause.

"I will see to it—so you be quiet and enough of this chatter!" Dr. Mahoney said, hanging up.

Mahoney might have thought that a few dollars and she was rid of the child. But then a postcard came. It was something unexpected— and the doctor was very careless not to expect it. This again seemed to force everything into the realm of whimsy—of events not controlled by a woman so used to controlling them.

"Here's a card for you," Ginger said, a week or so before the wedding. "It's from Cassie."

Mahoney snatched the card, like one might an indiscreet photo they didn't want a child to see, and turned to read it by the sunlight through the window.

Dear Abigail,
I hope all your plans are coming to fruition, as I believe they will. But I have to tell you a little secret. I feel guilty about it, because I want to make something of my life. You see, Noel and I were married last year. I do not know if he told you, or what it does to your plans. But he certainly pressured me into marriage. Like so many young girls, I have been done wrong by a man, just as you told us might happen. I will not break his confidence if you don't. But perhaps you should tell Ginger? Of course no one wants to break Ginger's heart.
                                        Love,
                                        Cassandra Avalanche

For minutes the doctor kept her back to Ginger. Then she gave a fatal "Ohh, that girl," and tore the postcard up. She turned her head, her lips trembling and asked whether Ginger had read the card.

"Of course not," Ginger said.

"Oh, that girl," she said again. "I believe she hates us."

"Why?"

"I tried to help—you know that, Ginger. Between her and you I worked day and night. Now she is fighting with the warden, whom I have a perfectly good rapport with, having counselled many of these young women. She is trying to say you stole Noel from her—at the drive-in years ago. But for your sake, your family's, and poor Noel's, I will handle it. You see, she broke his heart, and you healed it. She never thought you'd be able to. Now she can't stand it. She might say or do anything just to cause pain. If she does telephone here, do not listen to a word she says."

"I won't," Ginger said. "But maybe after she gets out she can come here for a while and get back on her feet. Maybe all she needs is love."

"Oh, nothing would please me more. But her envy of me and you might ruin that," Mahoney said. "Where's Noel? I have to speak to him just a sec."

And she went off to find her son, the torn postcard in her hand.

"How can you do that?" Ginger called after her.

"Do what?" Mahoney said, a little frantically, stopping dead in the center of the room.

"Love us all, love every one of us—after so many of us have hurt you?"

The doctor waved her hand gaily, continued toward the stairs, and did not turn around.

That Noel had done this infuriated her, made her less than cautious, made her want for once and for all to prove who she was.

"What is this about prosthetics?" Miles said, coming into the living room with his hands in his pockets one Friday afternoon, as sunlight splayed upon our carpet, showing the shadow of one maple leaf waving and dust undulating against my father's wrinkled grey pants.

"This is Ginger's new idea for money—get into the prosthetics business. How many people do you know need wooden legs?"

331

Two days later he asked me, "What would be the gain in sinking our money into the prosthetics business?"

I was not much bothered by this. And then one evening after supper, as I was brushing my teeth, I looked into the mirror and saw with a start an imp of Satan standing behind me, holding a towel in front of him. I turned around and there was no one there. A frame had moved out of focus and then back again, to reveal only a rack of yellow hand towels. And I realized that it was my first, my very first, hallucination.

I went downtown. It was late, and as sweet a night as I could remember. The lights glowed softly from the park, and the store lights made their front windows look like a splendid dusk attained.

Later in the tavern I heard the word—not prosthetics, but a new business venture by Dr. Mahoney.

In a state of shock I drove around in the rain in my father's old woebegone car. At dawn I came into the house, miserable and sickly, and went to bed. When I woke up, it was almost evening again. For a moment I had forgotten what harassed me so. Then I realized it like a brick hitting my face. The house was quiet and almost dark, with all the blinds drawn against the outside world, and a lamp was on in the far-off den.

I stood in the hallway, near the picture of my gram.

"It is not prosthetics, Father," I said.

I did not know where in the house he was, but it didn't much matter; we were very used to carrying on conversations like this.

"What is it?" he said.

I jumped, because he was standing right behind me, with a can of tomato soup he had brought up from the basement.

I told him first who our partner was: Gary Fallon. He had put in money as well. So you see, I said, this is a corporation almost.

"It is Gary Fallon—" I said. "Our little sergeant with the dishwashing machines—he is back in our life now. He and Ginger—well, with Dr. Mahoney as a guide—are the major partners in this."

"I see. And what is it we are in business about?" he asked, trying to read the soup label to find out its content of salt—or to find out if it contained alcohol. Who knows.

"About?" I asked.

"Yes—what are we about? I know at one time we were about movies like *Mary Poppins*, and *The Sound of Music*, and a drive-in theatre where I sold French fries—and had sales on hot chocolate when it got cold and wondered why every movie with Randolph Scott had a train and a mountain in the distance. What are we about now?"

"Prophylactics," I said.

He didn't seem to understand.

"French safes," I said.

He didn't seem to understand.

I made a motion as if I was lucky enough to be putting one on.

"Good God," he said.

"Quite," I answered.

We decided we would be silent. First, because we were too shocked to say anything. Second, for Ginger's sake it would be better than becoming hysterical. Finally, it had to be her deal.

As a matter of fact it had nothing much to do with us any more. Her adviser in this had been Dr. Mahoney, who had been an advocate for birth control and all proper procedures for years. Dr. Mahoney had something we did not have: a kind of licence to the moral higher ground of the eighties.

Now Ginger had a fiancé and a business and a prospective mother-in-law all caught up together. She was out of our life, just as she wanted to be. It might have been a dangerous place, but how would I know?

Ginger had not come to me, because she no longer trusted me.

I was sorry about this. I was sorry her freedom was so painful to her and to us. Remembering her from the time of her childhood, remembering my mother, remembering my grandmother, I began to speak one evening, not like the conservative that people thought I was, but like the progressive person I so wanted to be so I could exist in the world again. It seemed I could not exist now, for like my father I could not pretend not to know what I knew.

Yet I was angered at this, and desperately needed a scapegoat. And what better scapegoat than Father himself? Tapping my fingers on the windowsill in my room, while staring out at Dad's lilacs, I said, "This is her moment, her wedding, her life. Why should we torment her so?"

"I am not tormenting her," Miles said from his room.

"You don't have a decent bone in your body when it comes to her. You have tormented her and the things she loves all of her miserable little life."

"That is not true."

We were once again at opposite ends of the house, each of us drinking on our own, with the hall light on and music playing somewhere.

"You don't. You are a feeble father, a hateful father. When did she ever have a birthday? When did she ever have a friend for a sleepover? Nada, nada, and nada once more. No wonder she has run to the nurturing arms of Dr. Abigail Mahoney."

"Nurturing what?"

"Nurturing arms."

"I don't care what you think. I am not a miserable father."

"Are so."

"Am not."

"A very feeble and hateful father who thinks he has read a great deal."

"Have not."

"Have so."

(Long pause.)

"Have not."

"Why, may I ask, if I can ask, if I should be so bold as to ask—why didn't you learn how to play the piano?"

"Mom wouldn't let me."

"'Mom wouldn't let me.' What a sissy, a pansy—"

"Am not."

"Are so."

"Not."

(Long pause.)

"So you take it out on poor Ginger, who is my poor little sister—her happiest day, getting married, and you have been at her for ten months writing terrible apocalyptic letters."

"Terrible what?"

"Apocalyptic letters—getting married. For God almighty's sake, Dad, you should be ashamed of yourself. Your heart should be bleeding in gladness for her. But no, you have to stick the knife in and twist it up and down, because that's what people did to you. You are no gentleman, sir."

"I am so."

"You are worse than the worst than the worst, as far as I'm concerned. Gary Fallon is better than you, and I am glad he took Mommie out. I am glad, do you hear—I am glad."

No answer.

The tall grass was waving, and somewhere someone walking home, in the thick broken-hearted silence.

"I don't mean that you're the worst." For a moment I could not go on. "I don't mean you are the worst. I don't mean that about Gary Fallon either."

(Peevish reply.)

"Well, that's what you said."

"I didn't mean it."

"You said about Gary Fallon, you just said you were glad Mommie went out with him. You just said it."

"Didn't mean it."

"And how do you know what I was like when I was a boy? You don't know. How do you know how many times I was beaten and fought back and tried to protect Georgina? And tried to protect her and everything—and how do you know what I know—what cloth of progressiveness Mahoney has hidden her hide under? Don't you have any understanding? You don't know what I know—you do not know what I know, sir!"

"No, I don't—and I'm sorry."

"Well, let's lose our identity and all of us become a bunch of Drukens, for they are Drukens even though you might think they are Mahoneys. So I will lose what little identity I have left—such as it is."

"No—I don't want that! I'm sorry—I should not have said what I did. It was said it haste."

"Pardon?"

"I said, it was said in haste."

"I don't mind what you say about the people you know, and about me either, Wendy, for I have long been used to spite and false candour from the herd. But I tell you this—I am a gentleman."

"I know."

"And I will tell you one more thing."

I am silent. Silence reigns in the house for almost an hour. For almost an hour I think he is long, long in alcohol-induced sleep.

"She will slip up," came a whisper, like a tinge of horror across the carpet into my dark, soundless room.

THREE

My father said one time that among the refined, among the privileged, is a certain feeling that crassness has no place.

"So when it is seen—and it is seen—as in Kate Croy in *Wings of the Dove*," he said, "then is an added dimension of humanity laid down."

"What?" I asked.

"The common and universal magnet toward moral corruption that shows pettiness in the refined as a stain—yet forgiven as old-world virtue in certain settings."

But with Dr. Mahoney, crassness was expected, he said. "And the overlay of that," Father reminded me, "is to bully us into accepting it as a sign of vitality and a kind of moral virtue as well, that only the naïve—which is supposedly ourselves—you and I, Wendy, my dear—would not embrace—but is seen as experience in life's terrible lessons, which are promoted as necessary to understanding the very nature of what they themselves tell us is virtuous. It makes us middle-class lackeys, doesn't it? We are the prudes if we hesitate to embrace their world. Yet they rely upon us not to be as quick as they in embracing it—for if we do, we will know it as well as they, and they can no longer be certain of our hauling the wool over our own eyes, as Ginger and Gus have. Do you follow?"

"I do not know."

"Of course both groups seek the same thing in the end." He looked at me a long moment, disappointed that I did not grasp so quickly what he was saying.

"Money, son—both groups seek damn money from those whose blood they suck."

Though my father loved Henry James, I could not get myself though *Wings of the Dove*. I left it on my bed stand to accumulate dust as I set about destroying my life in bars.

Mahoney had been forced into action—by those phone calls from Cassandra. Forced to move much quicker than she would have preferred. Right at the moment when everything she had ever planned was coming to fruition, there was this catch: she was forced to rely upon someone else's idea. So everything for our poor doctor, in spite of a life of planning, was now up to whimsy.

Mahoney's proposition had come when Ginger was alone on an afternoon filled with rain. She was having a cup of tea out of Gram's old teapot when Mahoney came in to see her. The doctor was nervous, and whenever she was nervous she looked angry. She had been forced to see Fallon, for Cassandra now had something on her, just as she once had something on Joey Elias.

Gary Fallon had taken her into his confidence on condition that she come up with some money very soon. She had met him in the Palace Bar, and now his idea consumed her. For, even though she did not think of it herself, it was a good idea. It was easy; it might be perfect if it worked.

"We need the money now, before someone else jumps on the idea," Gary said. "I can very easily carry myself, but I need someone else."

"Noel will have money once he is married—or at least he'll have some access to it," Mahoney said, thinking aloud. "When would you need it—I mean exactly when?"

"You mean you're not interested in re-establishing Janie's theatre?"

"No, not at present. I was wanting something else. I was thinking Janie's theatre is part of the old world—and Ginger has to be delivered from the old world."

"I can't risk the wait," Fallon said, "because Miles wants to re-establish and has others on his side who will convince Ginger—"

"Ginger listens to me," she said.

"Then you better prove it."

The small doctor, with a slight hobble in her gait, went back home and spoke to Noel. Would he consider this as an investment?

He shrugged, for he left everything up to her. His plan was to get what he could and go away with Cassie. But he said, "Ginger told me that Miles needs help, and she wants to spend the money on him, to go away and dry out."

"Really."

"The idiot thinks you're someone he knew when he was a boy."

"I see," Mahoney said. "Well, I can handle Ginger, as long as you go through with our plan. And remember, it's Ginger we love."

Even if the plan was not entirely hers, it was a dream realized. And Ray Winch—one of the few to long suspect who she was—considered her now more brilliant than ever.

If she was who Ray suspected, she had learned on Joey Elias's knee what must be done to exercise a perfect Trojan horse. It had taken fifty years to establish herself as Joey Elias's principal protegé. Now she was a master—better by far, Ray acknowledged, than he himself. But what Ray Winch did not realize was this. She had no intention of starting a business at all.

At first she did not speak about the business opportunity. Taking Ginger's hand, she spoke instead of the theatre, of its grand and wholesome days, of other theatres now disappearing into the gaunt, tabloid kind of movies that existed, a debasement that she said my father had run at the last.

"I am glad we are out of that," she said, saying "we" circumspectly, even devotionally. Then she added, "Instead of exploitation, why don't we do something positive—for unwed mothers?"

"Unwed mothers? Well, of course," Ginger said. The rain pelted down outside. And Ginger was much like the rain. She had just paid for Gus Busters's rehab treatment in Saint John, where he was now in the Veterans Hospital. He had no one in the world, and Ginger could not refuse. Dr. Mahoney knew about Gus being in the rehab clinic, and had sympathized with Ginger while reminding her that she had other obligations. These obligations were to take care of the funds her grandmother had left her, to do something that her grandmother would be proud of.

"Besides, I think Gus and your brother want to do something together."

"What do they want?" Ginger asked.

"A disco, a place to go and drink," Dr. Mahoney said. "You know men. But I need someone with the assets, yes, but also with the verve."

"Verve," Ginger said slowly, sugaring her tea and smiling.

"It requires it, it requires a sense of social duty. Of course we will make a lot of money."

Ginger nodded again.

"Promise me you will keep this from your father."

"Why? I mean of course, but why?"

"Because of what they intend to do with your money. I mean, it is not up to me, it's up to you." She paused. " There is a time when you must stand alone. It is what Janie had to do against her own father."

"Of course, yes," Ginger said. Yet she was trembling with a fear she had not felt before. Although Dr. Mahoney herself felt excited and exceptional, and though Ginger didn't understand why they needed to rush ahead, or even why they needed to keep it from her father, she was sure her friend knew best. The idea of doing something clandestine made it more radical. But why was Ginger afraid—easy—this was exactly the current she feared, under every conversation they ever had—which said that Ginger would someday have to prove herself by spending money.

She had invested much in her relationship with Dr. Abigail Mahoney, and she knew she had lost her opportunity to back out.

The doctor insisted they must act soon—that very night if possible. "There is no time to waste. The first to think of this will be wealthy."

Ginger and Dr. Mahoney went to a meeting that night. In the back office of the adult video store sat two pudgy middle-aged men she hardly knew—Gary Fallon and a Mr. Conroy. The air was full of cigarette smoke and sweat, the same smell that had greeted my grandmother upon entering the office of Mr. Mahoney of the talking pictures almost sixty years before.

Ginger looked about for Noel, but he was not there.

Learning what the plan was, Ginger was more uncertain. She felt a cold shiver on her arms. But she had promised not to tell her father—and already there was the idea that she was doing something as revolutionary as her grandmother.

Ginger managed to ask, "Aren't there other, bigger companies?"

"Those are in the States," Fallon said. "We are in a position to take over the market in Canada."

"I see—of course."

She asked if they needed her just for the money.

Dr. Mahoney stood and got Ginger a bottle of water, uncapped it for her and sat back down. "Perhaps you are right," she said, "but say no and I will leave this building forever and nothing more will ever be said about it."

The men made no bones about it. Money was the thing she was to bring, and Dr. Mahoney was "allowing" her to. She sensed this gave her the one chance to remove herself. But the wedding was only a few weeks away. And all of Dr. Mahoney's plans—everything she had worked toward—had come to this. She had managed much, but the greatest of her achievements had been her ability to isolate the young woman sitting beside her.

There was silence.

"If a psychologist likes this, it can't be bad," Conroy said.

Ginger sipped her water. It was not water. Dr. Mahoney, sensing her nervousness, had given her gin.

Who would Ginger be betraying if she walked out? A woman who had come back to the river, every bit as noble as Janie King; her future mother-in-law, and a woman who had saved her from a bad marriage. For it was Dr. Mahoney who had saved both her and her mother, and Ginger was loyal if for no other reason. She thought of Gus down in the Veterans Hospital two hundred miles away, and how much she cared for him.

Yet what would happen if she walked out? She doubted they would love her as much as they did now. In fact, it was masterful timing by our psychologist. She knew of the investigation, and she feared Cassandra—now was the moment.

She bravely looked at her future daughter-in-law with concern.

"Perhaps we'd better go," Mahoney said. "Perhaps you aren't ready."

Ginger squeezed the doctor's hand. "Of course I'm ready."

"Okay then," Gary Fallon said. "We're ready too."

Fallon stated his case. If they acted quickly they could make a fortune with prophylactics. He was interested in the fortune. Abigail, he assured her, was interested in helping women.

Ginger paused, and then whispered, "Is Gary a nice guy?"

"I wouldn't introduce you to him if he wasn't," Mahoney said.

These three people were salesmen, and they might have been selling her a car.

So it did not matter if Ginger did believe. She wanted to believe. And she thrust the money into her friend's arms so she could prove she did. For she was compelled to, and this had begun not today or yesterday—but years ago, when the tough little woman had first laid eyes upon her. Ginger remembered their first meeting, and how Dr. Mahoney's eyes penetrated her soul.

And there was something else Fallon stated to Ginger—in a soothing manner: this, my dear, he said, was morally appropriate—in fact, if making money from this was immoral, then the world had no case, and there was no right or wrong. But if the world said there was right and wrong, good and bad, then this was certainly above all things good! She could go to the reserves and help the First Nations, or to poor people and help, and isn't that worth devoting time to! How could Ginger not want that?

She blushed and nodded, and looked at Dr. Mahoney, who was staring at her intensely, just as she had the first time they met.

When they went back to the house that night, the first person they saw was Noel, waiting in the den. He looked first at his mother, searching her face, and then at Ginger with a warm, inviting smile. For the first time she saw a conniving look in him, a cringing after his mom's approval, that was so unlike her father.

Ginger had to believe in her new occupation as radical activity. The doctor, who was her only friend, told her it was.

But my father whispered, in a state of hoarseness after a night of drinking, and lying with a towel to his eyes to stop them from watering, which they did now on a daily basis:

"Wendy, my dear, our Ginger has always been radical. Now she is just the same as the rest. She is just like them. She is playing at being, when before she *was*. Now she is only as a reflection, like Harris was." He waved the towel. "We have to get her back!"

"We all become like the rest sooner or later," I said.

"Well," Miles answered, still shaking the towel in front of his body, "if I can evoke a certain kind of temperament for a certain moment—is not Putsy more radical than the most radical of our new power dressers, the least self-serving of which would still demonstrate selfishness in a grand pox—so is that radical—is the search for power radical—supposedly it is. Supposedly it is supposedly, it is. But my mother never wanted it—and Putsy in some moment of despair chose sacrifice to power and was laughed at, hooted at, and condemned. Only to be seen as a charlatan and condemned—when the charlatans are very rarely condemned. My God, they are given parties and honours and awards, and are rarely condemned—and mankind walking in the rarefied air of the unprincipled who have changed our world and the very nature of truth."

"Condemned," I said, willing to listen to him as long as I was able to uncap the bottle and take a drink. (He made a short grapple for it and then let it go.)

"Very much condemned, Putsy was," he said, watching me pour a glass, "by her parents and by Joey. Envied by Rebecca, thought of as a charlatan by the bishop. And yet, though she healed no one, in a way she healed Uncle Walter of his hump, in a way she healed poor old Phil Druken of his shame, healed Joey Elias—for who prayed for him day and night? At the end he was saved by some intervention of Putsy. The intervention of Putsy—a good name for a play, that is—but you see what had Elias wanted—he wanted peace, like my father had in the end. He did not know how to achieve it. Putsy, who had no power in this world, had given the power away—the power to obstruct and oppress and hurt and destroy. Gave it up, Putsy had—found peace for him in the end." He looked at me in brilliant sheepishness.

"You mean that?" I said.

"I mean exactly what I say," he said, sitting up and pointing the sodden towel at me. "Out of the house in Dobblestein's mill yard came a saint who would never know she was, who had her teeth kicked out of her mouth as a child defending Rebecca, and was fucked by thirteen, and is now gone to her reward—a reward any of us would wish for ourselves, and few if any would work toward—God, would we want her reward unable though to work toward—!!!"

"And Dr. Mahoney—or Rebecca?" I said, taking the bottle again. He looked at it painfully.

"Rebecca is forgiven," he said, crumpling the towel and throwing it aside.

"By whom?"

"By me," he said.

"Does she know she has your forgiveness?"

"She doesn't. But more to the point, she does not know yet how much she needs it. However," he said, "I am more worried that little Ginger does not tumble and gets some return—for I am not going to mope or moralize on the position she has put us or herself in. Who am I to moralize? Why, if they came in shooting, I would say shoot!"

I thought this also. What right had I not to believe what she herself was willing to?

Two days before the wedding, Cassie was released from the Sleepy Hollow women's institution in Prince Edward Island. Cassie asked Noel to go and see her, and he made Ray Winch drive him down. All day Dr. Mahoney was trying to ward off Ginger's questions. But Ginger was frantic—where was he?

Noel told Cassie he was going to call off the wedding. He felt he could still get his hands on some of my sister's money.

Cassie, more politic, told him to wait. She said "If you are doing this for me, prove it."

"How?"

"I want a house out of it."

"Well, of course."

Then she brought up the reason she wanted to see him. He had brought down some PCP. She had been straight for months and did not want to remain straight.

"I can't do it with you," he said. "I'll be all fucked up."

"You have to," she said. "What am I supposed to do? Be left out of everything?"

He was afraid that Ginger would realize something. But he was more afraid of displeasing Cassie, and if truth be told, so was his mother. So in a small hotel room carved out of nowhere, in the middle of the afternoon, both did speed.

After he left Cassie he had to go with Ray Winch, who was his best man, to pick up the suit he was to wear. Noel stood among the mannequins in the darkness of the little room and felt miserable and detached. Seeing himself in a suit, in the change room with its pressboard walls and no bigger than a toilet, he became claustrophobic and violent and went into a rage. Ray Winch had to rescue him, fighting with the lady at the front of the store, while he half dragged Noel out.

Noel was angry that his mother would put him through this—angrier still that there was a man waiting for Cassie when he left her. So he came home wanting to tell Ginger everything.

Dr. Mahoney tried to stop him from seeing her, but Ginger rushed to him, teased him, tried to hold his hand. He was about to push her away when Ray Winch grabbed his arm. Noel winced. Something unpleasant had happened with that needle he had taken, and for the first time he felt sick.

Ray whispered in his ear, "Smarten up or you'll ruin everything."

Noel realized that breaking off the wedding meant breaking away from his mother and her plans.

"Do you think we will have a good life?" Ginger asked sweetly.

"If you want," he said, barely whispering, his eyes half closed, his lips dry.

"I do. It's just—"

"If I'm not good enough for you, then just call it off," he answered.

"You won't mind if I break up—call it all off?" Ginger said teasingly.

"Not in the least." It was on the tip of his tongue to say something about her mother and how much fun he had with her.

Ginger stepped back and looked at him.

"Call what off?" Dr. Mahoney said, vivacious and happy, coming into the room with a glass of wine.

Noel smiled and said, "Oh nothing." He staggered a little, and would not speak any more.

In a second, everything became crystal clear, in his face and his eyes. And Ginger knew.

He left the room. He went to the bathroom and took off his shirt. He remembered Cassie's smile when the needle wouldn't go in easily, how she turned away and laughed.

For the first time he felt pain, and he stared at himself in the mirror and saw himself no longer young or pretty, or even lucky. Whatever Putsy had tried to tell him was coming true, and there was nothing he could do now but watch.

Ginger looked at Dr. Mahoney, then at Ray Winch, whom she had never liked, with his tattoos across his fingers. Her heart was pounding. She felt she didn't know either of them at all.

The phone rang and Mahoney turned to go to it.

"Nerves," the good doctor said, the wine spilling a little as she took a drink. "Goddamn men and their second thoughts—nerves is all." She picked up the phone.

It was Cassandra, asking what she might wear to the wedding.

"You cannot possibly come," Dr. Mahoney whispered.

"Why not?"

"It wouldn't be good for Noel."

"It might be good for me," Cassandra said.

"You will have what I have out of this," Mahoney whispered. Turning sideways she saw Ginger staring at her. She lifted the wine and smiled.

"Caterers," she mouthed.

Ginger went to her room, shaking and shivering. What could she now do? She was in love with him, wasn't she? Perhaps she wasn't— perhaps she was only in love with Gus. But then there was the business and all that money. She turned her face to the side and saw the ancient prayer beads Putsy had left her. In fury she opened the drawer and threw them in, those old wooden beads from 1848.

———

The day before the wedding Miles cooked a ham. "To quell my desire to be one when I introduce the groom's mother," he said.

I told him of my hope that Ginger would be happy. He nodded as he took out the ham to baste it.

"I do I do I do—but if you have people stealing, you have people who believe they are more human than you are. Don't think for one moment that this is not what Joey Elias thought. His theft and his dislike were based on an intellectual superiority. What lamp will light our way—for it is swimming the river all over again, and will be long and dark from here to the shore."

He put the ham back in the oven and licked his fingers bare.

FOUR

The wedding took place at the courthouse, for reason's sake. The dinner took place at a small restaurant near the Enclosure.

My father did not eat, but had four gins, and was relaxed enough to stand and toast the groom's mother.

"She has been with me always," he said, "and I imagine will always be. I salute you." Then he looked at her a long time, almost to the point of embarrassment as he held his glass to his lips. Finally he drank.

"To Abigail!" people shouted, and waved and clapped. She raised her glass of champagne and drank, spilling just a little and laughing.

Miles staggered slightly as he sat back down. He gave me a sudden stare, as if I had said something.

"Yes?" I asked.

"Pardon?"

"What?"

"Yes—what," he said. "That's exactly it. What have I just seen that you do not see?"

"I don't know."

"Ah—Gary," he said in mirth (tragic mirth), waving to Gary Fallon. "A bright and blissful future for all."

"What's that?" Gary asked across the tinkling glasses. "What?"

"Bright and blessed future for all?" (Asked as a question.)

"Yes, yes—you're right."

"It's good to know this," Father said to me. "He has just quelled my fears and put a stop to my objection." Then he stood and shouted, "Hear, hear—my fears have been quashed!" He held his gin and saluted the crowd. A picture was taken. It shows my father, cuffs a tad stretched, looking Dr. Mahoney's way, and behind him a young boy of about six, looking awestruck at whatever it was that might be happening.

"Gary—Gary?"

"Yes, Miles?" Gary asked, not quite annoyed yet.

"You work with population control—I was wondering. You know there is this—ozone thing, and also climate control. We are either heading head down toward an ice age or a hothouse—not sure which. So after you quell the populace, then you should start on climate."

Gary nodded, a little sternly.

"And then of course there is my play," he said. He sat back down and said to me, "My God—I got away from myself, didn't I."

"What are you doing?" I said.

"There's nothing more here than meets the eye," he said.

"Well, isn't that fine—"

"But it's what meets the damn eye, son." He smiled. "We are all drunks."

"Who are all—drunks," I said.

"What is left of the King family. But there, you see, my prodigal son—and oh, if only she would come home." Then he became silent and morose.

Ginger had been drinking for more than a year now, and I could not stand it. I knew it was terrible to moralize over this with her, but still—she was my sister.

The wedding was horrible simply because it was a wedding. The jokes were raw, the conversation strained.

We drove back to the house, to the caterers, and the party, which was put on by Ginger, at her own expense, the way things are done when people reach a certain age—their independence leaves them vulnerable, and money becomes a sad part of their relationship with others, and it is not until an occasion like this that it is noticed as poignant, yearning and—the real word—solitary, like a stranger taking money out to pay a taxi driver on a sun-drenched street filled with empty sidewalk cafés.

There was a moment at the party when I knew we were the outsiders, even, or especially, Ginger. It seemed suddenly and almost fatally incongruous that this strapping man with the wild eyes would be married to this child—for I still considered her this. Had she heard what people were saying, that his loyalty to her was a joke, that he was doing it for the business, and that Ginger must have known and taken her chances anyway?

Lobsters and oysters and jumbo shrimp on ice, and sparkling wine. Her face beautiful. Still after all of that strife, beautiful.

"Keep an eye on him," she whispered, holding my hand lightly and then letting go. There were three girlfriends of hers from the convent, but I had not seen them in years and had forgotten their names. Perhaps Ginger had also. She seemed to get them as recruits, called up at the last moment to prove she had someone at her side.

If you looked at Ginger closely you could tell that this was not her first wedding. There had been a loss of innocence somewhere among us all. Most were falling into early middle age. Most of us had done things we would never admit to. Ginger was worried about Dad, but she herself could not stay away from the gin, and at one point stumbled and was held up by Noel.

Looking at my father, I saw a desperate innocence in him, compounded by his spiritual fall from grace.

The tables spread across the lawn with paper skirts, and bugs among the lights soft as fairy dust. Ginger turned to answer a child's question. This was Janie's granddaughter, in her early thirties. Still vivacious, beautiful, and craning her neck beyond the one she was speaking to, to see where her father was, and if he had fallen into the dessert dish as he did at a Rotarian function.

My father did not belong. Not only here, but to life. Something had happened in his life, and he had never belonged. Now his money had been lost to prophylactics; and that seemed to complete his alienation from any part of the world he knew.

"Taking a business away was not only symbolic of killing my mother, it is in essence killing my daughter," he said with a smile as he passed me by.

My sister's light green dress—the same colour as Dr. Mahoney's— left her solitary in the middle of the lawn.

I could have mentioned at that moment the sensation that something terrible would happen to Ginger, for this was the premonition I had, looking at her alone in the middle of the lawn. I thought that Noel might kill her. But I was no soothsayer, and no one in town listened to me anyway.

As night came on and loud music lingered from the patio, Miles watched with a kind of childlike gaze as people ate oysters, and then he watched Dr. Mahoney, as if trying to understand something. He walked away, then meandered through the crowd to look at her once again.

"So, you do think that these whatchamacallits that we are going to produce in droves and droves will come in handy and make us money, do you, Doctor?"

"Oh, Miles—absolutely," she said. "But your daughter is not doing it for the money. She is doing it for something else."

"She is not doing it for the money?"

"No, she is not doing it for the money Miles—she is doing it for the children."

"For the children?"

"Absolutely, Miles. For the children."

"Well— What I mean to ask is—and forgive me for asking it—but will there be children if she does it?"

"No. But that's the point, isn't it, Miles—all those little boys and girls suffering."

"Ah—the point is for them not to suffer?"

"That's absolutely right, Miles," Fallon chipped in.

"And the way for them not to suffer—here I mean, on this earth—is never to allow them a chance at it."

Gary and the doctor both smiled at the old disgrace that he was. Dr. Mahoney tried the diplomatic answer, knowing it was perhaps my father's old Catholicism that bothered him, the confessional and all of that.

"That is what Ginger is about. She is a beautiful child herself and now she helps poverty, abuse, all the things she knows causes suffering. All my life I wanted to do something decent, and now we have a chance. If we meet our projected sales we will be doing very, very well," she said.

"Just keeping dumb women from having kids—not bright women," Fallon said, happy to clarify his point.

"Very well," Miles answered, turning to Dr. Mahoney again. "With what you call projected sales, yes— Besides I know she is a beautiful child—I know she is not doing it for the money. I know she is only interested in helping others. But—"

"What, my dear?"

"These watchamacallits—are—well, legal? They weren't when I was a lad, but that was long ago and in another country."

Fallon laughed. Miles gave him a peculiar look and then looked away.

"Of course they are, Miles. It's a brand-new age now. And you should embrace the business. It's not like it used to be, when you were little. It has all changed. The whole world had changed," the doctor noted.

"Ah yes—a brand-new age of whatchamacallits. Yes, of course, I see. And of course I cannot see them in my mind's eye as anything but used product on the ground at my drive-in—so you see I have no moral higher ground, just the drive-in ground—ground down, so to speak?"

Gary wandered away, and Dr. Mahoney stayed politely, purse in hand but looking over his shoulder for an avenue of escape. My father took a desperate chance.

"I want to tell you that I always felt terrible for your loss—the triplets so long ago."

The doctor looked at him as if gauging his cleverness, but her toughness diminished.

"I don't know what you are saying."

"Willie, Sam, and Paddy Dan," he said.

Father paused, for he never in his life really wanted to give anyone pain. He saw her lips tremble just slightly.

She smiled at someone else.

"Do you, Doctor, know the story of my sister?"

"Georgina? Absolutely."

"I want you to know—I want you if no one else knows to know—all my life I have been sorry about your early life—the betrayals you yourself must have felt when a child alone."

"Thank you, but I don't know what you mean," she said almost fiercely.

The talk seemed to drift away over our great immortal river. My father paused, knowing he did not want to cause a sorrow that had been so freely given by others to him.

"I know. But about Georgina. Can I tell you something about that little casualty?"

"Of course. But there is nothing in the world I don't know about Georgina, for Ginger has told me everything."

"There are some things you might not know."

"No—I am certain I know everything," she said, insisting on her portion, her right to know more about us then we did about ourselves.

"Of course you do—Doctor—but I am asking a rather rhetorical question here. Do you think she would have traded a second of her life for anything?"

"Absolutely not."

"And she did suffer."

"I hope not too, too much."

"But it follows that she did."

"Well, perhaps—"

"Therefore, you see, Georgina is a perfect example—almost a required one. She would never have traded a moment of life even in her suffering. And I have had to live with that for many a year. So I am not at all against the whatchamacallits. In fact, at this point in life I am against nothing, carefree, glib abortion at the doctor's or dancing nude as beasts in moonlight. How can I disapprove, I who am the worst of all—the one true failure on the river? But still and all, suffering is the price of life, the price that all those sad children are willing to pay if we allow them. The price you have paid as much as anyone—Rebecca."

She gave a start, almost a fatal one. He bowed to her and walked up the gravel drive past many of the cars where small groups of men drank.

"Hello, Mr. King," Ray Winch said. He had been included in the partnership, given every cent he had, and now, exuberant about the possibility of new friendships and money, was vulnerable to any answer my father might give. Knowing this, my father refused to be unkind.

"How are you, son?" my father asked.

"Mr. King—we used to sneak into the theatre—did you know?" He nudged Gary Fallon, standing beside him.

"I knew, son, I knew."

"We used to wait by the exit door—did you know?"

Miles smiled. "Your father once waited by the door as well. I often left the door open for you, Ray," he said. "I often did that for you, boy, for I knew your circumstances better than you cared about mine."

There was a slight guffaw and then complete silence.

He circled back from the pathway through his hedges and came out beside Dr. Mahoney again. She caught him staring at her, and smiled, and then, with perfect resolution, stood for a picture, and then moved away with someone I didn't know. Miles grinned at me. He looked like Malcolm Lowry at this moment—indistinguishable from the bottle of Bols gin he was holding.

In the dark he was gone from me again.

I tried to keep an eye on him. There he was by a tree. There he was talking to Ginger's maid of honour about string beans and the best soil for them. There he was alone at the side of the house tapping his foot to some Hank Jr. music. "A Country Boy Can Survive." There he was watching from the back bushes, a glass of fulsome gin in his hand, like a spy, nodding to whoever would nod at him.

I could just catch his pale suit; I could just catch his head as his body weaved slightly in among the hundred guests, the street with a ribbon, and a heart with Noel's and Ginger's names. There was a shouting match between the two wives of the two lesser investors, who staggered off in opposite directions. Ginger came to me in a hushed excitement and explained that Miles was bothering Dr. Mahoney.

"I knew this would happen. You have to take him home. He'll make a scene with her, and she has done everything for my day." Tears sparkled at the corners of her eyes, but she too was almost drunk. I went and told Miles I wanted to go home. He told me he was ready enough to go, for he had snuck a bottle of gin in his coat, and the bartender was staring ruthlessly at him. We walked up the path toward the street.

I asked him if he had eaten today.

Not in four days, he said, except for licking his fingers when he cooked the ham. He checked the bottle to see how much was in it. It was three-quarters full. He smiled at his luck. The luck of the McLearys. The forgotten wedding of 1791.

I asked him if he wanted to have something to eat, and he said no. Or lie down?

"Of course not," he said.

He walked over with straightened dignity and offered the bride a kiss.

"Thank you for coming," Noel said. "She completely changed my life." It didn't matter to him if he was lying; lying was somehow part of his appeal, the cynical mirth in his face always assessing or accusing those he spoke to.

Dr. Mahoney caught up with us at the drive.

"Here," she said, and gave me a hug, with unfelt affection. Then she kissed Miles on his cheek. "We'll always be together—we're one family," she said. "And don't worry about what some people might say about our business. Not only is it legitimate but there is a moral here. That's why Ginger is so involved."

"Yes, I believe there is a moral here. And you and I, Doctor—well, our lives and our loves are intertwined. The most important people to me are somehow the most important to you."

"And I'm going to write that book," she said. "But it won't be naughty, so you don't have to fear."

"You would be the one to do it," he said, "for you've been where we have not been, and you have seen what we have not seen, and you know what we cannot know."

"Thank you," she said, with delight.

He smiled as well.

We were home, but he would not get out of the car. He was thinking of something. There was a feeling of pleasant self-destruction in him when he drank. The strange fact was, he was not to be trifled with whenever he decided not to be; and no Noel Mahoney or Ray Winch would ever bother him, once decided.

"I have not read Homer, I have not read Tolstoy," he said to me. "You have read both."

"I have."

"Who am I—Ulysses? Paris?"

I told him instead about Father Sergei, Tolstoy's hero who never was, and who wandered the last years of his life looking for peace.

"Well, that's who I will be," he said. "I will be a hero who never was—like Walter P. McLeary."

And he opened the door, and we walked in the balking rain toward the house.

For the first time in his life he turned all the lights out. It was the strangest feeling I have ever had.

"You have turned out all the lights," I said.

"Fine," he said.

(Pause.)

"What's wrong—"

"With what—"

"What's wrong!!!"

"You should not be overly anxious," he said. "You know what it is. Our poor Ginger married and convinced she is part of the solution to world overpopulation and venereal disease, an AIDS campaign in full blossom. That is what the child has taken to her heart, my prodigal girl. You see, she is a fighter for the right things—even though the reality is so dismal. That's what idealism tends to be—and what money will they ever make? None at all."

I did not answer.

"You realize that as well, Wendy?"

"Of course."

"And what do you think of Noel?" He didn't wait for an answer. "I will tell you about Noel. He does not care a bit for her. In fact, his dislike of her is evident—I assume it will be over shortly. Joey Elias did not get to marry Janie to cramp the style of our business, but Noel got to marry Ginger," he said almost peevishly as he removed a shoe and let it drop to the floor.

I rose and went into the living room. He was sitting, with his tie still measured in his defining Windsor knot, his pale hands wearing their three rings, his Rolex, keeping time in the translucent airy dark. One shoe still on. One sock impeccable. Thunder had started above his head, about our house—"and happy as the grass was green," I thought. I sat with him for thirty minutes as he simply stared into silence, holding the bottle of gin without taking a glass.

Finally he said, "She has told me—"

"Told you— What has she told you?"

"She has told me something between her and me that happened forty—no, fifty years ago or more, when I was a boy—no one else would know. She has told me—"

"What?"

"I knew she would," he said, being mysterious for effect. He opened his gin, picked up a glass, turned it over and poured it a quarter full, and handed it to me with an air of the professional drinker. He took another glass and poured the same amount for himself. Then he reached forward and clinked my glass. "I knew she would."

We had not, in fifty years, gotten any closer to that night, he told me. She was very clever, yet she could not die without one-upmanship. It was her way, he said, to let the world know how bright she was, or is. It was a confession, really.

"She had to tell me, and I've been waiting for it since she came back."

Detectives, police—no one knew. "Not even Kipsy Doyle," he said. "Although perhaps Kipsy got close. Kipsy knew things from one era were tied to another."

With research and months of investigation, he said, we had only gotten to the steps and didn't, or couldn't, look down to see what had happened in the old forgotten Regent Theatre. Going back along the street on that Christmas in 1930, we could see someone moving into the dark alley between the Biograph, now only a memory, and Elias's house, long ago torn down.

"Who was moving there—and what did she have in her hand?" He sat up straight and looked at his jacket sleeves to make sure they were impeccably drawn down.

I shrugged. I knew the question was rhetorical and he would answer himself.

"Rebecca Druken, sixteen years of age," he said, "holding the Christmas present, for she could never leave nice things alone. It was the clue she took away with her. No one would know of that present except Miles King. And she had to tell me."

"What present?"

"The present I bought my grandfather for Christmas in 1930. The present I put in his suit pocket at his house that day without even Janie herself knowing."

"And what present is that?"

"The four-leaf clover Dr. Mahoney was wearing today on her bosom."

I was more surprised at the word *bosom* than by the four-leaf clover or the idea she might have been under an assumed name and a murderer.

"To celebrate her son's wedding to my daughter."

(He paused.)

"Ginger helped her pin it on. I watched them, before I made the toast."

I turned cold and a shudder went through me, because I remembered it clearly.

"How do you know?" I said. "It could be anything—couldn't it?"

"I went to get the four-leaf clover with her before Christmas—I had saved my money and waited for her all day to take me to the store. All the way downtown she was irritated, hauling at my hand to keep up. 'I had no money to get anyone a present when I was yer age,' she said. I realized then how much she disliked me for that fact. In some ways I do blame her. She has always relied on the fact that those with a little don't blame her resentment. She tried the four-leaf clover on and said, 'Your granddad should wear it just like this.'"

"But maybe she kept it—stole it then?"

"No," he said calmly. "I wrapped it. I put it into the pocket of Granddad's suit jacket when we brought the suit to the house. I put it into his pocket just before I left. I might never have remembered buying it if she had not been so angry with my ability to. It was something that later allowed my heart to go out to Elizabeth Whispers. Does this not prove a Druken in our midst—maybe two?"

"I don't know," I said, though I did know.

"I put it in the jacket with his name on it. It was the same jacket he was wearing—the person who hit him over the head took it from him. It is the clue—or one of the clues I knew was out there and could not remember. You see, I did not remember it. I have spent forty years looking at pictures and trying to find out what it was. Today I remembered. Tonight I celebrate that memory."

Then he added, "Leon Winch might have gone there and hit him, but she went back, to find out for Elias, and she hit him again, to finish him."

He shrugged, as if to say it didn't matter if I believed him, drank the gin off in a draught, and poured himself another. He set the glass down and lit a cigarette. He looked with a kind of sprightly amusement at the smoke drifting up into the black between us both.

I paced the floor most of the night. Twice I went to the phone to telephone Kipsy Doyle, or Ginger's house, the bars, anywhere to let people know, while my father in the background simply said, "It isn't in a picture after 1938."

"What isn't?"

"The store where I bought the clover."

"So?"

"The family who owned it is dead and gone—everyone is dead and gone—so then they probably wouldn't have a receipt or any such bill of sale, h'm?"

The next morning I told Dad I was going to confront her about it. It was, after all, about my great-grandfather.

"No—don't," he said.

"Why not?"

"She will have an answer so pristine you will probably believe her and not me."

I went to the house anyway, and sat down with them for brunch. Noel and Ginger were leaving on Gary Fallon's boat for P.E.I. that afternoon. They were excited, and Noel was still fussing with his hair—he liked it the way his mom did it.

Dr. Mahoney came in from the kitchen with bacon wrapped in a dishtowel. She had repinned the four leaf to her blouse, as a memento to the celebration. I could not face it when I spoke, so I turned a little to the side.

"Where did you get that four-leaf clover?" I asked. There was a momentary pause, and I turned to see her eyes saturated with a kind of analysis—going back over the years, and years, tic-tac-toe of memory dominoes shuffling in her own gymnasium and falling down one by one to come to the moment. But when the moment was found, like ringing the bells in a slot machine, her eyes widened.

"Do you like it?" she said, fingering it slightly and smiling like a little girl.

"Sure," I said.

"Mommy always has nice things," Noel said, taking Ginger's hand.

"Do you want it?" she said suddenly, completely as if she was inspired by kindness toward me but in another way hurrying to get rid of it.

"No," I said (and then regretted saying this). She looked at the four-leaf clover and then took Ginger's hand.

"I found it here, in Miles's room upstairs," she said, "Who knows how long it was there? Someone told me it was a Christmas present to poor old Jim—Miles bought it or something. I could not think of not wearing it today. Did I do something wrong?"

"Of course not," I said.

She snapped a piece of bacon and smiled, and moved around the table, talking and laughing about the old days. She looked back at me once, with narrowed, searching eyes. Then she coolly laughed at something Noel said.

FIVE

Some months went by. My sister's life seemed fine, for there was not a thing she had to do for herself. Dr. Mahoney was always there, still spry at seventy, carting in groceries and making up lists, and helping redo a room for a child, with a grandmotherly devotion. But Ginger discovered things in bits and pieces.

Noel was spoiled, and wanted everything right away. He thought there would be a million dollars instantly. And Ginger felt it was her fault that they did not have a million instantly for him. So by the second month he openly pouted and ignored her, going away to visit someone. And most of the time she was left alone. She took to painting landscapes, and was quite good at it, and went for walks or bicycle rides by herself. Then she began to take yoga.

One day when Ginger came home early from yoga, Ray Winch was standing at the door with the doctor. He turned and saw her, and shook his head.

"What's wrong?" Ginger asked, looking at him, and turning back to her.

"Woman problems," she said, biting a strawberry slowly and watching him drive off.

What was wrong was simply that Ginger herself had no idea what was happening to her money.

In the triangle of people who had the most to say about the business, there was something very deliberate happening. Each of these people feared the other would take a good deal of the money and leave when things became difficult. Cassandra was telling each of them that this would be the case. She had levelled with Winch, telling him of Dr. Mahoney's intentions. She did this hoping Winch would cause a disturbance to prod everyone ahead. "There are probably no French safes at all, Ray," she told him.

She was also putting pressure on Noel to get what he said he could and leave. If he did not, she would tell the world of their secret marriage.

Gary Fallon, fearing Cassie also and fearing that she would get Noel to rob for her, was the most worried, for the money was the most he had seen. He also knew Dr. Mahoney simply assumed it was hers. "It's as much mine as it is that bitch's," he told Ray Winch one night.

Fallon believed Dr. Mahoney was deliberately trying to sabotage the business and leave with the funds. He tried to watch her and her son like a hawk, but it was impossible.

Only Ray Winch tried to get the business to go. He made phone calls, worked day and night. All the others just wanted to take the money for themselves, knowing by the seventh month there was no way any of them could get the business to work, not because it wouldn't work, but because of the mistrust they had for each other. Why, each of them deliberated in a private moment, should they sink so much money into a business when the money was already available—staring them in the face?

And thinking this, each one found a legitimate reason to mistrust the other and take his share. Cassandra in her talks to Fallon, who she said was her only link to her husband, whom she loved, told him that she suspected Dr. Mahoney. "She will leave you with nothing," she said.

Gary, who had known Cassandra from the time she was a child, had reason enough to believe her.

So in the ninth month something terrible occurred. Gary Fallon left them in the lurch, taking forty thousand dollars he was given to use for packaging and distribution of the sample product, leaving the creditors to hold Ginger accountable. He had struck first but he had not taken the largest portion. He could not get hold of that.

This is what Cassandra wanted. Now she begged Noel to take his money before it was too late. Whining and petulant his mother couldn't stop him. He planned his own business, with halogen lights and controlled heat to grow marijuana to sell in New York State. No one knew about this except Cassandra.

Dr. Mahoney was furious. She wanted him to close down his farm for his own safety. She told him that Cassandra was using them both.

He did not believe her.

"Damn you—they will start an investigation now," she said. "We only have a few more months before it comes crashing down—so prepare for that—and prepare to leave."

About this time, Ginger discovered that selling their product in Canada was, because of the provinces' different regulations, even more difficult than selling it into the States, and in the States they could not compete because they were far too small.

But Dr. Mahoney was in a position where she could not simply take this money and leave as Gary did.

Ginger paced the floor one night, waiting for the doctor to come in. When she did, Ginger started to speak, but the doctor said almost viciously, "Aren't we too sarcastic. It's not my fault."

Ginger had her summer dress on, and a small gold chain I had given her as a wedding present. She was alone in the centre of the room.

"Can we get our money back?" Ginger said. "I mean, if I want out of all of this?"

The doctor stopped on the stairs and said, "How should I know, Ginger?"

Ginger felt her throat catch and she started to weep.

But the good doctor went upstairs and closed her door—where my father used to sleep.

Ginger sat on the loveseat, shaking.

Noel hadn't been home for more than a moment in a month. Around the living room she could see mementoes of her wedding. And the next day was her first anniversary.

Outside she could see through the trees the Morrissey Bridge opening, and she remembered how Miles had construed an elaborate and complicated equation to prove the span should swing in the other direction. That compelled her to do something, anything. There was no sound in the house. It was as if there was no soul at the top of the stairs.

It took her three-quarters of an hour to climb those stairs built more than half a century before, when her grandmother and grandfather might have contemplated a happy, useful life in among the foxgloves doing the foxtrot. On each step she would stop and look up, wistfully taking the damp hair from her eyes, and brushing her tears away.

Finally at the top she knocked lightly.

"Abigail?" she said. "Are you sleeping or are you angry? Please don't be angry with me. Please. I'm sorry."

The door opened, and Dr. Mahoney, taking up the entire width of the door frame, arms spread to both sides and smiling, wearing the T-shirt, with the "I'm a Tough Nut" logo, and her hair covered in a gypsy bandana, said, "I need a good drink—don't you? I need to get blasted and forget my problems!"

"Yes," Ginger said automatically. "That's true—that's what I need. But we don't have any."

"Ha!" Dr. Mahoney said. "I'll never let you down, girl."

And she produced a forty-ounce bottle of gin. Though I should hold my tongue, for I have no moral claim on the betterment-by-abstinence crew.

"I love you, Abigail. Don't you know I find you a cross between Gram and Mom?"

"Of course I do. Can't you understand? Everyone is so jealous of us, it would be a miracle to keep their minds off saying things about you. So don't worry about it. Everything will turn out and we will go to bed next year at this time with a million dollars in our hands. Then Ray Winch will crawl back asking where his money is—and we will give him the cheque."

"I wish it was right now—just so I could say, 'See, I told you so.'"

"Oh, so do I."

"But I should tell Dad."

"Tell your dad? But he is the one who wanted to destroy you."

Within this conversation was another—a ploy not overt but subtly attached. And it said almost as an afterthought: that if they lost all, had everything taken away, and nothing left to show for it, they had done the right thing for society by investing in Ginger's idealism.

The doctor was sure Ginger would demand to see the one important piece of information: the accounts. It was through these bank accounts that Noel was siphoning off money and so was Dr. Mahoney. She didn't mean to. It was simply that she had to, because Gary had taken his share. So she must take hers. What might have worked as a profitable business if they had just listened to Ginger from the first was now completely doomed. And the one who did not know this was Ginger.

Dr. Mahoney was also selling some of Ginger's antiques.

But instead of asking any more questions, Ginger said she wanted to see Noel, and she began to cry.

Dr. Mahoney kissed her forehead. "We all want to see Noel, honey. I cry too."

The next day, her first wedding anniversary, Ginger went downtown and bought Noel a $698 watch, carrying it in her pocket for the moment he came home.

Two days later, Noel came home. He was in the bedroom taking something from the drawer when she handed him the watch.

"Do you like it? It's for our anniversary."

"Oh yeah—well—sure—it's great," he said. He had been expecting her to roar and scream at him, but she gave him a watch.

"Ray wants to speak to you," she said, squeezing him about the waist.

"Yeah, I heard."

He moved away from her. She saw at that moment each callow quality she had overlooked so long.

He put his watch on. "It fits."

But the news he revealed at supper was glum. And it seemed to Ginger, who knew how to read people when she had to, that this glum news was not at all unexpected by his mother. She could see this in how they cautiously looked at each other as they spoke. They had no distributor for their product, and because it was sitting in a damp warehouse, much of it had been damaged. The design and name they had come up with infringed on another product. That's why, Noel said, the prophylactics weren't wrapped. The real truth was, there were no prophylactics. Not one. Even the one in Noel's pocket hadn't been made by them. His money was lost too: the halogen lights had failed because of his power source, and the marijuana beds discovered by the RCMP. The rest he had spent on a house for Cassandra. Now he needed to take the little he had left to go away. He had come home to his mother for a loan.

"What do you think we should do, Noel?" Ginger asked. She sat in the same chair where there was so much laughter the morning after her wedding.

"We can sell off what we have to a larger producer. But they'd take it on risk and we'll lose much of our investment."

"Well, let's do that, then," she said, looking uncertainly from one to the other.

"Okay," Noel said, "if that's what you want."

"I want what everyone wants," Ginger said.

Noel nodded and lit a cigarette. He had that easy and clever way of sounding detached, and he was pleased with the way he sounded. But Ginger saw in his eyes a different look—it was a look she now remembered he had had when criticizing Gus Busters in front of her. She quickly looked at Dr. Mahoney. Of course! It had always been there, that look. The look that changed from delighted to predatory, always as quickly as one frame shifting to another in the millions of miles of movies our father had run.

Seeing this, Ginger tried to be firm. "Why don't we have a distributor—can't we afford that?" Ginger asked, banging her fist against the palm of her hand, just as my father used to do.

"Because Gary took the money for the distribution," Dr. Mahoney explained. "And Noel's been working hard doing what has to be done to get everything back in order."

"Ginger," Noel said, shaking his head, "that's what we have been trying to tell you, sweetheart. That's where I've been!"

"I know—but tell me again," she said, shaking, her nose running.

She was hoping for him to comfort her. He had not remembered their anniversary.

Noel, as sudden as a predator sensing weakness in prey, looked at Ginger as if it was her problem and her fault. This happened in his gaze in a second. It had happened the same way with certain middle-aged women he had left as well, after they had given him their money and their love.

Later Ginger waited for him in bed. But he was sick and shivering and wanted to spend the night on the couch. He had had these attacks before. His left arm was numb, and the only way he could feel well was to take more speed. Ginger went to him, but he pushed her back and demanded to see his mother. All that night he was weak and fevered, and Dr. Mahoney ran to him with hot towels.

My father learned most of this within walls of rumour and gossip, overhearing it on street corners as cars passed by in the night, and in bars where he drank alone in the middle of the day. The hilarity over Ginger was like before, only this time people were absolutely shameless in their rejoicing. He heard that Noel was using needles and, loyal to the end, tried to protect them both.

"How dare you," Miles would say, standing with drink in one hand and cigarette in his fingers, "how dare you speak of Ginger King to me in that vein. How dare you, sir."

"Who the fuck are you—her father?"

"I am—I am at that," he would say, slightly bemused, and ready with his fists up to defend her honour to the death, and being ignored because of his age and his condition, and because secretly there were enough people to react against the shamelessness of the tormentor's conduct.

"I am—I am the father of Ginger King, the husband of Elizabeth Whispers, and the son—do you understand, I am the son—of Janie McLeary. And you, sir, will not talk to me in this vein. If Noel

Mahoney uses needles as is so blatantly rumoured, he has a right to use them, as much as you do to mock it, sir."

He would walk home alone, and lie unconscious on the couch, wheezing into the wee hours where he would wake, bolt to the washroom and stand under the shower in his clothes. With water spilling over and across his peaked face (hat still on his head) he would shout out to me:

"Made a bit of a stir tonight at the Palace Bar—where they have that nice carpet, with the nightly duo singing the tolerable leftovers from the seventies—lounge lizards invaded it today—the godawful useless set who know politics a tad, and whose daddies were lawyers, smirking in that way they do, said something about your sister—I defended her—I defended Elizabeth—defended them both—they have me to deal with from now on, no more backsliding in my duties to protect my daughter. In fact am thinking, considering buying myself a nice well-adjusted shotgun, for defence of my home."

I would get him out of the shower and into bed, and sit beside him, in those nights with flecks of memory of Mom and Dad when they were young and we were wee ones, in the hobbled absence of sound.

My father would bring home these ruined draughts about Ginger, though she wouldn't see us.

"I would want to give money back to Raymond Winch if I could," Miles said, "even though I know that is the exact amount Noel and he took out of old Dingle's pocket while bashing his skull with pans."

SIX

Ginger was pregnant, and was alone in the house with Dr. Mahoney. Abigail, as far as I can tell, did not worry, for since childhood this was her life. She had never done another thing except play the game of the pea. And even in its failure this was her major victory.

But one night when Dr. Mahoney was out Ginger found courage enough to say to herself, "The money has to be upstairs—behind that door where Abigail lives. I will get it and give it to my father—it is his money. It is him we have betrayed."

For once she longed to help her father. There was no one in the house, and shadows fell across the chesterfield and the mahogany table. Most of the doors were closed. And there was a terrible feeling that she should not go into the doctor's room. But she found herself walking up the stairs. She did not want to go into the room because her action would prove to her a warranted suspicion.

But if she did enter she could not remain as close to her mother-in-law as she had been. This was the most difficult moment. Still, she decided she must go.

She found herself with the master key to all the upstairs doors of the house, which her grandmother had given her when she was fifteen. It was the one secret she had managed to keep.

She unlocked Dr. Mahoney's door, and walked into the room that had belonged to my father when he held on to the tree with his pigeon coop. The tree was still there. She kept the light off, because moonlight shone on the white bedspread and reflected eerily back at her. She did not know what she was searching for, but she began to open the drawers, carefully rummaging with her hands under linen and clothes. Her hand touched a package wrapped in plastic. She did not know what it was, and she pulled her hand away. She went to the closet. On an upper shelf she saw, to her amazement, the antiques that had been lying about the house, piled in a box. Abigail had taken them for herself. Some had belonged to Ginger's great-grandmother. She tried to reach these, but she couldn't.

Suddenly she heard a noise. When she turned around Abigail was staring directly at her. Her heart stopped. The doctor made no movement toward her. And then Ginger realized the mirrored closet door was hiding her from view.

Ginger crouched down, as the woman came over, brushed her hair and smiled into the mirror, turned and left the room, looking once, twice, stopping, almost deciding to come back. Then she walked right by Ginger again, and went to the window. She whistled at something, looking down at the ground. And Ginger suddenly realized the woman was whistling at the distance my father fell as a boy. Yet how could that be?

"Ginger?" she called, turning her head.

She went to the dresser, opened it and looked at something, then closed it quickly.

"Ginger, where are you?" she called. "Little pea brain?"

Then she turned and went back to the door. All of this took about thirty seconds. Closing the door behind her, she went downstairs.

Strangely Ginger felt if that woman had found her there, she might have killed her. But worse, she saw herself as herself walking arm in arm with Dr. Mahoney in front of her father, and smiling back over her shoulder, at his lonely solitary figure.

I asked my father about the four-leaf clover one day shortly after his escapade at the Palace, when he took on those bouncing sons of the old school lawyers, the Rotarian boys going off to their rewards as surely as he.

"Perhaps I have been mistaken about her all my life, do you think? I cannot prove a thing, you see. That's what bothers me. She has given me a clue, and I cannot prove it. It's something that she might not even realize herself any longer. Who knows? We are still involved in prosthetics—"

"Prophylactics, Dad—and I don't think they are slipping on as well as they once thought—"

But he had forgotten all about that stuff and did not know or pretended not to hear what I just said. I think "pretended" is the word, as he shuffled to the patio to have a drink and watch his hummingbirds suck the nectar from his flowers.

"I am certain, Wendy—they are trying to sell wooden legs," he yelled back at me, "Well, it's not a flying car, like poor Gus Busters once said he would build, but it is transportation—Ginger says she will help me out in anyway she can, as soon as she can—but the money is tied up—"

I was sure he would not live too much longer. Not the way he was now drinking. Let him go off to glory seeing wooden legs instead of French safes, I thought.

Ginger's heartbreak in this, my father reminded me, was the fact that she now had to mistrust the very woman whom she told us we must—we were morally obligated to—trust.

I saw Ginger downtown one afternoon, but she did not look my way. She had become a stranger, just another stranger on the street. She was pregnant and yet thin as a rail. Her eyes looked large and scared. I know that she thought getting pregnant would stop Noel from seeing that other woman, and would bring the money back under her control. I went home to a bottle of gin and five sleeping pills.

Two weeks later, Ginger was in the baby's room decorating. She was standing in the middle of the room with a length of wallpaper, when the doctor appeared. Ginger did not speak to her. The doctor had slapped her the night before, calling her spoiled rotten and accusing her of snooping in her room. She said she could tell something in her drawer had been touched. Ginger denied this but still felt the sting and the shock of the slap. And at that moment their relationship seemed to be over.

Today she turned and looked at her mother-in-law. Dr. Mahoney had a grave smile that Ginger had seen only in certain moments.

"I know we haven't been on the best terms lately, so I want to make it up. I have a present for you. I have kept it awhile—it's for your little girl."

"I don't know if I'm having a boy or a girl," Ginger said.

"It will be a girl for certain," the doctor answered, "and you will call her Georgina. Wouldn't that be appropriate? I picked these out some years back. Aren't they nice?"

She handed them to my sister.

"They're very nice," my sister said. "They are wonderful."

"Yes, they are," the doctor said. "As soon as I get to Montreal I will tell you what's happening. It wasn't your fault, but we lost some of our advantage. And I have to go and get it back."

"When are you coming back?"

"I'm leaving next week, but I'll be back quicker than a flash." Then the doctor hugged Ginger and said, "Remember what I said, concerning this deal we have. You are doing what is right. Only those jealous of you are trying to stop us."

Ginger smiled, for she had no one else.

The doctor was happy, and when she was happy, Ginger's heart was glad. After lunch, while Abigail was doing the dishes, Ginger went upstairs.

She was sitting in the big bare room that had once been Georgina's room—the room my father dressed her in on that day. Ginger sat on the floor with her knees tucked under her, thinking of Dad's garden.

Then quicker than a heartbeat, something terrible came over her. Something so horrible she could not move. She was staring at the present the woman had given her. It was on the wooden table at the far end of the room. A present solitary and non-verbal. Yet suddenly because of the history of her family, they told her something horrifying. Ginger the eccentric goofball, who had believed up until that moment that her life was one way, now realized Miles was right and her life was a completely different life. Completely and totally other than what she had thought as she was eating her lunch at the mahogany island in the kitchen.

She stared at the present for more than an hour, not moving a muscle, scarcely able to breathe. The present was like the Grecian urn, an inanimate mirror into past tragedy, from the age of our sad and courageous Jane.

Little purple gloves, wrapped in plastic to keep them timeless.

She stood, heard the woman below her singing. When she reached the banister she thought she would faint. She was as white as a ghost.

Rebecca Druken was humming a song, brushing her hair back, staring at her own reflection, her two suitcases open in the living room, waiting to be packed.

Ginger walked past her and left the house.

She came to me, and my father.

"What do you do," she said, "when you realize your entire life is a lie, and your father has told the truth?"

"You go and thank him," I said, a little sternly. But at that moment I had no idea what she meant.

"It's over," she said.

"What is? The business? Thank God you've gotten out of that business."

"Yes, and my entire life, it seems." She gave a kind of hopeless smile.

She wanted to find the picture of Georgina. It took us about three hours to locate. She looked at pictures like a puzzled school-girl, saying nothing at all to me, picking them up and tossing them aside, just as I had done a few years previous. Then we came across it at about five in the afternoon. There Georgina was at four years of age, staring with a halo about her, looking at the camera of Mr. Maurice, wearing the purple gloves. Ginger took the present from her coat and laid those same buttoned-up gloves on the coffee table before me.

What incensed Ginger was Gram had gotten them for her child. What incensed her was that Rebecca Druken thought she could get away with it; or perhaps she no longer knew where they had come from.

Ginger did not want to go back there any more. It was so horrible to her.

"You go back," she said. "You go back and put her out of my house—or I will get the police—I will get Kipsy. Call Kipsy for me, or Constable Delano. That's what we have to do—we have to get protection!"

She was shaking, her nose running, and she was crying for a tiny child she had never in her life seen. She sobbed with abandon for hours on end.

Then she phoned Kipsy Doyle and, still bawling, related as much as she could.

"There," Kipsy said, "we'll see to it now. It's over. Tell your dad it's all over now."

Fifty-five years after it had started.

Kipsy Doyle came to our house that night. My father did not want to listen and went to his room. Here in the living room—Kipsy explained how the police felt the deal was set up—how incidental it all seemed. How they all believed in it at first, and how they all turned on each other when things started to go wrong, suspicious each would get the bigger share.

"Rebecca Druken—is it her?" I asked.

Kipsy said she and the RCMP Officer John Delano now believed that it was. If it was she was already wanted on five or six charges, both here and in the States, under two or three names.

"She did not know Miles had a daughter when she came back—she had no idea. But when she found out she kept pushing Noel on you, hoping something would go wrong in your first marriage," Kipsy said. "When it did—they helped it along, let me tell you. In a way, she was the consummate matchmaker."

Kipsy laughed at this for a second but, seeing tears running down Ginger's face, said, "It's all over, Ginger. Don't think about it any more. They had to get rid of the screen. If they could topple one business, they could make your dad sell the other, and then they could use the funds. Besides, your marriage is non-binding—for in spite of his mother's wishes, Noel married Cassie in secret before he married you."

Ginger looked up at Kipsy, startled, and then put her head down again.

"Anyway, I don't think you'll see any of them again. You can thank your lucky stars. But," she added, "the money, your grandmother's money, is gone. All except for a few thousand, I think."

"I see," Ginger kept saying in a whisper, staring at the floor, mortified to appear so weak in front of her old adversary, "I see. Well, that's it, then. Thank you, Kipsy—thank you very much."

Kipsy nodded, closed her notebook, stood abruptly, and walked assertively to the door, her duty completed.

Then, turning and seeing Ginger with her head down, her fingers fumbling with one another, rushed over and hugged her for two solid minutes.

My father had been telling her all of this for years. That is why he couldn't stand to hear it now.

SEVEN

Within a week the business was over. The police issued a warrant for Rebecca Druken, a.k.a. Dr. Abigail Mahoney. They would have a hard time proving anything, Rebecca knew. She said she had picked the gloves up in an antique sale years before and was saving them for her granddaughter. And she said every business she was ever involved with was legitimate. Then she disappeared.

Ginger had a miscarriage.

Ginger tried to bring a lawsuit against Noel Druken. But no one knew where he was. Then a year later I heard that he was living on the street in Montreal, had hepatitis from a dirty needle, and he needed a new liver.

I kept this from Ginger, but told Father.

"He could have mine, for what it's worth. A tad overused, mine is, I suspect," my father said, without the least gloating, and a terrible sadness.

We sold what we could to pay what we must. Ginger was very astute in that regard. She was determined not to let the other investors down.

Roy Dingle's house was sold, Janie's house was empty, and we had to sell every piece of furniture. I saw my grandmother's violin during a Mendelssohn concert in Halifax, and my grandfather's piano sits today in a bar in Fredericton.

We lost Janie's house in the end. It was boarded up. My father was sitting on the steps one November day, and was told by a policeman to move along, that it was a historical property and he wasn't wanted there.

My father did not say, "I am Miles King, who was born here." The fresh-faced policeman wouldn't have known who he was.

I wanted things solved for my father's sake. And Kipsy took an interest in me, and I in her. So she listened to both my father and me for weeks, trying to distinguish fact from fiction—our lives, of course, were filled with both. Kipsy believed, from going over the old, faded files, that my great-grandfather was hit twice, first by a man, and then probably by a woman.

"There is one piece of the puzzle that might help—if we could find it," she said.

"And what is that, dear Kipsy of mine?" my father asked.

"The key, Mr. King—the long-lost key."

My father stayed at home and worked in his greenhouse. After a while he could not afford to pay the bills, even though Ginger took a job at the restaurant to help him. We sold our old bungalow.

Ginger and I moved into an apartment, where we began to look like the middle-aged people we have become. She started dating Gus Busters again, and I started dating Kipsy Doyle. We went out together often enough, and Kipsy helped me quell my happy habits, at least a little.

Miles lived in a room downtown, with a potted ivy and a geranium. Still, he took what he had and did what he could. He manicured his own nails, and drank a cheap gin, which he said was godawful. He still had his suits dry cleaned and tied his tie every morning into a Windsor, with thin practised hands. He had a budgie that sat on his shoulder when he went for walks, at times his jacket soiled by bird droppings that seemed compatible to his gait.

He read much of Matthew Arnold and some of Emerson, bought the complete works of Shakespeare, which he sometimes carried under his arm.

"Someday we will recoup our losses," he said, looking into the mirror and brushing his clothes off. "Someday I will see Miss Whispers again." And he added, "The modern agitation on behalf of women, Wendy, would not allow for our Janie, could not allow for such true independence, but did allow for Ms. Druken." He smiled and put the cloth brush aside. "But it is not sad Ms. Druken's fault alone."

It was the last he mentioned it.

But when they tore down the Regent to build the pizza parlour something good did happen in our lives. A strange thing, no doubt, cast in the winds almost three-quarters of a century before. Hidden in the wall, behind the sink of Walter P. McLeary's room was the one-sheet for *Frankenstein* starring Boris Karloff, which poor tormented Walter thought he looked like and hid so no one would make fun of him.

Gus Busters found it there and brought it home. We were about to store it away in a room when Kipsy said we should check to see if it was worth anything.

It took four months before we found out it was one of only three one-sheets from that movie left in the world.

"And how much will that gain us?" Kipsy said laughing.

"Two hundred thousand dollars," I said, pretending a yawn.

In fact, it got what Dad was hoping for his paintings.

It allowed him to buy Janie's house back, and we moved in as well.

We get along now, you see, for there is no sense not to. No sense in the world.

Rebecca Druken died in a rooming-house fire in Toronto in 1991. She had rented the room that week (mostly she was living on the street then) and became disorientated in the smoke and did not find the door. She was utterly alone. Small mementoes from her life in our town were found in her purse—odd little things, a spoon, a picture of Mr. Dingle's back yard in winter taken from the kitchen window, a postcard of the Morrissey Bridge, a matchbook from the Palace Bar. And my father's stamp collection that he had when he was ten.

That was all she had left of her life.

"Elderly transient dies in fire" was the caption in the *Sun*.

Hearing of it, my father burst into sobs and cried for hours. I suppose such terrible closeness can only bring love.

Ray Winch was left with Noel, whom he had promised to take care of. Noel, now forty, had liver disease, and came back here to die. No one he knew would give up any time to take care of him. His wife, Cassie Avalanche, said to him the afternoon he turned up at her door:

"You got caught."

Her cream complexion as wonderful as before and her smile callow and empty, she turned away and left him alone.

Noel was vulnerable without his mom. People who had been terrified of her were not one bit frightened of him, and left him bruised and bullied on many occasions.

My father, hopeless as he was, tried to protect him.

"You'd not do this if Rebecca Druken was here," he said. "You'd piss yourselves like kennelled dogs—get away from him."

Noel complained about his life, and his mother's betrayal.

Ray Winch carried him here and there, took him to the hospital, tried to keep him on his diet and medication.

Noel managed to write Ginger a short note after his mother's funeral telling her that someday their life would be repaired. The letter came in the winter snow. "We got mixed up over those damn French safes," he wrote.

She did not press charges, did not hear from him again.

Eight months later a car was travelling toward the Miramichi from Saint John, and Ray Winch and Noel Druken were in this car. Noel was driving and Winch was on the passenger side. They were planning to rob the Palace Bar, on Tuesday night, pay night, from the backroom's safe. They were both armed. They would, they believed, get enough money to live for a year. Winch did not think Noel would live much longer than that, though Noel was filled with plans.

As they were approaching the Enclosure, an argument arose over the money Winch had put into the business that went under and the money Noel had been foolish enough to give to Cassie. Ray was angry about this, and he was not a man you wanted to anger.

"Your mom lied about that, Noel," Ray said. Noel's face was the colour of a yellow flag, and pills that Ray continually reminded him to take were scattered all over the dash.

"We did what we could," Noel said. "If the scheme Cassie and I had had worked, I'd be rich."

"Yeah—and I wouldn't be—now I'm back to doing what I did when I was twenty—and it's your mother's fault!"

The car drove on around a turn. The argument continued, and Noel pulled the car to the side of the road and reached under his seat. A red maple shadowed the car roof, and a little stream trickled off to the right, where some sparrows flitted in among some pin cherries. Noel smiled, and reached for what Winch thought would be the skinning knife Druken was going to carry during the robbery.

Ray Winch fired my father's pistol, just once, into Noel Druken's head.

Noel's head fell against the dash, his eyes open, his hand under the seat clutching my grandfather's box of coins, compensation from his mother for losing it all.

It was brought back to our house and sits on the drawing-room table again.

I married the police officer, Kipsy Doyle, and my sister remarried Gus Busters, and the four of us live together, for the house is certainly big enough and we want to bring life back into it, as Janie would have wished.

Time passed, and Rebecca Druken was forgotten by us. The badness just all went away. The old part of our town, like Ripper's East London of my grandfather's boyhood, is no more.

Yet I was speaking to Kipsy one spring evening about my father's pigeons, and how they were buried by Rebecca and him in the yard. She looked at me as if I had stuck her with a pin.

"You stupid idiots," she said. "All you Kings are idiots!"

"Well, I know—but why?"

"You mean you can't see it? "

"See what?"

She grabbed Ginger by the arm and told Gus to get a shovel, and we followed her along the back path where my great-grandfather Jimmy used to drink. From there we entered my grandmother's lower yard.

It was at the corner near the rock fence, under the old purple ivy stems. A terrible wind whistled off the water, and Ginger said she was cold, so Kipsy, always laying down the law, gave Ginger her coat.

Upstairs I could see a shadow in the window—only a shadow but who knows, perhaps a ghost, perhaps Georgina herself, the little girl I've loved my whole life, looking at us one more time before she said goodbye.

Kipsy ordered Gus to dig, and my poor happy halting brother-in-law—who himself believes he will invent a flying car, and is working on it now—did so. He dug in three places and then a fourth, and finally he scooped up some remnants from the ground.

Harry Feathers was gone, and the box was nothing but splinters, and the only thing left wrapped in rotted cloth, that shone in the moon and in the wind, was the old Regent Theatre key.

"Eureka," Ginger said, and hugged Kipsy so hard she lifted her off the ground. For it was the weight of the world lifted from my father's shoulders after so long a time.

But it was a strangely unpleasant victory, wasn't it? And caused, I'm afraid, me to drink once more.

———

"We all walk the wibbily wobbily walk," Malcolm Lowry wrote. My father did that. Not a thing to prevent him from going to the liquor store on the last day of his life.

He poured himself a drink, he took out his mouth organ, and he played three songs: "It's a Long Way to Tipperary" for his father, George King, late of Blackheads Lane, and then, for his sister, Georgina, "Danny Boy," and for his mother, Janie McLeary, "The Risin' of the Moon."

There was fire and beauty and all good things in his sound.

He had an audience too. Little children across the street came to listen, crowding about him. His first audience since 1930. They didn't know he was Miles King the song-and-dance man, the soft-shoe shuffler, the bit of a dandy who strutted out at St. Paddy's Day and could pull Harry Feathers from his hat.

They listened in rapt attention nonetheless, with their hands folded together, tapping their shoes in our dooryard mud.

It was reported to me that as he played tears filled his eyes.

And then his sun went down.

ACKNOWLEDGEMENTS

The author wishes to thank his editor, Maya Mavjee, and his agent, Anne McDermid.